KU-033-735

Chris Bunch was part of the first troop commitment into Vietnam. Both Ranger and airborne-qualified, he served as a patrol commander and a combat correspondent for *Stars and Stripes*. Later, he edited outlaw motorcycle magazines and wrote for everything from the underground press to *Look* magazine, *Rolling Stone* and prime-time television. He is now a full-time novelist.

Allan Cole was raised as a CIA brat, travelling the world and visiting pretty much every global hot-spot before he was eighteen. Subsequently he has worked as a chef, a prize-winning newspaperman and a TV screenwriter. He has nineteen novels to his credit and has written more than a hundred episodes for television shows such as *Battlestar Galactica*, *The Rockford Files*, *The A-Team*, *Magnum, P.I.*, *Quincey*, *The Incredible Hulk*, *Walker, Texas Ranger*, and even *The Smurfs*. He currently lives in Boca Ranton, Florida, with Kathryn, his strongest supporter, and "Squeak"—the cat who rules all writer elves.

Find out more about Chris Bunch, Allan Cole and other Orbit authors by registering for the free monthly newsletter at www.orbitbooks.co.uk.

STEN 8
EMPIRE'S END

Chris Bunch
and Allan Cole

www.orbitbooks.co.uk

An *Orbit* book

First published in Great Britain by Orbit 2001
Reprinted 2002, 2004

A CIP catalogue record for this book is available from
the British Library.

ISBN 1 84149 083 0

Typeset by Palimpsest Book Production Limited
Polmont, Stirlingshire
Printed in Great Britain by
Mackays of Chatham plc, Chatham, Kent

Orbit
An imprint of
Time Warner Book Group UK
Brettenham House
Lancaster Place
London WC2E 7EN

To Everyone Who Was There
When
"Death came quietly to The Row"

BOOK ONE

INDIAN OPENING

CHAPTER ONE

THE RUINS OF the Imperial assault fleet fled through the "dark" between star clusters. There was one tacship carrier, two heavy cruisers, one light, their destroyer flotilla screens, and, in the center of the formation, auxiliaries and the troop transports carrying the battle-shattered remnants of the First Imperial Guards Division.

Flanking and closing the formation was the huge battleship *Victory*.

On its bridge, Sten stared at a strategic battlescreen, not seeing either the glow "ahead" that represented the Empire . . . nor the symbols to the "rear" that were the anarchy-ripped Altaic Cluster.

Two E-days earlier:

Sten: Ambassador Plenipotentiary. Personal Emissary of the Eternal Emperor. Admiral. Medals and decorations beyond count, from the Galactic Cross down, including Grand Companion of the Emperor's Household. Hero.

Now:

Sten: Traitor. Renegade. And, he thought, don't forget Murderer.

Among the symbols representing what was "behind" the *Victory* was one marking where the Imperial Battleship *Caligula*, its Admiral Mason, and over three thousand loyal Imperial sailors had been. They'd been slaughtered by Sten for following a direct order to planetbust the Altaic's capital world, an order issued in person by the Eternal Emperor.

"Boss, Ah hae a wee tip."

Sten's eyes—and mind—refocused. Alex Kilgour. Sten's best friend, a rather roundish looking heavy-worlder who probably knew even more about death and destruction than Sten.

"GA." Part of Sten's mind, the part always removed from the hue and cry, found it funny both of them still used slang from their now-long-gone days in Mantis Section, the Emperor's supersecret covert-operations unit. Go ahead.

"Giein' thae y' hae no 'sperience a' bein't an outlaw, y'r entire life bein't spent singin' hymns an' such, p'raps y' dinnae ken Robbie Roy types hae noo time t' be pausin't an' smellin't th' flowers i' thae dinnae wan' a halter an' a neck-stretch."

"Thank you, Mister Kilgour. I'll get my thumb out."

"Dinnae fash, lad. Any wee service, y' hae but t' snivel."

Sten turned away from the screen. Around him, waiting, was the *Victory*'s bridgewatch. The top elements of his long-serving personal staff, who were in fact more Sten's own private intelligence agency than striped-suiters.

Twenty-three Gurkhas—Nepalese mercenaries famous for serving only in the Emperor's private bodyguard—but these had volunteered for special duties: guarding the life of their ex-CO, Sten.

Otho. Six other Bhor. Squat, shaggy monsters with long beards, yellow fangs, and ground-brushing knuckles. They seemed happiest either tearing an enemy in half the long way or else doing the same to his bank balance in a shrewd mul-tiworld trade. They were also fond of eddaic-type poetry. There were another hundred of them elsewhere on the *Victory*.

And, most important, left to last, their commander:

Cind: Human. Expert sniper. Descended from a now-obliterated warrior cult. A highly respected combat leader.

Beautiful. Sten's friend and lover.

Enough bean counting, he thought. Kilgour had been right: a wolf could never chance lying in a sunny clearing listening to the bees buzz—not unless he'd suddenly decided on a new career as a fireside rug.

"Weapons?"

"Sir?" The young woman was waiting. The lieutenant's name, Sten recollected, was Renzi.

"Bring your people back to general quarters. Commander Freston"—this was his longtime personal com officer—"I want—oh, clot. Cancel."

Sten remembered. "Both of you," he said, raising his voice. "And anyone else interested—listen up.

"Things have changed. I just declared war on the Emperor. Which makes me a traitor. Nobody's required to obey my orders. No one who remains loyal to his oath will be harmed. We'll—"

His words were interrupted by the ululation of the GQ siren as the weapons officer obeyed Sten's first command.

That was one answer.

Freston made another: "Pardon, sir? There was some static there and I lost you. Your orders?"

Sten held up a palm for Freston to stand by.

"Weapons, I want all Kali and Goblin stations at full launch-readiness. Some of our Imperial friends might decide to bag a renegade. Plus there were four destroyers escorting the *Caligula*. If any ship begins an attack, put a Goblin in the vicinity and blow it off as a warning."

"And if they keep coming?"

Sten hesitated. "If they do—contact me. No Kali launches will be made without my orders, and any launch will be controlled by either myself or Mister Kilgour."

The Kalis were operator-guided shipkillers.

"That's not—"

"*That* is an order. Follow it."

"Yessir."

"Commander Freston. Patch me a secure link to General Sarsfield on whichever transport he's riding." Sarsfield was the Guards' CO, and the next-ranking officer to Sten. Freston touched keys.

"One other thing," Sten said. "You've been through C&S school?"

"Yessir."

"You have any really terrible sins in your past? That'd keep you from being the very model of a shipcaptain? Ram the admiral's barge? Shine the ship's cannons with carbolic acid? Bootleg the beer? Badmouth the beef? Boast about buggery?"

"Nossir."

"Fine. They tell me pirates get promoted a lot before they get hanged. The *Victory*'s your ship, Mister."

"Yessir."

"Don't thank me. That just means you'll probably be next after Kilgour for the high jump. Mister Kilgour?"

"Sir?"

"All offwatch personnel to the main hangar."

"Yessir."

And then Sten noticed Alex's hand move away from the small of his back. He might have been fingering an old war wound around the caudal vertebra. Kilgour was not—his hand had been touching the butt of a miniwillygun, hidden in his waistband. Alex took no chances: loyalty to the Emperor in the abstract would be acceptable. But if anyone attempted to fulfill that promise to "defend the Empire and its welfare onto death," they would be prime candidates for martyrdom. And most likely Kilgour would loudly admire their fidelity at the wake.

A screen cleared. Sarsfield.

"General, you're aware of what's happened?"

"I am."

"Very well. In view of events, you are now the ranking officer of the fleet. Until you receive differing orders from the Empire, I would suggest you continue the present course toward the nearest Imperial worlds.

"I will advise you that, regretfully, any attempt to interfere with the *Victory* or its movements will be opposed with maximum force. However, none of your ships are in danger if they obey these instructions."

The old soldier grimaced. He took a deep breath, and

started to say something. Then he changed his mind.

"Your message is understood."

"Sten. Clear."

The screen blanked. Sten wondered what Sarsfield had been about to say—that none of the Imperial ships had one-quarter the firepower of the *Victory* nor were they skippered by deathseekers? Or—and Sten cursed at himself for still having a bit of romance in him—Good luck? It didn't matter.

"Jemedar Lalbahadur?"

"Sah!"

"Turn out your people. I want them as flanking security."

"Sah!"

"Captain Cind, I'd also like your people dancing attendance?"

"They're already drawing weapons," Cind said.

"Commander—pardon, Captain Freston, have the captain's personal boat ready for launch. We'll steal you another one somewhere." Interesting, Sten thought, how quickly one could lose that stifling straitjacket discipline the navy held so dear.

"Yessir."

"Mister Kilgour? Shall we go draw the line with our saber and see if anybody's in an Alamo kind of mood?"

Alex hesitated.

"Sir, i' y' wish. But thae's another wee matter . . . a matter o' security . . . Ah think Ah'd best—"

"Oh Christ!"

Suddenly Sten remembered security. He had no idea what Alex was hesitating about—but Sten had recollected two trump cards of his own. If they still held value. He unsealed the front of his combat suit and lifted out the thin pouch that was hung on a tie around his neck. He removed two squares of plas.

"You people stand by," he ordered.

Sten hurried across the bridge to the central computer station. He told the two operators to clear out of the cubicle, pulled a security screen around the station, and slid a key-board out.

Touched keys.

The station was one of the three on the *Victory* that could access ALL/UN—the central Imperial computer net that reached every Imperial command on every world and ship of the Empire.

Should, Sten thought, rather than *could*.

Most likely the *Victory* had been cut out of any access to anything, just as the Eternal Emperor had cut Sten's usual direct line into his quarters.

Weeks passed. Months. Decades. Sten knew his body could have been carbon-dated before the screen suddenly cleared and ALL/UN blinked at him, then vanished.

Then: ACCORDANZA.

Sten input the *Victory*'s code.

Another long wait.

The next thing he would see would be the simulation of a stiffly extended human middle finger and STATION REJECTED.

Instead: ATELIER.

Sten input the program on the first plas chip. Again, a wait, then, BORRUMBADA. Damn, he thought. They accepted it. Once again: ATELIER. The second chip was fed in. And again Imperial All Units accepted the program. Now we pray a lot, and hope both those little bastards work their magic.

The chips were a gift from Ian Mahoney, Sten's former commander in Mantis, Fleet Admiral, and, for aeons, the closest thing the Eternal Emperor had for a friend. But Mahoney was dead now—accused of treason by the Emperor and executed.

It's a great pity, Ian, Sten thought, you couldn't come up with one of these for yourself—and deploy it before the Eternal Clot killed you. He caught himself. No time for that, either.

Sten pulled the security curtain aside and found Alex waiting. "Ah'm thankin't you f'r warmin't th' chair frae me, boss. Noo, i' y'll get gone?"

"Yessir, Mister Kilgour, sir. Out of the way, sir, right away, sir. Can I have someone send in tea, sir?"

"Clottin' liquid fit only t' flow through th' veins ae sassenachs. Ah'll hae a dram in a wee." And Kilgour pulled the curtain closed.

Sten started for one of the slideways connecting the bridge to the battleship's central transit tube and thence to the hangar near the stern. Without orders, the Gurkhas, willyguns at the port, were trotting behind him.

Cind and her Bhor were waiting at a junction. She motioned them, and the Gurkhas, to move on ahead.

For a moment, she and Sten were alone at the bend of a corridor.

"Thanks," she said, and kissed him.

"For what?"

"For not asking."

"Asking what?"

"You are a clot," she said.

"You mean—"

"I mean."

"But I never thought that you wouldn't, I mean—"

"You're right. I stay volunteered. Plus I never took any oath to any Emperor. Besides, I know how to pick a winner."

Sten looked closely at her. She did not appear to be either making a joke or trying to build his morale.

"My ancestors were Jannissars," she went on. "They served tyrants who hid behind the lie that they were the voice of a god they'd made up.

"I swore if I could become a soldier, I wouldn't be like them. Matter of fact, the kind of soldiering I dreamed about was helping get rid of all those bastards like the Prophets. Or like Iskra. Or the Emperor."

"Well," Sten said, "you told me that before. And now I guess you'll get your chance. Or at least a good shot at going down in noble flames."

"Naah," Cind disagreed. "We're gonna kick his ass. Now come on. You've got a sermon to preach."

Sten stood on the winglet of a tacship, looking down at the nearly two thousand beings—those sailors of the *Victory* not absolutely required at weapons stations or to keep the ship alive, plus the remainder of his embassy staff—spread out around him. He didn't think he was doing a very good job of preaching tyrannicide. He tried not to look up at the hangar's overhead catwalks where Bhor and Gurkha marksmen waited, in case someone planned any nonverbal objections.

"All right," he finished. "That's the situation. I shoved the Emperor's face in it. There's no way he can let me vanish and pretend nothing happened. Which I'm not going to do anyway.

"I won't say what comes next. Because I don't think any of you should volunteer to remain with me. If there's anybody down there who's good at running progs or who stayed awake in battle analysis, it's easy to come up with a prediction.

"I've got the *Victory*, and maybe some beings somewhere who believe the same as I do. Which is, that it's time to fight back. This, I plan to do.

"I've been serving the Emperor for most of my life. But things have gone nuts. Like the Altaics, for instance. All right, those poor beings were blood-crazed. And have been so for generations.

"But we're the ones who made it fall apart. We're the ones responsible for turning turmoil into bloody chaos."

Sten caught himself. "No," he said, his voice dropping so that those in the back had to listen hard. "I shouldn't say 'we.' You, me, all of us, did our best.

"But our best wasn't good enough. Because there was one being who was running his own program. The Emperor. We followed his orders—and look what it produced. And I was not going to let it be covered up with a planetbuster.

"That's all I think I should say. We'll have the captain's own boat ready in a bit. It'll cross-connect to the rest of the fleet. You've got about one ship-hour to collect your gear and board.

"Do it, people. You'll live a lot longer if you stay with the Emperor, no matter what he is and no matter what he does. I have no other choices left. You do.

"One hour. Get yourselves out of the line of fire. Now. Anybody else, anybody who's had enough of serving a madman who's hellbent on turning the Empire into chaos, like the chaos we just left—move over against the hangar baffle.

"That's it. Thanks for helping. Thanks for your service. And good luck to all of you, no matter what you choose. Dismissed."

Sten turned away. He pretended to be busy talking to Cind, but his ears were full of the low rumble of voices, and then the clatter of bootheels on the decking.

Cind's eyes weren't on him, but beyond, watching for a potential attacker.

Then the voices and movement stopped.

Sten made himself turn around. He blinked in astonishment. Before he could ask, Cind told him.

"The first people to move were your staffers. I'd say, maybe nine out of ten will stick. You've really corrupted them."

"Hell," was the best Sten could manage.

"No drakh," Cind agreed. "Plus you have what I'd estimate is two-thirds of the swabs. I thought nobody in the navy *ever* volunteered. But I think you got a whole bunch of prospective rebels."

Before Sten could do anything—like fall on his knees and thank a couple of the Bhor gods that the *Victory* had been blessed/cursed with over a thousand brain-damaged crewmen—a com blared:

"Sten to the bridge! Sten to the bridge!"

There was a slight note of emotion in the talker's voice—which meant that almost certain and immediate catastrophe loomed.

* * *

"These six screens are patch-ins from the *Bennington*'s internal com. They came right after the first contact."

Sten glanced at them—they showed weapons stations and missile-control consoles, all deserted.

"I am not assuming they're realtime casts," Freston continued.

Sten looked up at the main screen. On it was the *Bennington*, the tacship carrier that was the heaviest ship in Sarsfield's fleet. Flanking it were two specks that a readout ID'd as destroyers. Headed directly toward the *Victory* at full drive. Either Sarsfield had ordered a suicide run, since there was zero possibility the carrier could play hitsies with a battlewagon, or else things were getting weird out there.

"I have," Freston said, "six Kali stations manned, tracking and holding at four seconds short of launch."

"Replay the first transmission from the *Bennington*."

Freston brought the cast up on a secondary screen.

It showed the *Bennington*'s bridge, which looked as if it'd been the focal point for a bar brawl. The officer onscreen had a bandaged arm, and her uniform was torn.

"*Victory*, this is *Bennington*. Please respond, this freq, tightbeam. This is Commander Jeffries. I have assumed command of the *Bennington*. The officers and sailors of this ship have rejected Imperial authority, and are now under my orders. We wish to join you. Please respond." The screen swirled, and the message repeated.

"We also," Freston said, "have a cast from one of the DDs—the *Aoife*. The other one's the *Aisling*. They're both Emer-class." He indicated a projection from *Jane*'s on another screen, which Sten ignored.

"Their cast is shorter, and key-transmitted *en clair*. As follows: '*Aoife* and *Aisling* to join. Accept Sten command. Both ships homeworld Honjo Systems.' Does that explain anything, sir?"

It did—barely. The Honjo were known as supertraders throughout the Empire. And they were cordially hated. They were ethnocentric to a ridiculous extreme, dedicated to the maximum profit but absolutely loyal to whatever master they'd agreed to serve—as long as that loyalty was returned. They were also lethal, nearly to the point of race suicide, as the privy council had found out during the Interregnum when they tried to steal the Honjo's AM2.

Sten had heard rumors that since the Emperor's return the Honjo felt, with some degree of justification, they hadn't been rewarded properly (which meant monetarily) for their loyalty to the Empire.

"Divert the Kali watch from those two ships. Contact them as soon as I finish, tell them message received and stand by for instructions," Sten ordered. "We'll find out how far they're backing us in a bit. Get me through to this Jeffries on the *Bennington*."

The connection was made quickly. And the conversation was short. The *Bennington* had, indeed, mutinied. The captain was dead; five officers and twenty men were in the sick bays. About thirty percent of the crew, now held under arms, had remained loyal to the Empire.

"Request orders, sir," Jeffries finished.

"First," Sten said, thinking fast, "welcome to my nightmare, and I think you're all insane. Second, get all loyalists ready for transshipment. If you've got a supply lighter, use that. Otherwise, disarm enough tacships if that's the only alternative. Third, keep your weapons stations unmanned. Sorry, but we're not in a position to trust anyone.

"Fourth, stand by to receive visitors. Fifth, get your navcoms set up to slave to this ship's command. We're going to travel some, and you'll convoy on us. That's all."

"Yessir. Will comply. Standing by for your personnel to board. And . . . thank *you*."

Sten blanked the screen. He didn't have time to wonder why another set of idiots were volunteering for the death chamber. He looked around for Alex and found him, sitting back from the main console, looking smug. Kilgour surreptitiously crooked a finger. Sten, wanting to growl, went over.

"Y'r pardon, boss, but afore we move on, Ah hae a report . . . We're still rich, lad."

Sten repressed the suicidal urge to kick Alex. What the hell did that have to do with—

"Since we're in a hurry, Ah'll keep th' input short. While y' were doin't y'r usual job ae inspirin' th' idjiots, Ah hit our bank accounts.

"Another thing a wee outlaw needs is liquid'ty. So all our assets Ah could lay th' fast touch on, I dumped into an old laundry bank frae th' Mantis days."

Sten started to say something, but then realized Kilgour wasn't being greedy—revolutions, like politics, are fueled by credits and fail for lack of same nearly as often as they do for not providing a proper alternative. Sten would need all the credits in the known universe if he was even to survive this war, let alone win.

And Kilgour had not exaggerated about their riches. Years earlier, when they were prisoners of war of the Tahn, their ex-Mantis companion Ida the Rom had pirated their accrued pay and pyramided it into vast riches. They were wealthy enough for Sten to have purchased his own planet, and for Kilgour to build half-a-dozen castles and surrounding estates on his home world of Edinburgh.

"Then, thinkin't thae'll prob'ly be someone followin' that trail, Ah then rescrubbed th' gelt t' Ida, wi' a wee message t' stan' by an' expect th' pleasure ae our company, fat cow thae she is. Ah think we'll be needin't th' gypsies afore thae skreekin't an' scrawkin't is o'er.

"Plus Ah drop't a wee line t' our king ae th' smugglers ae well, although Ah dinnae ken i' Wild's dropbox is still good.

"Thae's all, boss. Noo, y' hae some work f'r me? Ah'm assumin't we're noo bein't sensible an' findin' a badger's den an' pullin' it in a'ter us."

Alex was on his feet and at attention. Sten nodded appreciation.

"You've got that right. Besides, the Emperor would just send badger dogs after us. So we won't bother. Grab about half of the Bhor and get over to the *Bennington*. Make sure they're real sincere about things."

"If not?"

"Do whatever seems right. But if it's a trap, make them bleed, not us. I'll keep two Kali stations launch-ready until you say otherwise, and I'll keep one flight of tacships out on CAP."

"Ah'm gone." And Kilgour was.

Sten wanted to take a deep breath and come up with a plan—but there was no time to do anything other than react. He went back to Commander—now Captain—Freston.

"Okay, Captain. You heard what we're doing. We'll have all three ships slaved to the *Victory*. I want an irrational evasion pattern on the nav computer."

"Yessir."

"I want one flight of tacships out around the *Bennington*. And I want another flight . . . gimme a hotrod—whatsername, La Ciotat—in charge . . . one light-second back of the formation, also slaved to the *Victory* as rear guard.

"Every time we hyperjump, we'll leave one of the *Bennington*'s Kalis behind, manned by one of Renzi's officers. I don't like being followed."

"Yessir."

"Now, get me double-ganged to those Honjo hardheads."

"Aye, sir. Do we have a final destination?"

Sten didn't answer.

Not because he didn't have an answer, but because one secret of being a live conspirator was never telling anyone anything until just before it happened. In fact, he had two, now that true miracles had happened and he had not just a ship, but the beginnings of a fleet.

The first one he hadn't exactly decided on. But it would be close to center stage, since all good rebellions require some kind of Bastille-bashing to get started.

The second?

Mahoney had shouted "Go home," as he was dragged off to his death.

And Sten had finally figured out exactly where Mahoney meant. Even if he still had not the slightest idea why or what.

Or so he hoped.

CHAPTER TWO

RANETT DUG HER elbow into a sleepy-eyed clerk's ribs, trod hard on a naval officer's toes, and, with practiced carelessness, dumped hot caff on a bureaucrat's swollen paunch.

As she punched through the crowd, she strewed apologies in her wake: "Pardon . . . So sorry . . . How clumsy of me . . ."

If anyone had been awake enough to notice, they would have seen that Ranett moved with the oiled ease of a combat veteran. She slipped through the crowd at full tilt. Leaping across openings. Forcing gaps where none existed before. All the while she kept her eyes focused on her eventual goal—the enormous doors leading into the Arundel Castle pressroom.

At the door she was brought up short by a black uniformed mountain. The golden insignia on the guard's sleeve was an ornate *I* with an *S* twisted around it like a snake. Wonderful, her mind snarled . . . Internal Clottin' Security.

She flashed her sweetest smile. Guaranteed to melt the hearts of most reasonably heterosexual males. "Excuse me, please . . ." Ranett started to duck under his arm and slip into the pressroom. Inside, she heard a briefer's dry voice. The clots have already started, she thought. I'll skin somebody's hide for this.

Again, the IS man barred her way. "Press only," he snarled.

Ranett kept the sweet smile pasted on. "Then, that means

me." She whipped out her credentials and held them steady for the big stupe's beady eyes. He looked closely at the credentials, then at her face. Taking his damned good time.

"Looks like you, all right," he said. Then he gave her a malicious grin. Double wonderful, Ranett thought. A media hater.

"You still can't go in."

"Why the clot not?"

The IS man jolted. The sweetness on Ranett's face was gone now. Her tone dripped icicles. But after the moment's hesitation, the guard failed to take warning.

"Orders, that's why," he growled. "The briefing's already in progress . . . No one may enter or leave until it's over."

A heartbeat later his self-satisfied smile was replaced with a look of pure terror as Ranett unleashed her pent-up fury.

"Get out of my way, you pumped-up little scrote," she snarled. "You let me in there this instant, or I'll fry your pubes for breakfast."

She let him have it for a full one and a half horrible minutes. Scorching him and the wall on either side with blasphemies and foul threats equal to anything the IS man had ever heard—up to and including introducing him to the Emperor's chief torturer.

As each second of the ninety dripped away like a full year, the name on the press ID started registering in his tiny brain. The woman flaying him alive was a legendary newsbeing. Ranett had covered the Tahn wars from the front. Survived the nightmare years when the privy council ruled. Produced prizewinning livie documentaries that even he had watched in awe. Mighty government and corporate chieftains had been known to flee like small boys caught in dirty little acts when she showed up with her recording crew.

When she paused for breath—or new inspiration—the IS man did his best to ooze out of her way. He was busy deserting his post—he'd rather face his hyena-voiced sergeant than this woman—when he heard the big doors hiss open, then closed. He looked behind him. Managed a breath . . . long and shuddering. Ranett was inside. He was safe until the press conference was over. And clot his orders.

Fleet Admiral Anders—Chief of His Majesty's Naval Operations—did a little mental swearing of his own when he saw Ranett duck into the crowded room and cozen some young fool out of an aisle seat.

Up until now, the thing had gone perfectly. When he had first gotten news of the drakh that had hit the fan in the Altaics, he had put his press crisis officers into motion before he had even gotten orders from the Emperor.

The admiral's critics—all silent now—believed him far too young for his post. Also too consciously handsome and smooth. A man who had climbed quickly to the top through political talent, rather than military. In fact, his combat medals had all been won by staged fly-ins to recently cleared enemy territory. He had fired many shots in anger, but all skillfully executed memos and press releases.

His first act as Chief of Naval Operations had been to create the emergency press-pool system the beings before him were operating under. The rules were simple: (1) Only newsbeings credentialed by his office could attend a Crisis Briefing. (2) Only questions pertaining to the "facts" presented in the briefing would be entertained. (3) Only authorized spokesbeings were permitted to be questioned. (4) Any violations of the first three rules might be deemed a breach of Imperial security and all parties prosecuted for treason.

Still, there were certain realities to handling the media. Some of the beings before him were stars as popular as any livie heart-throb. And they commanded salaries of such size that they were powerful corporations in their own right.

Fortunately, most of them were tame. One part of Anders's genius was he recognized that even a gadfly must join the institution it torments to become a rich and famous gadfly.

Ranett didn't fit this mold. She was merely famous. She had no desire for wealth. Cared nothing for her fame . . . except as a powerful tool to be used to get her way.

Which was why when Admiral Anders drew up the list

of reporters to be called, he was forced to include her name. But it went on the bottom. Careful instructions were given for the call to go out too late for Ranett to attend.

But here she was. In clotting person. Despite the hour—Anders had purposely set the crisis briefing for two E-hours before dawn—Ranett looked frighteningly awake. Unlike her punchdrunk colleagues who yawned and nodded all around her, halfheartedly bending an ear as Anders's pet briefing officer continued the jargon-laden drone.

". . . So much for the history and physical makeup of the Altaic Cluster. You will find planetary thumbnails, relative-grav data, and time-conversion charts in the materials we've already handed out," the officer said.

"Also included is a fact sheet on the four principal races: the Jochians and Torks. Both human. And the Suzdal and Bogazi. Both ET. It will be helpful to recall that the Jochians are the majority race. And each of the races harbored historical hatred of the other."

There was a dry rustle of documents as the officer moved on. "Next . . . the political backdrop. The details are well known to you all. However, to sum up. Anarchy threatened when the Emperor's trusted ally, The Khaqan, died. He was a member of the Jochian majority. It was unfortunate the heavy workload and detail-driven nature of his duties prevented The Khaqan from grooming a successor.

"The Emperor appointed Doctor Iskra—a prominent Jochian scholar and devoted citizen of the Empire—as the new leader . . ."

Ranett was getting the range now. She could see by the glazed look on her colleagues' faces that nothing important had been said . . . yet. But they were over an hour into the briefing. The dry lecturer in front of her was only one of several who had come before. Obviously, all of them had outlined equally unimportant facts. It was certainly not news that things had gone into the slokhouse in the Altaics. A leakproof news blackout had been slammed down for some time now. Ranett herself had just returned from an attempt to visit the sector. Her ship had been ordered back to Prime by someone very powerful, just short of its destination.

She quick-checked through the sheaf of press materials she had snagged on the way to her seat. Found the Crisis Briefing Agenda. Sure enough, the first items listed on the agenda came under the heading of Background. That was followed by Crisis In Focus: Fleet Admiral Anders, Chief of His Majesty's Naval Operations. This was followed by a Q&A. Nowhere on the agenda—or in the other material in the folder—was there a hint of exactly what this crisis briefing was all about. Except for the fact it had something to do with the Altaics. And it was probably military, since the briefing was being conducted by the Chief of Naval Operations.

If Ranett was the type who whistled, she would have done so right then. There was some deep drakh about to come down. In her experience weaving through the maze of Imperial politics, good news was announced immediately. Bad news was shunted to the end.

She caught Admiral Anders dart a glance at her. He was clearly stewing over her presence. Gooood! She gave him her nastiest grin. Anders pretended to ignore her. Turned his solemn attention back to his briefing officer.

". . . the greatest difficulty," the man was saying, "proved to be the numerous heavily armed forces at the command of the several highly volatile races. To begin with, a diplomatic effort was launched to meet with the commanders of the hostile forces arrayed against Dr Iskra. And, as quickly as possible, Imperial forces were sent in to assist Dr Iskra in keeping the peace. Those forces were commanded by one of the Emperor's most capable and loyal officers—Admiral Mason . . ."

Ranett's alarm bells started ringing. Why the lavish praise for Mason? She had also caught the past-tense phrase: ". . . forces *were* commanded." Then the alarms grew louder still. The briefing officer had unaccountably left out the name of the man who had headed the diplomatic mission: Plenipotentiary Sten. She knew Sten was one of the most prominent beings on the Eternal Emperor's staff. The poor sod, Ranett thought. To her mind, Sten was either being set up as a scapegoat or was bound for execution. She wondered if maybe it had already happened.

". . . Despite the many difficulties," the briefing officer continued, "we are happy to tell you today that the situation in the Altaics has stabilized. Order has been restored. Some time in the near future, we expect to be able to permit free travel and communication with the cluster."

Riiight! Ranett thought. She knew when she was wading in drakh thigh-deep. "Near future" most likely meant . . . never in her lifetime.

"That concludes the background portion of the agenda," the briefing officer said. He made with an insincere smile. "Thank you for your attention, gentlebeings. Admiral Anders will now bring us up to date on the latest developments. Please give him a warm welcome."

There was a scattering of applause as Anders came forward. This frosted Ranett. She noted most of the applause came from the star anchors. Human or ET, they all looked alike to Ranett—gorgeous, rich, and self-satisfied.

"This is a solemn moment for me, gentlebeings," Anders intoned. "It is with heavy heart that I announce to you that one of our own has betrayed all that I . . . and the hundreds of thousands other members of the Imperial forces . . . stand for."

Ranett leaned forward. Here it comes, she thought.

"Only hours ago, Admiral Mason stumbled upon a plot to overthrow His Majesty, the Eternal Emperor."

A loud rumble erupted from the press corps. Anders held up a hand for silence. And got it.

"The coup attempt—using the disturbances in the Altaic Cluster as a screen—was uncovered only moments after it was launched. Admiral Mason engaged the perpetrators. And shattered them . . .

". . . Losing his own life in the process. As well as all hands aboard his ship."

The rumble turned into a thunderclap. Newsbeings were on their feet shouting for attention. Ranett stayed in her seat. Intent on Anders. She noted that his left cheek was twitching. And his eyes were overly bright. Her conclusion: the Admiral was a lying sack.

Again Anders signaled for silence. Again he got it. "The coup was masterminded," he said, "by a being we all believed to be loyal . . . a man who proved to be secretly nursing an insane desire to murder our Emperor, and once again bring disaster to the Empire.

"Plenipotentiary Sten! A man who once had the Emperor's love and trust.

"You will be pleased to know that although this intergalactic outlaw survived, his forces have been destroyed or scattered. As we speak, they are being hunted down one by one."

Now, Anders skillfully allowed himself to be overwhelmed by questions.

"Any word on this villain's whereabouts, Admiral?" one of the overpaid anchors shouted.

"None that I am allowed to verify," Anders said. "But rest assured, Sten—and his underling, Alex Kilgour—can run. But they can't hide."

"Were any of the rebel forces in the Altaics involved?" came another question.

"Again, I am hampered by concerns of Imperial security. I can say, however, that Sten was heavily involved with the rebels in the course of his duties."

"Is there any danger of the conspiracy spreading?"

"I can't say no to that. But, I can say I believe we have it localized. Internal Security will be following up all leads."

It's witch-hunt time, Ranett thought.

"What were Admiral Mason's total casualties?"

"I'm sorry . . . Again, security concerns prevent me from answering. Except to say all hands aboard his flagship died in the cowardly attack."

"How many of Sten's forces have been killed or captured?"

Anders shrugged. "I repeat my last . . . Imperial security, and all. I promise all of you these questions, and all others, will be answered . . . in the fullness of time."

Ranett dipped into her bag of tricks and pulled out her favorite—the Donaldson. Her practiced bellow blasted over the other questioners. "ADMIRAL ANDERS! ADMIRAL ANDERS!"

She could not be denied. Anders sighed. Motioned for her to GA.

"What evidence do you have against these alleged conspirators?" she asked.

Anders frowned. "Evidence? I told you . . . There was a coup attempt." He tried laughing at her. "I know it's early, Ranett, but we do wish you'd pay attention when we speak."

"I heard you, Admiral," Ranett snarled. "But, I assume . . . If this Sten is captured—"

"*When*, Ranett. When!"

"Your qualification, Admiral. Not mine. Regardless. If, or when, Sten—and this Alex Kilgour—are captured . . . what proof of a conspiracy exists? For the trial, I mean. For example, did you monitor any conversations? Discover correspondence between the alleged perpetrators? Witness them meeting with known enemies of the Empire? That sort of thing."

Anders sputtered. "Dammit. They attacked and destroyed Admiral Mason's ship! What other proof do you need?"

Ranett wasn't buying. "An honest prosecutor might ask for more than your word, Admiral," she said. "Surely you can see that. Show us pictures of the attack, for example. Transcripts of bridge-to-bridge communications. Whatever proof you have."

"I'll have to plead security concerns again," Anders said. "You'll have those things . . . eventually."

"In the fullness of time?" Ranett said.

"I couldn't have put it better myself," Anders said.

Ranett knew, at that moment, no one had any intention of capturing Sten. Not alive, at any rate.

The admiral buried a smile and started to turn away.

"One other question, Admiral . . . if you please."

Anders buried a groan. "Go ahead, Ranett. *One* more."

"Does this incident with the plenipotentiary indicate a severe weakness in the diplomatic corps?"

Anders was honestly stumped. "I don't understand. This is an isolated incident. One man acting in league with a small group of deranged individuals. Nothing more."

"Then what about Ian Mahoney?"

Anders purpled. "One has nothing to do with the other," he snarled.

"Oh? Wasn't Ian Mahoney assigned to the Altaics as well? In fact, wasn't he Plenipotentiary Sten's superior at one time? And wasn't he just executed? Also accused—with great fanfare, I might add—as a traitor? And, like Sten, hadn't he too spent a lifetime in service to the Emperor?

"Come on, Admiral. Either one and one equals two or we have a coincidence that at the very least indicates dissatisfaction with Imperial policy. Loyal and able beings who have spent their entire careers fighting the Emperor's battles aren't suddenly transformed into traitors. Unless there is something seriously wrong."

"Writing an editorial, Ranett?" Anders growled.

"No, Admiral. Just asking questions. That's my job. Answering them is yours."

"I won't dignify your remarks by responding," Anders said. He turned to the rest of the newsbeings. "And . . . I warn you all . . . The area your colleague has just encroached upon is forbidden under the crisis-briefing rules. She—and the rest of you—*will* confine yourself to asking and communicating only those details authorized under those rules. Do I make myself clear?"

The press room was oddly silent. No one looked at Ranett. Angry enough to peel and parboil Anders, Ranett opened her mouth to bellow one more stinging question.

Then she saw the deadly look in Anders's eyes. Saw an Internal Security officer move forward, getting ready for a word from the admiral. Her jaw shut with a snap.

She smiled, shrugged, and buried her head in her notes.

Ranett was a survivor. She would get her questions answered—one way or the other.

As the press briefing broke up and everyone hurried out of the room, Ranett thought about Sten one more time.

Poor sap. He didn't stand a chance.

CHAPTER THREE

"I AM AFFLICTED with fools," the Eternal Emperor roared. "Overpaid, overstuffed, smirking, self-satisfied fools."

A variety of beings quaked in their footgear as the Emperor detailed his displeasure. There was Avri, the young woman with the very old eyes, who was his political chief of staff. Walsh, the handsome but exceedingly stupid boss of Dusable, who was the Emperor's toady in Parliament. Anders, the admiral who had run afoul of Ranett at the press conference. Bleick, the Emperor's chamberlain. And scores of other beings—uniformed and otherwise—were scurrying about the yawning Imperial chamber or hanging their heads in shame as the Emperor railed on.

The Emperor towered over Anders. Blue eyes shifting to the color of cold steel. "What kind of a press conference was that, Admiral? You're supposed to be an expert on that sort of drakh. God knows, you can't pour piss out of a boot when it comes to *real* military business."

"Yessir," the Admiral said. He was drawn up, heels locked, like a raw recruit.

"And *you*, Avri . . . You were supposed to gameplan this

thing with pube brain, here. I gave you the spin on a gilt-edged platter, for crying out loud."

"Yessir," Avri said. Licking lush lips with a nervous tongue.

"People, I do not have time to explain basic politics to you," the Eternal Emperor gritted. "Traitors—the privy council—put this Empire in its worst shape in two thousand years. And I barely pulled it out *that* time.

"Now I'm saddled with debt, harried by mewling allies, and every time I turn over another rock, a new kind of traitorous slime crawls out.

"In my view—which, dammit, is the only view that counts—Sten is the worst of the lot. I nursed that snake at my bosom for his whole clotting life. Gave him honors. Riches. And how does he repay me? Conspires with my enemies. Plots my murder. And when discovered, he slaughters innocent sailors, and one of the best admirals in my service, in a cowardly sneak attack."

The Emperor's voice lowered. He shook his head. Weary. "Now, *that's* a spin, dammit. Guaranteed to turn a drakhhouse into a palace. Not so very hard, is it?"

"I'm very sorry, sir," Anders said. "I don't know how that reporter—Ranett—got in."

"Oh, just shut the clot up, Admiral," the Emperor said. "If you can't make a plan that can stand the test of somebody with a little smarts, then get out of the clotting business."

"Yessir."

"Avri, it's damage-control time. I want *all* newscasts blanketed by our spin doctors. Hit the Op Ed programs extra hard. 'Face The Empire.' 'Witness To History.' 'Countdown.' That sort of thing.

"I especially want you to get into the pants of that Pyt'r Jynnings clown over at K-B-N-S-O. Half the Empire watches that piece of drakh he calls 'Nightscan.' I don't know why. Guess he makes everybody feel smart because he's so damned dumb."

"Right away, Your Majesty," Avri said.

"You! Walsh!"

The dimwit that was the ruler of Dusable blinked into semisentient awareness. "How . . . uh . . . may I be of . . . uh . . . service, Your . . . uh . . . Highness?" he managed.

"I want those lazy sods in Parliament stoked up. Some kind of condemnation vote. Calling Sten and that Scots sidekick of his every filthy name in the book. And if that vote isn't unanimous, I'll nail your guts to a post, Walsh. And lash you around it."

"Yessir," Walsh gobbled.

"One other thing. Get ahold of Kenna. I have a little personal business I want him to transact."

"Right away, Your Highness," Walsh said. Kenna was possibly the sharpest old pol on Dusable. A world whose politics were so crooked infants gurgled the word "mordida" before they learned to say "momma."

"Anders. I want all firstline forces on this. I don't care what fleets you have to strip. Sten *must* be found."

"Yessir."

"Bleick!" His chamberlain snapped to. "I want—"

He stopped in midorder as the door hissed open and Poyndex, his chief of Internal Security, entered. His face was grim. Bloodless. A man bearing bad tidings. But the Emperor was too angry to immediately notice.

"Where the clot have you been, Poyndex? I told you I wanted that info on Sten and Kilgour immediately, dammit. Not tomorrow. Not the day after. But now, dammit. Now!"

Poyndex glanced quickly around the room. Then back at the Emperor. "I think we need to talk in private, sir."

"I don't have time for games, Poyndex. Spit it out."

Poyndex hesitated. The Emperor's eyes got a sudden spooky glint in them. Clinical paranoia was Poyndex's diagnosis. "If you insist, Your Majesty," Poyndex said. "But I would be remiss if I didn't warn you one more time. This should be discussed in private. I strongly urge you to reconsider."

The Eternal Emperor turned to his people. "Get out."

They got. With feeling. In moments the room was empty. The Emperor looked back at Poyndex. "Okay. Now report."

Poyndex stiffened. "I regret to say there is nothing *to* report, sir. All files on Sten and Alex Kilgour have been wiped clean."

"Say clotting what?"

"It's as if they never existed, sir." Poyndex's heart was hammering as he delivered the news.

"That's not possible," the Emperor said.

"But I'm afraid it's true, Your Majesty," Poyndex said. "Even the Mantis computers have been penetrated. There is no record of Sten—or Alex Kilgour—in *any* record system in the Empire. I don't know how it was done. I've got every tech in IS working around the clock. The only thing we know for sure is it had to have been done by a very high placed insider."

The Emperor stared at Poyndex for a long, uncomfortable time. He turned and palmed a switch. His personal computer terminal winked into life.

"Fortunately," the Emperor said, "I keep my own files for just this reason." He laughed. Without humor. "When all is lost," he said, "you have to depend on yourself."

His fingers flashed across keys, beginning the search.

"I *used* to have a staff I could depend upon," the Emperor said. "Mahoney, for one. Sometimes I regret I had to have him killed. Ian was a strong right arm, that's for sure." The Emperor, who normally appeared to be a man in his mid-thirties, suddenly seemed very old to the IS chief. His handsome features drawn. His voice high-pitched . . . and weak.

The Emperor looked up at Poyndex. ". . . The same with Sten. I tell you, Poyndex, the trouble with traitors is they tend to be your best people." Another humorless laugh. "Maybe that's what old Julius was trying to tell Brutus."

"Pardon me, Your Majesty? I have no knowledge of these beings. Should I have IS put this Julius and Brutus on your Personal Enemies list?"

The Emperor grunted. "Never mind." He muttered to himself. Just loud enough for Poyndex to hear. "That's the other thing . . . No one to talk—"

He suddenly broke off. "What the clot?"

"Something wrong, sir?"

The Emperor hammered keys. "No. I probably should have—Holy drakh!"

The Emperor bleared up at Poyndex. "My files . . ." he gasped, "they're . . ."

Poyndex glanced at the screen. Saw the display. "STEN, NI. KILGOUR, ALEX. NO FILES ON RECORD. PRESS ONCE FOR ANOTHER REQUEST."

The IS chief staggered back, as flabbergasted as his boss. The Eternal Emperor's personal files on Sten and Kilgour had been wiped absolutely clean.

The Emperor's heavy fist smashed on his desk. "I want Sten, dammit! Get him, Poyndex. If you don't, I will. And I will personally put his head on a stake next to yours."

Poyndex fled. And as he went out the door, he swore he could hear a growling, as if a great hound were snarling after him.

CHAPTER FOUR

"GOOD EVENING, GENTLEBEINGS. I'm Pyt'r Jynnings. Welcome to this week's edition of 'Nightscan.' The news program that examines the crucial issues of our time.

"Tonight we focus our full hour on an event that has stunned the Empire. At the heart of this broadcast is a disarmingly simple question . . .

"Sten: Traitor, or Misunderstood Genius?

"To my right, Professor Knovack. A renowned Imperial historian and expert on parliamentary power brokering. To my left, Sr Wiker. Former speechwriter for the Eternal Emperor. Current ambassador to the Tahn worlds.

"Professor. We'll start with you. What is your response to the question?"

"Oh, he's a traitor. No question about it."

"What about you, Sr Wiker?"

"I couldn't have put it better myself, Pyt'r. Sten is definitely a traitor."

"Ah! Agreement! And . . . uh . . . so soon. Goodness me. Well, let's explore the other side of the coin, then. Professor?"

"I went first before."

"Ha ha. Too true. Well, Sr Wiker, what's fair is fair. Now, tell us . . . do you think Sten is a misunderstood genius?"

"That's an interesting question, Pyt'r. And I've come prepared to discuss it all night . . . if I have to."

"Good. Good."

"But, before we do, I think we have to talk about the nature of this man."

"Oh? Did you know Sten? Personally?"

"Good God, no! Uh . . . I mean . . . I know *of* him. And I most certainly know *his* type."

"Please share these insights with our viewers."

"To begin with, he has enjoyed the favor of our Emperor his entire life. True, he performed some service. Valuable service, some might say."

"But, would *you* say that?"

"I think that's . . . uh . . . open to interpretation. More importantly, he has been the recipient of a host of honors. So these services—however one might characterize them— have certainly been repaid. Besides these honors, he has also been blessed with great wealth. Thanks to his friendship with the Eternal Emperor."

"How do you react to those statements, Professor Knovack?"

"I think this . . . this . . . traitor approached our Emperor in a rare moment of weakness. After that awful business with the privy council. And our beloved Emperor mistook his ambition for love and loyalty. And now it seems . . . the Emperor was . . . was . . . nurturing a snake at his bosom."

"Very well put, Professor. Your reputation as a phrase-maker has once again been assured . . . Any comments thus far, Sr Wiker?"

"I think we're forgetting those poor Imperial service beings who were the victims of Sten's traitorous and cowardly action. Especially Admiral Mason. Think of his family! Think of how much agony they must be in at this moment."

"A most excellent point. I think we should all pause for just a moment. A moment of silence, if you please. Out of respect for Admiral Mason's family and the crew of the *Caligula* . . ."

As the vid recorders whirred for the billions of K-B-N-S-O viewers, the three men solemnly bowed their heads.

The director's voice whispered in Jynning's ear. "For clot's sake, Pyt'r. Not the silence business again!"

The anchor whispered back into his throat mike: "Shut the clot up, Badee. You're not the one who has to fill an hour with these two scrotes."

"Well, think fast, bub. We've got fifty minutes to go."

"Cut to a commercial, dammit."

"You gotta be kidding," Badee said. "Who'd advertise on a piece of drakh like this?"

"How about a 'Give Blood' spot, then?"

"Oh, maaann. Another house ad. Okay. If we gotta. On the count, then . . . One . . . Two . . ."

At that moment a porta-ram smashed through the studio doors.

"On the floor," Sten shouted.

"Move't, or lose't, mates," Alex thundered.

Jynnings, his guests, Badee, and the livie crew gaped for a full two seconds. Sten and Alex strode over the ruined double doors, willyguns at the ready. Behind them, Cind led a contingent of Bhor and Gurkhas.

"It's Sten!" Jynnings uttered in absolute awe. "And Kilgour."

Sten motioned with his weapon. "I said, Down!" He fired, blowing a largish hole in the news anchor's desk.

Much diving for the floor commenced, Jynnings denting his wavy head against the desk. Only the director had the presence of mind to whisper into his mike: "Holy mother . . . we've *got* our hour! Keep rolling, fools. Keep rolling."

Sten advanced, just out of pickup range. To his right, an emergency door creaked open. Sten saw a flash of many uniforms. Guards. Then the air shattered as Cind put a burst through the doorway. Howls of agony. The uniforms vanished.

A burly man stepped out of the shadows, swinging a heavy light standard.

"Ooops, there, lad," Alex said, catching the light housing with one hand. Giving it a yank. "Y've made a wee m's-take." The grip stumbled forward. Alex dropped the light and hoisted the man off the floor. With one hand. "'Tis noo i' y'r job description, mon. Y'r lucky Ah'm noo a taleteller. Ah'd put a bug in y'r shop steward's shell, otherwise."

The man's eyes bugged out. Alex hurled him. A loud crash as the goon hit, and monitors cascaded around him.

Alex turned back to Sten. "Ah, think w' hae their attention noo, wee Sten . . . I's showtime, folks."

Sten stepped in front of the camera.

"Gentlebeings," he said. "Fellow-citizens of the Empire . . . My name is Sten. The subject of this broadcast. I am addressing you live from K-B-N-S-O . . ."

Anders gulped like a fish as he watched Sten address the Empire. The man he sought was speaking from the station's main broadcasting center—in an orbit only a half-an-E hour from Prime World. His propaganda-centered mind immediately caught the full impact of the blow Sten had just struck.

The man was standing virtually in the center of the Emperor's stronghold. Waving a rude finger at the mightiest military force in history.

". . . The Emperor has branded me and my colleagues a traitor," Sten was saying. "History will judge if this is true. Just as history will judge the Emperor. And I promise you it will judge him harshly. My fate does not matter. It is your fate you should be thinking of at this moment. And your children's.

"I accuse the Emperor of betraying *you*. . . His people. You work in near poverty. While he enjoys lavish entertainment. As do his favored cronies. You labor in cold, in heat, in near darkness. While the Emperor's favored bask in the light of plentiful AM2.

"The Emperor has betrayed you. Only one of many crimes. I will detail those crimes over the coming days: Star-chamber justice. The imprisonment, torture, and execution of beings whose only sin was to trust their Emperor . . ."

Anders recovered and turned to his aide, Captain Lawrence. The woman's face was a mask of confusion.

"Scramble the fleet," the admiral barked. "I want to see a hole in the sky. And I want to see it quick."

"But . . . all the civilians at the station—"

"Clot the civilians. I want that man dead. Now, move it!" The captain rushed into action.

Anders turned back. Sten was still talking. Good. I'll see you in hell, you son of a bitch.

Alex signaled to Sten. A finger across his throat. Time to get the clot out.

". . . The list of the Emperor's sins is far longer than I have time to detail. I suspect his fleets are on the way now. So, I haven't much time. Except to say this:

"I, Sten, declare war on the Eternal Emperor. And I urge you all to join me in this crusade. He's left you nothing to lose. And *all* your freedom to gain.

"Thank you. And good night."

Sten lifted his weapon and turned the camera into molten metal and plas. The station jolted again and again, as Sten's forces blew their strategically placed explosives. No innocents would be hurt. But it would take many months and even more credits before K-B-N-S-O broadcast again.

Sten prodded Jynnings with his toe. The man whimpered and looked up at him with terror-stricken eyes. The anchor was sure he was staring a madman in the face.

"Thanks for the loan of your program," Sten said.

"Sure," Jynnings squeaked. "Anytime."

Cind shouted, "We're three seconds behind schedule."

Sten nodded, and sprinted through the blackened hole posing as a doorway, his team behind him. The last out was Cind. She paused and fired a long burst around the room to add to the terror and confusion. Molten metal and plas dripped from smoking walls.

Then she was gone.

Jynnings raised his head from the floor. "Thank God," he breathed. "I'm safe."

"Who cares," the director said as he scrambled to his feet. "You realize what we just broadcast? I tell you, the numbers we get on this baby are gonna blow our competition out of the water."

Badee looked around at the ruins of the studio. Humming to himself. It was gonna be easy street all the way, now. He would have his pick of any job in the livie business.

He wondered if there was a com line undamaged. He had to call his agent. Real quick.

All the alarms were hooting warnings as Sten and the others dived aboard the *Victory*. Within minutes, Sten was on the bridge. Captain Freston's face relaxed slightly.

"Just in time," Freston said. "We've got a whole clottin' fleet after our tender young hides. Led by a big clottin' battleship . . . the *Nevsky*. Permission to run like hell, sir."

"Negative," Sten said, scanning the incoming blips. There

was just enough time. "I want to thin out a little of the competition, first, Captain."

Sten swiveled to Lieutenant Denzi. "Weapons?"

"All Kali and Goblin units at full launch-readiness," she reported. The woman was ready to fight.

Sten hated to disappoint her. "I'm afraid I'm going to have to do the honors, Lieutenant," he said.

He raced for a Kali station. He called out to Captain Freston as he pulled on the helmet. "When I say go . . . go, dammit!"

Freston nodded. He wouldn't need to be prodded. The monitors showed the *Nevsky* coming fast, accompanied by half-a-dozen cruisers and a forest of destroyers.

Sten's hand automatically armed the missile, then fired. His point of view was black space pricked with flares of color rushing by him as the missile hurtled out.

There was a cruiser bearing down on the *Victory*. Behind it he could see the battleship. There was just a chance he might slip his Kali past the cruiser. But Sten opted to play it safe. Especially when he saw the cruiser's missile bays' gunports yawn, ready to fire at the *Victory*.

Aboard the *Nevsky*, Captain Leech faced a similar problem. His battle monitors showed the *Victory* in a parking orbit to the side of the orbiting livie station. An alarm indicated an enemy Kali honing in on his lead cruiser. And that the cruiser blocked any possible shot at the *Victory*.

Then he saw the solution. The livie station.

Leech had become addicted to an ancient Earth game when he was a young officer on his first lonely outpost. It was called "pool." Why, he didn't know. One didn't puddle water on the green felt table. In a clutch, one of his favorite tactics was a "power break," which called for smashing the white cue ball into its brothers with all his strength. The results were messy, but sometimes miraculous.

The livie station before him presented a similar situation. A direct hit on the station would produce an explosion that would, at the very least, damage the nearby *Victory*. The bigger the blast, the greater chance he had to disable or even destroy Sten's ship.

It never entered Leech's mind it took a minimum of two thousand beings to run a livie station of K-B-N-S-O's size. His orders, after all, were to get Sten. At all costs.

A rush of orders to his weapons officer put his plan into action.

Moments later, three nuclear-tipped missiles spit from the *Nevsky*'s tubes.

Freston had never heard of pool. But he was blessed with a remarkably quick mind. When the enemy missiles winked into life onscreen, he at first thought the captain of the *Nevsky* must be incompetent. Their trajectory would take them nowhere near the *Victory*. His mind swiftly calculated their course . . . the livie station? What the clot? Then he got it.

There was no time to warn the station. Much less Sten, who was hunched at the Kali controls, his mind racing along with the missile he'd aimed at the enemy cruiser.

Freston's hand smashed down on the drive controls.

The cruiser jumped up at Sten, as the Kali closed. He thumbed controls, the image blurred, and his mind was falling away . . . back . . . back . . . back . . .

The Imperial missiles struck the station simultaneously. The nukes detonated. Two thousand beings ceased to exist.

Radioactive debris shrapneled outward. In moments the *Victory* would be riddled.

Sten plunged into awareness just as the *Victory* crashed into hyperspace. Kilgour's face bleared at him. Pale and worried. Behind him was an anxious Freston.

"Tell us y'r name, lad," Alex said.

"Say clottin' what?"

"Y'r name. 'Tis a wee test."

Sten snarled back. "Kilgour, if you don't get your haggis breath out of my face, I'm going to stuff you into a ship's stomach along with the rest of the porridge."

Kilgour turned back to Freston. A big smile wreathed his round face. "Aye, he's fightin' fit. Altho' his slangin' c'd use a bit o' work."

"What the clot's going on, Kilgour?" Sten demanded.

"W' hae to' leave, wi'oot waitin' on th' order ae our comin't, nor f'r you t' bash th' cruiser. Th' mad Emp hae stuck his foot in th' drakh i' whae's goin't on, young Sten."

"I repeat my opening remarks, Kilgour. What the clot is going on?"

"Th' Emp's blow' it up his pet livie station."

"What the clot for?" Sten was gaping.

Alex made a motion with his heavy-world shoulders. It was a shrug that came in a massive wave.

"P'raps he dinnæ like th' panto."

CHAPTER FIVE

EYES ONLY

NODIST

NONONIMP

NOFILE

PERSONALLY DESTROY POST RECEIPT

ACKNOWLEDGE TO ORIGINATOR VERBAL ONLY NOREC

DOCUMENT ID: None (vice Originator)

TO: ALL IS STATION HEADS
   DESIGNATED/CLEARED EMBASSY SECURITY STATION CHIEFS
   OTHER PERS DESIGNATED BY P. OR HIGHEST

FROM: POYNDEX, HEAD, INTERNAL SECURITY

1. All stations have received orders for the immediate apprehension of STEN, (NO INITIAL). No task is to be given higher priority by IS personnel unless specifically notified otherwise by P. or designated subordinate.

2. This task is to include the apprehension or deactivation, by any means necessary, of all involved co-conspirators; both those identified to date in Imperial Bulletins and those who are clearly participants but not yet named.

3. To this end, you are authorized to commandeer or requisition any Imperial resources whatsoever, WITH HIGHEST AUTHORIZATION with no justification for actions of this nature required to normal-channel suppliers.

4. In addition, ANY intelligence of any nature pertaining to STEN, NI, and KILGOUR, ALEX, is to be forwarded to this station, PRIORITY ONE-ALPHA. Particularly sought is physical descriptions, habits, hobbies, speciality areas (civilian and otherwise), places where above are known to have frequented, in short, ALL data concerning above two individuals.

5. No, repeat no screening of raw data relevant to (para. 4) above is to be made.

6. (Para. 4) and (para. 5) are not to be discussed with local authorities nor any conventional division of Imperial Intelligence.

7. Any request for data in the area of (para. 4) cannot be answered at this time, and IS chiefs are advised to avoid mentioning reasons to anyone in (para. 6). This is due to some confusion and doubling of input, caused as an act of sabotage by STEN, NI, or some other conspirator yet to be discovered and indicted. As complete data becomes available on STEN, NI, and KILGOUR, ALEX, it will be immediately disseminated to all levels.

8. Under *no* circumstances is the information in (para. 4), (para. 5), (para. 6), and (para. 7) to be conveyed with any personnel formerly associated with the discredited Mercury Corps, nor, most particularly, with Mantis Section. In addition, any inquiries as to STEN, NI, by former operatives of this branch, especially Mantis Section, must be reported *immediately*, Priority One-Alpha, to P.

9. If possible, STEN, NI, is to be apprehended secretly and immediately prepared for transfer directly to Prime for trial. No information is to be released, particularly to media.

10. If, however, apprehension is made by operatives other than IS, and publicity is inevitable, STEN, NI, is to be charged with HIGH TREASON, MURDER, CONSPIRACY and ATTEMPTED REGICIDE. Other charges will be filed after STEN, NI, has been transferred to Prime World and is in high-security custody.

11. In the event of contact with STEN, NI, and apprehension is not possible, or in the event of attempted escape after apprehension, immediate termination *must* be made.

12. As a corollary task, all IS operatives are ordered to devote maximum attention to uncovering the degree of conspiracy attempted by STEN, NI. However, under no circumstances is this investigation to be regarded as a "hunting license" to remove other enemies of the Empire. This task is too important and too immediate to be allowed to broaden to such a degree, although operatives should maintain files on the above matter for eventual attention.

13. Successful accomplishment of this most vital mission will not only be deemed in the Highest Traditions of Internal Security, but a personal service to the Eternal Emperor himself, and so rewarded.

FOR THE ETERNAL EMPEROR

P.

CHAPTER SIX

THE SCHOOL OF fish broke the surface, scattering spray against the face of a wind-whitened wave, then skittered down across the trough.

Their flight was pointless. Death was close.

The sea exploded as the great creature arced out of the water in front of the school, mouth gaping as it inhaled the leader. A monstrous flipper crashed and two more of the half-meter-long fish writhed, then floated limply, momentarily stunned.

The com buzzed, and Rykor's focus on her alfresco midday meal was shattered. But she didn't answer immediately. Instead, she deliberately devoured both fish before they could recover, thoughtfully analyzing their taste.

Yes, she thought. These were not from our farm-spawnings. Yet another ground is breeding back to its proper level. True wild fish can always be distinguished. The taste is . . . more . . . more . . .

Pondering just what it was more of, the being that was the Empire's most gifted psychologist rolled on her back, oblivious to the raging hurricane and the below-zero-C temperatures. Rykor's flipper waved over the bone-induction com that fitted closely around her neck. Neck was an arbitrary designation—Alex Kilgour had once observed that "it hae t' be th' lass' neck, since some'at keeps her head frae bangin' into her chest, aye?"

The caller was one of her assistants, in the luxurious quarters/office she'd had lovingly built that some insensitive sorts compared to an arctic sea cave.

"I do not," Rykor rumbled, "particularly appreciate being interrupted in midmeal. Lunch, as the humans say, is important."

"There is a priority message from Prime," the assistant said, new enough to be somewhat awed by this communication from the Imperial capital. "It requires that you stand by for special duties, at the command"—and his tone grew more hushed—"of the Eternal Emperor himself."

Rykor stiffened. "What sort of duties?"

"The message was not specific. But it said the duties would almost certainly be protracted, so you are advised to bring a gravchair and pack accordingly."

No mention of the late Ian Mahoney, Rykor thought. Nor of the recently outlawed Sten. Nor did the message suggest that perhaps the Emperor—or more likely his new head of secret police, Poyndex—might also be interested in why Rykor had conferred recently, in the greatest secrecy, with one Sr Ecu, Diplomat Extraordinaire.

Bad, bad, very bad.

"And how am I to get to Prime?"

"An Imperial ship has been dispatched. I have a confirm from the spaceport that its time of arrival is within two E-days."

Worse and worse, Rykor thought.

"Shall I reply, or wait for your return?"

"Advise that . . . advise that you are still attempting to contact me."

"Received. But . . ."

"For your own sake, if you are recording this conversation, I would suggest you blank the record immediately. By the way, that is an order."

"Are you returning now?"

Rykor thought hard. She had two E-days before the ship that could only be carrying Poyndex's gestapo and an arrest warrant arrived. Time enough.

"I am. But only momentarily. For these new duties, I shall require some time to myself, out here at sea, preparing and focusing my energies."

"Of course," the still-bewildered assistant said. Like all aquatic races, Rykor's race needed the sea not only for physical health and nourishment, but for psychic replenishment as well. "I shall have your usual travel pack ready."

"Very good. I am returning. Close transmission."

Rykor, without waiting for acknowledgement, shut the com off and bulleted back toward her home.

Two days.

Time enough for her to pack bare necessities and get to the in-atmosphere flier she had concealed underwater not far from the cave, the flier she had bought a few years earlier, when she sensed that somehow the Empire was going very wrong.

All of her expertise about intelligence was theoretical, but she had spent long years advising Mahoney when he was head of Mercury Corps and then Sten. She knew any conspirator worth his cloak always had a back door.

The rest of the back door was a small yacht she had hidden in a remote warehouse at a tiny spaceport on the other side of her world. She had two days until their arrival, then perhaps two more days while they fruitlessly searched the winter oceans for Rykor on her mythical wanderjahr—and then they would know she had fled.

Long enough, she hoped.

She even had a refuge—with the being that had first come to her with the horrid suspicion that the Eternal Emperor had gone insane.

Sr Ecu caught the updraft that rose close to the vertical, sunbaked cliff and allowed it to loft him out of the twisting canyon, high into the sky.

Before him, centered in the vast valley, was the towering spire of the Manabi's Guesting Center.

Sr Ecu had delayed his passage as long as he dared, following the course of the canyon as it wound its way toward the valley. He could dawdle no longer.

He'd taken his time in responding to the summons not out

of rudeness—among the Manabi's qualifications as the Empire's diplomats and negotiators was an overwhelming sense of what could only be termed decency—but so he could make sure his carefully prepared lies would still stand up.

He also felt a relatively unfamiliar "emotion," to use the human term. Fear. If the slightest suspicion fell on Ecu, the Manabi's main protection, absolute neutrality, would not help him stay alive.

Ecu himself had broken that political and moral neutrality some time ago, when he had determined the Eternal Emperor was no longer qualified to rule, and that the Emperor was, in fact, destroying the Empire he had created. He'd then sought out Rykor, for confirmation of his theories and that he was not the first Manabi to go insane.

And then he had sought out Mahoney and Sten, advised them of the situation, and, still worse, announced he, and therefore the entire Manabi race, would be willing to assist in any attempt to prevent the seemingly inevitable collapse of the Empire.

Now Mahoney was dead and Sten was on the run.

Just ahead could be the instrument of Ecu's own dissolution into the nonmaterial racial presence. He wondered just who the Emperor's inquisitor would be.

Ecu's long black body, red-tinted at the wingtips, three-meter-long tail ruddering skillfully, floated toward the Center. Ecu found his senses at peak. Perhaps, he thought, because this could be the last time he experienced the quiet joy of his home world. At times he wondered why he'd ever chosen his career, a career that took him away, off Seilichi and its lake-dotted single supercontinent and occasional jagged mountain ranges.

Perhaps he should have stayed, and been no more than just another philosopher, drifting in his world's gentle winds, thinking, teaching. His early sketches at forming a personal dialectic were stored on a fiche somewhere underground, where the Manabi kept whatever machines and construction necessary.

The only artificial constructs to show above Seilichi's surface were the three Guesting Centers, and they existed only as a courtesy to whatever non-aerial beings chose to visit the planet. And they were intended to appear, as much as possible, like huge natural extinct volcanic necks, with the landing fields hidden in the "crater."

The Center sensed Ecu's approach, and a portal yawned. Ecu flew inside, tendrils flickering. He found traces of the signature scent he used, and followed those traces to the assigned conference room.

Inside, sitting very much at ease, was the Emperor's emissary.

Solon Kenna was even fatter and more benevolent appearing, if in a bibulous fashion, than Ecu remembered. Those who had taken Kenna as an obese caricature of a stupid, crooked pol over the years had generally not survived in the political arena long enough to correct their thinking.

Now Kenna was on Seilichi, as the Emperor's hatchet man.

"It has been long."

"Too long," Kenna said, coming quickly to his feet and smiling. "I have been sitting here, lost in thinking of the marvels of Seilichi." Of course Kenna pronounced the word correctly. He still showed the regrettable love for flowery speech the Emperor had noted years ago. "I should have found occasion to journey here many times, especially now that the Empire has returned.

"But . . ." He shrugged. "Time creeps up and past all of us. And I have had my own concerns. You know that I am preparing my memoirs?"

"Those will be most interesting."

Ecu was being more than polite—he was constantly wondering why humans had such a love for the convolutions of dishonest politics when, from his race's point of view, a direct approach was far more likely to work. Not that the Manabi ever allowed this belief to hamper their appreciation for circumlocution, nor their abilities to practice it. So, indeed, if those memoirs were in fact produced, Ecu would be fascinated by how many ways Kenna could find to avoid the simple fact that he was, and had been since he was a baby ballot-box-stuffer, Crooked to the Gunwales.

"But now I am here on business," Kenna said, mock-mournfully. "The business of the Eternal Emperor." He slid a card from his pocket, and the Imperial emblem glowed to life, keyed to Kenna's pore patterns.

"Regarding Sten, I would imagine."

"You imagine correctly."

"Of course," Sr Ecu said, "I will render what service I can. I see no problem in cooperating, since my race's neutrality has never extended to a confessional seal about criminals—which Sten is, correct?"

"Of the worst order," Kenna agreed. "He betrayed the Empire—and for no reason that anyone can ascertain except personal ambition."

Kenna tried to look pious, a laughable attempt. It was supposed, the Manabi knew, to look stupid, and the witness then encouraged to think Kenna the same, never noticing the razor gleam from his piggish eyes.

"Ambition . . . something that makes mockery of us all, as the poet said."

"Sten," Ecu mused, as if assembling his thoughts. "I frankly know very little, since the time I spent in his company was rather . . . frantic, might be the correct word.

"The Tribunal and the privy council was far more on my mind than anything else. But, as I said, what help I may render, I shall. But I'm puzzled, frankly. Considering all the time Sten passed in Imperial Service, I would think your . . . I mean Imperial . . . records would be far more thorough, even considering that the greater percentage of his career was spent in . . . irregular pursuits."

Kenna frowned—and it seemed this expression was honest. "I thought so, too. But evidently not. Or else the Emperor needs to cross-correlate what records he has. Or, and this is the most likely, he's dredging for any scrap that can bring this traitor to the bar."

"Where would you like to begin, then?"

"Would you consent to a brainscan? A machine and the finest technicians of Internal Security are aboard my ship."

Ecu jolted, wingtips involuntarily twitching. A brainscan was not only the ultimate mental rape, but likely to produce longterm psychic damage or death, even when performed by the most highly skilled operator.

"I will not," Ecu said firmly, after he recovered. "While I have served the Emperor, I must officially remind you that I was never in his service, nor were any others in my race. And we have our own secrets, of course, which are not of the Emperor's concern."

Kenna nodded acceptance and reached to a side table. On it were the refreshments the Manabi had provided—Kenna's favorite brandy from Dusable, a glass, and a tray of snacks, supposedly intended to sop up the affects of alcohol, actually chemically synthesized to compound them.

"The Emperor said you would decline, and told me I was not to press the point. He did, however, add—and this is off the record, so if you are recording this meeting you are requested to so cease—the following, and I am quoting directly:

"'When Sten is apprehended, tried, and brainscanned prior to execution, any being involved with him or his conspiracy, no matter if they're neutral, will be considered a personal enemy, and dealt with accordingly.'"

"That," Ecu said, feeling proud that his wing tendrils did not even flicker slightly at the threat, "is not the most diplomatic statement I have ever heard the Eternal Emperor make."

"These are not diplomatic times," Kenna said. "And he takes the threat of Sten and the others far too seriously to waste time with niceties. However, my personal apologies for the bluntness, even though I was merely the messenger. And I also wish to apologize for the amount of your time I am now going to consume, since the Emperor wants *everything*.

"I must now advise you that this conversation is being recorded. You have a right to counsel, legal advice, and medico-watch to ensure you are not under any influence, physical or pharmacological."

"I understand, and thank you for the dual apologies," Ecu said. "But for me, at present, there is nothing but time. Shall we begin?"

He carefully began his story. He would tell it very slowly, with great exactness, and the tale would take several days.

And at the end of each day he would carefully check his story, Kenna's reactions, and what should come next with his own mentor, hidden far below the conference room in one of the Manabi's laboratories.

Rykor.

Chief (Investigative Division) Lisa Haines came suddenly awake—but made no move whatsoever.

First . . . ears.

Nothing.

Smell. Nothing.

What, then?

Motion. Her entire "houseboat" moved slightly.

She opened her eyes a pinhole.

Moonlight filled the large single room of her home—a McLean-powered barge moored several hundred meters above one of Prime World's forest refuges.

The room was empty.

Her husband, Sam'l, snored gently beside her.

Haines's hand slid to the side of the bed. Down the side of the watertube mattress. Touched the butt of the mini-willygun. The always-loaded gun was in her hand and the safety slid off.

Again, the houseboat swayed.

Someone trying to climb up one of the mooring cables? Yes.

Haines was in bed/Haines was suddenly crouched, naked, combat stance, in the middle of the floor, gun ready. Confirmed. She was alone.

She snaked to an armoire, took out and pulled on a one-piece phototrophic coverall. The coverall, like the pistol, was strictly Imperial-issue, and not even a police chief like Haines was entitled to own either one. But, as always, cops don't follow the laws they enforce.

Haines had been expecting this.

Now to confirm.

She slid to the door leading out to the houseboat's deck, and opened it a notch. Then she took a pair of light-amplifying goggles from a hook beside the door and pulled them on.

Daylight. A little green, but daylight.

Out, onto the deck.

The houseboat swayed again.

Not yet. First worry about . . . she scanned the darkness of the hillside across from her. Nothing. She switched modes, into thermal imaging, and looked again. Ah. A tidy little glow over there. Several beings.

The command post, she speculated. That's what it would be, if what she had been anticipating was in fact happening.

Or else the kingpins, allowing for the other possibility—that some of the gangsters she had harassed and crucified regularly over the years were coming to wreak revenge. Unlikely. Crooks only looked for nonprofitable vengeance in the livies.

Haines switched the goggles back to light amplification, went flat, and slid forward, peering over the edge.

Quite correct.

Someone . . . three someones . . . were coming up the mooring cable. Skilled climbers—but as they climbed, the cable unavoidably swayed, and the houseboat jerked minutely. All three someones wore identical phototropic coveralls, combat vests, and holstered pistols. Some kind of special-ops team.

All right, Haines thought. What you were hoping wouldn't happen is happening. You've worried about it from the time you heard Sten was named traitor—she came close to god-damning her ex-lover—and there is no way you are going to stand still for a brainscan or any of the other lovely devices you have heard Internal Security is using for "deep interrogation." Not you. And *by God*, not Sam'l.

A whole clotting lifetime being on the right side of the law, and just because of a minor love affair—all right, a major love affair—way back when and you're now a crook.

A completely unknown fragment drifted through her mind, translated from some long-forgotten tongue: ". . . where every cop is a criminal/and all the sinners saints . . ."

She shot the first climber in the face.

The crash of the detonating round echoed into the stillness, and the man dropped soundlessly, straight down, cleaning off the second infiltrator as he fell.

A scream, and Haines was rolling back to the doorway, flipping open the cover of what appeared to be an outdoor power socket but was a switch, switch closed, and . . . thank the Lord for the blessing of paranoia—the three saddle charges blew her mooring cables in half.

The third climber shouted in surprise, then fell silently to his death as the houseboat, unanchored, lifted like a balloon under the power of its antigrav generator.

Now, Haines thought, let us hope these 'nappers didn't want to disturb my neighbors' sleep with nasty old overhead aircraft, because we're screwed if there's top cover.

Inside, she heard grunts as Sam'l woke, crashed to his feet, and evidently walked straight into a side table.

"What the hell . . .?"

He was no Sten, no cop, no soldier, took half an hour to grunt awake enough to be able to hit the ground with his hat, and Haines loved him for all of those reasons . . . and a lot of others.

The nightwind caught the houseboat and sent it spinning over the forest. Haines heard crashes from inside as paintings

came off the wall and plates shattered. She went inside, one
hand steadying against a wall as the boat started drunken
sashays through the air.

"A kidnap team," she announced, even though in his present stupor it would probably take Sam'l several minutes to
define kidnap. "All of them in uniform. Imperial thugs."

Sam'l, astonishingly, was suddenly quite alert.

"Oh," he said. Then nodded.

"Well, I suppose it had to happen," he said. "Although I
wish we could think of something more . . . active to do than
just running."

"First we run," Haines reminded him. "Then we hide.
We'll have all the time in the world to figure out paybacks."

She crossed to a chest, opened it, and took out two personal "chutes"—steady-drain McLean packs with harness
that would drop an average-weight human safely from any
distance up to two kilometers before the batteries went dry.

When the houseboat hit about four klicks altitude, they'd
go out the door and free-fall half the distance to the ground,
targets too tiny—she hoped—to be picked up by Imperial
sensors. Sam'l was the one who'd taught her that sport.

Time enough for paybacks. Yes. With luck there would
be, she thought, but didn't say it aloud as she helped Sam'l
into his rig.

Even now, even in the darkest part of the night, the tower
still was a muted rainbow at the end of the gorge.

Inside, Marr and Senn slept uneasily, curled around each
other. They looked almost the same age as they had been
years earlier, when they were *the* Imperial caterers and Sten
a young captain, in charge of the Emperor's Gurkha bodyguard. Perhaps their fur had darkened slightly, to a deeper
gold. But nothing else had changed. The two Milchen, finan-
cially stable in their retirement, still loved beauty and love
itself. The lovers were not only Sten's friends, although it
had been years since they had seen him, but they had thrown

the Grand Party after which Haines and Sten had become lovers.

Marr suddenly woke. Sat up. Senn whistled questioningly, huge eyes blinking.

"It was but a dream."

"No. A gravcar. Coming up the valley."

"I see nothing. You were just dreaming."

"No. There. Look. It's coming without lights."

"Oh dear. I feel those fingers touching my soul. Cold. Cold. At night, without lights. If it stops, we do not answer."

Marr didn't respond.

"I said, we do not answer. In these times, with the Emperor not as he was, only a fool goes to the door after midnight. Those who move by night are not friends."

Silence. The gravcar had stopped outside.

"The cold is stronger. Don't you feel it?"

"I do."

"The bell. Who is it?"

"I don't know."

"Don't turn on the lights. Maybe they will go away."

Marr's slender hand moved through the air, and, outside, four single beams marked the parking area.

"You fool," Senn snapped. "Now they know. Who are they?"

Marr peered out. "Two. They are human. One is a man. The other a woman. I don't know the man . . . the woman looks familiar."

"Yes. She does. Marr. She is carrying a gun. Turn out the light."

"I know her," Marr announced. "She is that policeperson. She called me on some vague pretense just days ago. I wondered."

"Which police . . . oh. Haines."

"Yes. The one who loved Sten."

"Then she is a fugitive. The Emperor must want to question anyone who knew him. And she must know something, or else she would not flee."

"Senn. Think. Would you not run from that horrid Poyndex? The one who personally murdered Mahoney?"

"Turn out the lights. Come back to bed. We do not play human politics.

"See? Now they are turning away. Someone else will take them in."

Marr did not answer. He thought he could hear the crunch of footsteps outside and below, in the parking area.

"I once was told," he said slowly, "by a human, that if he was ever given the choice of betraying a friend or betraying his country, he hoped to be courageous enough to be a traitor."

The two leaned close to each other, their antennae twining. Senn pulled back.

"All right," he said. "But don't try to talk to me about loyalty and all those other complicated human emotions. You just want to have houseguests to cook for again."

His hand moved in a semicircle.

And suddenly the tower of light glowed in full life, welcoming Haines and Sam'l.

CHAPTER SEVEN

ONCE AGAIN THE Eternal Emperor's chambers were jammed, the air freshers working overtime as he barked orders to the flowing stream of staff members.

"Avri."

"Yes, Your Highness?"

"What's the status on the K-B-N-S-O operation?"

"Not good, sir. I've got our best spin doctors working on it. But nobody's buying our angle."

"Which is?"

"That it was a quote tragic accident end quote triggered by Sten's attack on the station. That we were merely trying to quote protect the innocent civilians end quote."

"Change 'innocent civilians' to attempting to 'limit collateral damage.'"

"Thank you, sir."

"Then I want you to set a backfire."

"Like what, sir?"

"Easy. The airwaves belong to the Empire. Which means me. Inform them I'll yank their licenses to lie if they don't start telling more of mine."

"Yessir . . ."

"You sound doubtful. What else is bothering them?"

"They're scared. Afraid Sten will raid them next."

"No problem. Anders."

"Yes, Your Majesty."

"Hustle up some spare ships and troopies. I want all the major Imperial broadcasters ringed. I want a net a flea couldn't get through, okay?"

"Yessir. But, we don't have that many to spare. What with the budget cutbacks. And the heavy commitments to help stabilize our weaker allies. Then there's the garrison forces. We've got them spread all over—"

"*Find* them, Anders. Just find them."

"Yessir."

"One other thing."

"Sir?"

"I'm not forgetting your fine Italian hand in this station foul-up."

"No sir. I take full responsibility, sir."

"Shut up, Anders. And while you're doing my bidding, I want you to think about a nice post I can send you to after this whole thing is over. An island, someplace. A cold island. And make it small, while you're at it. No more than a kilometer in any direction. Now, get busy."

"Uh . . . Yes, Your Majesty!"

"Walsh."

"Yes, Your Highness."

"What's the status on the AM2 tax bill?"

"I'm not sure we have enough votes to carry Parliament, sir."

"What's the hangup?"

"The Back Benchers are arguing that the tax increase goes against your promise."

"Big deal. They break promises all the time. Why can't I? It goes with the territory. Which is politics. Which is nothing more than lies and damned lies."

"Yessir. But they don't feel the same now they've given up their independence. We offered AM2 at bargain-basement prices if they became Dominions of the Empire."

"Sure, I remember. I also remember that I'm the boy with the hand on the AM2 nozzle. I'm the sole supplier. Ergo, I get to set the price."

"Yessir. I know that, sir. It's the other members of Parliament. They say they've all got deficits that are choking them."

"Well, tell them they're going to have to join the club. Because that's why I've got to have my tax increase. My treasury is tapped out. Nary a bone in the cupboard. I can't believe those people. Clot, I'm the one with the whole burden. Without me, they've got zip. I figured six years of being under the thumb of the privy council would have proven that."

"True, Your Highness. But I've heard some whispers in the halls that maybe things weren't so bad, uh, when you, uh, were gone, and the privy council was running things."

"Don't worry about whispers in the hall . . . Kenna?"

"Yes, Your Majesty."

"I want you to help Walsh on this."

"Delighted, sir. As always."

"I want Dusable behind me when it comes to a vote. I want a big push. And I want a bigger vote margin. Unanimous would be nice, but I'll settle for 99 percent."

"I'm not sure that's possible, sir."

"Dusable is one fat and sassy system right now, is it not?"

"Yes, Your Majesty."

"I've made you guys a principal AM2 depot. Which means you get to skim all you like."

"I protest, Your Majesty. The good citizens of Dusable—"

"Knock it off, Kenna. If you weren't stealing I'd be suspicious. Point is, I've been giving you all the goodies. Made you one of the top jewels in my crown. Now it's time to pay the piper. And get out the vote."

"I'll do my best, sir."

"That's not good enough. Theft is required. And arm breaking. I want this Parliament brought into line. At least until it recesses. I can always pack it with more of our own people afterward."

"Consider it done, Your Highness."

"Bleick."

"Yessir."

"You're working with Poyndex on that high priestess character, aren't you? What was her name?"

"Zoran, sir. High priestess of the Cult of the Emperor."

"That's the fruitcake I mean."

"Yessir. I have that assignment."

"What's going on? I was expecting a few godheads in my pocket by now. I badly need to boost my image with the ignorant masses. Damn, but the poor can be hard on a ruler. We've got riots all over the place. Bad for business.

"A few temples built in my honor could restore faith in the economy, and seriously trim this depression."

"To be frank, sir . . . I haven't had much luck with the woman. She's either not available, or, when she is, she talks in circles and giggles a lot. I think she's crazy."

"Like a fox, Bleick. She's a nut, for sure. But she's smarter than most people in this room. Tell her I'm getting tired of pouring credits into her organization. With no return."

"I spelled that out for her, sir. In absolute no-nonsense terms."

"Hmmm. I smell a skunk. Fine. Forget her. Exile her or something. Tell her it's time for her to reflect on the Spheres. Tell Poyndex to have her sent to her proper reward. Something quick, and not painful. Then suborn her second-in-command.

"If that doesn't work, keep going down the list until you find somebody with big eyes and a small brain. Talk to Poyndex. He'll know what I mean."

The door hissed open. Poyndex entered—with the pinched bad-news look on his face again.

The Eternal Emperor made immediate motions for his staff to make themselves scarce. They did.

"Sit."

Poyndex obeyed, sitting stiff in his seat, almost at attention. The Emperor pulled a bottle of Scotch from his desk. The ancient Earth whisky had taken him years to reinvent. He poured a glass and braced himself with a long swallow. The Emperor pointedly didn't offer Poyndex any.

"Okay. What's happening this time?"

"It's Sten, sir."

"I figured that. What about him?"

Poyndex leaned forward across the desk. The man was honestly bewildered. "Sir. My people have been over every connection you gave us a hundred times. And we've come up with many more. But, it's no dice, sir. No one, but no one, knows him, sir. Except in passing. We've brainscanned people. Had them worked over by experts. But as near as I can tell . . . Sten doesn't have a friend in the Empire."

The Emperor *woosh*ed, then took another heavy slug of his drink. Poyndex noted that his once-clear features were getting puffy and there was a small red web of a blemish beside his nose.

"That doesn't scan," the Emperor said. "Even the lowest being in the Empire has at least *one* friend. Even the misguided attract their own. Or, I should say, *especially* the misguided."

Poyndex turned his hands palms up. "It's true, just the same, sir. The real trouble is, with all the records on Sten and Kilgour wiped . . . we don't have much to go on."

"Except my memory."

"Which is excellent, sir. The few breaks we've had have all come from you."

The Emperor stared at Poyndex, reading his face. No. The man wasn't catering to his ego. He meant it. The Emperor wondered for a moment if maybe he was beginning to lean on Poyndex more than was healthy.

Beings could get very dangerous ideas . . . if one depended on them too much. Only Poyndex, for example, knew of the bomb that had once been planted in his gut. A bomb wired to that . . . that *thing*.

That great ship, out there beyond the Alva Sector, through the discontinuity.

The great ship that controlled him.

The Emperor's mind shuddered at the thought of the ship with the white room and the disembodied voice that spoke to him.

He shivered. Took another drink. Then he remembered. Correction: former controller. It was Poyndex who'd set up the special surgical team that had removed the bomb from his body and cut his link with the controller.

Another drink. Yesss. Much better now. He was the last Eternal Emperor. Until the Empire's end . . . Which would be?

Never.

He pulled himself together. "There's only one thing to be done, then," he said. "Somehow, I have to make more time. Get an interrogation team on standby. Every spare second I have, I'll devote to my memories of Sten. Any detail the team digs up from me, you can get cracking on immediately."

Poyndex hesitated. "Are you sure that's wise, sir?"

The Emperor frowned. "I *know* it's not wise. I've already fallen into the jimmycarter, for crying out loud. Micromanaging every detail in my empire. Next thing you know, I'll be going over the damned newyear's greeting list with Bleick. But . . . dammit . . . what choice do I have?"

"Sten is just one being, Your Majesty," Poyndex said. "Let us deal with him."

"I can't take that chance. Sten is the symbol of everything that's gone wrong. Citizens have no faith. They won't follow orders. They question my every pronouncement. When I'm the only one who really cares about them.

"Who else can take the long view? I mean the *really* long view. I see things not in years, but generations."

The Emperor fell silent a moment. "No. This is something I have to do," he finally said. "Damn his eyes!" And the Eternal Emperor drained the glass.

CHAPTER EIGHT

HOME.

It was strewn across a thousand thousand kilometers of space, a slowly whirling sargasso of industrial junk.

Vulcan.

Sten stared at the ruins through his suit's faceplate. The sound of his breathing seemed loud.

This was the hellworld where Sten had been born, an artificial factory planet built and run as a violent, dangerous industrial plant by The Company. His parents, Migrant/Unskilled laborers, and his brothers and sisters had died here, killed by an executive's callous decision about secrecy.

The boy that was Sten exploded into futile rebellion. He was caught, and sentenced to Exotic Section, an experimental area where the workers were assured of a slow, painful death. But Sten survived. Survived, learned to fight, and—his fingers touched the deathneedle sheathed in his arm—"built" his knife from alien crystal.

He had escaped Exotic Section, and become a Delinq, living in the secret ducts and deserted storehouses of the planet, trying to stay one theft ahead of The Company's Sociopatrolmen and brainburn. He had met Bet here, his first real love. And here he had been saved from death by Ian Mahoney, coldcocked after a blown raid and drafted into the Imperial Guard.

Mahoney had again "volunteered" him—this time from infantry assault training into Mahoney's own covert force: Mantis—where he learned the dark alleys of intelligence and the darker skills of secret violence. How to kill any being without leaving a mark. Or, more importantly, how to seduce or corrupt them into your service, without them ever realizing they'd been used.

And then Mahoney had sent him back to Vulcan with Kilgour and the rest of his Mantis Team. Mission: destroy the man who killed Sten's family.

His first great success. In the course of that destruction, Sten, three ETs and three humans, including Ida the Gypsy, had created and led a planetwide revolution.

That minirising brought in the Imperial Guard, and Sten's team came out, Sten himself on a life-support system.

He had never found out what happened afterward to Vulcan. And he had never wanted to know. He assumed that new management had come in Vulcan as an only slightly less lethal factory.

Evidently not, he thought, looking at the shambles in front of him. Or, anyway, not for very long. Even if it was needed for defense during the Tahn war, the privy-council era would have made Vulcan unprofitable—AM2 had simply become too rare and expensive to waste running a heavy-industry vacuum-based plant.

Vulcan had been abandoned, looted, and gutted. At its height it resembled a junkyard anyway—factories, quarters, and warehouses had been built, used, and discarded without being wrecked out.

But now it looked as if the gods of Chaos had looked on man's work, found it amateurish, and decided to improve matters.

Somewhere in this scatter would be—or so Sten hoped—whatever secret Mahoney had guided him toward.

At first, when Sten considered Mahoney's cryptic shout, he had thought of Smallbridge—the world Sten had bought some years earlier that was the only home he had ever known, besides Imperial Service.

Improbable. If Mahoney meant "home" to be something useful to Sten—best theory: a weapon against the Emperor—he would not have stashed it in a place known to Sten's friends and enemies. Plus, to the best of Sten's knowledge, Mahoney had been on Smallbridge exactly once, and that was to warn him the privy council's goon squad was on its way. Not exactly time enough to build a hidey-hole.

No—not Smallbridge. It was far too obvious—even considering a purloined-letter device—for an Irisher as subtle as Mahoney.

And so Sten had forced himself to look up the interstellar coordinates to Vulcan and issue the orders. Even if nothing is here, he thought, this is an adequate temporary hideout. Destroying Thoresen had been a nonrecord Highest Authority mission, which meant Vulcan's importance and its relation to the Grand Traitor wouldn't show up, even on Sten's fairly accurate, highly classified Mantis file. Sten, experienced soldier that he was, was operating on the assumption that Mahoney's trick program hadn't worked and the Empire knew everything.

Of course, there's yet another possibility, his mind went on, spinning further into the double- triple- quadruple-think that eventually drives all counterintelligence types into the gaga ward. If the Emperor's got a real fine memory, and has put together his own private termination file, then he's just liable to remember the orders to destroy that mysterious Bravo Project on Sten's home world.

"Lad?"

Sten came back to the present thankfully, before he took

this feedback nonthinking any further and attempted to disappear down his own throat.

"Ah dinnae want to seem like Ah'm noodgin', but i's gettin' on, 'n Ah'm noo lookin't forward t' bein't a Resurrection Man. Shall we be gettin' at it?"

The Mantis soldiers who had died on Vulcan—Jorgensen, Frick, Frack—had been friends of Kilgour's as well. Alex himself had almost died, defusing a nuke.

Sten nodded, then realized there was no way Alex could see the gesture through the thick alloy helmet.

"Let's move."

He touched controls and sent his suit jetting forward, on its tiny Yukawa drive, toward the main clump of wreckage—Vulcan's central core.

He was probably being foolish, but rather than use one of the deep-space worksuits—which were really small spaceships with a tiny bicycle-type seat and room enough to scratch when and where it inevitably itched—he and Kilgour had corseted themselves into fighting armor.

Vulcan, he had rationalized, might still have a McLean generator on, and some gravity. Or maybe its whirling bulk would give some weight, and it would be better walking rather than trying to fly the canister-shaped deep-space suits through the corridors.

Behind him the *Victory* hung, with the destroyer *Aoife* as screen. He had ordered the *Bennington* and *Aisling* to proceed directly to Sten's eventual final destination, after his minifleet had spent several ship-days after the raid pursuing nonrational trajectories, eluding pursuit.

Beyond the *Victory* he also had a full flotilla of tacships on CAP around Vulcan.

A trap was unlikely.

But Sten had not lived to his present age without being careful, native caution his training had amplified. One commandment, going back into prehistory and old Earth, was from an odd unit called Rogers' Rangers—"Don't never take no chances unless you have to."

The question now was, Where in this scrapheap was he to look?

"Sten." It was Freston, back aboard *Victory*. He had demoted himself from captain to man the com board and was sitting on an open-miked tightbeam caster to the suited men.

"I've got a transmission."

"Where?"

"From Vulcan. A very weak broadband signal's coming from the core. Weak, and erratic. Like an SAR beacon that's running dry. I've gotten a triangulation from the *Aoife*. On your orientation, it's at twelve o'clock, near the tip."

"That was called the Eye," Sten advised. "Stand by."

He braked the suit, killing velocity and steering toward Alex, aiming himself so his suit's own directional com pointed directly toward Kilgour.

"Ah heard," Alex said, without preamble. "An' thae raises more sarky questions thae i' answers. If Mahoney left somethin' aboot, p'raps he'd bolt a wee transponder to it. T' make life simpler f'r us.

"But Mahoney whidny hae left i' runnin', i' i's a truly deepy darky secret, aye? He would'a keyed it t' go off frae somethin' or someone when thae got close. Playin' Cold an' Warm wi' the bairns, as it were. Nae t' mention battery life an' such, which i' Freston's watchin' his gauges, seems to be runnin't doon."

"Possibly," Sten agreed. "Which means that somebody else set it off."

"Wi'out knowin' it or wi'out bein' able to retrieve th' goodies. Or th' whole thing's boobytrapped an' th' mad bomber had nae th' patience t' let us find his handiwork blind an' then blowin't ourselves oop."

"Right. Which gives us something to really worry about— once we're onboard."

"Aye. Noo. Home's been narrowed, assumin't we're thinkin't correct, an' yon beepitybeepity's noo a wild signal frae some bit ae forsook electronics."

"Agreed. Home's somewhere in the Eye. Something that we knew about. Or I did, anyway. Our hideout—that old liner—was around there. Nope. DNC. Mahoney wouldn't know about that. Maybe his old office, when he was spying out the land, pretending to be a recruiter? Maybe—but that does not compute easily, either. Mahoney wouldn't chance us remembering where it was, which I don't . . . Oh clot," Sten said.

"Aye. Th' main man. Duke, or Dynast, or wha'e'er he'd dubbed himself."

"Baron. Thoresen." That name he'd never forget. In a final duel, Sten had taken on the murderer of his family bare-handed—and killed him.

His quarters had been just at the top of the Eye, in a pala-tial dome that covered Thoresen's office, garden, and quar-ters.

"That's it. But we'll not go in direct. Nor hang up here being big fat targets anymore."

Sten put full drive on his suit and, Kilgour in his wake, eye-calculated a trajectory that would intersect Vulcan just above the old ship-porting area. He would not chance that dockyard—that was too easy to booby-trap.

To one side, as they flew "over" Vulcan, was the great rip in the planet's skin where the laboratory that was Bravo Project had been until Kilgour's bombs went off.

That also meant that somewhere below Sten was the cramped apartment he had grown up in. For all he knew, the muraliv that haunted him might still be mounted on the wall, the snowy landscape on a frontier world that his mother had sold six months of his life for, a muraliv that had broken in less than a year. Sten had unconsciously duplicated that scene in reality on Smallbridge—a cluster of domes sitting in his planet's arctic regions.

No. He would not—could not—go there. It would be too much.

He shut that part of his mind off. They were closing on Vulcan.

Sten landed on a bare stretch of hull. Finger-point. Make me a door, Alex.

Kilgour took a prepared charge from a carrying case, extended its small legs, and clipped the charge to Vulcan's skin. He started a timer, then motioned Sten away. Alex, demolitions expert that he was, pushed off into space unhurriedly and hovered a safe few meters away.

The timer went to zero, and the charge blew, blasting a stream of molten metal through the hull in a widening cone. It was a violent but relatively silent way to B&E. No air *whoosh*ed out. Vulcan—or at least this part of it—had lost its atmosphere.

Kilgour the perfectionist then trimmed a few ragged edges, ripping them off with his hands. Massively strong heavyworlder that he was, he almost certainly could have done it without the suit's pseudomusculature cutting in. But he felt lazy.

They winkled through the hole.

Blackness. Both of them turned on their helmet spotlights. They were in some kind of machine shop.

Sten pointed himself back through the hole.

"Inside," he broadcast back to the *Victory*. "No prob. Tag on. Moving."

He set his suit's inertial navigation system as a guide toward the Eye, in the probable event of Vulcan's twisting corridors getting them lost, and they started out. His "tag"— a transmitter broadcasting on an unlikely freq—would tell the *Victory* where, in this metal maze, they were.

Zero air, zero gravity.

It was quicker to use the suit's drive and "fly" toward the Eye. Sten wondered what the seventeen-year-old Delinq that had been Sten would have thought, given a bit of clairvoyance, seeing somebody actually fly inside Vulcan.

He would probably think it wonderful and then promptly figure out how to use the newly accessed dimension in a raid.

It was tempting to increase their speed, particularly when their course led through some of the huge open assembly lines. Tempting—but that could be quickly fatal if there *was* a trap. Or if something jagged lurked at the end of an insufficiently braked swoop.

They moved on, "up" into the docking area. Huge ship-size airlocks yawned into vacuum, and fittings had been roughly cut or blasted off. The scavengers hadn't bothered to close the doors behind them.

A slideway—or where a slideway had been. Someone had ripped the alloy top away, exposing the aircushion plates below. The slideway led due "north"—toward the Eye.

Suddenly there was a great gap, a rip of metal extending through several decks directly out into space. Here was where one of the Imperial assault ships had deliberately smashed into Vulcan's skin, making a breach for the Imperial Guardsmen to pour through.

"You should be within range of that broadcast," Freston's voice whispered. "Tune Six-Three-Kilo-Four." Sten obeyed on a secondary com. He heard it. A whine that broke off now and again, and whose note rose and fell. It did, indeed, sound like a search-and-rescue transmitter whose power was about dry.

Now they were close to the "top" of the Eye, close to Thoresen's dome.

Even though he wanted to go faster, Sten forced himself to slow. Ahead was a great door. One of the periodic emergency barriers—airlocks—intended to keep an accidental rupture from dumping Vulcan's entire atmosphere into space.

Alex started to push on it, then caught himself before Sten could warn him.

Resistance. How interesting. That probably meant there was atmosphere on the other side.

And then Six-Three-Kilo-Four fell silent.

The link to the *Victory* opened, and Freston began a transmission, probably to tell Sten what had just ceased happening.

"Received," Sten said in a whisper. "Break 'cast. Monitor. Do not transmit. Click code."

He'd always known it couldn't be this easy.

Kilgour curled his hand, and his willygun slid down on its harness. A lifted eyebrow. Shall I blow the door, boss?

Headshake no. Motion—back.

Sten hit the cycle button.

Grindingly, the lock emptied its air back into the main chamber. He started forward, and Kilgour waved him back. Cover . . . and Sten did. Alex moved forward and ripped the door open, spinning back flat against the corridor's wall.

Nothing. Inside. They forced the outer door closed again.

Now they were well and truly trapped. Both of them shut off their helmet lights. Being an obvious target was one thing—there was no necessity to put a spotlight on the bull's-eye.

Cycle.

The grinding stopped, but the light that would signal ATMOSPHERE EQUALIZED did not go on. Burnt out. Possibly.

Nor did the inner door open automatically.

Sten pushed at it, and it reluctantly slid aside.

They were in Thoresen's dome.

Both men were crouched on either side of the lock, weapons ready. Sten could feel his suit press against him from atmospheric pressure outside before it adjusted. So where had the atmosphere come from? Was Thoresen's dome built so well that it held air after being abandoned all these years? Not clottin' likely.

He looked at a gauge. Neutral gas, 75 percent; oxygen, 18 percent; garblegarble trace gases. Oh really. Half a percentage of carbon dioxide. Exhalations from an oxygen-breathing creature? Possibly.

Breathable—no gases analyzed.

Pressure half E-normal.

There was enough light from the stars and a far-distant sun through the dome's skylights for Sten to see without needing his helmet light.

Kilgour pointed and Sten saw the piled racks of empty oxygen containers. That was where the atmosphere had come from—a hand-carried flask at a time.

Thoresen's dome was huge. Envision a jungle, now pet-rified when it lost atmosphere sometime ago. A garden. Up ahead would be Thoresen's office/living chambers. Sten and Alex would have to fine-comb the dome, their task compli-cated because they had no idea what they were looking for— nor if it was even there.

Sten turned on an outside microphone and listened. Nothing. He of course did not chance opening his faceplate and breathing the dome's atmosphere, no matter what his suit's analysis told him.

He went into the chamber.

In front of him was the twisted, desiccated drought night-mare that had been Thoresen's lush forest.

Very strange, trying to move silently, as if he were walk-ing point for an infantry patrol, deep in a planetary jungle. In a spacesuit. Toe first . . . touch, test the ground under you, heel down, full weight down, other foot lifted straight up, brought forward slowly, close to Sten's center of gravity . . . toe touching . . .

The dead boughs twisted up around him, agonized arms stretching for, never to reach, the far-distant stars.

A crunch. Sten tensed and looked down.

Gleaming bones.

He remembered. One of Thoresen's "pet" tigers. The one he'd killed with a desperation thrust-kick with both legs, crushing its throat. Sten shivered. He was the one who should have died.

Kilgour followed Sten. He, too, looked down at the tiger's skeleton, then, without realizing it, at Sten's back. Clot, he thought. Ah heard th' story, but really didna believe it. Ah ne'er, ne'er woulda gone f'r it.

Somewhere across the dome, Sten heard a noise. Or thought he did.

He froze, waiting. Nothing. He chanced a look back at Alex. He could see Kilgour shake his head from side to side through the faceplate. He'd heard nothing.

Sten continued on.

He half expected to find Thoresen's skeleton next, rib cage shattered where his heart had been torn out, still beating. But the body would have been removed and given some kind of burial, or at least dumped into space.

Wouldn't it?

Here was the wall where Thoresen had hung his weapons collection, everything from an archaic flamethrower to a broadax. The racks were empty, weapons most likely souvenired by the victorious Guardsmen as they poured through the dome.

Over there. Thoresen's office. The huge slab that had floated, held invisibly up by McLean generators, was canted against one wall.

And then Baron Thoresen walked out of the gloom.

Sten's willygun was up, finger pulling through to full auto, mind screaming, *Goddammit, you aren't there, you aren't there you're dead goddammit or by Christ you're going to be because there aren't any ghosts full magazine right in the middle of that clotting robe, right between where those skinny arms are stretching out for my neck . . .*

He heard the baron's voice through the open mike:

"Don't kill me. Please don't kill me."

A scratchy, wavery old being's androgynous voice.

One thousand out of one thousand normal people would have already opened fire. Nine hundred and ninety-plus Guard-trained combat-experienced soldiers would have, too.

Sten's finger came off the trigger.

"Don't kill me," the old voice said again.

Sten's helmet light slashed on.

In front of him was an emaciated man, ancient skeletal claw arms and hands outstretched, trying to ward off the death he saw from the suited killer in front of him. The few strands of hair left sprayed wildly out above his head.

"I won't hurt you," Sten managed.

The old man *was* wearing a set of Thoresen's formal robes, the same sort Sten had seen him wear once, when delivering the mock-pious funeral oration for his parents. Stolen from Thoresen's unlooted wardrobe?

Sten lowered his weapon.

Kilgour did not.

He crabbed sideways, around Sten.

"Who're you?"

His voice, amplified, boomed through the chamber. The old man winced.

"Please. Please. Not so loud."

Kilgour brought himself back out from *Controlled Panic— Lethal Mode*, and his outside speaker control down as well.

"ID yourself."

"I'm not anyone. I'm Dan Forte."

"Where's your ship?"

"I don't have a ship. The others have the ship. They left me here. They said I had no right to live. They said I was . . . it doesn't matter what they said I was, does it."

"Somebody stranded him," Sten wondered. Alex nodded— he guessed so.

"Ah wonder whae th' lad did t' get marooned?"

"Maybe we don't *want* to know."

"Aye. Dinnae y' turn y'r back on th' rascal."

Kilgour went to Forte—the man flinched—and swiftly, expertly, checked him for weapons. "He's clean, metaphoric'ly speakin't . . . but Ah'd noo be openin' m' face-plate t' hae a sniff."

"How long have you been here, Dan?" Sten asked.

"Not long. Not long." The old man started laughing, and then singsonging: "A bottle here/A bottle there/A ratpack here/A ratpack there/Breathe it out/Breathe it in." His singsong stopped.

"You know, the sun is going to die. They are going to kill it. The Tahn know things like that. What they know/They always know/What they do/They always do."

"Laird hae' mercy," Kilgour said. "Th' puir clot's been here since durin't th' war!"

"And I watch," Forte went on.

"I always watch."

"Take me with you. Please. Don't leave me. There was another man. He wore a suit. Like yours. He had a gun. Like yours. I was afraid to ask him. He had a gun. But I was young, then. And afraid of more.

"Now I'm not afraid. There's nothing to be afraid of. Is there?"

Kilgour let his sling snap his rifle back against his chest to carrying port arms.

"No, old 'un," he said heavily. "Thae's nae t' fright y'self. W're nae but friends."

"That man," Sten said carefully. "Did he leave something here?"

Forte quivered.

"And Moses smote the rock twice . . . and the congregation drank . . . and the Lord spoke . . . because you believe me not, to sanctify me in the eyes of the children . . . ye shall not bring this congregation into the land."

"Uh . . . we believe you, Dan."

"Then strike ye against the wall!" Forte shouted, waving.

Alex and Sten looked at each other. Sten nodded. Alex shrugged, aimed his willygun against the wall Thoresen had hung his weapons on, and snap-fired four times. Once against each corner of the wall.

And it crumbled and fell, as one piece.

Behind the wall, high-piled in a hidden chamber that could have been built by Thoresen or Mahoney, was the Secret. Stack after stack after stack of identical file-storage cases.

Sten rushed forward. Knelt in front of one case. It was neatly labeled, in Mahoney's militarily perfect handwriting:

ASSASSINATIONS, SUCCESSFUL
Official Denials
Suppressed Evidence
Rumors Circulating Following
Personal Theories

Another case:

THE SECRET YEARS
System Politics
Murders Ordered
First AM2 Supplies Provided by
Philanthropic Foundation Institutes

Yet another:

THE "CIBOLA" EXPEDITION
Scientific Journals—Expedition Suggested As Possibility
No Other Info Available
No Hard Data Could Be Found
Personal Theories Only

Sten realized what he was looking at.

He didn't know—and suspected Mahoney didn't either—if these cases held The Secret that would destroy the Eternal Emperor—or even A Secret that might help. But he *did* know these cases contained enough dangerous data for the Emperor to be willing to sacrifice most of the Imperial Guard to recover. These were the notes for the never-written biography.

After the Eternal Emperor had been assassinated by the privy council, Mahoney had found it expedient to retire, and begin plotting the destruction of the council. As a cover he announced that, in deep mourning for his old leader and friend, he would write the Eternal Emperor's complete biography. At first, just a cover. But as he had told Sten, Mahoney would have been quite happy being an archivist instead of a general, and so his files got larger and larger, more and more thorough.

The thought floated up: perhaps if Mahoney *had* become a researcher he would have lived longer. But he shut that idea out.

The cover had become a fascination, as Mahoney discovered that *all* biographies of the Eternal Emperor were fraudulent, either authorized or unauthorized. Deliberately false data had been given; incompetent writers, researchers, and foundations had been encouraged while capable ones were shunted aside.

Mahoney found many, many versions of given events, versions that had been deliberately created by the Empire and used as red herrings.

Sten had wondered what the Emperor had been trying to hide, and Mahoney had retorted, "Damned near everything, from where he came from to how he got where he is . . . I'll just mention two of the murkiest areas, besides where the clot the AM2 is. First is that the son of a bitch is—or was, anyway—immortal.

"And the second thing is . . . he's been killed before."

Sten had scoffed—and Mahoney had offered to show him the files sometime. But events moved too fast and too bloodily, and the one time Sten had thought about those files, he had decided they were certainly explosive, and that anyone interested in staying on the Emperor's fair-weather side would probably be wisest not even considering their existence.

Or, as the Z-grade livies put it, just after the scenarist had failed to come up with an even vaguely believable explanation for all the drakh he had come up with earlier, "There are some things in this universe, boy, man was not meant to know."

All right, Sten thought. But this time man's gonna find out.

Because Mahoney, in a way, died for these files.

Sten got to his feet. He started to key his com, to order the *Victory* to send down a cargo lighter and some strong deck apes. He—or somebody, anyway—would begin analysis when they reached their intended destination, Sten's intended base of operations.

"You're my friend, aren't you?"

Sten remembered Forte—and, when he called the *Victory*, he told them to send down a bubblepak stretcher, with the interior controls sealed.

Dan Forte, completely insane, would either be cured, if that was possible—and Sten would dedicate all resources he had to help—or else given a long, happy life in whatever luxurious asylum Sten could put him.

Because he had very possibly given Sten the keys to the Empire.

CHAPTER NINE

"YOUR SUCCESS THUS far has bordered on the miraculous," Sr Ecu said.

"Correction," Sten said. "It's been nothing but a series of *real* miracles. But, I can't keep on counting on smiles from the gods. I need a goal. And a plan. All I've been doing is shooting and scooting in the dark."

"I can see how operating without a plan would be especially disturbing to you, Sten," Rykor said. "You always were a being in search of structure."

Sten laughed, unfazed by this instant bit of analysis from the Empire's most eminent psychologist. "Another delusion destroyed. Here I always thought I was a real seat-of-the-pants kind of a guy."

"Oh, but you are," Rykor said. "I remember the first profile I drew up on you. Your inventive skills were among the best I've ever seen. But you tend to be displeased if your actions must take place in a vacuum. It's a typical trait of most special-operations experts. You like the illusion of complete freedom. But there must be structure just the same."

Water splashed as she eased her bulk in the tank. "In the

past, it was service to the Emperor that provided that structure."

Sten shuddered. All too true.

"Guilt is not necessary in this situation," Rykor said, reading him like a crèche-level fiche. "It is my own misfortune to share some of these same traits. I too found comfort in the bosom of the Emperor."

As Sten mulled this over, one of Sr Ecu's tendrils whiskered out to touch a hidden switch. A small 'bot bearing a tray churned out of an alcove. In a moment, Sten was gratefully slugging down stregg.

"I hate to sound like an old-fashioned dipsomaniac," Sten said. "But boy did I need that. Thanks."

Sr Ecu's tendrils wriggled with humor. "The circumstances cry out for inducements. Besides, Rykor and I are ahead of you. Appropriate stress relievers have been added to the atmosphere. As well as to that liquid our largish companion is lolling about in so casually."

Rykor barked and ducked her head under the spiked water. She emerged again, lips parted between her big tusks in what Sten was sure was a grin.

"That's why I'm being so pedantic," Rykor confessed. "I tend to be pompous when I imbibe."

"I see I have some catching up to do," Sten said. He raised the stregg. "Confusion to our enemies," he toasted. He drained the glass and refilled it.

Although Sten's situation hadn't improved, he was feeling much better. It had little to do with the stregg.

He'd left his minifleet tucked away offsystem while he made this visit to Seilichi to seek Sr Ecu's counsel. Sten had immediately been whisked to the hidden chamber beneath one of the planet's Guesting Centers.

Finding his old friend Rykor waiting there was not only a surprise, but a bonus. Having two beings like Sr Ecu and Rykor on his side made him feel that the odds had shifted slightly in his favor. Now he figured he only had a ninety-nine percent chance of winding up quickly and horribly dead.

He gulped more stregg. As he did, a sudden thought jolted him. "Sr Ecu, do you *usually* keep stregg on hand? Somehow I can't imagine that many diplomatic types with a lust for this evil Bhor brew."

More tendril wriggling. "No. It's for you. And you alone."

Sten puzzled. "I can't imagine why you'd keep it in stock. The last time we met, I rejected your invitation. I was pretty damned firm about what I intended to do next. Which was to get the clot out of the Emperor's way and bury myself somewhere. And mind my own business."

He was referring to Sr Ecu's secret visit to the Altaics, bearing proof from Rykor that the Emperor had gone mad. The Manabi had urged his help. Sten had given him a definite no.

"I said I had faith in you. I laid in the supply of stregg as soon as I returned."

"I am in a room full of beings," Sten said, "who know more about what I am going to do next than I do myself."

Rykor woofed through her whiskers. "Illogical. But understandable in the circumstances . . . Oh, brother. There I go being pedantic again . . . Still, I hope the thought gives you no distress."

"No. I just hope the Eternal Emperor isn't as good at calling my shots as you are."

There was no answer to this. Silence for a moment, as each being contemplated various sins and partook of his or her own favorite brand of poison.

"Back to that visit, Sr Ecu," Sten finally said. "I assumed at the time that when you asked for my help, you had something in the works."

"Ah . . . The illusive plan," Rykor burbled. Before Sten could react, she added, "Which is a very natural assumption for two fugitives such as ourselves."

She hoisted herself higher in the tank. Waved a flipper at Sr Ecu. "You do have a plan, don't you, my dear friend? I would hate to think I was facing a life on the run. It's difficult to dodge about for someone of my needs . . . and size."

Sten buried a sudden hilarious image of Rykor ducking in and out of dark alleys, hauling her tank behind her.

"Actually, I don't," Sr Ecu said. "I'm a diplomat. Not a soldier. And I fear this situation requires military action first. Negotiating, later."

"The Emperor won't negotiate," Sten said. Flat. "Even before . . . when he was—" The word stuck in his throat.

"Normal?" Rykor completed it. "How can a being with apparent immortality ever be normal? No. He was mad all along. I understand that now. Something only made his condition worse . . . A judgmental word, I realize. But I think it applies."

"Here is the situation as I see it," Sr Ecu said. "I speak for the Manabi, now. All our progs come to the same conclusion. The Empire is finished. The future will be nothing more than a slow, miserable descent into chaos.

"We predict the bloodiest wars in the universe's history. Starvation and plagues on an unimaginable scale. A complete collapse of all societies and cultures. In the end, we will all end up where we began. As barbarians.

"All the progs call for only one solution. The Emperor must relinquish power. Quickly. Because all progs also indicate delay will produce the same disastrous results. To use diplomatic jargon, 'The window of opportunity is very small.' We act now. Or it will soon close."

Sten had been too battered by recent events to be shocked by this doomsday prognosis. It all made very tired sense. "Fine. The window's open. How do we get through?"

"I have nothing I can dignify with the word *plan*," Sr Ecu said. "But I do have a proposal . . ."

"Thank God. Let's hear it."

"All over the Empire, many beings feel exactly as we do. Perhaps all they need is encouragement. Now . . . You have forces at your command. What if you waged a guerrilla campaign? A series of blows that would arouse the citizens everywhere. Many of them might join us.

"When the pressure builds until the Emperor can no longer

bear it, we make an offer. We demand he abdicate . . . or agree to a constitutional monarchy. There have been successful governments of that type in the past. He would be Emperor still. Have all the glory. But not total power."

Sten's hopes sagged. "We don't have a prayer for that," he said. "You're right. Sr Ecu. You're no soldier.

"Here's the reality. The Emperor holds *all* the cards. The only reason I've kept my head on my shoulders so far is because he's still in a reactive position.

"He may be mad, but he's certainly the smartest being I've ever met. The Empire's enormous. So it takes a very long time to come up to speed. If the Emperor wants to throw a punch, thousands and thousands of details have to be dealt with first.

"But, believe me, when that punch lands—which it will, and I guarantee he won't miss—we'll all be bloody smears on the pavement."

Rykor rolled in her tank, spilling water over the side. "He's right, Sr Ecu. I've lost count of the number of operations the Emperor has consulted me on. And that was how it always came out in the end."

"Another flaw," Sten said, "is even if we could bring that much pressure to bear, he'd never agree to step down now. Much less share power. Why should he? He's the Eternal Emperor. Practically a god to some beings."

"No wonder," Sr Ecu said, very grim. "He appears immortal. A key definition of godhood as I understand it."

"I really doubt that," Sten said. "No one can be immortal. Claudius proved that."

"But we all saw what happened when the privy council struck," Sr Ecu protested. "All over the Empire, billions witnessed him die. Then . . . six years later . . . we were there to greet him, you and I, when he stepped off that ship. As if he had risen from the dead."

"Mahoney said it's happened before," Sten said. "Several times. And each time he was assassinated, according to Ian, there was a very large explosion. Just like this last time. As if he had a bomb implanted in his body.

"Also, each time he was quote killed endquote, he returned approximately three E-years later. This time it was six. The longest it has ever been."

"But you don't believe our late friend?" Sr Ecu said.

"I have to admit Ian knew more about the Emperor than any other being alive. I have whole cases of research he compiled aboard my ship. When there's time, we plan to go through it. See if there are any weaknesses we can uncover.

"But as far as immortality goes . . . No. I don't believe it. He's as human as I am."

"Then how do you explain what happened?" Sr Ecu asked.

"I don't," Sten said. "The historical facts say it occurred. Natural facts say it can't. I'll stick with nature over history every time. History has been known to lie."

"Now I know what the Christians were envisioning when they invented Hell," Rykor said. "We are living it. And are doomed to stay here until the end of time. And after listening to Sten, I see no possible solution."

Sten sipped absently at his drink. Scattered thoughts were beginning to coalesce. He slammed the glass down. "We're going to try, dammit!"

"But how?" Sr Ecu wanted to know. "I'm afraid your argument has convinced me. I'm with Rykor. There is no hope."

"Maybe just a sliver," Sten said. "But forget about trying to make His Highness see reason. Emperors, he's told me time after time, don't need to *see* reason. They *are* the reason.

"Therefore, we either have to capture him . . . or kill him."

"This is the part I always like," Rykor burbled. "Goal setting. It makes one feel so satisfied."

Sr Ecu said, "But you just explained—quite logically, I should add—that the Emperor is too powerful for us to defeat."

"We have to keep making his size work for us," Sten said. "Keep him in a reactive position as long as possible." He drummed his fingers on the table. "If we can draw his forces out . . . stretch them to the limits . . . then . . . in theory . . . size won't matter. We look for a hole—or make one, dammit—and punch through. We don't have to take all the pieces. We only need to kill the king."

"Assuming all these impossible things become possible," Sr Ecu said, "we are still left with the same dilemma as the privy council.

"Without AM2, the Empire will collapse. You know as well as I that all modern industry and transport is based on that substance. And only the Emperor knows its source."

"The privy council spent six years trying to find it," Rykor agreed. "And they didn't come close."

"I've thought about that before," Sten said, remembering a late-night talk with Cind after they had first suspected the Emperor had gone mad. "I'm not so sure it's that bad a fate. To live without AM2, I mean. When we were running out—during the privy council's reign—things were bad, true. But at least a whole lot of beings were learning to fend for themselves."

"It will be the end of interstellar travel," Sr Ecu said. "Which means we will all quickly become strangers again."

Sten shrugged. "Maybe it'll be good for us. Starting all over again. Besides, maybe someday somebody'll figure a way to synthesize AM2."

He filled his glass with stregg. "Of course, it'd be easier if I can get him alive. Toast his toes, or something. To get the secret of AM2 out of him."

Rykor shifted her bulk. "One large problem . . . just to add to the others. What if you're wrong about the immortality aspect? What if there's another big blast—I'm assuming you'll take this in consideration and stay at a safe distance—and he disappears. Only to return. A few years later."

"I still think it's a trick," Sten said. "Sleight of hand. Or maybe he does it with mirrors. Whatever. If I can pull this chess match off—and pin his royal behind—I promise you that whatever cosmic misdirection he's been pulling won't make me look the other way."

"I see no other choice," Sr Ecu said. "Speaking for the

Manabi—and I do have that authority—I pledge our complete support."

"I'll need it," Sten said. "I'd appreciate it if you can lay the diplomatic groundwork. Obviously with total secrecy."

"As a matter of fact," Sr Ecu said, "I put out a quiet word or two already.

"There are many natural allies . . . the kind that come with some successes. Your attack on the broadcast station was a good start. Actually, the fact that you are still eluding the Emperor's minions is an even better one."

"I'll try to keep it up," Sten said dryly.

"What about me?" Rykor asked. "How can I assist in this grand crusade?"

She burped daintily. "My, but that's an interesting potion, Sr Ecu. I must acquire your recipe."

Sten rose to his feet. "Rykor, my gentle sot, you're coming with me. We're going to put that tricky brain of yours to work skewering the Eternal Emperor."

"Ah ha. I fight at last. To arms! To arms!"

When they rolled her tank aboard the *Victory*, Sten's newest gallant warrior was snoring blissfully.

CHAPTER TEN

"WE APPEAR," STEN observed, "to be trapped."

Cind grunted at him, still recovering her breath.

"Was *this* on the aerial?"

"Negative. Or if it was, I didn't pick it up on the viewer."

"Doesn't matter, really. Other than we're going to have to do some serious backtracking."

He slid out of his heavy pack, nearly falling on the steep icy slope. Backtracking? He glanced behind him.

Way, way, *way* down below, he could see the double herringbone tracks of their skis, leading up the slopes toward this clotting excuse for a mountain they were stuck on. About two kilometers before, the gradient had become too steep, and they had strapped their skis to their packs and put on crampons. A klick after that, the two of them had roped up as the grade grew steeper still.

Two klicks . . . one kilometer . . . that was the distance in a direct, near-vertical line. In actual travel, they had been off their skis since just after dawn, and the day was getting late. And they had better reach a decision on what to do next quickly—Sten would rather not spend the night in a sleeping bag that he would have to anchor to keep from sliding off the mountain.

If for no other reason than that he had designs on Cind's virtue . . .

Sten had arrived at his planned base of operations—the Bhor home worlds in the Lupus Cluster—without encountering any Imperial warships. Next, he would prepare his specific campaign and go to war.

He still had to get approval for using their worlds from the Bhor Council. But at least he had been greeted with cheers, invitations to drunken feasts, and volunteers who wanted to join him killing someone, anyone.

However, it took time for the Bhor elders to assemble, and even longer for them to reach a decision, given the Bhor tendency to endlessly explore any aspect of anything—all spokesBhor welcome. Which was probably a legacy from the severe lack of entertainment in their primitive days during long arctic nights.

Rykor herself had wanted some time and privacy to consider what could be done, from her perspective, against the Empire.

Neither set of Sten's potential allies had materialized. Not that there was any guarantee they would—both the Rom and

Wild's smugglers might have realized an alliance with Sten was more likely to produce death than freedom.

And Sten's troopies—from his embassy assistants to his Bhor and Gurkha heavies to the Imperial sailors—had suffered through a very long tour. Essentially no one had had any time off since they had arrived in the Altaics. Even the Gurkhas were tired and weary of blood.

Tired beings make mistakes, and Sten could afford none.

He spread his four ships out among the Wolf Worlds, hid them well on rural airports, and gave his troops some R&R. Sten worried his presence among the Bhor would be discovered by the inevitable Imperial agents, but Kilgour had told him not to fash. He already had a Plot, and would take care of that little matter before his own vacation. Which involved Otho, vast amounts of stregg, and whatever trouble he could get into.

Cind had the op order for Operation Vacation already drafted. A conventional lover might have looked for tropical oceans and romantic islands with ten-star resorts and twenty bow-n'-scrapers for each guest. But Cind was a descendant of the Jann, had grown up among the Bhor, and was a hard, experienced field soldier. To her, vacations meant the wilderness—and Sten's own ideas weren't that different.

The Bhor home planet was still glacial, even though the Bhor had reluctantly removed some of the glaciers as civilization and the birthrate increased. Scattered across the world were volcanic "islands"—oases in the midst of freeze. Most of them had been settled aeons ago by the Bhor, but there were still a few that were unpopulated.

Cind had planned on kidnapping Sten and taking him to one of those, and had been trying to figure out which of the possible areas could provide the best skiing and even some winter climbing. Sten had taught Cind rock scrambling, and she was determined to become at least his equal and, she hoped, his master.

She had found something better on a recent aerial photomosaic. Not on any map. Completely unknown. All that was necessary to get there was to grab a pilot and a gravsled and they could be there in an hour.

Cind sneered. That, too, was no vacation. Getting there was half the fun.

And so, carrying packs heavy enough to give them the trail staggers, they had Kilgour drop them off where the dirt path ended, with a promise to return in five days to pick them up—or start the search parties in motion.

Among the reasons their packs were so heavy was that neither Sten nor Cind fancied carrying dried rations—they could stay in the barracks and on duty and get ratpacks. They were willing to break their backs carrying some other, minor creature comforts.

Their route on skis through the foothills to the base of the mountain. Where the mountain steepened, they would follow the course of a generally frozen river upward, through a gorge, to Cind's secret spot. Since the maps of the wilderness were rotten, they would navigate from the aerial.

And so it had been—until they reached this place not too far below the mountain's summit, where the river went vertical, and became thirty meters of frozen-solid waterfall. They were trapped.

This was a helluva fix she had gotten him into, he thought. And so observed.

"Shut up," Cind said helpfully. "I'm trying to figure out if we can slither back down this slope to that ravine we passed an hour or so ago. And maybe go up that to the summit. Then we could drop back down to where we want to go."

"That sounds like work."

"Stop whining."

"I am not whining. I am sniveling. How much rope do we have?"

"Seventy-five meters."

"Dammit," Sten swore. "See if I ever play climbing purist again. Right now a couple of cans of climbing thread, jumars, and a grapnel would be welcome. Or a stairway. But ooookay, we'll do it the hard way."

He unclipped from the rope, set his pack down where it hopefully wouldn't start sliding all the way back down to the foothills, reroped his harness, took a deep breath, and started climbing.

Up the ice of the waterfall.

"I don't like this," he muttered. And he didn't—the only reason Sten knew that ice cubes could be climbed was because he had seen it done once in a livie and also because he had once spent a weekend with one of his instructors in Mantis—and whatever happened to her, he wondered—who had been a nut on climbing waterfalls when the temp went below zed Centigrade.

He had come off twice and had to be near-hoisted to the top, he remembered. No. His memory was wrong. None of the four of them had made it that long and bruised weekend.

Follow Cind's advice. Shut up.

It wasn't that bad, he thought. No worse than, say, dangling by your hands and having to do a pull-up every two minutes.

At least the ice is good and frozen. Don't have to worry about any kind of a spring thaw.

And you've got a good place to stand every now and then. As he was doing at the moment.

"What's that called?" Cind wondered from five meters below him.

"Suicide," Sten panted. "Front-pointing."

His good place to stand consisted of two front metal spikes of his crampons—alloy plates clamped to his boots that had vertical two-centimeter-sided spikes around their edges and horizontal ones sticking straight out from the toe.

One foot suddenly *skriiich*ed out of the ice, and Sten went back to dangling. He twisted back and forth for a while, getting the hang of things, did another pull-up, reached out for a hand-hold, found a handjam, kicked in his free boot. Half a meter farther up.

Two wheezes, and try it again.

And again. And again.

Eventually, there was no ice above his hand to grab, and he flailed a little. Hand moved to one side. A rock projection. Rock? Such as no more waterfall?

No more waterfall.

Sten pulled himself to blessedly level ground, and rested. Then he tied off, and shouted down to Cind.

First came the packs, tied to the rope and hand-over-handed up. More wheezing. Not only getting old, but old and weak, Sten thought.

Now for Cind. He waited—in spite of an impatient shout—until he'd gotten *all* his wind back. He wouldn't mind losing a pack, but . . .

Cind tied on.

"I've never done this before," she shouted.

"All the girls say that."

Cind started climbing. Naturally, Sten thought in some disgust, she's a natural. She swarmed up the waterfall as if it were liquid and she an Earth salmon in spawning season. Nor was she breathing very hard at the top.

"I didn't know you could even *do* that."

"All the girls say that, too."

Sten shouldered his pack. Helped Cind on with hers. They were next to a frozen pool, rocks sticking through the ice. Sten noticed the ice looked hazy the further back it got.

Just ahead of them—not more than fifty vertical feet—a cloud drifted toward them of a draw. Wonderful. Now they'd be climbing in a fog.

Sten was wrong: the rest of the climb—a gentle walk on level ground—took only four minutes.

They moved through the draw, into a winter paradise. The draw opened into a tiny valley. Shrubs. Grass. Wild-flowers.

"Well, I'll be go to hell," Sten marveled. To one side of the valley a hot spring bubbled, its water flowing across the minimeadow and joining the larger river, still hot enough to melt the ice. Pools dotted the course of the spring's flow, and they were anywhere from boiling to frigid, the farther away they were from the spring.

Sten thought it was almost worth the climb.

The steaming springs drew them—but both of them knew the unchangeable ritual: first shelter, then fire, then food, then fun. Shelter was easy—snap three sets of shock-corded wands together, slide them through slots, and their tiny dome tent was up. They staked it down for security. Fire was also not a problem—their stove was a Mantis-issue item no larger than Sten's palm. But it was AM2-fueled and could run at full blast for at least a year without a recharge. Sten took it from his pack and set it near the tent, between a circle of small rocks that his small fold-up grill would sit on. Food? They skated on that one for the moment—their muscles were sorer than their bellies empty.

Or at least that was the pretext.

"Damn, but these rocks are cold."

"Of course they're cold. Get in here where it's warm."

Sten, naked, slid into the pool near Cind.

"What," she asked, "is in that bottle?"

"You will observe what appears to be a standard alloy campflask, which disgusting people who espouse clean living and good thoughts probably fill with some sort of healthy soyagunk. But some subversive clot happened to dump the organic glop, and fill it up with stregg."

Sten uncapped it, *whooo*ed, put the cap back on, and tossed the flask to Cind.

"There are three more like it in my pack."

"Oh, boy. I brought two myself," Cind said. "So much for the clean life." She drank.

Sten eyed her lasciviously.

"They float!"

"Brilliant observation. You're only just noticing, and we've been together how long? Is that why they made you an admiral?"

"Yup."

"What a guy to go Empire-toppling with," Cind said. She rolled over and kicked against the rocky wall of the pool, sealing out into its center.

"Hey, you can almost swim out here in the middle."

"Uh-huh."

Sten had no interest in swimming. He lay on his back in shallow water, parbroilingly close to where a stream of water bubbled into the pool. Years of trouble and blood seemed to wash out of his body and mind.

"I think," he managed, "every muscle in my body just turned to rubber."

"Oh dear."

"Not quite. Come here, wiseass."

"Observant, romantic, and complimentary to boot. Well, here I am. Now what?"

"There . . . like that. Now. Down a little."

Cind gasped as Sten arched his body. He moved his hands up, across her breasts and moved her up, into a sitting position across his body.

And then neither of them had any words.

Dinner, somehow, never was prepared.

The only light in the world was the tiny candle hanging from the tent's ceiling, glowing through the tent's thin red-synth walls.

"I . . . think," Cind managed, "that I am dishrag city for the rest of the night."

"I didn't suggest anything."

"Then what are you doing?"

"Just . . . sort of stretching."

"Yeah. Right."

"I read someplace once that you didn't need to do any moving. That you could focus your attention, concentrate, and *whambo*."

"I don't believe it."

"I never lie. It was called Tantric or Tentric or something," Sten argued.

"At least you're trying it in the right place. Hey. You're moving."

"No, I'm not. You are."

"I . . . am not. Would you . . . at least slow down? Hey! If you try to put my leg up there, I'm . . . liable to get burnt!"

Sten blew the candle out.

Neither Cind nor Sten woke the next day until very late in the afternoon.

"How long do we wait, Mister Kilgour?"

"A min. An hour. A lifetime," Alex said with complete indifference. "Intel's noo frae th' impatient."

The com tech, Marl, shifted. Perhaps she was impatient, perhaps she felt a bit strange, stuffed into the gravsled's shell rear between the beefy Scotsman and an equally looming Bhor police constable. The amount of room available was further decreased with the jam of electronics.

But she didn't say anything—Alex had handpicked her as being the most likely candidate for intelligence training of all the *Bennington*'s com crew.

Kilgour already had an extensive spookery section as part of Sten's embassy team, plus some likelies he had spotted among the *Victory*'s crew and trained on the Altaics. But he needed more. Marl was a good candidate, he thought. Enough time in life and the service so she wasn't still a mewling infant. And built proper, not like the wisps Sten seemed to favor. Not that Kilgour would consider doing anything— romancing a subordinate under your command was about as unethical to him as, say, inviting a Campbell up to your castle for a drink. But he could look.

A box clicked. A needle swung. A screen lit. A sweep swept. The gravsled was a disguised mobile locator.

"Ah-hoo," Kilgour said in satisfaction. "See whae Ah said

aboot patience? Oh whistle an' I'll come t' y', m'lad. Right on schedule."

"First lesson. I' y're t' be a spy, Technician, dinna be stickin't t' any schedule. Nae y'rs, an' 'specially nae y'r control's. He/she's more worried't aboot makin' dinner than whether you're blown. One a' y'r few real weapons i' bein' unpredict'ble. You lad's signalin' away like a clockwork mouse."

Quite suddenly all the gadgetry went to respective zeros.

"Nae quick enough," Kilgour mourned. "Ah'll say third floor, back. Whae's your call, Paen?"

The policeman keyed his com, linked to a second locator. "Right."

"Ah," Kilgour said. "Jus' th' lad we thought. Human, t' boot. Another lesson. I' y're runnin' field agents, ne'er use your own people i' y' can recruit locals. They're nae as easy to spot."

"And," the technician-in-training said, "if they get blown, you don't lay awake as if it were one of your own."

"Y're learnin'. Y're learnin'. Noo. Let's go visiting."

The agent, who was using the cover name of Hohne, was carefully combing gel into his hair when the door came down. He spun away from the mirror.

"Help! Police!"

"Button it!" the Bhor snarled. "I *am* the police!" He held out his ID shield.

"Who are you? Who's he? What do you want?"

Kilgour wasn't listening.

"Const'ble Paen," he said casually. "I' y'll pick up yon door, an' prop it up, wi' you on th' other side, Ah'll be wantin' a wee word wi' this fine, upstandin' young man."

The policeman followed orders.

"You don't have any right—" the man said.

"Tsk," Alex said. "First mistake. Lass," he said to the technician, "he had his game right th' first time. Full a' prop' it outrage thae his privacy's been invaded. Which he should'a kept oop, an' shoutin' aboot how some clottin' human dinnae hae jurisdiction here i' th' cap'tal ae th' Bhor."

"I want to see some kind of warrant," the man said firmly.

"Thae's no warrant," Alex told him. "Y're nae under arrest. Thae's noo record ae police activ'ty i' this district t'night."

Hohne paled, then recovered.

"Aye," Alex said. "Thae 'tis th' price ae spyin't. But thae's a price y' ken already, Sr Hohne. Y're noo a baby spy, y're the senior Imperial agent i' th' cluster. 'Sperienced, an' thae. Although Ah mus' admit thae Ah noo c'nsider you lads frae Internal Security fit t' wipe th' arses ae th' lowliest Mantis bairn. But thae's m' prejudice. Noo. Let me ap'rise y' ae where y' stand. In th' middle of a deep, deep bog, my friend.

"Dinnae be talkin' an' sit y'self doon while I 'splain. Oh. One wee thing thae'll pertain. Ah hae *all* y'r net rounded up an' in a holdin't pattern."

Hohne followed orders and sat down while Kilgour went on. The Empire had quite naturally always spied on its friends and allies as well as its enemies. As every sane power had done throughout history. With Internal Security having replaced Mercury/Mantis, and the Emperor's new fears, the spying grew more intense.

Sr Hohne was, indeed, a senior operative for IS, which really wasn't that impressive, given that Internal Security was a newcomer to espionage, crippled by the Emperor's and Poyndex's decision that no one from Mercury Corps was capable, loyal, or honest.

Hohne had been in the Lupus Cluster for some time now, working under the cover of a native crafts buyer/exporter. The cover wasn't exactly original.

Bhor Counterintelligence knew, of course, that they were being spied on. Just as their own External Bureau spied on anyone it could. Most of the subagents Hohne had been running were Bhor or, if they were human, at least natives of the cluster. Only their Control was from outside—a wretched mistake in Kilgour's estimation. Field Control should also have been a Bhor, and whoever was running the net should stay safe in the Imperial embassy.

But the Emperor trusted no one, and neither did Poyndex. In the Lupus Cluster the Imperial embassy was staffed by numbwits and timeservers.

The field agents reported—regularly—to Hohne. Their broadcasts or drops had been monitored or picked up, copied, and then replaced for pickup for some time by Bhor CI. All the Bhor lacked was Hohne. Not that they had tried for him particularly hard—the Empire and the Bhor were still technically allies, although the cluster was under Imperial suspicion, just as anyone or anything who'd had the slightest contact with Sten was a potential pariah.

Kilgour had taken only a few hours at CI headquarters to work out a pattern for the Imperial field agents, and found they worked on a schedule. Reports were to be filed by X time/date, whether the spy had gotten any hard data or not. A response would also be provided—another no-no—at Y time/date at Z location, different from the drop box, so the still-unknown Imperial wasn't a *total* yutz.

Now to find Control. Kilgour worked on the assumption of like slave, like master. A broadband sweep found unknown transmissions being tightbeamed toward a known Imperial base "near" the Wolf Worlds, transmissions that were "trapped," logged, and then located.

Which was what led Kilgour to Hohne's apartment.

"So," Kilgour finished, "since zed a' y'r reports aboot ex-Imp sailors rootin' around th' Wolfie Worlds hae got throo, y'r master'll be gettin' concern't. He'll be wantin' a report, mos' rickety scratch, aye?"

"You want me to double."

"No. Ah *wan'* very little. A pint, a dram, a lass, a side ae smoked salmon no bigger'n y'r ego. You are *goin't* t' double, lad. Y' hae no choice. It dinnae matter whae reason y' hae f'r spyin't, f'r gold, f'r th' flag, or f'r y'r own reasons. Y're noo workin't f'r Alex Kilgour."

"There's no way," Hohne said, "that I'll help you cover Sten and your treason. I imagine you want me to sit here and file reports that this clottin' cluster is 152 percent

Loyalist, that nobody's ever seen Sten out here, nobody's ever heard of him, and they'd spit on his grave if he did show up."

"Twa points, mate:

"First, Ah dinnae wan' y' t' lie aboot th' cluster. Nae like that, at any rate. Nae. 'Tis dangerous oot here. Y'll be wantin' more agents. Agents by th' squad, by th' pl'toon, by th' bleedin' clan i' y' can score 'em.

"Second, y'll be helpin' me. Ah hae nae a doubtin' shadow a' thae, an y' should no either. An' Ah'm sure it'll noo take but hours til y' ken th' wisdom ae my words, an' reck wha' a *fine* laird Ah am.

"Aye? Ah. Y' still dinnae believe me.

"Mister Paen, i' y'd step in? Y' c'n take th' lad wi' you. Ah'll be wantin' further words wi' him a' another time."

Not gently, Sr Hohne, Internal Security, was removed.

"Will he come around," Marl asked.

"Oh aye," Alex said, as their civilian gravsled took them back to where Kilgour and his team were quartered. "He'll sit i' th' wee dungeon, contemplatin' his sins, which are many, an' his future, which i' bleak, an' he'll come aroun'. Spies bein't th' failed bein's they are, they always do. T' make sure, th' Bhor'll play some awful tapes ae pris'ners under inter'-gation, screamin' ae they're flayed alive an' forced t' listen t' political speeches.

"Ah'm quite th' screamer, gie'en good recordin' tech-niques an' a wee throat spray. Y' see, y're learnin', Marl. F'r openers, y' hae learned th' virtues ae patience. T' elaborate, Ah'll noo hae a parable. Are y' religious, lass?"

"Nossir. But my crèche was."

"Then th' fable be e'en closer t' y'r heart. Seems thae was a man. Nae a puir man, nae a laird. But he's livin't i' a wee house, an' he dinnae like it, but he canna fin' th' money frae a bigger one.

"So he hears aboot a wise man. Ver', ver' wise, he is. An he determines t' consult thae' wise man.

"Bein't wise, a' course it's a t'rble journey t' find him. But eventually our hero climbs t' th' top ae th' mountain where th' magi hangi't his beanie, an' he pleads, 'Great One, what c'n Ah do? M' house i' wee an' Ah canna stand it.'

"Th' wise man thinks, an' asks, 'Hae y' a coo?'

"'A coo?'

"'Aye, a coo.'

"'Aye, Ah hae a braw Hereford.'

"'Move it i' y'r house.'

"An' th' wise man refus't t' say more, i' spite ae th' man's pleadin't an' cryin't. So th' man goes back home, an' aye, it's e'en more a t'rble trek.

"An' he's thinkit, an wonderin't, but he knows th' wise man's truly wise, an' so he moves his coo in t' sleep wi' him. An' his wee house is e'en wee-er.

"An' he canna stand it. So he goes back, t'rble journey thae it is, all th' way t' th' wise man, an' again asks th' question.

"Th' wise man thinks, an' then he says, 'Hae y' a goat?'

"'A goat?'

"'Aye, a goat.'

"'Ah hae a goat.'

"'Move it i' th' house, too.'

"An' once again, th' wise man refuse't say more.

"So th' man, noo puzzled sorely, wander't back t' his wee home, an' thinkit. But 'cause th' sage i' truly wise, he move th' goat i' wi' him an' th' coo.

"An' noo he *truly* canna stand it, f'r his house is e'en smaller.

"So again, he goes back t' th' wise man, an' asks f'r help, sayin't 'Ah hae a wee house, noo wi' a coo an' a goat i' it, an' i's bleedin' crowded, an' Ah canna stand it.'

"An' th' wise man think't, an' then he says, 'Hae y' chickens?'

"'Chickens?'

"'Aye, chickens.'

"'Aye, Ah hae chickens.'

"'Move 'em i' th' house. Come t' ponder, i' y' hae ducks, an' swans, an' pigs, hae them i' the house ae well.'

"An' despite th' man's pleadin', th' wise man sayit noo more.

"But th' man goes back home, an' puts th' chickens in th' house. An' noo i's worse, i's so bad i's intolerable. Thae's no room left i' th' house f'r th' man, i's so crowded.

"An' he journeys back yet again t' th' wise man, an' says, 'Ah canna stand it! M' wee house hae naught but animals i' it, an' there's noo room ae all f'r me! Noo, Ah'm pleadin't, help me!'

"An' th' wise man sayit, 'Go home, an' take all th' animals oot ae th' house.'

"An' thae's all he'll say.

"An' th' man rush't home, an' clear oot all th' animals, an' y' ken whae he discovered?

"He still hae a wee house.

"But noo it's *entire* full ae animal shit!"

Marl stared at Kilgour for long moments. She had been warned. She should have known. But . . .

"What does that have to do with patience?"

"Y' listened all th' way through, di'nt y'?"

Cind was the first to spot Kilgour's gravsled as it sped up the dirt track toward them.

"It's over, isn't it," Sten said, just a bit sadly.

"It is. It was time to come back anyway, since we were out of stregg. But we've still got three containers of the herbed anchovy pâté, right here in my pack with the dead soldiers. We could've stayed out another week on that wonderful taste-budtingling delight you had to go and discover."

"So I made a mistake. The label made it look trick. Cut me some slack—I'm the one who brought the adobo."

"True, and forgotten if not forgiven," Cind said. "Now, all we have to do is explain why we're sunburned in places nobody gets sunburned climbing rocks."

"The cover story is that we were learning how to ski nekkid. Not that anybody better ask."

Sten turned serious. "Thanks, Cind. Five days—I wish we would have had five fives. This'll be something to remember in a few weeks.

"When things . . . heat up again. A good reminder that it doesn't have to be crazy all the time."

Her answer was a kiss.

Sten pulled her tight. And the gravsled grounded, so neither of them had to continue the thought that something like this might never happen again for them.

They had expected just Alex. Instead, Ida ploomped out of the front passenger seat beside him. She was even fatter than the last time Sten had seen her, and her brightly colored gown was even more expensive. Obviously her vitsa— family/band—hadn't completely lost its senses, and she remained as chieftain—Voivode.

She may have been fat, but she unloaded from the gravsled as smoothly as she had moved years ago as a Mantis operative with far fewer years and kilos.

Of course, she did not greet Sten with any sort of compliment, any more than she would have met Kilgour without an insult.

"You are still disgustingly outdoorsy," was all she said. Then she looked Cind up and down.

"So you are the one."

"I don't know," Cind said. "What is the one?"

Sten intervened. "Ida, since when are you vetting my life?"

"I always did, imbecile. You just weren't smart enough to realize it."

"Oh."

"She appears all right," Ida judged. "A good companion. A man should not sleep alone. Nor a woman."

"Th' coo's snapp't, gettin' all sentimental an' a'," Kilgour said. "Pinch'd m' thigh on th' way out."

Ida merely sneered at Kilgour's cheap lie.

"Greetings out of the way," she said, "can we get out of this clottin' snow and somewhere close to a fire and some alk?"

The four loaded, and Kilgour lifted the gravsled back for Otho's castle, where Sten was quartered. Ida—who hadn't, of course, offered to get in the back and let Sten ride up front—swiveled around to eye him.

"So. It is finally time to end all this nonsense with the Emperor, eh?"

"You go right to it, don't you?" Sten said.

"Enough is enough. It was barely tolerable back then for the Rom, with all these laws and beings with their borders and boundaries who start wars for this clot who dubbed himself Emperor. And back then all of them were considered sane, at least by the thinking of the gadje. We Rom always knew better. Freedom cannot be served by making laws and fences.

"The Empire had become too much for us, even before that bastard on Prime went mad. There had been discussions at tribal gatherings of this. Perhaps it is time for the Rom to move on."

"To where?"

"Beyond." She gestured upward, forgetting about the gravsled's roof and putting a minor dent in it. "Beyond the Empire, beyond where it stretches now, beyond where it will ever reach. It is time to search out treasures and beings we can't even imagine. This little Empire has suddenly become hard to breathe in."

Sten suddenly had a dizzying, entrancing vision of swirling, unknown galaxies, stars, and systems whispering the invitation to adventure, instead of this seemingly endless series of wars and slaughter. Beyond. It drew his soul like a magnet.

"Load the ships with our most precious and compact trading goods, fuel them and slave some barges as tankers, and set a one-way course," Ida continued. "I have heard stories some Voivodes have already convinced their tribes to move on, and it is true that some vitsa are not seen at council anymore. After all, it is said we Rom did not originally come from the worlds of men."

She turned back to the subject at hand. "But that is a matter for later, after we have killed this gadje who's called himself Emperor too long. Here is the situation for us Rom, Sten. We have come to serve the star of freedom. Which, at least for the moment, means you and your allies. If that changes—or if *you* change—then we shall reevaluate the situation."

"Thank you," Sten said. "I accept."

"We hae also," Alex said, without taking his eyes from his piloting, "heard frae Wild. He offer'd t' set doon, but Ah advised him to hang offworld. P'raps th' fewer who ken we hae a bargain wi' th' king of the smugglers, th' better it might be."

"Good," Sten approved. "We'll send one of the Bhor ships up to pick him up and any lieutenant he wants for a strategy session when it's set."

He settled back in his seat.

The forces of rebellion were gathering . . .

"I have," Sten began, "what, for want of a weaker term, might be a plan. Or at least the beginnings of one."

The seven beings listening to him were dwarfed in Otho's great banquet hall, which could easily hold two thousand Bhor in cheerful riot.

The hall would have satisfied the most critical Viking as an acceptable place for *Valholl*, even though the roof wasn't made of war shields, and there wasn't a goat with aquavit-flowing teats handy. Far overhead were monstrous wood-beamed ceilings, with skylights in the roof, now snow-covered from the driving storm outside. Four huge fire-places that it seemed a tacship could park in roared at each corner of the building, and the AM2-powered radiators that provided the real warmth were hidden behind false stonework.

Thick carpets covered the flagstone floors, and the walls were hung with war and hunting trophies. The furniture— long tables and benches—were as solid as anything else in

the hall. Necessary, when an acceptable way for a Bhor to
deliver a categorical syllogism's conclusion was with a
knobkerrie.

This was a high-strategy preliminary planning session.
Listening intently, and sipping only non-alk drinks (although
Otho kept looking thoughtfully at his great stregghorn and a
barrel of the deadly stuff on a nearby table) were Freston,
who represented Sten's minuscule conventional military
force; Ida; Wild, who would carry as much or as little of
Sten's plans as he chose to the loose group of smugglers and
confidence men who considered Wild's advice worth taking;
Otho, who, even though he had formally retired as Head of
the Bhor Council to serve as a mercenary soldier under Sten,
was still regarded by the Bhor as an elder statesman; Kilgour
and Cind, Sten's closest aides; and Rykor. No one except
Cind and Alex knew about Sr Ecu, and that the Manabi were
now part of the conspiracy to overthrow the Emperor. Rykor
would report whatever was necessary to Ecu, back on Seilichi,
who hopefully would *never* be publicly seen as one of Sten's
chesspieces.

"Here's what we want to do, and forgive me if I get a
little obvious. So far, we have the Empire in a reactive position. We want to keep things that way as long as possible,
because the minute we slow down, we'll get squashed like
bugs.

"We'll hit the Emperor every chance we get—but we don't
ever want to hit him in the predictable places. The bastard
is smart, and he's got people almost as smart working for
him.

"So we'll bash him in unexpected places . . ."

"Like K-B-N-S-O," Otho rumbled approvingly.

"Right. Any of you who come up with wide-open targets
like that, feel free to add them to the pot. We'll also want to
be hitting the Empire in embarrassing places as well. For
instance, if anybody knows where the Empire's main supplier of toilet paper is, that could be a viable target.

"We won't be able to hit him with a knockout, but maybe

we can dazzle his ass with some fancy footwork and jabs and get him to stumble over his own feet, in which case we'll kick hell out of him while he's down.

"We want the damage to be as public as we can make it. We want to make him look like a mess. I'll stick with the stupid hand-combat comparison—I want him to be wandering around leaking blood from some good solid eyebrow slashes. Fat lips. A shiner on each eye. An ear chewed off. Like that.

"If we can get him mad, that's all to the good. I don't think he's that stupid, but we can try. When we're thinking of these raids, also consider how they'll play to anybody who might be an ally. For instance, we've already got two Honjo ships. Believe me, their actions will be quietly praised on their home worlds. With any luck, we can get the Honjo to declare openly for us, if we can convince them the Emperor's a loser. Rykor's handling that, and the rest of the propaganda, which we'll get back to in a minute."

Sten broke off for a minute, and drained his mug of tea.

"The second priority will be AM2. We want to steal it, destroy it, divert it. I'm operating on the premise that the Emp is the only one who knows where it comes from, or how to make it if it's synthetic. Fine. We're gonna mess with that capability. And we want to take as much of Anti-Matter Two as he's trying to give his toadies, and pass it along to our allies. We'll get specific about that later.

"Kilgour will be running the intelligence end. So anything you pick up on AM2, even if it's a weird rumor that it's really the Emperor's crap and smells like attar of roses, put it in for analysis and possible addition to the databank.

"Same deal for anything on the Emperor himself. Any stories about where he came from, what he's done, girlfriends, boyfriends, sheep, goat, or octopi he used to get romantic with back in the dark ages . . . anything, anything, anything. This is a critical part of the whole campaign, and we'd like to keep it fairly quiet that we're putting together a personality fiche on the Emperor. So don't be putting anything in writing to your intelligence staffers. It'd be too easy for our Eternal Opponent to start a disinformation campaign as an ambush.

"Don't ever forget—the Emperor himself is our target. We're going to capture him if we can, and convince him to see the light if we can. But more likely, we're going to have to kill him. That's also *sub rosa*, of course."

"Sten?" It was Freston.

"GA."

"Right now the Emperor is staying on Prime. The few times he's been offworld have been unannounced and on the run. Is that right, sir?"

"Aye," Alex agreed. "Th' lad's holed up in his wee castle. Which i' a stronghold Ah dinnae think w' can take on an' reduce."

"Agreed. We've got to smoke him into the open."

"Good luck," Wild said cynically. "He did not get to where he was by doing what *anyone* wanted him to do."

"We're still going to try. More in a shake on that.

"We want him out, in the field, where we can nail him. And once he's in the open, we'll smash him."

"Admirable," Ida said. "But my vitsa'll want some nice specifics before we start wadin' through the gore. Such as how we're gonna winkle the clottin' Emperor out of his nice, safe shell."

"Rykor?"

"We're going to embarrass him out," Rykor said. "First you gentlebeings will set the stage. Make his forces appear foolish. Make his generals and admirals appear incompetent. Every time you can win an engagement, that victory will be publicized. Publicized on two levels.

"The first is the open one. We must tell the truth, no matter how painful it is. With luck, the Emperor will play into our hands with his own propaganda. One of the many faults the Emperor has evinced of late is a large and growing ego. If anyone questions this, look at his Imperial stupidities in the Altaic Cluster.

"Egomaniacs, just like power-seekers, can never be satisfied. So we hope that the Emperor's people will take any victory or accomplishment, and go big with it. The technique is called the Big Lie, and the theory behind it is that if you tell a great enough falsehood, the listeners will, at most, argue over its size, not over its truth.

"This is correct in some instances, but not when its practitioners are completely watchdogged. And every time they blow trumpets for their latest untruth, someone points that out immediately—using nothing else but the truth. The eventual result will be that *all* information from that Big Lie's parents will be questioned and disregarded, which is just what we plan to do with the Emperor.

"But our side *must* always tell the truth."

"A frightenin' concept," Alex said.

"Don't worry, Mister Kilgour. That's only with white propaganda—stories that clearly emanate from our side. Gray and black . . . you'll still have the ability to try to outlie even the Emperor himself."

"Ah dinnae ken i' Ah'm *that* bonnie . . . but Ah'll gie i' a wee shot."

"As for black propaganda," Rykor continued, "this is what Sten was referring to earlier. We shall spread some awesome rumors. Stories that the Emperor in fact never returned. If we can get him out of Arundel, and present at a battle, rumors will spread that he was killed in that battle. There will be stories that he is mentally, morally, or even physically crippled. We shall play to the worst of human male fears in *that* particular area."

"Small things," Otho rumbled. "The Emperor is a warrior. He cares not if there are back-alley rumors he is a eunuch."

"Small things," Rykor agreed. "I shall tell you a joke, Otho. Do you know the difference between the old Emperor, the new Emperor, and the privy council?"

"I do not."

"If somehow all three entities were aboard a ground

vehicle, and were informed the vehicle is stalled, their responses would be as follows: the privy council would have ordered the controllers be shot, the crew sent into exile, and someone new brought in. The old Emperor would have ordered the problem investigated and then the most competent crew members given promotions and the vehicle be put under way once more. The new Emperor would pull down the shades and pretend the vehicle was still moving."

Otho considered, then politely chuffed a minilaugh. "As you said, Rykor, a small thing."

Cind got it. "Uh-uh," she said. "Isn't the point of the story to get beings thinking in terms of *old* and *new*? Which ices the whole Majesty of Ages, Eternal Emperor belief?"

"Just so. Once we have accomplished that mental division, then the stories, the back-alley rumors, will start to be believed.

"Another area—I think it is profitable for us to look at this Cult of the Emperor that has been tacitly encouraged. Once you have two beings convinced that the immaterial exists, and can affect the material, you can then make one proclaim the other a heretic. Possibly you can even convince the first being that the new deity is, in fact, the antigod.

"Beings, particularly humans, will harbor the most imbecilic thoughts and commit the most appalling acts in the name of whichever god they've created and decided to worship . . . But I am sorry. I run on."

"Not at all," Sten said. "You, at least, have a specific campaign. At this point all I have is some generalities and a possible first target. Gentlebeings, the floor is open for ideas, suggestions, and stupid ramblings."

"All a which," Kilgour said, "is vasty improved wi' a whiff ae th' grape. Or stregg. Boss, whae are y' drinkin't?"

Sten shook his head. "No thanks. Somebody's got to drive." He was starting to realize that among the many things wrong with being the one for whom the buck stops, a fairly high degree of sobriety was one.

As it happened, the only drinkers were Otho, Kilgour, and

Freston, and Freston stopped after one heavily watered glass of alk.

Otho looked them up and down, then growled. "Wonderful. Simply wonderful. By my mother's beard, I appear to have cast my lot with a group of bluestockings."

And he promptly drained the great horn and refilled it, determined to compensate for this shame single-handedly.

The session did not break up until nearly dawn. It had been productive—and that possible first target was a definite.

As everyone yawned toward their quarters, and a few hours of unconsciousness before the Dream would be broken down, bit by bit, ship by ship, duty by duty, weapon by weapon, ratpack by ratpack, into an operations order.

Cind lingered on and caught Otho's eye. He nodded, knowing what she would ask.

He filled his horn and grunted a question. Cind nodded, and Otho filled one for her.

"When will we gather?" Cind asked.

"I have already heard from the elders. They wait on our convenience."

"Soon," Cind suggested. "Do you know what you will say?"

Otho's brows furrowed. His great fangs bared. He snarled. To anyone not familiar with the Bhor, it would have been taken as at least a threat, at worst the beginnings of a possibly cannibalistic attack. Cind knew it to be a smile.

"By Sarla and Laraz, I do. But it is not what I had planned. By my father's thawing buttocks but I am surprisingly thick at times. But now I have the words, and shall cut my beard if necessary to make the elders listen."

Beard-cutting was the way the Bhor had of bringing a matter to an immediate "vote" in front of the assemblage—and something that, if the "vote" did not go in the favor of the beard-cutter, would almost certainly result in his dismemberment.

"Yes, I now have the words," Otho repeated.

"I shall inform the elders, and we shall meet at nightfall of this day. Advise Sten and the others to remain in their quarters after dusk. I do not mean to embarrass great warriors such as them—but this business must be done with only our people present. Time has run out for the Bhor to continue as they have been."

And that was all that Otho would tell Cind.

Near dusk of the next day, the Bhor arrived, singly and in groups. "Trickled in" might be a correct phrase, but tsunamis never runnel. Cind was one of a handful of humans—all natives of the Lupus Cluster, and all high-rankers in the Bhor military—permitted at this enclave. She, like the others, wore full battle harness.

Otho had the great tables laid out for a banquet, and sideboards held cold roasts and dishes for late arrivals. Everything had been presliced, since a Bhor political discussion did not need further encouragement by allowing edged weapons.

Great barrels of stregg were set out at strategic intervals. Which meant arm's length.

At full dark, the subject was formally announced by the Bhor elders: Should the Bhor declare against the Empire? If so, should they declare independence and war openly—or merely back Sten to the hilt, protesting innocence all the while and declaring anyone whose name/profile showed up on a WANTED poster a renegade?

That ancillary topic was taken care of rapidly. In spite of the brawling style of the Bhor, they were not imbeciles—and the mere mention of the size of the Imperial fleets, the existence of planetbusters, and the probable willingness of the Emperor to deploy those weapons sent a cold chill across the great hall.

Even the greatest warrior may have a mate and offspring, and somehow hope to still have a home he/she/Va might return victoriously to.

Then the major issue was mounted.

By midnight, several topics had been discussed:

Whether it was wise for the Bhor to involve themselves with *any* cause with a human at its helm.

Whether Sten was in fact human or a Bhor reincarnated under a curse in that puny body.

Whether Alex Kilgour was actually a Bhor (passed by acclamation).

The most successful way of thawing frozen buttocks.

Whether, if the motion to go to war against the Empire failed, the Bhor ought to declare war on *someone*, since the new warriors were little other than mewling milksops.

Whether the W'lew Peninsula still contained any wild stregg.

Whether the W'lew Peninsula offered better fishing than C'lone Bay, assuming you could not find any stregg.

Whether the problem with the Eternal Emperor could be settled by a chosen Bhor warrior challenging him to a winner-take-all duel to the death.

Six tables had been broken, two over Bhor heads. Twelve warriors were on their way to hospital. Cind was nursing a black eye and bruised heel of palm from a badly conceived but extemporaneous rebuttal. Five very promising duel challenges had been issued. Seven warriors had been tossed through a window into a snowbank to sober up.

The Bhor were merely getting started—this was the first big issue to come up in several years, and it might be a week before it was settled, assuming the stregg held out and there were Bhor still left unhospitalized to argue.

Otho had enough.

The elders had already attempted to manipulate the "dialogue" toward Otho, with small success. Otho waited until Iv'r was in midperoration, surprisingly close enough to the subject at hand, being a diatribe that even the best of the Imperial Guard would not be a worthy adversary to the Bhor, no matter how greatly they outnumbered the race.

Iv'r, a longtime friend of Otho—Otho'd once bested him in a trial of endurance over the stewardship of a disputed arctic oasis—saw him fondle his beard, knew what Otho would do as a last resort, and yielded the floor to a "point of order."

This meant he knocked another Bhor unconscious, who'd been shouting claims about the shortness of Iv'r's mother's beard, and sat down.

Abrupt silence.

Otho began. These were parlous times, he said. The Empire had turned murderous, and its leader no more than a beardless dacoit. The Bhor must respond to this threat in a new fashion, or face obliteration. Otho reminded them of how they had been following their ancient enemies, the stregg, to extinction, courtesy of the prophets of Talamein and their swordsmen the Jann, before Sten came to the Wolf Worlds.

Now it was time to choose—and there could be but one choice.

"The choice is yours," Otho bellowed, roar booming back from the ceiling high above, "and it is clear. Or have we become a race who flees across the ice from a stregg?"

That put the matter in quite a clear light. The Bhor would declare for Sten.

Iv'r's shout rose above the clamor: "Then let us choose a leader. The greatest warrior of all, to lead us in this battle."

Pandemonium. There were those who agreed, those who disagreed, fearing tyranny—although choosing a single warchief in an emergency was a respected Bhor tradition—and most loudly those who knew they were the only possible candidate for the post.

Iv'r began chanting: "Otho! Otho! Otho!"

Eventually others started chanting as well.

Otho's bellow went to sonic boom—and he got the silence he wanted, or at least the noise reduced to mere agony level. "No!"

That got *real* silence.

"I am old," he began.

Shouts agreeing or disagreeing. Otho paid no mind. "I

will assist, I will aid. But I am in the nightwinter of my life, and this struggle might go on for years. I wish to serve in the coming conflict as but a simple soldier. Or, perhaps, battleforce leader.

"I said we must respond to this threat of the evil Emperor in a new fashion, and that I meant. Which means someone who can look beyond our cluster, and see what is best, and convey that vision to our elders."

Otho should have built his "nominating" speech to some kind of "Happy Warrior" peak. Instead, he stepped off the table, filled his stregghorn, poured it down, stregg spilling across his chest, gasped for breath, and jerked his thumb across the table.

"Her."

Her, of course, was Cind.

A very long silence, followed by an even greater bedlam.

Cind, after she recovered, attempted to argue. She was but a human. She was still young, and not fitted for this honor. She was—

Whatever else she had tried to stammer went unheard. And the bleat went on.

Near dawn, the controversy was settled. Those still conscious who knew and respected Cind's battle and leadership abilities, plus those who were intrigued by the novelty of a human speaking for the Bhor, "won," although the field looked less like a political debating chamber than Hattin from an infidel's perspective.

Cind would speak for the Bhor.

She went to wake Sten, wondering how he would take the news.

Sten, of course, was delighted. First that the Bhor had declared, and second that they had picked such a talented and capable leader. He also found it funnier than hell that he and a Bhor were bedpartners. Although he did suggest she must immediately concentrate on beard-growing.

Alex Kilgour had not slept that night either. Near dawn,

he found himself outside, on one of the fortresses' high battlements. A sentry saw him, started to challenge, then recognized him and left him to his thoughts.

The storm had broken, and the stars gleamed cold overhead.

Kilgour stared up, his eyes going past the strange constellations of the Wolf Worlds, far into interstellar space, toward the unseen galaxy that held his home star and system.

Edinburgh, where he was Laird Kilgour of Kilgour, with castles, estates, and factories. A hard three-g world, that bred hard men and women.

A world that Alex suddenly felt he would never see again.

An' whae ae thae, he reminded himself. When y' took th' Emp's shilling, wae it noo wi' th' knowledge th' service would likely put y' in y'r grave, as it did y'r brother Kenneth? Or, ae best, leave y' crippl't, like Malcolm?

Aye. Aye. But th' gutcrawl thae y'll noo live t' bear th' corpse ae th' Emperor t' his final rest i' a hard one.

But would y' rather die abed, years hence, wi' y'r mind a snarl ae th' past, y'r body withered an a', snivelin't graybeard?

Alex shivered, as his mind laid out all the paths before him, and all of them led only to his death.

He shivered, and it was not the cold.

Then he turned and went inside, to his chambers.

I' death comit, was his final thought, ae th' wee Jann put it, S'be't.

W' hae a war t' fight i' the meantime.

CHAPTER ELEVEN

DUSABLE WAS ONE E-year away from its quadrennial elections. At stake: the office of Tyrenne and two-thirds of the seats on the Council of Solons.

All across the big, densely populated port planet—the industrial and political linchpin of the Cairene System—the upcoming elections were heatedly debated. Even the big news of the Imperial hunt for that traitor, Sten, was buried in an avalanche of pontificating and speculation on the livie newscasts.

Everyone from sewer worker to industrial baron was testing the political winds. Parents discussed the chances of Tyrenne Walsh and Solon Kenna at the dinner table. Joygirls and joyboys spread the mordida thicker among the local cops. Ward bosses counted and recounted the promised votes. Dirty tricksters pored over graveyard registries. Even children were recruited from the crèche play yards to snoop about the wards for scandal.

Politics, the Eternal Emperor was fond of saying, is big business. On Dusable, it was the *only* business.

Patronage was the axis upon which the world spun. It was unlikely there was a being on Dusable whose existence didn't depend upon it. Cops were tithed by their precinct captains for prized mordida-collecting beats. Business owners bribed inspectors for their licenses. Unions traded influence for featherbedding jobs. Even dishwashers sold their votes to become pot wallopers. And pot washers paid mordida just to keep on scrubbing.

In short, Dusable was the most corrupt planet in the Empire. But in its fashion, the system worked. A citizen careful to always back the right horse was assured a chance of a happy life. Only the losers plotted and schemed to "throw the rascals out."

When the Eternal Emperor had made his long and twisted return from the grave, it was a Dusable election that had given him his first large step up to the throne. Since then, he'd repaid that debt many times over.

To begin with, Walsh and Kenna owed their current exalted status to the Emperor's not-inconsiderable political savvy. He'd stolen the election from Tyrenne Yelad—a boss with three decades of experience in ballot-box larceny.

But the Emperor was a fervent believer in that ancient law of politics, "He who was with me before Chicago . . ." and had ladled favor with a heavy hand.

Against this backdrop Solon Kenna hit the stump. Electioneering as if the big date were a week away, instead of a year, even though all his advisers said the election was in the bag. They pointed out that Dusable had never been so prosperous. The landing orbits of its big shipping ports were jammed. Factories were working twenty-four-hour shifts. The GNBI (Gross National Bribery Index) at record levels.

AM2 was not only plentiful and cheap, but the Eternal Emperor had gifted the system with a brand-new AM2 depot—servicing two vast sectors in this area of the Empire.

Kenna refused to be soothed. As the president of the Council of Solons and the power behind Tyrenne Walsh, he had a great deal to lose if there were any miscalculations. Which was everything. Kenna had no intention of repeating Tyrenne Yelad's most crucial error: overconfidence.

He approached his first major speech of the campaign season with special care.

To begin with, he chose a friendly audience—the Cairenes division of the giant shipping union, the SDT. The union had been one of Kenna's power bases since his days as a rookie member of the Council of Solons. The brawny shipyard workers could always be counted on to deliver, whether it was votes, hefty campaign-chest contributions, on-demand wildcat strikes, or strong-arm good squads to raid rival wards.

Next, he dipped deep into his private war chest to provide the entertainment. There would be three hundred refreshment tables, creaking under the weight of tons of food. A hundred more would serve as open bars. A central stage was erected, and scores of musicians, comedians, and scantily clad dancers were pressed into service for dawn-to-dusk entertainment. Fifty tents were thrown up at the edges of the big main shipyard and staffed with teams of patriotic joygirls and joyboys, who were called on routinely during the quadrennials to give their all for Dusable.

Finally, he put gentle pressure on the Emperor to provide him with suitable ammunition for his speech. And the Eternal Emperor, Kenna was pleased to tell his aides as he mounted the platform to address the assembled SDT members, had come through with more than he could have hoped for.

The roars of greetings that met Kenna were loud enough to drown the sounds of an inbound liner. He stood for long minutes under the rolling thunder of applause and huzzahs. He affected an attempt at interruption—a weakly raised hand for silence. Then the hand fell . . . Helpless before the enthusiasm of his admirers. As a newscaster's camera pushed in for a close-up, Kenna flashed that humble grin he had perfected over decades of working the hustings.

Three times, Kenna attempted to halt the applause. And three times, he had to bow to the will of the masses and accept their praise. On the fourth attempt, Kenna made a small hand signal, which was instantly picked up by the shill captains, who passed the word to their minions peppered heavily in the crowd to cool down. This time, the applause and glad shouts slowly diminished to a hush.

"I have one question before we get started," Kenna intoned, his voice blasting over the portaboomers. "Are you all better off today than you were four years ago?"

The crowd noise was even louder than before. A news

tech watched the needle of his popularity meter bang against the max peg and hold for a full minute. He nudged his anchor, whose eyes saucered. It was a near record.

Then the claque brought the crowd to a hush again, and Kenna continued.

"It is with great pleasure and humility that I stand before you once again to ask for your support," he said. "Now, my worthy opponents think I'm a fool for rubbing elbows with good, honest, working beings such as yourselves . . ."

He allowed a space here for a growl of anger at his snobby "worthy opponents." The growl came on schedule.

"But I say to them, without the working class, where would Dusable be?"

A shill shouted a carefully crafted impromptu from mid-crowd: "In the drakhouse, that's where!" The crowd hooted laughter.

Kenna made with the swamp-beast-eating grin again. "Thank you, sister!" More laughter from the crowd.

The smile was replaced with Kenna's patented frown, in which his two gloriously thick eyebrows met in a dramatic, inverted V. "There's change in the wind, my friends, and no one, but no one, knows it better than the working being. And of all the hard-laboring folks of Dusable, it is the SDT Union which has led the vanguard in promoting these changes."

It took no prompting by shills to get a deafening shout of approval here. Kenna waited until it died of its own accord.

"Now you all know I'm not one for false humility," Kenna said. There was laughter. "But, I'm going to have to be honest with you good people here.

"These winds of change I'm speaking of have graced Dusable with the greatest prosperity in its history. Full employment. Record wages. Prices at near-record lows.

"All these things we've enjoyed partly because of the enlightened leadership of Tyrenne Walsh . . . and my humble self . . . but, there is really one being all of us have to thank for our good fortune. And that is . . . the Eternal Emperor himself."

The crowd went wild at this. Shouting. Pounding on one another. On and on it went, the shills working the lines with fervor. This time the news tech's needle pegged out for one and a half minutes.

Kenna stepped in again. "My opponents say all the benefits we have received since that historic day when the Emperor revealed himself among us, is charity, pure and simple."

There were loud boos at this. Kenna smiled in acknowledgment, but pushed on. "They say Dusable is at the beck and call of its master, the Eternal Emperor. That since we've become a dominion of the Emperor, we've abandoned our traditional independence."

The crowd hooted.

"You've heard all these lies, and more," Kenna continued. "But, the truth is, Dusable is being listened to for the first time in its history. And I mean *really* listened to. We can hold up our heads in all the great capitals of the Empire now. And who does the Emperor turn to for advice in these trying times? Why, our own Tyrenne Walsh, who labors as we speak in the great hall of Parliament on Prime World."

Kenna sipped at a special throat-soothing drink as the crowd applauded.

"Yes . . . Dusable owes a great deal to the Eternal Emperor. There's no doubt about it. But, the Emperor owes us as well. And in these trying times, he needs us more than ever. I spoke to him personally, just the other day, and he told me to thank the people of Dusable for their undying efforts for freedom.

"And he said he especially wanted to thank the workers of SDT. He said he wanted you all to know that without the great shipping unions of our Empire, all his struggles would be for naught."

The crowd took forty-five seconds to thank the Emperor back.

"But as you all know," Kenna said when the applause waned, "the Eternal Emperor is not just a being of words.

And I'm here to tell you this day, that once again he's putting his thanks into action."

Kenna lofted a large, old-fashioned piece of parchment. The news cameras pushed in to show the Imperial seal at the bottom. Then panned up to Kenna.

"First off, our brand-spanking-new AM2 depot—orbiting now high above our blessed world—has just been raised to a Triple A rating!"

The crowd really took off on this. A triple A rating would bring even more business and work to the port.

"But, that's not all," Kenna said. "Along with our new rating, comes an even greater responsibility.

"My friends, I'm pleased to announce the Emperor has diverted an enormous AM2 shipment from a less deserving system. The amount is enough to supply all the needs of this entire sector for two E-years.

"As we speak, this AM2 shipment is approaching Dusable. And when this shipment is safely stowed away in our state-of-the-art depot—constructed, I might add, by our own talented people—Dusable will be able to rightly boast of the Emperor's respect and faith in us.

"For, from this glorious day forward, Dusable will be the only supplier for AM2 in this sector. And that, my friends, is anyone's definition of loyalty repaid."

The applause, cheers, and general pandemonium greeting this statement rolled across Dusable's capitol. Beings in distant wards looked up and wondered at thunder on such a cloudless day.

Aboard the *Pai Kow*—sixty-seven million miles away— the cheers became a sudden blast that nearly cracked the com unit's speaker cells.

Captain Hotsco chopped the volume, chortling to herself over Solon Kenna's lavish promises of AM2 aplenty. She hit a monitor touchpad and Kenna's face—silently mouthing the words of his speech—became a small window in the right-hand corner of the screen. Space filled the remainder.

Hotsco scanned the monitor, singing, "Mushi, mushi ano nay, ano nay . . . mushi, mushi ano nay . . ."

Then she saw it. Lights winked at three o'clock.

"Ah so desca." Hotsco laughed. "Come to Momma, bright eyes." She glanced at Kenna's round face, still flapping its jaws to the union masses. The captain gave Kenna a mock salute. "Solidarity, brother!"

Fingers brushed touchpads and Kenna's face vanished. The winking lights shifted to dead center. And the monitor snapzoomed in.

Hotsco sucked in her breath as the robo "train" came into view. The lead element looked like an Imperial battleship chopped in half. In a way, it was. The ship had been turned out decades ago in one of the late, not so great, Tanz Sullamora's yards. The command and weapons part of the ship had been buzzsawed, a new nosecone installed, and now it consisted almost entirely of engine. Tractor beams ringed the center. Starboard was a hump that was the brains of the ship.

The sole job of this giant engine was to tow the eighty-kilometer formation of barges trailing behind.

Hotsco started an automatic count of the container ships, then quit in awe as the sum reached into the scores.

And each and every one of them was filled with the most precious substance in the Empire—AM2.

Captain Hotsco, part-time pirate, full-time smuggler, was gazing upon a dream prize. The value of the AM2 train bound for Dusable's depot was unimaginable. Even allowing for a Kenna lie involving the quantity—clot, cut it in half—Hotsco knew she was looking at not one fortune, but as many as the number of ships in the convoy.

And it was just sitting there for the taking. Okay, she couldn't get it all. But she could certainly cut out enough to buy two or three systems the size of the Cairenes.

Wild would be livid enough to cut her pretty throat.

Clot Wild.

But, what about that cute Kilgour? It was his intelligence

that had turned up word of the AM2 shipment. She had fallen in lust with the tubby Scotsman as he had laid out the plan to Wild and a group of his captains—which had included Hotsco.

The drill was for the smugglers to use their normal runs to the Cairenes—usually carrying expensive illegals for the pols and their cronies—as a cover to sniff out the AM2 train.

It was a damned good plan, too. Proof was looking out at her from the monitor.

And there was no one, but no one, around to know.

But if she followed her instincts, she might never learn the answer to that age-old question of what lies under a Scotsman's kilt.

Clot the kilt.

Look at all that AM2.

After all, she hadn't promised anything. Not really. She had only said she would take a look. And she was looking, wasn't she?

Then a terrible, dream-souring thought trickled through. What would she do with it? Who could fence that amount? And if she tried dribbling it out, someone would eventually fink. And the Imperials would soon be hot on her trail.

Clot the Imperials. Hotsco had practically been born on the run.

Yeah . . . But . . . She had never had to run from entire fleets. Which is what would happen. All that AM2 double-damned-guaranteed it.

Oh, well.

Hotsco decided to do the honest thing—no matter how much it hurt.

To cheer herself, she thought of Alex's broad, smiling face. And that short kilt.

She quickly coded the message, including the coordinates of the AM2 supply train. Then she sent it in one short, powerful blast.

Hotsco waited for two, or three breaths.

Her com unit bleeped.

It was the *Victory*.

Message received.

Hotsco quickly shut down and scooted out of the area, thinking, I hope you're worth it, Alex Kilgour.

Dusable's new AM2 depot was the size of a small moon. In looks, it resembled a quartered sphere. Each "slice" was placed in the corner of an imaginary square, then linked with its sisters by enormous tubes. All traffic and freight flowed through these tubes. Laid over this configuration was an elaborate spiderweb of com lines, repair walks, and pipes carrying everything from industrial liquids to recycled air and sewage from the life-form units.

The depot normally required six hundred beings to operate. But there was nothing normal about Dusable. Even here, parked in high orbit, the rules of featherbedding applied. There were twice that number lazing away when the AM2 shipment arrived.

Most of them were asleep. Or partying in the rec center. Kenna's announcement hadn't been a surprise to the depot people. They had been alerted days before to get ready for the shipment. Not that there was much to do. The depot was almost entirely automated.

A sleepy operator noted the approach in his log. He half checked that all automatic units were functioning, and then returned to his bunk and spooned up to his joyboy's smooth back.

For a moment, he thought about waking the lad for a little fun. His loins stirred mildly. Then sleep overtook him, and he was snoring away.

On the monitor, the image of the giant AM2 train closed in. Then it stopped as the convoy reached a synchronous orbit with the station. Signals went out. The com board lit up with computer-exchanged messages.

The first container units separated from the train. They moved in a slow arc toward the depot where 'bot units waited to snag them and guide them aboard.

If the operator had been looking, he would have seen one of those AM2 container units detach itself from the convoy and scoot away from its fellows.

The depot's shadow fell across the scene. And all became darkness.

"I'll never be able to hold up my head in the stregg halls again," Otho mourned.

"It'll do you good," Cind said, as she jockeyed the phony barge away from the pack of container ships closing on the yawning main depot bay.

"You could stand to lose about eighty kilos. Get your girlish figure back."

"By my mother's beard, you have no heart, woman," Otho said—keeping an eye out for the patrol boat it was his job to track.

He figured they had about fifty-five minutes before it completed its routine circuit.

"I, Otho, have been ordered to do a thing that is less than glorious."

"Poor baby," Cind mock-sympathized.

She was getting used to the controls now. It had been awkward at first. After all, she was basically piloting a hulk—except it had been gutted, and a standard ship's lifeboat hidden inside. The only clue that the container wasn't standard was the slight cutout in the stern for the boat's drivetube. It was so battered from millions of light-years of travel that only a close inspection would reveal the exit bay the *Victory*'s sailors had cut out with torches under Kilgour's direction. The lifeboat contained herself, Otho, and half-a-dozen Bhor warriors.

"When my good friend Sten informed me that our first target was the quisling politicians of Dusable, I thought my old heart would break with joy," Otho said.

"By my father's frozen buttocks, I thought, but this is a true brother of the stregghorn. For there is nothing a true Bhor loves to hate so much as a politician. And here I was offered a whole planet of these vipers to slay.

"I tell you, Cind, I dreamed of a long-old age, spinning the tale of all the thick political skulls I cracked. Their blood would flow like stregg at a blessing. The only sorrow I foresaw was that there would be so many souls to drink to hell, I would not live to honor them all."

"Quit trying to soften me up, Otho," Cind said. "First off, you're not that old. Secondly, you've done more than enough killing to boast for six lifetimes. So, forget it. I'm not going to suddenly feel sorry for you, and say, 'Well . . . if you feel so strongly about it, dear . . . let the slaughter begin.'"

"A slaughter wouldn't be necessary," Otho said. "If only I could crush a throat or two, I would be satisfied. A happy Bhor."

"No," Cind said. "And that's my last word on the subject." Just then, the container coasted against one of the depot slices. It bumped once. Twice. Then she had it steady against the steel walls.

She applied small bursts of power, edging the container along the station's hull. Finally, it came to rest against a repair port. Cind locked on.

"Now, let's get inside," Cind said. "And remember, Otho . . . No killing. We're freedom fighters, remember? And a bloody trail of innocent civilian victims makes for a lousy image."

"If you insist." Otho sniffed. "I suppose I'll become accustomed to these modern ways in time."

A few blurred minutes, and they'd peeled the sealed port door with a small charge and were inside.

Cind clicked her com unit twice. A moment later, there was a return click from the *Victory*.

Step one complete.

Cind had never seen an AM2 depot in person, much less been inside one. Onscreen, the mission had looked easy. The schematic Kilgour had ferreted out of a reference library showed a very dull, functional structure. Only its purpose

was dramatic. A storehouse and distribution center for the
most efficient power source ever discovered.

The schematic showed that almost the entire depot was
devoted to this purpose. There was only AM2 in the Imperium
X-shielded bays. Living and work quarters. And a big-son-
of-a-clot computer to keep things humming along.

Onscreen, it looked easy . . .

Cind glanced around the corridor she and her squad were
slipping silently along. Nothing but gray walls, gray ceiling
and floor, bathed in a faint glow of indirect lighting. From
the repair port, the corridor ran straight for half a klick. Then
it elbowed to the left. A quarter of a klick more, and they
had reached the central computer.

For a change, Cind thought, the practice looked as easy
as the theory.

Then they reached the elbow. Turned. And it quit being
easy.

"By the curly hair on my dear mother's chin," Otho
groaned, "it looks like the inside of a streggan's lair."

His comparison was quite accurate. The streggan—a
mortal enemy of the ancient Bhor, now hunted to extinction—had lived in deep caverns reached through elaborate
mazes scraped out of rock. To this day, the Bhor played a
complicated game based on those legendary mazes.

Cind was looking at something very similar. Dusable's
engineers had only partly followed the schematics. Instead
of one corridor leading in a single direction, the main tunnel
split a dozen times.

There was not a clue which entrance she should take.

"How much time do we have?" Cind asked, a little desperate.

"It doesn't matter," Otho said.

"Dammit, it does. If that patrol boat—"

"You have surpassed your old mentor in many things," Otho
said. "But I see there is still some things you can learn. By my
father's scrawny backside, I tell you . . . that gives me hope."

His brows beetled fondly at Cind. "A maze," he said, "is

a thing of purpose. The purpose can be to amuse, or to hide."

He glanced at the tunnels snaking out before him. Shadows deep inside each one indicated other corridors celing off to who knew where. "The beings of Dusable," he said, "most likely are concerned with the second. From what I have heard, the politicians have almost everything to hide."

"Why would they want to hide their central computer?" Cind asked. "I would think quick access would be important."

Otho nodded. He strode down the center tunnel a short distance, thumping on walls. Solid. Then a hollow sound. He lifted a belt torch from his harness and quickly cut a small opening.

Otho peered inside. Then he chortled. "I knew it." He waved for the others to join him.

Cind peered into the hole. There was a large compartment beyond, stacked with crates and barrels of contraband.

"The depot serves a double purpose," Otho said. "To store AM2 for the Empire. And to enrich the black marketeers of Dusable. You see. I was correct. As usual."

"Well, good for you," Cind said. "But that still doesn't tell us which corridor to take."

"Oh . . . *That*. No difficulty at all," Otho said. "I was merely curious as to the purpose of this puzzle."

"You mean you know the way?"

"Certainly. These dimwits of Dusable would have chosen the most basic maze design. We take the tunnel on the far left. From then on, no matter what opportunity presents itself, you always choose the left. Eventually, we will arrive."

"If you're wrong," Cind said, "then we could be lost for hours. The entire mission blown. Not to mention our own buttocks being held against the fire."

"You doubt me? I, Otho. The master of the maze game?" Otho's red-rimmed eyes were wide at her lack of confidence.

Cind hesitated, then shrugged. "Lead on," she said.

Otho did. They moved quickly down the left-hand corridor, which twisted and turned and then spread out into many other possible routes. But Otho always chose the left.

Sometimes this route would dead-end. And they would have to retrace their steps. Then plunge on.

Suddenly, the corridor made a left elbow like the first that had confounded them. Ahead was a door. Behind the door came a gentle hum of electronics.

With high drama, Otho waved a hand at the door. "Our destination," he intoned. He beamed at Cind, expecting a gush of admiration.

Cind simply nodded and raced for the door. She unsnapped a listening device from her harness. Put it to the door and bent an ear. A moment later, she signaled the all-clear, palmed a switch, and the door hissed open.

Light flooded across the elaborate computer that controlled all functions of the AM2 depot.

Cind plunged inside, went directly to the computer. She stared at the various options, touched some keys, grinned, and then took a programmed fiche from a beltpouch and fed it into the machine.

Otho and the other Bhor took their preplanned security positions. "The young are so rude, these days," Otho complained. "They do not see value in the experience of their elders. Why, when I was a stripling—too young to drink stregg unless it was in my milk—my mother would have skinned me for showing so little respect.

"Oh . . . well . . . No sense complaining. At least I had the joy of playing the maze game."

He thumped his corporal's back. "Was that not a most splendiferous achievement?"

Before the corporal could respond, there came an incredible shrieking wail, followed by a loud hooting of alarms.

Cind sprinted out of the control center as the computer voice blared down the corridor and sounded all over the depot.

"The depot has just been impacted by a meteorite. Point of impact, the main AM2 storage center. An AM2 explosion is imminent. All personnel are ordered to abandon the depot immediately. Use emergency procedures 1422A.

Do not panic. Repeat do not panic. Impact."

"Let's get the clot out of here before they do," Cind shouted. And they raced away—this time bearing to the right as they wound their way back through the maze.

All over the depot, beings scrambled for the lifeboats. As the alarms hooted and the computer advised them not to panic, they scratched and fought for positions aboard the boats. In a few minutes the depot had emptied. And a small area of space was filled with lifeboats hurtling for the safety of the planet's surface.

Cind's container craft quietly kicked off.

She clicked her com three times.

Mission accomplished.

Aboard the *Victory*, Freston keyed acknowledgment. Then he gave swift orders for the *Aoife* to scoop the team up and head for home.

Freston turned to Sten. "Ready, sir."

"Proceed."

As the AM2 train and abandoned depot swung in their orbits, the *Victory* suddenly appeared out of hyperspace. Missile ports swung open, baring the *Victory*'s teeth. Six Kalis spat out.

Before they struck, the *Victory* was gone.

On Dusable, there was no sound as the Kalis hit home and set off the massive AM2 explosion. Kenna and the thousands of SDT workers still gathered at the shipyard election party were suddenly aware that something was different. It was an odd, swimming sensation as all objects suddenly lost dimension. As if they had all been transported to a world of dots on paper.

They looked up at the sky. And it was gone.

All they could see was blinding white light.

There were loud screams. The crowd wavered as a gut-gripping hysteria swept over it.

Kenna fought for self-control. He raised a hand—to plead for calm.

Then all was abruptly normal. The white light gone. Dimension returned.

Kenna sucked in breath. Then his heart jammed against his ribs as he saw the enormous vid screen at the edge of the crowd wiped clean of his transmitted image.

Another man's face looked down on them. Vague familiarity clawed at his memory. There were loud, frightened mutters from the crowd. Then Kenna knew.

It was Sten.

"Citizens of Dusable," Sten's voice boomed. "I bring you grim news. Your leaders have callously chosen to gamble with your lives. And they have sold your right to be a free and independent people to the Eternal Emperor. And now you are his slavish allies."

Kenna shouted frantically for his tech to wipe Sten's face from the monitor. But it was no use. And it wasn't only at the shipyards that people were hearing and watching Sten speak. The broadcast was overpowering all transmissions, all freqs on the planet.

"Considering Dusable's importance to the Empire of Evil, I have no choice but to remove it as a threat to me and all freedom-loving beings.

"The first attack has already been launched. We have destroyed the AM2 depot the traitor Solon Kenna was boasting about. We have also destroyed the AM2 shipment that was the price your Judas leaders set for your betrayal."

The crowd was transfixed, hanging on every word that fell from those gigantic lips on the vid screen. Kenna was looking for a bolt hole.

"My forces are launching a series of attacks on your world," Sten said.

People in the crowd looked wildly about, as if missiles were going to fall at any moment.

"However," Sten said, "it is not our wish to harm innocent civilians. Therefore, I now give you warning on which military targets we shall strike. I urge you all to abandon those areas immediately."

Sten held up his doomsday list. And began to read out: "In Ward Three, the arms facility . . . In Ward Fifty-six, the tooling facility . . . In Ward Eighty-nine, the shipyard . . ."

Kenna and the union minions didn't wait to hear the rest of the list. Sten had just named the shipyard where they all stood and gaped.

Screaming, weeping, calling to forgotten gods for mercy, the crowd poured out of the yard and raced away for safety.

Kenna was too scared to be ashamed to be among them.

The missile swooped lazily out of the sky, dropped to twenty feet above the broad boulevard, and slowly made its way along the avenue, on a hastily installed McLean drive. Broadcasting as it went:

"Warning. I am a Kali missile. I carry a low-yield nuclear device. Please do not interfere with my progress. I have no wish to harm innocent civilians."

All over the street, beings scurried for cover. Windows slammed as the missile cruised by at second-story height.

In one apartment, a child reached out with a stick to touch the missile. His mother grabbed him just in time and pulled him back.

In Ward Three, the workers at the targeted arms factory dashed out of the sprawling complex. Fleeing on foot, grav-car, and occasionally on one another's back.

A Kali slowly approached, skimming over their heads.

"Danger. Danger. I am a Kali missile. My target is this arms factory. Please clear the area immediately. Do not panic at my impact. I am set to explode in fifteen minutes."

Still broadcasting, the Kali sailed through an open door of plant headquarters.

A plant supervisor watched in awe as the missile entered the main work area. Then settled to the floor.

"You now have fifteen minutes to evacuate. Please leave

at once. I have no wish to harm innocent civilians . . . You now have fourteen minutes and fifty seconds to evacuate. Please leave at . . ."

The supervisor and his team needed no further prodding. They ran.

At a bearing factory in Ward Forty-five, a missile was buried up to its nose in a crater.

". . . please abandon this area. I am armed with twenty-four explosive devices. The first will detonate in one hour. Please do not return to the area after the first explosion. The other explosives have been programmed to explode every hour on the hour. Warning. I am a Kali missile. Please—"

A burly ward boss, frustrated at being cheated out of contracted overtime, rushed forward. Swinging a two-meter-long hunk of steel.

He connected. Then disappeared from the face of Dusable as the Kali exploded.

Two factory buildings collapsed as the force of the blast hammered out. But only the ward boss and four of his crew were dead. Good sense saved the thirteen thousand other workers. They had fled long ago.

Dusable's biggest shipyard was now empty of politicians, hangers-on, and sentient life. Scattered all over were hundreds of abandoned freighters, transports, liners, and private flitters.

Kalis rained down. These fell with no warning.

In two awful minutes the yard was a smoking hole. Surrounded by twisted frames and molten metal.

And every launch pad had been turned into craters. The port would be useless for decades.

Sten studied the damage on the monitor. Image after image of destruction leaped up at him.

Factories gone.

Smoke and fire bursting upward from other points as delayed explosions went off.

Not just one, but thirty shipyards in total ruin.

It would be a long time before Dusable would be a threat—or a support to anyone again.

As the mind-clouding scenes of destruction swept by, he had a sudden, giddy moment. He felt lightheaded. Powerful.

Almost . . . godlike?

For just a heartbeat he knew what it must be like to be the Eternal Emperor.

Sten shuddered and turned away, disgusted at himself.

Captain Freston stopped him just as he was about to exit the bridge. He had a puzzled frown on his face. "A strange thing has happened, sir," he said.

"Go ahead."

"That AM2 shipment? Well, according to the com officer, just before the missiles hit, there was an odd transmission."

"You're sure it was from the ship?"

"Yessir. I double-checked it myself. The message was coded. Naturally."

"Where was the signal being sent?" Sten asked.

"That's even stranger, sir," Freston said. "I've run the coordinates over again myself. And I keep on coming up with the same answer."

"Which is?"

"To nowhere, sir. It was being beamed to nowhere."

BOOK TWO

POISON
PAWN

CHAPTER TWELVE

STEN'S HAMMER BLOW to Dusable caught the Eternal Emperor completely unprepared. As Sten had hoped, he was still in a reactive mode, concentrating his energies on the massive hunt he had launched for the ragtag band of rebels.

When word of the attack was flashed to Arundel, the Emperor went into instant overdrive. Military and political aides were scrambled. Whole fleets were diverted to guard other AM2 depots. Diplomats were yanked from their posts and flung across the Empire to shore up weak alliances.

The hunt for Sten was doubled and then redoubled again in intensity.

Before he ordered any of these things, however, the Emperor cracked down with the heaviest news blackout in the history of his reign. All over the Empire, news organization CEOs got the word: there was to be no mention of Dusable or the Cairenes until further notice.

The Emperor's emissaries didn't bother mentioning what the penalty might be if the edict was violated.

They left it to the corporate chieftains' vivid imaginations.

But between the orders and their implementation, there fell one brief moment.

A journalistic no-man's-land . . .

"This is Ranett reporting live from Dusable.

"A terrible blow was struck against the Eternal Emperor today, when the fugitive rebel leader, Sten, launched a surprise attack against the Emperor's most important ally.

"In one swift action, Sten's forces destroyed a crucial AM2 depot, along with what local sources claim is two E-years' worth of AM2 supplies. The attack was followed up with a devastating series of surgical strikes against key military and transportation facilities.

"High officials on Dusable say it will be a decade or more before these facilities can be rebuilt . . . if ever.

"Eyewitnesses to the attacks say Sten's forces appeared to purposely avoid civilian population centers. Casualties to civilians were described as extremely minimal.

"The precision strikes apparently lasted only a few hours. But during that time, sources in Dusable say, this once-thriving port planet was effectively eliminated as a key transport and energy-storage facility.

"The devastation wrought here—which experts say will easily mount into several trillion credits—may have an even broader impact on the Empire at large.

"High-placed sources say Sten's raid did even greater damage to the Eternal Emperor's prestige. Many allies, they say, will question the Emperor's ability to guard his friends against similar action.

"One source said the humiliation the Emperor suffered, and the David versus Goliath image the rebel Sten—"

Ranett reeled back as her image on the monitor shattered into a blizzard of interference. The shriek of a powerful jammer howled from the speaker cells.

She wasted no time deciphering what had happened. Actually, Ranett was mildly surprised her broadcast had been allowed to run so long. At best, she had hoped to deliver the first two graphs of her report before the Emperor's censors pulled the plug.

Ranett punched in the commands that would blast her small ship from its hiding place in a grove near Dusable's now-ruined main port. The craft was a luxury yacht she'd muscled out of a businessman who owed her big-time for keeping his name out of a series on slave labor.

In reality, her inaction had been no favor at all. Crucial

evidence had been lacking to really nail the scrote to the wall. It was a missed opportunity she had always regretted. But the injustice would now be corrected when Imperial agents hunting Ranett knocked on his door with the registry numbers of his yacht.

Ranett laughed at the thought of the little pube's well-deserved misery. Then she got busy getting the clot away from Dusable. She would go to ground. Just as she'd done before, during the privy council's reign of terror.

There she would remain until the heat was off. She had no illusions. It was likely she would have to remain in hiding for the rest of her life.

As the ship broke free from Dusable's gravity and headed for the first stop on Ranett's elaborate escape itinerary, she reflected on the report she had just filed.

Unfortunately she would never be able to follow up on it. In her view this was almost certainly the opening shot in the greatest news story in the Empire's long, tortured history.

Bigger than the Emperor's assassination. Bigger than his return. Bigger than any war.

The Eternal Emperor, she thought, might have just met his match. The impossible had now become a slight probability.

The romantic side of Ranett's weatherbeaten soul wondered what would happen if somehow Sten won the fight.

Would he then rule in the Emperor's stead? Quite probably. If so, would Sten be that mythical beast fuzzy headed scholars called "an enlightened ruler"?

Give it a rest, Ranett, she snarled to herself. There's no such thing as good guys and bad guys. Just those who are in. And those who wanna get in.

No way was this Sten character any different from the others.

First chance he gets, he'll screw us all.

Avri believed she had seen anger many times in her life. But nothing in her wide experience among the powerful had prepared her for the Eternal Emperor's face.

His skin was a ghastly white, his brow ridged with pent-up fury. His eyes shifted back and forth in their sockets like great hunting birds tracking their prey.

The most frightening thing of all was the rictus grin upon that face.

The second most frightening was his complete calmness.

"This is the time for cool heads," the Emperor told his assembled staff. "Hysteria never improves a crisis. We have to approach our problems as if they were routine irritations.

"Now, to business . . . Avri? What's the mood in Parliament?"

Avri jolted, nerves jangling from being called upon first. She recovered quickly. "Not good, Your Highness. Tyrenne Walsh had to return home fast, of course."

"Of course," the Emperor said, maintaining that odd overly mild tone.

"No one is saying anything openly . . . but I spotted a lot of shuffling positions among your allies. And lots of quiet conversations with the Back Benchers."

"I'll rein them in," the Emperor said. "After all, who do they have to run to? But I get your drift, Avri. I'll work up some programs to stiffen their spines.

"Meanwhile, hit the floor expressing my sorrow and concern. Deplore anything you think needs deploring. Promise them plenty of forces. Lots of hands-on support. Oh, yeah. Make some noises about Sten being brought to justice any minute now."

"Yes, Your Majesty," Avri said. "But . . . next to Sten . . . what they're most worried about is the AM2 supply. They're saying things were bad before Sten struck. But, now . . . I don't know . . . They're pretty edgy about the future."

The Eternal Emperor curled a lip into that rictus grin again. "I'll take care of the AM2. And *that's* a promise they can count on.

"As a matter of fact"—the Emperor indicated his personal com center—"I put new shipments into motion not fifteen minutes ago. The first convoys ought to be arriving fairly soon."

"Yes, Your Highness. They'll be delighted to hear that, sir."

"Poyndex?"

"Sir!"

"That broadcast from Ranett . . . Any prog yet on how many of my subjects it actually reached?"

Poyndex tried very hard not to show his relief. He had expected much screaming over that slip-up. Still, like Avri, the man's calm demeanor worried him.

"Yessir," he answered. "And the news is equally bleak in that direction, Your Highness. Although the damage from the initial broadcast was not as bad as we feared.

"Only about 6 percent of the available audience were tuned in at the time. The big problem, sir, is that copies of her report are the hottest thing anyone has ever seen in the underground market."

The Emperor waved, seemingly unconcerned. "Okay. So some pirated copies got out. Couldn't pick up more than another three or four percent viewership from that."

"I wish it were true, sir," Poyndex said. "The figures are more like 20 percent . . . the first day. Then—in their jargon— it almost instantly hit breakthrough."

Poyndex paused and swallowed hard for what he had to say next.

"Go on," the Emperor said.

"Yessir . . . Uh . . . They're figuring that within two E-weeks more than 80 percent of the Empire will have seen Ranett's report."

Absolute silence from the Emperor. Poyndex and the other beings quaked as they waited for the expected explosion from the absolute ruler of the known universe. He remained perfectly still for a long, agonizing moment. As if, Poyndex thought, he were consulting some demon deep within.

The Emperor stirred in his seat. He forced a slight chuckle.

"Not the most wonderful news, I'll admit," he said. "However, as I said at the beginning of this audience, this is no time to focus on the negative. If we act in a calm, deliberate manner, this crisis will soon pass. I've been through this sort of thing before. And it always ends the same. My enemies dead or in disorder. My subjects praising my name."

The Emperor's eyes swept over the small crowd in the room. "Of course, there will be a great deal of blood spilled meantime. There always is."

He stopped. As if he had forgotten their presence. Absently, he reached into the desk drawer. Pulled out a bottle of Scotch and poured himself a drink. He sipped. Musing.

Then he began to speak again. Very quickly. Conversationally. But it wasn't the people in the room he seemed to be addressing. It was more like he was having a late-night talk with a few old friends.

It scared the hell out of Avri. Like the others, she stood quite still. Instinctively they knew this was no time to draw attention to themselves.

"I blame myself for Sten. What could I have been thinking? From the moment Mahoney brought him to my attention, I believed I saw a young man with vast potential. Potential to serve me. I should have seen how badly flawed he was. And that flaw was ambition.

"Amazing how you can miss something like that. Because we're talking about an ambition that goes far beyond any kind of norm. Yes. I can see it now. He wanted my throne all along."

The Eternal Emperor sipped at his Scotch. "Yes. That explains it. Sten is quite mad. And he's been mad all along."

For a moment he fixed his gaze on Poyndex. "I believe that explains it, don't you?"

Poyndex did not make the deadly mistake of hesitating. "Absolutely, Your Highness," he said. Fervent. "Sten is quite mad. It's the only possible explanation."

The Emperor nodded. Absently. "I suppose he rationalizes his actions, however," he said. "Very few beings like to think of themselves as having evil intent . . . He probably thinks I'm mad as well."

His eyes darted to Avri. Like Poyndex, she did not falter. "If he thinks that, sir," she said, "he *must* be insane."

Again, the absent nod. "Of course, his view will have some public appeal," the Emperor said. "Albeit limited."

"*Very* limited . . . if at all," Poyndex said quickly.

"Ah, well," the Emperor said. "Bleak economic times seem to always draw out the worst in a monarch's subjects."

Cold laughter.

"There seems to be this persistent point of view in any age that times of plenty are normal. Hard times an aberration. Usually caused by the rulers of the offending state."

The Emperor topped up his drink. "Actually, the opposite is true. In most times . . . for most beings . . . life is sheer hell.

"And they give us—their rulers—even greater hell for somehow failing them."

The Emperor lifted his rictus grin at Avri. "But it would be bad politics to point those facts out to them, of course."

"I agree, sir," she said. "Promises are always better than getting into pocketbook negatives."

He motioned for her to come to his side. She did. An arm snaked out and drew her closer. He began stroking her slowly. Avri flushed. But no one dared notice. They kept their eyes on the Emperor as he continued.

"Still . . . the pressure is tremendous on a ruler to deliver the impossible." Avri shuddered. Fear, not desire, as the caresses grew more intimate.

A bitter laugh from the Emperor. "And . . . if we should falter . . . it is the monarch who gets the blame . . . Our subjects desert us."

The Emperor shook his head mournfully. "But it isn't good for a monarch to dwell on these things. Otherwise . . . his subjects will drive him—"

He stopped, staring into nothingness. Then his eyes blazed to life again. He shouted, "God, I wish my subjects had a single throat. I'd slit it, without a thought."

All around the room, hearts jumped. Poyndex found

himself staring into the Emperor's eyes, pinned there, frightened to keep looking, yet frightened to look away.

Then he realized the Emperor wasn't seeing him. His face was blank, his thoughts inward. A creak of swivel chair as the Emperor turned away, his eyes lifting to take in Avri.

Suddenly, he pulled her into his lap. Fingers fumbling at the fastenings of her clothing. Avri instinctively twisted to help.

Poyndex made frantic motions to the staff. Very quietly, they slipped out of the room. He was the last to exit.

But just before he was safely gone—

"Poyndex?"

He spun. Avri was sprawled naked in the Emperor's lap.

"Yessir."

"That wish was not original with me," the Emperor said. Absently, he traced a finger along Avri's flesh.

"Nossir?"

"It was from one of my colleagues . . . a long time ago." The finger stopped its trek. Thumb joined against finger on tender flesh.

"His name was Caligula."

"Yessir."

"A much-maligned ruler, in my opinion. He had no head for money, of course. But in many ways he was very talented. Unfortunately, the historians tend to focus on his personal habits."

His pinch bit deeply into Avri's flesh. A small moan of pain escaped from her lips.

"Very unfair," the Eternal Emperor said.

"Yessir."

The Emperor's eyes dropped back to Avri, Poyndex forgotten.

"Lovely," the Emperor said.

Poyndex stepped quickly away, letting the door hiss shut. Just before it closed, he heard Avri scream.

CHAPTER THIRTEEN

THE CAL'GATA, SR Tangeri, whistled shrilly, breaking the long silence that had hung across the chamber while he'd considered Sr Ecu's words. The whistle signified mild amusement and interest.

"I see," the being went on, "why you chose your words with such care. It would be entirely too easy to misunderstand what you just said, and interpret your words as a very subtle inquiry as to whether the Cal'gata have any particular dissatisfaction with the Empire as it has been reconstituted since the Emperor's return."

"Fortunately," Ecu said, "I knew I was not speaking to a being of lesser intellect, so I have no fears whatsoever about being misunderstood."

Tangeri whistled again, the Ecu allowed his tendrils to flicker, also showing appreciation for this fencing match that had gone on for nearly two E-hours. It was a pity, Ecu sometimes thought, that all of the recreations Ecu found intellectually stimulating, such as historical analysis or the human game of go, made Tangeri's black/white fur bristle in boredom; and Tangeri's own pastimes, such as fourth-level equations in topology, mapping a posited universe containing an additional, fictional, eighth or ninth dimension, Ecu thought intellectual masturbation.

The only common ground they had was the subtleties of diplomacy. Each of them knew, however, that he was actually only humoring a friend: in a "real" contest, there would be no contest at all.

The reason the Manabi were preferred to Tangeri's race as the Empire's diplomats was their innate pacifism and neutrality. The Cal'gata had no problem, if they saw an advantage to their species, in getting involved, even if it meant wading through blood up to their incisors.

"If I understand a passing reference of a while ago," Tangeri continued, "you brought up the name of this human, Sten. I further understood you to imply that his quixotic and kitlike gesture of waving his private parts at the Empire was seriously meant."

"Your understanding is not too distant from what I said," Ecu said. "Pray continue."

"Most romantic. One being against the Empire. Or so it would appear. Do you know, I have run some analyses of late, based on the data you were kind enough to send me under sensitive cover. The data I'm referring to is the amusing situation you created that the Empire is destroying itself. You have a rare ability to synthesize fiction."

Both of them knew the Empire's kamikaze rush toward doom was no fiction whatsoever.

"From your data, as I said, I made some extensions. Sheerly in the spirit of the mental exercise you created. I will give you an abstract if you wish.

"But briefly, given the proper conditions, which I posited, it is indeed possible for one being—such as this outlaw Sten—to shake the Empire. If the Empire failed to respond correctly to this minor stimulus, it is not inconceivable this would produce a multiple-loop feedback situation, and that the ensuing oscillation, if continued for a not-particularly-extended period, might bring the entire system to a halt or—accepting ultimately favorable conditions and no successful damping—its destruction.

"Most interesting."

Tangeri fell silent and stroked his long face-sensors with a tentacled paw, then sat motionless braced on his tail, a fat, furry black-and-white tripod. He could maintain this immobility for hours and days if necessary or desirable.

"That *is* interesting," Ecu agreed. "And I would like to see your equations. Strictly for their amusement value, of course. But you mentioned something I perhaps did not understand."

"My most sincere apologies. I find the older I get the more likely I have become to use circumlocutions or even inaccuracies."

"No," Ecu said. "You were most clear. I would merely be interested in what you generally mentioned as 'favorable conditions.' If you could be more specific?"

"I posited many such," Tangeri said smoothly. "Perhaps the most fascinating was if this Sten made a secret alliance with another race, one that normally maintained, or tried to maintain, neutrality when it came to Empire-wide politics."

"Ah?" Ecu wondered if Tangeri's point would be to expose the Manabi as being on Sten's side. No. He would hardly take pride in doing something which was that obvious to the Cal'gata—Ecu had done everything except put up a flagpole and run Sten's battle emblem up it.

"Yes. I further envisioned a large race. Somewhat warlike."

Sr Ecu floated, completely motionless.

"A race that had also been loyal to the Emperor during the Tahn war, and one which maintained hostile neutrality during the Interregnum."

This was it! This was why Ecu had made the long journey to this world in secrecy.

"Mmm," Ecu said. "Could you possibly have added to this hypothetical race that after the Emperor's return they were hardly rewarded for their loyalty, perhaps because the star clusters they controlled, no matter how numerous, were far from the Empire's heart?"

"More than two hundred and fifty such clusters." Sr Tangeri whistled sharply, and the fencing match was over. "Some of our most respected beings were murdered by the privy council. We lost two million during the Tahn war.

"And now we are forgotten. Our AM2 supply is tightly

rationed. If it were possible to burn wood in stardrive chambers, we would be exploring that as an option.

"Yes," Tangeri went on, his whistled speech losing its sharpness. "The Emperor has set and locked his controls for the heart of some great sun. The Cal'gata will not make that journey with him.

"Contact your Sten. Tell him what I said. All we lack is enough AM2 to fight the war. Ask him what he needs. Ships. Fighting men. Factories. Whatever.

"The Cal'gata are declared. And even if we are wrong, and this rebel Sten is destroyed, bringing some or all of the Empire down with him into near-barbarism, that will still be better than the absolute chaos which is the only thing at the end of the Emperor's path. Tell him that, as well."

Two hundred and fifty clusters sounded like a massive host, Ecu thought, after he had returned to his ship to rest and prepare for the next day's formal banqueting. But to the enormity of the Empire, which swept across many galaxies, it was little more than a company-size formation.

Still, it was a beginning.

He floated next to a wallshelf—what the free-floating Manabi called a desk—and sorted through papers a courier ship had delivered while he was negotiating with Tangeri.

Being a disciplined creature, he first went through official fiches, but his vision kept straying to the small pile that was personal—fiches from colleagues, friends, and one female exbreeding partner. And something else. Something that shimmered.

He could stand it no more. A tendril slipped it from the stack, and held it up. The small fiche swirled a kaleidoscope of light at him, colors washing across the surface of the fiche in waves.

A commercial solicitation. He should have expected something like it. The question was, how had whichever business sought his custom found Ecu's private shipping code? He looked more closely.

The return code was hand-scribed. Marr and Senn? Ecu thought, then remembered. The former caterers for the Imperial Household. Ecu remembered them with pleasure. He, like almost everyone who had encountered the lifetime-bonded same-sex lovers, had been enchanted by the two Milchen. He had first encountered them at a formal banquet and been impressed that they had not only gone to the trouble of finding and synthesizing examples of the Manabi's native diet, but also to the trouble of somehow finding out some of Ecu's favorite "dishes." He had also been invited to a couple of parties at their famed "tower of light" home that was in an isolated sector of Prime.

But why would they contact him? They were, if memory served, in retirement.

He touched one of the sensitized areas.

Two small holographs hung before him. Marr and Senn. Their antennae waved.

"We send you our fondest greetings, Sr Ecu," they chimed, then vanished. A personalized advertisement, then.

Aromas floated up to him, aromas of a great kitchen. A tiny holograph of a steaming platter appeared next. It vanished. Another hologram, this of a formal banquet table.

Ah. They had evidently begun some sort of catering operation, and no doubt thought Sr Ecu was somewhere near Prime and might wish to take advantage of their services.

How odd, he thought. They could not need the credits. But possibly the boredom of a long retirement had driven them back into the business world.

The table disappeared, and again Marr and Senn appeared. They confirmed that they were now available for custom catering. And they offered—

There was a chime. Ecu glanced at a wallchron and realized he was late.

He looked at the play time on the fiche and was surprised. There was almost thirty E-minutes' play time left. What had Marr and Senn done, list their complete menu and how all the dishes were prepared?

Very strange. He set the fiche down. He did not have time to go through the rest of Marr and Senn's message. He was already encroaching on time that could be best spent readying himself for Tangeri's gathering.

But he hesitated, his attention still drawn by the fiche. No. This *still* did not make sense, as his mind occamrazored away.

Very, very odd indeed.

But he was now *very* late for the banquet . . .

Perhaps later.

The convoy slid through hyperspace, eighteen troopships, with only two picketcraft as forward escorts.

They were unaware of the two sharks lying in ambush, only light-minutes away.

"Like a school of cod," Berhal Flue, commanding officer of the rebel destroyer *Aisling*, said to his brother berhal, Waldman, aboard the DD *Aoife*. "Blinded by the sun and swimming happily into the shallows toward the net.

"Or," he corrected his analogy, "toward the spearman."

"Tactics, sir," Waldman asked. He was one class-year junior to Flue, despite their common rank as berhals.

"As we agreed," Flue said. "Hit them and split the formation."

"One pass and gone?"

Flue hesitated.

"Most likely. But stand by for emendation."

"Sir? I think it most unlikely that this convoy is almost completely unescorted. Perhaps we might lay doggo until it passes, make a full globesearch to make sure there are no surprises, and then hit them from the rear?"

"My orders stand, Berhal," Flue said shortly. "If they sense us, they could scatter. We have an opportunity here to strike the first great victory for the rebellion. And for our names to ring across our home worlds forever."

Waldman, like most Honjo, had less interest in glory than in honorable survival and profit, but he made no further protest.

"At your timetick," he said, and turned away from the screen.

The crew of the *Aoife* was already at general quarters waiting for the command.

Ship-seconds ticked away . . . and zero flashed.

Both destroyers went to full drive and "dove" on the convoy.

Aboard the Imperial ships, alarms yammered, and the two picketcraft shot between the attackers in a useless if brave attempt to at least slow the convoy's attackers. They were instantly obliterated.

And then the wolves were among the sheep, and the "flock" split, fleeing in all directions as rebel ship-to-ship missiles sought them out. As the destroyers swept through the disintegrating convoy, both skilled captains brought their warships close enough to the Imperial spaceships for chainguns to be employed, even if for only a few nanoseconds.

The *Aoife* and *Aisling* cleared the far side of the convoy.

Four troopships no longer existed; three others had taken crippling hits.

"One more sweepthrough," Flue ordered. "Then take individual targets and we'll destroy them in detail."

Waldman again thought of protest. This was not only against common sense, but against Sten's direct orders. When he had sent them out on their roving commission, with instructions to create as much havoc as possible, it was with the direct command to never take a chance. "You have fast ships," Sten had said. "But that gives you no license to sail in harm's way. We are only four—the Bhor units are still forming and unready for combat. Fight hard—but come back!"

Before Waldman could decide whether to say something, the rear-lagging escort appeared onscreen.

Four Imperial light cruisers, and eleven heavy destroyers.

Honjo screens flashed a warning.

There was neither time nor need for Flue to shout orders. Both rebel destroyers went to emergency power, set irrational zigzags into their computers, and set final orbit for the pre-arranged RP.

Weapons officers launched Kalis as a rearguard action.

And the Honjo sailors prayed.

One destroyer flameballed as it took a solid Kali hit, and the bow of one light cruiser vaporized.

But prayer wasn't valid—or whatever gods controlled this sector of hyperspace were more interested in slaughter.

The Imperial ships counterlaunched.

Both destroyers sent out a barrage of Fox countermissiles. But there were too many launches.

Waldman flashsaw: Screen A: Imperial Kali closing on the *Aisling* . . . Flue's onscreen face, eyes widening . . . prox detectors howling.

And the screen to the *Aisling* went blank as the tightbeam severed.

"The *Aisling* is hit, sir," Waldman's OD said, completely tonelessly as he'd been trained. "Wait . . . wait . . ."

Waldman ignored him.

"Nav! Orbit! I want a collision course with the *Aisling*'s last position."

"Sir!"

"Wait . . . wait . . ." the officer of the deck monotoned. "Clear screen. No sign of *Aisling*, sir."

"Thank you, Mister. Powerdeck, I would appreciate it immensely if you happen to have a few extra PPS hiding back there."

"Missile closing," Countermeasures reported. "Impact . . . seven seconds . . . countermissiles failed to engage . . . four seconds . . ."

And the *Aoife* swept through the near-empty vacuum where the *Aisling* had been. Near-empty, but full enough to confuse the Kali's controller, as she lost contact with her missle and manually detonated the bird.

A miss. An Imperial officer at Central Tracking tonelessly reported the *Aoife* was still intact. Still under drive. A second launch went out.

But it was too late. The *Aoife*, tail between her legs, outran first the missiles and then the pursuing destroyers. The Imperial cruisers were far "behind" in her "wake."

Seven ship-minutes' battletime.

Imperial casualties: Two light escorts destroyed. One heavy destroyer destroyed. Four troopships destroyed. One light cruiser crippled beyond repair. One troopship abandoned and blown up after survivors were evacuated. One slave-towed to a shipworld and then scrapped as hopeless. The other two would require long months of repair before returning to service.

Almost fifteen hundred Imperial sailors as casualties.

Seven thousand trained Imperial soldiers were corpses.

Against:

One rebel DD destroyed.

Two hundred and ninety-three Honjo rebels dead.

A smashing victory for the Empire.

Sten gloomed back from the memorial for the *Aisling*'s dead. Christ. He was very glad that Berhal Flue was an exploded corpse on an endless orbit to nowhere. Because, if he had survived, Sten would have had him shot.

He had been tempted to relieve Waldman as well, and would have if he wasn't concerned about losing whatever support he had on the Honjo worlds.

Instead, he declared the dead Honjo martyrs to the revolution, announced that a new warship would be named the *Flue*, and ordered medals and bonuses in all directions for the sailors of both ships.

Privately, he told the officers of the *Aoife*, the *Victory*, and the *Bennington*, and his Bhor officers-in-training that if anyone else fancied himself a General Kuribayashi they should so announce it now, and he would save them the bother of having to cut their own bellies after an appropriate amount of suicidally-brave resistance. Sten would be delighted to perform that duty right now and avoid the summer rush.

He made particular emphasis to the Bhor. They had a

strong interest in self-preservation, as did any trading culture. But there was that species fondness for berserker rages, and Sten wanted no more memorials for a while.

He put that aside.

Ran his strategies once more. Was there anything more he could do at the moment, beyond what plans were already in motion? He thought not. Recruits from the Cal'gata clusters would be slipping secretly into the Wolf Worlds shortly, and Sten was braced for the howl of outrage when he began stripping veterans from the Bhor escort ships and his own vessels for training and command cadre.

He still needed somebody to analyze Mahoney's files. At first he'd considered Alex, but he needed the Scotsman mobile and heading up his intelligence branch.

The worst thing about beginning a revolution, he thought, was being so light in the ass when it came to Available Personnel.

What little he could think of, and what he could logically carry out, given his limitations, was being done. An image crossed his mind: a huge massed ball of collapsed material from the heart of a pulsar. Hung from a cable. And Sten was a midget, swatting at that ball with a feather.

Very good, he told himself. Any other mental images occur to you that'll cheer you up?

There was one. Hunt up Kilgour and Cind and chew on a bit of stregg. Two, actually. Chasing Kilgour out after a while and nibbling on Cind's toes for a month or so.

Cheered, he sought out his compatriots in revolution.

He found them packing.

Cind explained. She might speak for the Bhor, but they were an engine—actually a juggernaut—that mostly ran of itself. Her other ostensible duty, bodyguarding Sten, was already well covered by the Gurkhas.

Besides, she had suddenly felt her horizons open, even before Otho had used his ploy—and was starting to see the limitations in just being a headbanger and tactical leader of headbangers.

She had become interested in AM2, and found a possibly unique avenue of exploration, Cind went on. The privy council had looked very hard for the material, and found nothing. She was investigating—as best she could from this distance and without being able to get near Prime—any trail they had gone down.

"A' firs'," Alex interrupted, "when th' lass told me aboot th' notion, Ah crook't a wee brow an' wonder't why, since th' council went up blind alleys, 'stablished, what's th' in'trest?

"An' a course Cind remind't me thae's no better way t' save time thae t' know whae y'r pred'cessor did wrong, an' y' noo hae t' waste time duplicatin' th' effort."

Cind continued.

The initial investigation hadn't produced much of interest, and she was wondering if maybe the time *was* wasted. Then she ran across, in a declassified overview of the council's final months, that they'd appointed a special energy czar—with the title of AM2 secretary. A Sr Lagguth, who had suddenly vanished not too long after the first full-member meeting of the council in some time, a meeting, rumor had it, that was an emergency called to deal with the AM2 crisis.

"So," Sten wondered. "He probably stood up, announced 'I ain't got none,' and they geeked him."

"Maybe," Cind said. "But he was taken under Kyes's wing first."

Kyes. The ET artificial-intelligence specialist, who'd also disappeared, shortly after the council lifted Poyndex from his post as head of Mercury to a seat on the council itself. No explanation for that disappearance, either.

Sten had, in fact, investigated as part of his general work investigating the council. He'd discovered that Kyes's race was symbiotic, its real intelligence provided by a parasite. In time, the parasite claimed its due, and a Grb'chev went into drooling senility. Kyes, well past that well-known age, had most likely been discovered one fine morning watching sunlight crawl across a windowsill, murmuring "It's shiny," and been quietly medevacked to the Grb'chev Home for the Terminally Bewildered.

"Possibly," Cind allowed. "The Cult of the Eternal Emperor believes he was taken directly to commune with the Holy Spheres, whatever the hell they are.

"However, consider what we have here. Kyes, a computer genius, and his cohort, another specialist in the field. Both interested in AM2. Oh yes. One further thing. When Kyes became Lagguth's rabbi, all data that the council had stored on AM2 was removed. It vanished, too."

"Uh-uh," Sten said, alarm signals going off. "I think your report's a mickey. The Emperor had somebody wipe those files—*after* his return. And then put out the fiche you're using as disinformation."

"Could be," she said. "However, I'm off to Lagguth's home world. Just to ask some dumb questions. Unless you have something better in mind?"

Sten did—but it wouldn't further any cause beyond his own morale.

"And you're going with her," he inquired of Alex.

"Thae's a big clottin' naaaaaay, ae i' Ah was a foalin't mare. Ah'm off t' see th' weasand. Or whae Ah hope i' th' Emp's windpipe, at any rate.

"Th' lass' thinkin't makit a wee bit ae sense, Sten. An' Ah took th' same tactic. 'Cept Ah went peepin't aboot th' Emp. Y' rec'lect whae we were i' th' Altaics, oop t' our pits i' ter'rists, y' were skreekin't frae th' Emp and c'dnae get a response? A'ter Iskra massacreed th' students?"

Sten did. Very well. He had made call after call on the secure hotline between the embassy and the Imperial palace on Prime. The Emperor, he had been told, was indisposed.

"I always thought," Sten said, "that he was just ducking me. For some reason I never figured out, and haven't really considered since."

"Aye. Mayhap th' Emp dinnae want t' chat wi' y', lad. But Ah took th' trouble ae checkin't. Thae's still secure lines onto Prime, i' y' hae old friends who retired frae Mantis t' a sin'cure wi' Imperial Communications, aye? An' more mates who've gone int' private security.

"In'trestin' thing Ah hae discovered. Aboot th' same time, though no one's runnin't ae timetable, th' Emp wen' t' Earth. Wi' no notice, wi' no fanfare."

"Why?"

"Ah c'd nae find e'en a theory. But i' dinnae wash thae he'd gie himself a fishin't vacation whae th' drakh's hittin' th' fan e'erywhere. Th' lad's nae prone t' kenn'dy oot ae th' wee'est prov'cation.

"An' one other wee thing Ah hae heard, fraw m' sources wi'in th' Emp's soldiery. At aboot th' same time ae th' Emp wae goin't fishin, some laddies frae th' service wae detached, on spec'l duties, t' th' Imperial Househol' itself. EOD laddies."

EOD—explosive ordnance disposal. Bomb-defusing and countermeasure experts. Why would the Emperor want them on Earth? Sten thought for a moment, then nodded. It was time to filter somebody onto Earth and find out what the hell had happened.

"Ah'm away," Alex said, seeing the nod. "Altho' Ah dinnae hae pleasure i' this. Thae's bad thoughts oop thae, i' th' mist an' th' fog."

There were. Sten had led an assassination team against the privy council onto Earth, where they'd held a summit meeting at a palatial retreat up Oregon Province's Umpqua River from the Emperor's old fishing grounds.

Of the ten beings in the contact team, Sten had been the only survivor. And all of them had been longtime Mantis operatives, friends as well as fellow operatives, of Sten and Alex.

Another place, like Vulcan, with blood-drenched memories.

"Are you looking for anything in particular?"

"Ah hae no leads. Just wanderin' aroun' keepin't m' nose up i' th' air an' m' arse doon. Ah ask't Sr Wild i' Ah c'd borrow a wee ship an' a pilot.

"He's loan't me ae zoomie, an' a pilot he's claim't b' be

one ae his slinkiest. Human lass, nam'd Hotsco. Wild's say-in't she volunteer'd. So we ken she's brain-damag't.

"Ah hae spokit t' her. Pretty, i' y're fond ae th' slender lassies wi' wee hips an' boobies an' a waist y' can span wi' one paw. M'self, Ah always fear't Ah'd gie romantic an' snappit such a one i' half. But, since she's noo hard on most human eyeballs, Ah'll us't th' old deep-i'-love duo ae m' cover. I' anybody'd believe this Hotsco, wi' her hair hangin't doon t' below her waist an' flashin't eyes, hae an' int'rest i' a tub like m'self, aye?"

Bhor Intelligence would monitor Alex's work while he was gone, and he had appointed Marl, his agent-in-training and the Bhor Police Intelligence Specialist, Constable Paen, as acting case officers on his personal project, the counter-agent program he was running through the successfully dou-bled Hohne. The Imperial spy had seen the light, just as Alex had predicted to Marl, after only a few cycles at the bottom of one of the Bhor's more colorful prisons.

"So. Everything's goin't tickety-tickety, like a wee sewin't machine. Worries me, 'cause we're noo i' a sewin't machine.

"An' noo Ah'm off? D' either ae y' wish t' kiss me 'bye? Ah brusht m' fangs nae more'nt two epochs gone."

Instead, Sten bought him a farewell drink. Or two. Cind found time for one herself.

He loudly mourned, over the stregg, that he had now dis-covered the problems of being a figurehead. He never got to have any fun.

Cind patted his cheek.

"It's like the old song goes," she said. "'You just stand there looking cute/And when something moves you shoot.'"

Just stand there, Sten thought.

Like hell I will.

Ida, too, was disobeying Proper High Level Leadership Rule Three, SubParagraph D: Keep a Lotta Grunts Between You And Where The Bullet Goes Bang. Sten had determined to keep the Rom in the background as long as possible, and use them as deep-cover recon and for surreptitious transport of small attack forces. Eventually they would be blown—but Sten hoped to get the maximum utilization from the traders before they were exposed as the Emperor's enemies.

That, of course, meant that Ida herself shouldn't even consider going operational.

Ida had come up with a Grand Scheme, one that Sten had heartily approved of. She hadn't bored him with details such as who was the field agent who would plant this "bomb."

Ida planned to plant the Fiendish Thingie herself. Romantics, or those who had never spent any time around Kaldersash, might have thought she was providing a noble example by leading from the front or, possibly, indulging in some homesickness over the old glory days of Mantis.

Of course, the reality was that Ida had seen vast opportunities for the initiating agent to make Noble Profit, a reality Jon Wild also sensed instantly.

And so a grossly overweight and overbearing woman, accompanied by her mousy husband, arrived on the trading world of Giro. It appeard that he had the money, but she had the clout. But since they arrived with several millions in hard credits, E-transmitted one day after their arrival, no one cared about their personal arrangements.

Civilizations, human or otherwise, tend to accept certain fictions. One of the most convenient is that securities—stocks, bonds, and the like—actually have some relationship to the actual prosperity of the government/corporation they're issued by. The Bourse, Wall Street, Al-Manamah, the Drks'l System, all have worked about the same over the centuries.

Ida had figured out a long time before that the two best rules of security trading are: (1) Avoid the perceived wisdom, and (2) The stock is not the company. Her non-Aristotelian approach to the market as pari-mutuel system had made her several squillion credits.

One of the many odd facts she had collected in her periodic economic looting/maiming expeditions was that Giro was one of the worlds specializing in securities/finance where the entire system's main computers were housed.

Ostensibly, however, Ida's—and oh, yes, her husband's—reason for being on Giro, instead of using one of the brokerage houses on her—unnamed—home world to trade was that she liked to be in the center of things. That also wasn't particularly interesting to anyone.

She and Wild made their grand entrance one morning, when the trading firm of Chinmil, Bosky, Trout & Grossfreund opened. Ida had chosen the firm carefully, not for its massive size and far-scattered branch offices, but because CBT&G were known for their "liberal" interpretations of the Empire's security laws. Ida knew that a white-collar crook is one of the easiest to hoodwink. He's not only convinced he's the first to come up with whatever scam he's running, but is convinced that everyone else, from the coppers to the marks, are utter fools.

Ida and Wild announced their intent of increasing and broadening their holdings beyond their home system, and mentioned the huge amount they were prepared to play with, and were rapidly passed through the hands of a receptionist to a junior trader to a senior trader to a partner, Sr Bosky himself.

Ida pretended to listen to his advice, accessed a central terminal, and began buying. And selling.

Talking in a steady stream as she did:

"Sr Bosky, now, if I do as you advise, and go long on TransMig, keep what I have in Cibinium, consider this new issue of Trelawny . . . Jonathan, stop fidgeting, we know what we're doing . . . ah, getting out of Soward five percent municipals . . . see *that* quote . . . I could have told them . . . good advice, Sr Bosky, as I was saying that I consider Trelawny, although the prospectus hardly seemed to be complete—"

She had completely lost Bosky in one-half an E-day.

Ida sneered inwardly—she figured anyone as crooked as Chinmil et al were, most especially a partner, would have to be able to see which walnut Ida's pea was under for a day or so. But she continued her prattle as money went here, there, and everywhere.

Bosky was tempted to tell this annoying woman to go away—but he noticed that within two trading days, Ida had doubled her investment.

He started listening. Hard. And spending his own, and the firm's, money, chasing Ida's investments.

Of course, what Ida was really doing with her capital was very different than what Bosky thought, but it would take at least one cycle for the confusion to subside and Bosky to figure out just how many megacredits he had lost.

He also failed to notice that Wild, in the chatter, had been unobtrusively feeding a program into the firm's main computer. Stage One. It took one E-week to get the program exactly positioned.

That night, Stage Two was mounted. Ida and Wild, well after midnight, slid out of their hotel suite to a completely clean and anonymous gravsled Wild had procured and lifted into the night.

The next day, Ida got the obligatory terrible message from home. A cheap, hack, dumb device that'd get her busted out of Basic Extraction Tactics 101 at any spy academy. But businesspeople, in spite of loud boasting that they study history/espionage/military strategy, in fact do nothing more than memorize enough catchphrases to convince their fellow drinkers they're Tigers.

Ida promised Bosky they would return shortly.

And they departed on a great luxury liner, a liner they immediately left at the first planetfall, where they picked up one of Wild's ships that had been prepositioned for them. Then they disappeared completely. Even the ship they had used for their escape was completely wiped and given new registry, from engines to nav equipment to hull numbers. That was but one of the cultural specialties of the Rom.

Even before they had gotten off the liner, Stage Three, a completely automatic program previously fed into one of

CBT&G's smallest branch offices half a galaxy away, activated.

All of Ida's investments were liquidated immediately into hard currency, and the credits E-moved. Later investigators managed to follow the money through three laundries before the trail vanished.

Both Ida and Wild, already rich enough to consider hiring Croesus as a flunky, had trebled their personal fortunes. They had made so much, in fact, that Ida had felt almost guilty, and made Sten and Kilgour an additional bundle, just for recreational purposes. "How clottin' nice it is," Ida observed, "to be able to do well by doing good, or whichever way the grammarians say I should put it."

Stage Two went off, predawn, just as the market opened for the next trading "day."

Literally.

Twenty-six small but exceptionally dirty nuclear demolition charges blew Giro's automated computer center—which meant the Empire's main securities computer—off the face of the planet. The charges had been designed and built by Kilgour, the super-mad-bomber, before he had wandered off on his own mission.

Total casualties: one custodian who had passed out in a mess area instead of clocking out in a mess area, and a handful of security goons.

Nanoseconds later, the disaster rippled out, across livie channels and business "wires." Panic. Who . . . why . . . what could anyone . . . how could anyone . . . anarchy . . . atrocity . . . against the rules of something or other . . .

The market free-fell hundreds of thousands of points. And then instantly recovered, as sanity returned.

The horror was not that horrible. There were backup computers, of course. And certainly the monster who could even think of destroying a staple of civilization wouldn't know that.

The main backup computer went online.

Wild's program began running.

A junior trader saw it first, as he activated his workstation. The screen, instead of giving him a market display, showed a portrait of the Eternal Emperor. Scowling. In full uniform. Finger pointing directly at the clerk. The voicesynth boomed, "YOUR EMPIRE NEEDS YOU." And the image hung there, hung there, and the trader swore something about clotting politicians and clotting—stopped, broke off, looked guiltily around, since Internal Security had begun investigating the business community, and rebooted.

The rebooting activated Ida's virus, and quite suddenly the Empire wanted *everybody*, and everybody swore to themselves just as they swore when the omnipresent antipiracy warning came on their screen when they fired up their stations and then *they* rebooted. . . .

. . . and the virus spread some more. Spread and grew and spread and grew . . .

. . . and the backup computer system blew, and, as it blew, sent the virus on to yet another backup system.

The Empire's securities trading network went to La-La Land.

It was almost a full cycle before any trading floor approached normalcy. The first panic reaction of a good capitalist is to go for the gold. Liquidate everything into something secure.

Orders went out—but could not be implemented. Several exchanges were closed for trading. Banks declared holidays. Some very healthy corporations were forced into bankruptcy as shareholders dumped their holdings. And, conversely, some truly hemorrhaging entities were not only given a prolonged lease on life, but able to establish themselves firmly as successes. Traders sometimes had to actually keep notes— in *hand* writing. Buy/sell orders were handled verbally and manually!

Sten was quite pleased. Especially since Ida's grand scheme produced the desired end result: as investors liquidated, and bought into safety, which of course was the AM2-secured Imperial credit, those credits became more expensive as they became scarcer. And for a while, no matter how many credits the Empire's main bankers dumped out, the crash seemed unstoppable. Eventually the Empire's emergency financial dumping worked and the pendulum stopped swinging.

But the midget had swung his feather—and the ball had moved. It was yet another beginning on another front of Sten's total war.

Sten was rather morosely preparing himself a solitary meal, trying to remind himself that the best revenge is living well. Yet another pastime he had sort of picked up from the Eternal Emperor.

His meal was, by description, a simple Earth sandwich. Its filling would be a rib-eye steak from a steer.

But it may have been the Ultimate Steak Sandwich.

Earlier that day, before the paperwork and Go Higher And Hither orders had a chance to consume him as usual, he'd cut diagonal slices in the three-centimeter piece of meat. The steak went into a marinade—one-third extra-virgin olive oil, two-thirds Guinness—the remarkable dark beer he had been introduced to just before his last face-to-face meeting with the Eternal Emperor—salt, pepper, and a bit of garlic.

Now it was ready for the charbroiler.

He took softened butter, and beat a teaspoon of dried parsley, a teaspoon of tarragon, a teaspoon of thyme, and a teaspoon of oregano into it. He spread the butter on a freshly baked soft roll, foil-wrapped the roll, and put the roll in to warm.

Next he sliced onions. A lot of onions. He sautéed them in butter and paprika. As they started to sizzle, he warmed, in a double broiler, a half liter of sour cream mixed with three tablespoons of horseradish.

Next he'd charbroil the steak just until it stopped moving, thin-slice it on the diagonal, put the meat on the roll, onions on the meat, sour cream on the onions, and commit cholesterolcide.

For a side dish he had thin-sliced garden tomatoes with a vinegar/olive oil/basil/thin-chopped chive dressing and beer.

The com signaled. It was Freston.

He asked if Sten's com was shielded and scrambled. It was, of course. Freston said he had just finished an interesting analysis on that strange signal that had been beamed into nowhere from the lead ship in the AM2 convoy as it arrived in the Dusable system and robotically realized it was under attack.

Sten decided to wait until Freston was finished before eating his ass out and reminding the officer he was no longer a technowonk communications specialist but a combat leader with his own ship, and to leave his clottin' com techs alone.

The signal, Freston went on, didn't go to nowhere. It went to a dead system, somewhere between forgotten and lost. Freston had chanced borrowing one of the Bhor ELINT ships, bread-boarding their sensors into some measure of the sophistication he was used to in his access to the Empire's best gear, and then sneaking the ship into the dead system.

On one world the ship had found a small relay station. He didn't chance ordering a landing or trying any electronic probings, since he surmised the station would be booby-trapped.

He started to explain what he thought he had accomplished. Sten didn't need one. Freston had traced the mysterious robot AM2 supply convoys back one stage.

Sten surmised that the robot convoy would appear in this particular system from its origin in a still-unguessed place and receive either a GO, NO GO or DIVERT COURSE from the relay station, and, depending on the signal, either continue to Dusable or whatever other AM2 depot it had been intended for, or divert to a secondary destination, or . . .

Or any number of interesting possibilities.

"Is the ELINT ship still in-system?"

"That's affirm," Freston said. "I ordered it to lie doggo,

all passive receptors on full, and not to attempt any active sensing without a direct order from me."

"Were there any transmissions when the Bhor ship first arrived?"

"None reported."

"Have there been any since?"

"Technically, none," Freston said. "However, the electronics ship has recently reported increased power output from the station on all lengths. As if it's coming up from standby."

Freston's reaming—and Sten's dinner—was forgotten.

"Is the gear on the ELINT ship good enough to pick up another transmission like the one you flagged off Dusable?"

"Easily."

"What's the distance?"

"You could be there in three E-days."

Sten grinned: Freston knew his boss. "Okay. Is the *Aoife* ready to lift?"

"Affirm."

"I'm on the way. Tell its skipper—"

"Waldman, sir."

"This is his or her big chance to step off his sex organ for that convoy disaster. I want couplings ready to hook a tacship up to the *Aoife*. And I want you to set up a tightbeam com, set up to link between the tacship and destroyer. Yesterday."

"Yessir. I assume you'll be commanding the tacship?"

Sten started to nod: *Of course*. Then he caught himself. Come on, son. You're busting common sense in the chops enough, already. Don't be a complete grandstander.

"Negative," he said, to Freston's surprise. "I want a drakhhot pilot—And I've got just the candidate. Out."

Sten went out the door of his quarters before the com blanked.

The Gurkha sentry outside was one count into his present arms and Sten was gone, a flicker that might have been a waved return of the salute in his wake.

Sten had a helmet bag in one hand, weapons harness—pistol, ammo, cleaning kit, kukri—over one shoulder, and a daypack carrying three days' rations and toiletries in the other, three things that were never more than an arm's length from him.

Ida, unintended, *had* set an example.

Now was the time to scrape off some of the rust.

The three greatest talents a diplomat must have, Sr Ecu had realized a century or so earlier, was to never take things personally, to always look pleased when served what was generically dubbed rubberchicken on the banquet circuit, and most importantly to endure boredom.

Not just the boredom of long, droning conferences while amateur pols tried to score points as if governing were Beginning Debate, but also the boredom of endless hours traveling.

Ecu had wondered how spaceship crews, particularly on the torchships in the early days, kept from going berserk, and researched the matter. Reading of the murders, mutinies, and worse aberrancies, particularly on the pre-stardrive longliners, told him they didn't.

Now, on this long flight back from the Cal'gata worlds, especially as his ship was under enforced com blackout, he had started to feel like perhaps mutinying a little himself, even though he tried to remind himself that boredom was not an emotion the Manabi felt, and that the way he was feeling could be no more than a conditioned response from all the decades he had spent around humans.

Still, he was getting what he had heard described as the Jeabie Heabies.

He had viewed every livie aboard the small yacht, read every book available, written reports and progs beyond count, and they were still four ship-days out from Seilichi.

Finally his ennui led him back to Marr and Senn's flier.

He had wanted to look at it before, but had refrained. Thinking of the succulences that the two Milchen could concoct might be the last straw, especially considering the less-than-inspired rations the yacht's bellyrobber served up.

Ecu now thought he could tough out the four days before real nourishment would become available.

Again he touched the sensitized area, and again Marr and Senn appeared and greeted him by name. Again the wonderful scents floated toward Ecur's tendrils.

And again the two beings announced their catering service and began presenting a menu.

Ecu's senses flickered. Trouble. The menu was being presented in a perfunctory drone, as if Marr and Senn had been forced into this new business through economic desperation. But that could not be. Perhaps—

Both holographs stopped. Marr and Senn looked at each other.

"That's time enough for anyone busybodying through your mail to get bored," Marr said.

"I can only hope," Senn said. "Sr Ecu, we need your help. I trust it is you who is viewing this, and that some others—"

He shuddered and crouched, as if an icy windblast had caught him. Marr moved closer, protecting.

"—some others," he went on, after collecting himself, "are not.

"We are in trouble. We need to contact Sten. We are not aware if you know where he is, and the only reason we are sending this is because the two of you worked on that Tribunal, back in the awful days of those five beings whose names I will not pronounce.

"This is our only hope. We need Sten to help us. And someone else. I cannot mention the being's name. But tell Sten that the being is someone he will remember. Tell Sten to remember the party and what came later. In the garden. The black ball against the moon that happens but three times a year. The being does.

"If Sten remembers, tell him that this being is in trouble. The being is being hunted by the Emperor. We—"

Marr interrupted.

"We have *heard* where this being is," he said. "And if the Emperor learns of our knowledge, we too will be hunted. We do not know this being's exact location. We feel that even now a net is being cast, somewhere out there, by beings who intend us harm. Sooner or later, if that fisherman keeps casting, we shall be netted."

The beings moved together, finding what little love and security was left in their universe, and fell silent.

"We should say no more," Senn said finally. "Tell Sten of our problem. Ask him if he can help. He will know where we are. We do not have any suggestions.

"But . . . but tell him this. Tell him he must not chance all. We say this, and his friend says it as well. If help might risk his crusade, he must not try to help.

"Sten *must* not be defeated."

Drakh-hot pilot Hannelore La Ciotat had wondered—as much as anyone might wonder in a profession where two of the prerequisites were an inability to talk without moving one's hands and concern for the future a mild curiosity about what the O-club's got for its dinner special—just why she had joined the rebellion.

No one but her fellow rebels knew she had been Sten's pilot when he had ambushed Admiral Mason and the *Caligula*. And even if accused, she probably could have skated on that, and claimed to be in fear of her life if she disobeyed his commands. Instead, she had been one of the first of the *Victory*'s tacship pilots to throw in on Sten's side.

She settled on three reasons: First, that the Empire to her was represented by lard-assed senior officers who never could understand the tactical importance basic to underflying every single bridge that ran through the middle of her planet's capital world at mach speed, officers who would one day insist that she park the ship and start flying a desk. Second was that Sten was a pilot too, and spoke her language. Third was that she surely would have more combat time and flight hours with the rebellion than sticking with the monolithic Imperial forces.

She shied away from the fourth reason, which was Why The Clot Not, because that might imply that pilots are frequently lacking in any sense, let alone that of the common type. Especially tacship drivers.

She listened to Sten's briefing aboard the *Aoife* with some degree of skepticism, which Sten noted with amusement.

"You have a question, Lieutenant? Sorry, Captain. Congrats on the promo, by the way."

La Ciotat shrugged. More stars on the shoulder meant only more credits on the O-club bar payday night since sergeant-pilots and admiral-pilots still flew the same ships— and bore in.

"Last time you had this great plan," she began as tactfully as she knew how, which meant not very, "it was, 'Hey there, Hannelore, let's you and me ambush a battlewagon.'

"Dumb, dumb, truly dumb, but we blindsided the clot, and got away with it. Now you want to try again, except even bigger. As I understand it, my tacship, supported by one lousy non-Imperial tincan—"

Sten interrupted. "The *Aoife*'s only there to pull our tails out of the crack. She won't be there for the binga-banga-bonga."

"Even more wonderful. One spitkit, *not* supported by one lousy non-Imperial DD, to jump an entire convoy, a convoy carrying what's only the most important resource the Empire's got, and you think we're gonna accomplish the mission?

"Hell, I don't think we'll limp away, let alone do what you've got in mind. Who's gonna take care of the escorts?"

"There won't be any."

"Hoo. You weren't listening . . . by the way, what the clot do I call you? Besides 'sir'? I mean, what's your post-rebellion rank? Leader? Hero? I assume you've given yourself more tabs than just clottin' Admiral."

"Try Sten. No rank. No 'sir.'"

"Right. Anyway, you're saying the Empire lets its goodies travel unescorted?"

"I am."

"Sten, I gotta question how good your skinny is."

"You can question the intelligence and you can ask, La Ciotat. But you aren't going to get an answer. Need-to-know and all that."

La Ciotat stared at Sten for a long moment. "I'm not hot for your carcass," she finally said. "Nor needing any kind of an adrenaline rush. But I'm thinking I'm gonna be party to this silly-ass operation. So it's gotta be that I was born twins, and Momma said drown the dumb one and Daddy blew it. Okay, skipper. I'll brief my crew.

"They're gonna love this. Fearless Volunteers Into the Valley of Slok and all that. One of these years I gotta ask them before I toss them into the crapper, I guess."

Just beyond the dead system, Sten, La Ciotat, and her crew boarded the tacship, the *Sterns*. The com link was opened between the *Aoife*, the *Sterns*, and the Bhor ELINT ship, the *Heorot*, still monitoring from its silent parking orbit not too far off the relay-station world.

And then they waited.

La Ciotat, as was her custom before battle, retired to the tiny cubbyhole that was the captain's cabin, which meant on a tacship a closet-size room with a pulldown desk. But a cabin for all of that—there was a drawcurtain that everyone on a tacship called a door. She depilled from head to foot and bathed in water she had brought over from the *Aoife*'s supply, water that had been augmented with aromatic oils from her home world. She painted her face in the ancestral battlepattern of her house, and then cleared her mind of evil, of lust, of desires.

She was ready for battle.

She wondered what Sten—who occupied the only other cabin on the tacship—formerly belonging to the XO and engineer, given up at their request—was doing. What customs did *his* world practice? If any?

She considered the possibility of imminent nonexistence.

And the ramifications if she were to pull on a wrap, slip through the curtain, walk two meters to the next compartment, tap politely, and . . .

She caught herself. She went through the exercises again, forcibly clearing lust or ambition from her mind.

Besides, what was she worrying about, knowing that the void only beckoned her enemies, not her? She put on a fresh flightsuit and tried to sleep.

Sten, in the next compartment, slept deeply. Woke. Ate. Thinking of nothing except the taste of what he had put in his mouth, the hum of the air freshers in the background, the drone of the ship's internal power, the small jokes and large laughter at the mess table, as all thirteen beings on the *Sterns* waited for battle, trying not to snarl at or massacre the being beside them.

He slept once more. Perhaps he dreamed.

If he did, his mind chose not to record them when he woke to the yammer of the GQ siren.

He glanced at the overhead telltale. It was less than four ship-days since he had arrived insystem. Freston might have crystal balls and talent beyond that of being a mere battleship commander.

Heorot: "All stations! I have incoming—"

Aoife: "At battle stations!"

Sterns: "We have them."

Sten, from *Sterns*: "All stations! Maintain silence!"

The three ships watched the huge convoy bulk out of hyperspace toward them.

AM2. Twice the size of the convoy the rebels had ambushed off Dusable.

A com officer on the *Heorot* picked up a convoy relay-station blurt—a response to the convoy's initial inquiry from the planet. He resisted a temptation to run an analysis. Instead, he reported the transmission.

"All stations," Sten said calmly. "All recorders, all sensors on full. Stand by . . . stand by . . . stand by . . . *Now!* Captain! Full drive!"

La Ciotat obeyed. The *Sterns* flashed toward the monster convoy.

The com officer on the *Heorot* "saw" the convoy panic. Nothing physical happened, but the convoy began broadcasting on many frequencies.

"Ms La Ciotat," Sten went on, "I would like a Kali launch . . . individual control . . . area target . . . convoy on main screen . . . on my command . . ."

"Ms Castaglione," Hannelore said in turn to her weapons officer.

"Acquired. . . ."

"Target acquired, sir."

"Launch," Sten ordered.

"Fire."

The huge shipkilling missile lurched out of the center firing tube of the *Sterns*.

Screens flashed on the *Heorot*.

"We have a convoy-station 'cast," the Bhor com officer reported. "We have a response from the relay station . . . direction unknown, power strength massive . . . we have a signal transmitted on EM subspectrum . . . unclassifiable single spectrum . . . computers suggest between Omicron Sub Two and Xeta Three . . . no known previous use of spectrum by any known—*by the clottin' beard of my clottin' mother!*"

The fairly irregular interjection from the com officer occurred as his screens told him that the entire convoy had committed seppuku, a monstrous blast as if a star had gone nova! The explosion was beyond even the cataclysm that had resulted when the smaller AM2 convoy off Dusable had been hit by the *Victory*'s Kalis.

A second later, another screen showed him the robot relay station on the dead planet had also self-destructed.

Aboard the *Sterns* all screens overloaded and blew out.

Finally, one emergency screen cleared. It was a tertiary screen, 'casting from the Kali missile. It showed a great deal of nothing. Castaglione ran the pickup through all available bands.

Nothing but parsecs and parsecs of parsecs and parsecs.

La Ciotat forced herself to appear quite calm, as if a thousand-ship convoy suddenly blew itself up in her sights every E-day or so.

"All right," she grudged. "Your intelligence is One-A. But what a piddle-poor excuse for a battle this was."

Sten didn't answer immediately. Instead, he picked up the open mike on the three-way circuit.

"*Heorot. Sterns*. Six Actual. Trap? Angle?"

"*Heorot*. Affirm both."

"Do you have a receiving station?"

"Negative. None known. Analysis will continue."

"*Sterns* clear."

And now Sten smiled. "It was clottin' wonderful," he said.

"So what did we get?"

"We've got," Sten said accurately, "an Emperor with a major case of the hips, which is almost a case of the ass. We've just cut off a big chunk of the AM2 he'd be doling out to his cronies and allies. A *big* chunk."

His smile grew larger. La Ciotat looked at him skeptically—she wasn't sure she was hearing all of it.

She wasn't, although the fact that merely jumping out of the bushes and shouting boo had been enough to make the Big Bad Wolf drop dead of heart failure was significant—and certainly a tactic that could be repeated indefinitely, if they could continue finding the courses of the AM2 convoys.

Sten was realizing that one of the Eternal Emperor's primary weapons—that *no one* but the Emperor was permitted to get close to wherever AM2 came from—was a double-edged sword. Just as the shutdown of AM2 subsequent to the Emperor's disappearance would destroy any coup, so, too, Sten's boo-shouting could wreak economic havoc on the Emperor himself.

Possibly. Or at least until the Eternal Emperor figured out a response.

More importantly, the *Heorot* had recorded a second, equally mysterious signal to nowhere, this time from the relay station.

· If they could home on its target . . . Sten would be one step closer to finding the AM2.

And one step closer to destroying the Emperor.

CHAPTER FOURTEEN

41413 . . . 31146 . . . 00983 . . . 01507 . . .

Far beyond the stretch of the most sensitive sensor, far beyond the Bhor picketlines, an Imperial destroyer, modified into a special-missions delivery craft, dumped a tacship into space and fled.

The tacship, completely unarmed, its weapons systems replaced with massive electronic suites, slid toward Vi, the Bhor home world and capital of the Lupus Cluster. There were just five crewmen aboard, plus one Internal Security agent, fresh from her training and initial intern assignment.

09856 . . . 37731 . . . 20691 . . .

It found a parking orbit offworld, hiding behind one of the planet's moons until the ordered time came around.

Then, under partial and muffled drive, it set a landing trajectory. A somewhat unusual one. From the ground, it would appear that the tacship was coming "straight down," toward one point on the planet—a wilderness near the capital city. Speed was kept low to reduce skinheating and subsequent infrared printing by Bhor scanners.

It was still waiting for the correct moment, which came when one of the great Bhor intercontinental suborbital transports lifted from a field and bellowed for nearspace.

The tacship went for ground, using the cover of the transport's electronic, infrared, and physical turbulence.

On board, the dispatcher waited next to the spy. The compartment was lit with eye-saving red nightlights.

The spy was heavy-laden, McLean pack on her chest and a backpack containing a weapon and a travel case that would pass unnoticed as a civilian's valise. Inside the case were clothes, normal espionage gadgetry, plus a great sheaf of Imperial credits and Bhor currency.

Strapped to her leg was the heavy dropbag containing that most necessary and dangerous tool of a spy, a transmitter/receiver. The com buzzed.

"Coming in on Delta Zulu," the tacship pilot announced.

"Aye, sir," the dispatcher said.

"We're at dropspeed. On approach."

The dispatcher felt the tacship chop power and level out of its dive.

"Aye, sir. Hatch opening."

The dispatcher touched a button, and a circular hatch yawned. There was moonlit night and, far below, gleaming snow. Two corrugated steel plates slid out, into the middle of the open hatch. To one side, the dispatcher could see the flickering from the Bhor transport's stern as it drove on and upward, unseeing.

The spy shivered. But the compartment was heated.

"Looks cold down there."

"Your friends'll be waiting," the dispatcher soothed. "Now. Position."

The spy stepped onto the plates. She swayed in the airblast from the hatch, then recovered. As trained, she locked her hands tightly on the two handles of the McLean pack. One of them held the drive activation switch.

"Count thirty before you drop your bag," the dispatcher reminded. The spy nodded, not really hearing.

The com buzzed.

"Ten count . . . nine . . . eight . . . seven . . . six . . . five

. . . four . . . three . . . *GO!*"

The steel plates snapped back into their housing, and the spy plummeted down toward Vi. The dispatcher keyed the mike, as the hatch slid shut.

"One away, sir."

"Affirm. Return to your post."

The tacship lifted toward space. The temptation was to hit full drive and hare away. But the tacship pilot was a professional—the drive signature at full power would very likely be picked up, wasting all the trouble they'd gone to for the insertion. The dispatcher looked down, at the now-closed hatch.

"May all your eggs," he said, "be double-yolked."

A spy needed all the luck that could be wished for.

43491 . . . 29875 . . . 01507 . . .

Marl, now promoted out of tech ranks and commissioned as ensign, and the Bhor constable, Paen, watched one of the nightscreens in their gravlighter.

The image blurred, and Marl touched a button, and the picture was razor-sharp.

"You would not ever get me leaving a perfectly good tacship in flight," Paen observed.

"Nor me," Marl agreed.

The message had been coded and blurted out from Vi toward an Imperial Intelligence receiving station, located as close as safety would permit to the Lupus worlds:

41413	urgently
31146	require
00983	additional
01507	agent(s)
. . .	
30924	reports
32149	s
37762	t
11709	e

23249	n
03975	begins (beginning?)
26840	plans
41446	to use
37731	system(s)
03844	the basalt has come in again
. . .	
09856	delivery
37731	system
20691	m
. . .	
43491	will
29875	recover
01507	agent(s)

Marl was particularly proud of 03844, since she'd observed that Hohne was not exactly the most skilled of coders. Kilgour had been right in thinking Hohne a bit of an amateur since he was using an extant code. It wasn't significant to Alex that at least Hohne had chosen a prehistoric system, dating back to the dark ages when idiocies like obsidian daggers and onetime pads had been used.

She figured the Imperial who decoded the message would swear a lot, scratch his/her/its head(s), reconsult the code fiche, substitute 03843, meaning *for a base*, and the message would make sense. The mad Scotsman would be proud of her sneakiness.

Damn, but she was starting to miss Alex. When he got back, now that she was commissioned and all, and he was technically not in her chain of command, she planned to cozen him into drinks, dinner, and . . . who knows?

If nothing else, she wanted to find out the truth about that title, Laird Kilgour of Kilgour. If he was really some kind of baron, what was he doing in this revolt, instead of sucking up to the Emperor?

"The human looks cold," the Bhor said, not a shred of sympathy to his rumble.

"She does."

Marl felt momentarily empathetic for the doomed spy drifting toward them, still about a kilometer above the ground. She pushed it away. The woman has a choice.

"More stregg?" Constable Paen asked.

"I say again my last—humans can't be swilling stregg like you folks, and still function."

"Kilgour can."

"Kilgour isn't human, either."

"That is true."

Paen drained his cup—a duplicate in miniature of a drinking horn—folded it, and put it away.

"Shall we collect our new friend?"

Both beings slid out of the gravlighter, careful to not shut the doors behind them—the sound of a slamming door carries forever on a silent night. Around them, hidden in the blackness of this thicket, were twenty heavily armed Bhor policemen.

Above them the spy touched buttons, and her rate of descent slowed as much as the McLean generator could overcome gravity. The age of the fantasized strap-on-your-back personal flier still hadn't arrived, even with the antigrav capabilities of the McLean system. But at least it had replaced all varieties of the incredibly dangerous parachute.

The spy directed her descent toward one end of the huge open meadow that was the dropzone, the final end of delivery system M. Below her was tranquil forest. Far, far away—at least five klicks, she estimated—she saw the lights of a tiny farmhouse.

Just as planned. No ambush waiting.

Perhaps, she thought with a chill, her friends—the Imperial spymaster whose cover name was Hohne, or his chosen representatives—weren't at the rendezvous, either. But, that was not a problem. She would go to ground for one planet-day as instructed. There were rations and heat tabs in her case, and her jumpsuit would keep her very warm.

Even if they didn't materialize then, she would still be all right. Bury the jumpsuit and McLean pack, and make her way to the capital city. She had memorized three alternate pickup points.

Groundrush—under twenty-five meters—as she swung toward the snow.

She forced her eyes off the earth below, earth she knew had needle-sharp stones just under that innocent-looking snowy blanket, and onto the horizon. She suddenly remembered the dispatcher's warning, and her hand slammed the knob on her harness, letting the dropbag unspool on its five-meter cord so it wouldn't still be attached to her leg on the landing slam.

The bag with the transmitter dropped less than half a meter when the ground came up and smote the spy.

She did a classic three-point PLF: toes, knees, nose . . . and the pain crashed. She blurted, then buried an outcry and lay motionless in the snow.

"Clot," Marl swore, as the police spread out toward the spy. She and Paen hurried toward the sprawled agent. "If she ruined the com, I'll use the thumbscrews. We're two back now as it is."

Building a replica of one of the Empire's secret, compact superpower transmitters took a great deal of time—time when a spy would be out of circuit and would have to come up with some explanations when she reopened contact.

And there was no question in Marl's mind that this agent would eventually be tamed. Or else she would be brainscanned for her code phrases, contacts, electronic "fist," and then executed.

Only three Internal Security agents had chosen Patriotism and the Road to Tyburn so far—three of the twenty-nine whom Poyndex had ordered into the Wolf Worlds in response to Hohne's bleating about Sten's imminent arrival.

The other twenty-six were quite comfortable in quarters on various worlds that weren't quite prisons but were certainly not freedom, broadcasting exactly what they were fed.

Marl, and through her, Kilgour, and through him, Sten,

were running the Eternal Emperor's entire espionage net in the Wolf Worlds.

Just as Alex had planned.

Some time before, a colleague of Rykor's had been given an unusual assignment. A specialist in military recruiting, she had been ordered to prepare a campaign intended for the defeated Tahn worlds. At first Rykor had thought the idea somewhat unsavory, but she was pragmatic enough to realize that the military always recruits from its defeated and most generally downtrodden enemies.

But her colleague had gone on to explain that her orders had specifically stated that the campaign was to focus around a resurrection of the old Tahn samurai culture, a deathway the Emperor had sworn to extirpate after he had defeated the Tahn.

Interesting—and Rykor found it aberrational that the Emperor could believe that poverty could be cured by putting the poor in uniforms. But there was more to the concept than just that—and a full analysis revealed another indication of the Emperor's growing psychopathy. He was evidently building an army that he planned to use. Since there was no known external foe requiring a huge army to stand off, this newly restructured military would have as its purpose to destroy the enemy within. In other words, the citizens of the Empire.

Since the Tahn Way encouraged xenophobia, a racial superiority, the belief that mercy was a weakness, and the firm conviction that the strong had rights over the weak, this new model army of the Emperor's would be barbaric.

Rykor had subtly investigated—and found that other worlds with their own feral cultures were suddenly the focus of Imperial recruiters.

Very interesting.

Fortunately the campaign was very easy—at least easy for a being with Rykor's skills in mass psychology—to destroy.

Rykor had swept up every psychologist or psychological

student she could find who was able to fulfill some fairly basic requirements: Do you like to travel? Do you mind being alone? Can you tell a necessary lie without feeling guilty? Can you take on a job that you will not be able to see the results of? Can you accomplish a task and accept that you will not be rewarded immediately? And so on and so forth.

It was unfortunate she wasn't able to field battalions of counterpropaganda specialists, as she would have had she still been serving the Eternal Emperor.

But the antitoxin to this murderous psychological virus spread rapidly enough by itself. It worked because it addressed the Emperor's campaign at the root—and contained just enough truth to be unpleasant.

For instance, one of Rykor's volunteers was named Stengers. He was given a clean background and inserted on an Imperial world where he traveled openly as a student of sociology to Heath—the former capital of the Tahn. It was purest chance his wanderings were just behind an undercover Imperial Recruiting advance man, and just ahead of the recruiting team itself.

All Stengers did was ask some puzzled questions, especially to those young Tahn who were considering taking the Imperial shilling.

Questions such as: "Well, if the Emperor wants you to rise up and redeem the honor of the Tahn, why does he want you to serve so far from your home? It is hard to gain honor in the darkness, as one of your own proverbs states."

Sometimes, he was a bit more direct: "Interesting. You say that eighteen Tahn from this farm district alone have gone off to serve? And none of them have returned from Imperial duties? Two of them have died? How sad to die, so far from home, serving someone who seems to never notice such a sacrifice."

Or closer to the bone: "If the Emperor suddenly thinks so highly of the Tahn, and their elders, why is this district pig-drakh poor? With all of the Empire's riches, why are we shivering in front of this peat-bog fire? Why, the world I come from, which is no richer than this, and I live far in the hills, has AM2 heating in every home. I don't understand."

Or brutal: "Seems to me a pretty good way for the Tahn to never amount to anything if the Emperor's taking your best and sending them out to the fringe worlds to die."

Stengers and his fellows planted livie items, a revival of carefully chosen Tahn war ballads that centered around the belief that the Emperor and all his minions were worms beneath a Tahn's feet . . .

The next overall recruiting report to Prime contained some disappointing statistics about the sudden drop in volunteers to the Eternal Emperor's armed services . . .

Sten had cautioned Kilgour to be most careful on Earth. Even though the blown mission on the Umpqua River was against the privy council, security beings are security beings. There was a very good likelihood that the goons who would be wandering around the near-abandoned hamlet of Coos Bay, which Sten and Alex had used for their base, might still be carrying the same occupational specialty but serving another master. Gestapo is gestapo, as the seemingly meaningless archaism put it.

No problem, Kilgour swore. He planned to stay well away from the province of Oregon. Alex hoped that the secret he was looking for—the purpose of the Eternal Emperor's mysterious trip to Earth—was far, far away. In this case, far away meant the nearest full-range spaceport.

San Francisco, California's biggest city, boasted a population of almost 100,000. The young lovers—Hotsco, at least, qualified—claimed to have arrived in California Province on a shuttlehop into one of the desert retirement communities to the south, around the tiny province capital of Santa Ana. From there they had boarded one of the luxury gravcraft that swept over the San Joaquin Marshlands at the hamlet of Bakersfield, and leisurely found their way north.

Actually, Hotsco's smuggling ship was parked fifty meters underwater in the city's great bay near the Isle of Pelicans.

One beep from Hotsco's transponder, and robot rescue would be inbound.

Playing tourist, they took lodgings in one of the new pseudo-Victorian guest houses that were being built in the wilds atop the Twin Peaks. They marveled that there had once been a bridge across the headlands, and listened as visionaries told them one day the straits would be bridged again. They declined an invitation to hunt a man-eater in the overgrown jungles of what had once been a park. They listened to arguments as to whether the foothills of the Mission District should be cleared—some swore the low mounds were rubble from high-rise buildings that had fallen in some great quake. They danced in the restoration of a huge clifftop mansion patterned after one that had been destroyed pre-Emperor and three monster earthquakes ago.

They politely refused an invitation from two rather lovely human females to join them in sexual ecstasy, in the Lovedance of the Ancient Merkins. Free. Alex thought Hotsco looked interested and then somewhat disappointed when he reminded her that, generally, new lovers are in love for a while before kinks occur. He did make a mental note to himself that the woman appeared to have interesting recreational ideas.

And they ate. Crab they caught themselves with a rented pot near another ruined bridge which led directly across the bay. Long loaves of wonderfully sour bread. Broiled fish. Raw fish artfully arranged on pats of rice. Rack of lamb. Chicken roasted under a brick. Alex, never a sybarite, let alone a gourmand, thought of changing his ways.

And they talked. Talked to anyone and everyone. Especially in the bars and hangouts around the small spaceport just south of the city. Alex claimed to be a freelance import/exporter in the luxury trade, and Hotsco his new business/life partner. What, they wondered, did people think could be exported from Earth, considering that it was Manhome, that would interest customers throughout the Empire? More specifically, what *could* be exported—legally and morally?

Six E-days—and Alex smiled to himself: these really *were* Earth-days—later, without anyone seeming to realize that they had been grilled, Kilgour found his being. A customs official, someone with a sense of mission—which meant a built-in nose for a grievance, especially when it meant that someone had used higher authority to avoid proper procedure. Tsk, Kilgour assured her. Neither of them would ever . . . kind of thing that's despicable . . . business must be run in a proper manner . . . matter of fact, Ms Tjanting . . . one of the more terrible things about my own profession . . . some traders . . . even heard stories of very high officials bending the laws . . .

The pump didn't need much priming.

Very high officials, indeed. Straight from Prime, in fact. And during the time frame Alex was interested in.

Customs, through Earth Spaceship Control, had been notified that the province of Oregon was closed to all nonstandard inatmosphere and nearspace traffic. Which mattered not at all to Tjanting. She knew that the Emperor had his estates up there, and what he, or his people, chose to do was none of her concern. She might have been curious, being a good citizen, if the Emperor had been present. But of course, he had not been there.

How did she know that, Alex wondered?

Well, there would have been something on the livies, wouldn't there? But that wasn't why she was red-arsed, though. If the Eternal Emperor knew what liberties had been taken in his name, Tjanting knew, he would not be pleased.

About two weeks before the announcement, Tjanting went on, a commercial transport had grounded at San Fran, intending to clear customs at this entry port and then proceed immediately to its final destination—the Imperial Grounds some hundreds of kilometers away. She boarded the ship and immediately found things unusual. The ship was immaculate, and the crewmen followed orders as if they were in the Imperial Navy. But that was sheer conjecture. What had upset her was the cargo.

The skipper of the transport had, at first, refused to allow her access to the hold, claiming that what it contained was a classified cargo—property of the Imperial Household. But there was no paperwork to verify his claim. He could be carrying any sort of basic supplies to the river complex, supplies that the Emperor, like any other citizen, would have to pay duties on to the Earth government.

Tjanting insisted he open the hold—or else she would call for security and impound the ship and cargo and arrest the crew. The captain yielded gracelessly.

The cargo was medical—sophisticated equipment and supplies, as if someone were establishing a very small, but very superb, surgical ward. Or so, Tjanting said, a colleague specializing in med supplies had told her when she called back and read him the bill-of-lading fiche.

The problem wasn't that the cargo was dutiable—it probably wasn't, under humanitarian grounds. The question Tjanting had, and the one that wasn't answered, was why was this equipment necessary? Customs was also responsible for quarantine and health. Was someone in the Imperial Household ill? Or needing some kind of surgical help? For all she knew, there was a plague breeding.

She reported the matter to her superiors and was told to wait. They would contact the Emperor's staff in Oregon. That took minutes—no one in Oregon knew of such an incoming shipment. Tjanting was sure she had uncovered a strange sort of smuggling ring whose members had the maximum amount of gall.

Then another call came from the north, and before her shift ended, she was hauled in and reprimanded severely for what her supervisor called "unwarranted snooping into the business of the Eternal Emperor." Tjanting was also told she had a nasty reputation for being a busybody, and had best correct this character flaw lest it cause a downgrade on her next efficiency hearing.

By now the woman was seething, and Alex soothed her, and bought her another drink—a truly awful concoction of a sweet liqueur called Campari, charged water, and a brandy float on top. It was a monstrous waste of cognac, Alex thought, but said nothing.

So, while Hotsco covered for him with chattered sympathy, Alex mused: Jus' afore th' Emp dances on, some laddie wants t' set up an OR. An' it's gowky to conceive th' Emp's retreat nae has a wee medical kit an' such. So, somethin' special mayhap wae intended, aye? An op'ration?

On th' 'Ternal Emp'rer himself?

A wee bit ae surgery thae's carefully kept under th' rose . . . ?

Aye. 'Tis odd. 'Tis ver' ver' odd, Kilgour thought.

Actually, 'tis ver' simple, he realized, considering the presence of the bomb-disposal experts at the Emperor's compound. Surgically implanting a bomb in somebody wasn't unknown to Kilgour—the ruse had been used successfully by fanatics before. Kilgour had also heard of brave beings having a bomb installed inside them before they went on a suicide mission, to prevent any possibility of capture, torture, and exposing their fellows.

However, taking a bomb *out* was a new twist. And this is what he now thought had happened.

Mmm, Alex mused. So. Noo we' ken where th' boomie thae goes off whae th' Emp dies com't frae, aye? I's installed i' th' loonie's gut, p'raps where th' 'pendix was. I' dinnae matter. Th' *real* puzzler i' who put th' clottin' thing in, i' the first place!

Th' further an' further Ah dig an' delve, Kilgour mused, th' less an' less Ah knoo thae's f'r certain.

Ah well. I' y' want'd a life where thae was naught but th' abs'lute, y' coulda been a WeeFreesie. Or stay'd a common so'jer.

Alex refused to continue. Reasoning from insufficient data almost invariably produces suspect conclusions. He would think more on this later.

They fed Tjanting a couple of drinks, then announced that they had to get back to their hotel.

Tjanting watched them leave. After a moment, she frowned, and a queer expression crossed her face.

Halfway across the Empire, two men were drinking raw alk and knocking the shots back with homebrew in a portabar not far from a construction site. One man was a contact welder, the other a bank vice president, slumming.

"You heard," the welder began, "about what happened when the Eternal Emperor picked up a joygirl? First time he says I'm gonna ravish you and make you moan. He does and she does.

"Then he says I'm gonna ravish you and make you scream. He does and she does.

"Then he says I'm gonna make you *sweat*. And the joygirl pulls back and says Huh? And he says because the next time's gonna be midsummer . . ."

The banker chortled politely. "Way I heard it, the Emp just thinks that there's some things a man's gotta take care of himself. And in his case, it's th' little stuff."

The welder returned the compliment of laughter, turned serious. "You never notice, Els, that the Emperor never shows up on a livie cast when he's somewhere doin' something ceremonial with a woman?"

"Why should he?"

"No reason," the welder said. "But if you was top dog, I'd assume there'd be a ton of honey trying to lurk on you, right? Like if you got promoted Chief Suit tomorrow?"

"Maybe. But my wife'd have words about that."

"Something else the Emperor's lacking."

"Maybe that's why he lives forever," the banker suggested. "He's just saving his precious natural resources."

"Assumin' he's got any."

Both men snickered, and attention was drawn to the livie screen and the gravball match's third quarter just beginning.

Both "jokes" were the work of Rykor's staff. Funny or not, they were intended to accomplish just what they were doing: to reduce the Eternal Emperor's image of omnipotence. In this particular instance, quite literally.

These jokes, and a hundred hundred others, coupled with some really nasty whispered rumors and legends, were moving through the Empire at a speed slightly above stardrive.

The nighttime ritual was for Alex to check their room to see if they had been blackbagged or bugged. Then he would wash up in the fresher. Afterward, Hotsco would get showered and powdered and join him in the great, old-fashioned feather bed. But only to sleep. Alex, the professional and the moralist, would never dream of taking advantage of a cover. Nor was he attracted to the slender young woman. Not at all his type.

Or so he lied at increasingly frequent intervals.

He lathered and scrubbed, luxuriating in the soft water that needled against his body, remembering times and missions when there was no water for anything but drinking, and barely enough for that. He turned to adjust the shower from NEEDLE to BLAST, and a giggle sounded in his ear, a giggle whose Alex's expert ear sonared at two centimeters' distance.

"Move over," Hotsco said. "And give me the soap. Your back needs washing."

"Uh, lass . . ."

"I said, move over."

Alex did as he was told. Hotsco began scrubbing his back, soap moving in slow, sensual circles.

"I'm not looking," she said. "But I have a wager on what a Scotsman has under his kilt."

"Aye?" Alex said, a smile beginning to grow across his face. "An' y'd like t' feel someat thae's twenty-five centimeters? Reach under m' sporran twenty times."

Hotsco laughed. Her fingers moved on. Traced a red, ragged trough on Kilgour's biceps.

"What's that?" she wondered.

"Thae's where Ah zigged like a clot when Ah should'a zagged. Wounds are a good way t' keep y'r ego frae gettin' overweenin't.

"Lass, thae's noo m' chest y're scrubbin't."

"That's all right," Hotsco said dreamily. "That's not the soap, either."

"If Ah turn aroun'," Kilgour said, his voice a little husky, "Ah'll be startin' t' take th' wee game a bit seriously."

"Mmm."

Alex turned, reached down, and lifted Hotsco in his arms. Their lips met, and her legs closed around his thighs.

A bit later, they got out of the shower. They had to use Kilgour's robe as a towel, since the fresher looked like the site of a water-main explosion.

Outside was the moon shining on the bay and the dying lights of San Francisco.

"An' noo," Alex said, "we'll hie ourselves t' th' feathers, an' Ah'll noo hae t' worry aboot whether m' McLean powers are runnin't dry."

"Is *that* what you call it," Hotsco wondered. She crossed to her dresser, picked up a tube of aromatic oil, and slowly began rubbing it into her skin, smiling over her shoulder as she did.

"'If y're th' lass wi' th' soap," Alex volunteered, "dinnae it be justice if Ah'm th' lad whae goes slip-slidin' away?"

He took the tube from her, squeezed some oil on his fingers, and then, suddenly, his instincts cut through the lust. He flipped Hotsco sideways, across the bed. She thudded into the feathers, too startled to shout—and the dressing-table mirror exploded.

Kilgour backrolled to the door, came up, pistol magically in hand, kneeling, braced . . . three rounds crashed as one . . . and out on the balcony the assassin's chest exploded.

Someone or something crashed against the door, and Kilgour sent three more AM2 rounds through it, the wood wisping and charring. There was a scream outside.

Alex grabbed the tiny transponder that was their only back door, shoved it in his mouth, and scooped up Hotsco in one arm. He took two gigantic steps across the room, shattering what remained of the balcony door's framework, high-stepped onto the balcony, and jumped. Hotsco yelped.

It was seven meters to the grassy turf below, and as Alex fell, he twisted his body, feet together, and used the uni-formed cop who was gaping up at him as a trampoline.

The cop's ribs snapped, and he screamed a bloody gargle. Kilgour collapsed to his knees, absorbing the shock of the landing. Then he sprang back up, and, without pausing or dropping either Hotsco in one hand or his pistol in the other, hurtled toward the brushy cover around the inn.

An AM2 round exploded turf next to him—so, i's th' Emp's boyos, Kilgour recognized—and he spun and, with-out bothering to aim, pumped four rounds back up into the room they had just vacated.

Then he was juggernauting again.

By the time the pickup/hit squad of San Francisco cops and Internal Security operatives recovered, the white blur that was the naked heavy-worlder had vanished into the scrub.

Sirens ululated then, and lights flashed and coms crack-led.

But Kilgour was gone.

Two kilometers away, Alex stopped running. He estimated that he was somewhere in that great jungle close to the end of the peninsula, where tigers who had been freed from the zoo aeons earlier stalked the night.

The tiggers, he decided, would hae t' take their risks.

"Ah'm in no mood t' be trifled wi'," he announced softly. "Ah had plans f'r th' remaind'r ae th' evening."

Even though Hotsco had grown up on the far side of what most beings called the law, she was not used to this sort of thing—especially when it came at a blur of lightspeed. But she was clotting damned if she would lose face in front of Alex.

"I assume," she said, "the Empire just caught up with us."

"Aye," Alex said. "Thae hae willyguns. Th' custom's lass narked on us. Ah dinnae catch her last name, Hotsco. Dinnae y' ken i' it wae Campbell?"

He seemed completely oblivious to the fact they were both stark naked—and that their sole assets, against a city and a world that would be raising a hue and cry against them, were a pistol and a transponder.

"What next?" Hotsco asked.

"W' hae twa choices," Alex said. "First, an' most palatable, i' w' hunt doon th' two lassies ae th' Lovedance ae th' Merkins. Thae'll noo blanch ae th' sight ae a couple ae young lovers comin't t' them ae th' Laird made them. An' we c'n continue whae we barely—sorry, lass—begun't till th' heat dies doon. I' y' hae their card?"

"I left it back there," Hotsco said. Her shock had died away, and quite suddenly she found this whole situation funny. "In the hotel. You want me to go back for it?"

Alex considered.

"Nae," he said, straight-facedly. "Twas nae but a passin' fancy. Option two. We'll work our way t' th' docks, an' either steal a curragh, or else swim oot t' thae island ae th' big-jawed birds. Alcatruss?"

"Swim. I can't swim."

"Nae problem, lass. Ah'll need but one arm t' be bashin't th' sharks away. Ah'll hae y' wi' th' other, an' th' bangstick between m' fangs. A braw measure ae a Scotsman.

"Kickin't wi' m' feet an' steerin' wi' th' rudder th' Laird provided. It canna be more'n a klick 'r twa awa'. Brisk, refreshin' dawn swim. Ah hae a strong desire t' gie back t' th' wee game y' w're teachin' me wi' a minimum ae time loss. Shall we?"

He bowed formally, took her arm, and they started south, toward the fishing village.

Fleet Admiral Anders, the Imperial Chief of Naval Operations, looked at the progs on the five wallscreens, then at the sixteen fiches projected across his desk. His face was impassive, just as he had learned a proper war leader should look in his moment of decision.

He was not sure what he thought, since he was, or so his Intel chief had assured him, the first to see, let alone have the chance to analyze, this data. After all, there was just the possibility, his mind thought vaguely, that the Eternal Emperor had not been jesting when he said some time ago that when the Sten problem was over, Anders would find himself in command of two rowboats and a tidal bank on some forgotten planet. He really didn't want to make another mistake.

He decided to start with skepticism. Because he was a man of lists, that was the way he worded his doubts.

"Give me," he said, "three reasons why I should believe that this system—Ystrn—will be the jumping-off point for the traitor Sten's next raid? And why, in fact, does your intelligence suggest that Al-Sufi is, in fact, the target?"

Anders's Two, Sheffries, wondered whether she was supposed to come up with three reasons or six, considering that he had asked two separate questions. In either case, she was disappointed in her clot of a boss. She had three threes ready.

"One: Al-Sufi is one of the three largest AM2 distribution centers in the Empire. Two: Sten has already hit one such depot. Three: Revolutionaries with limited means, such as Sten—"

"That should be the *traitor* Sten," Anders interjected.

"Beg pardon. Traitors like Sten, who have little in the way of combat ships and troops, normally become enamored of spectacular targets. Particularly if those targets appear to provide the maximum damage to the enemy, sorry, the home worlds, they're rebelling against. The term is 'panacea targets.' In other words—"

"In other words," Anders went on, "he somehow had a small measure of success against Dusable, which is why he'll hit Al-Sufi next."

"Thank you, sir. You summarized my thinking admirably.

Four: The Al-Sufi/Durer battle, commonly called Durer by the masses, was one of the Emperor's biggest victories during the Tahn war. Therefore it makes perfect sense that the traitor Sten would want to ruin this image.

"Five. Since Sten was evidently, although we still have incomplete data, not serving with the Imperial forces during the Al-Sufi/Durer battle—"

Anders waved Sheffries to silence. "Very well," he said. "You have convinced me.

"Three fleets will be required for this operation. Alert my staff. I shall brief them on what the oplan shall consist of."

"Three fleets, sir?"

"Exactly. I propose to obliterate, at one stroke, this rebellion. So I shall wish all of my sailors to be aware of their participation in this moment of destiny."

"Sir. My plus/minus of accuracy on the prog is only eighty percent. And I haven't run *any* progs as to whether Sten—I mean, the traitor Sten—would be personally in charge of the raid."

"Of course he would," Anders said impatiently. "I would. You would." He smiled. "The Eternal Emperor will be very glad of this news. When the traitor Sten is finished, Sheffries, I shall personally see that you are rewarded with flag rank."

Sheffries managed to express delight, saluted, and was gone. Wonderful, she thought glumly. And if anything goes wrong, it'll be, Commander Sheffries, would you mind crossing your legs? We only have three nails . . .

Sten was plotting the "raid of Al-Sufi," and just how the rendezvous point in the Ystrn system should appear, when the EYES ONLY message from Sr Ecu, on Seilichi, was hand-carried up from the message center.

He swore, found a decoding machine, and keyed in pore pattern, retina flash, personal code, and all the rest.

Then he scanned the covering message and that appeal from Marr and Senn.

Clot. He knew who the other being was. Haines, of course.

Yes, he remembered only too well, his body stirring, the party and the garden and the black ball against the moon.

It made sense that the madman who called himself the Eternal Emperor would be rounding up anyone who knew Sten for brainscan.

He was glad that somehow Haines had escaped the net. Then he wondered if the Emperor and his satrap Poyndex had cast again, and gotten her. Or if they had widened their quest and gone after Marr and Senn, after they had sent the "flier." Yet a third and even more likely possibility was that Poyndex's IS elements had discovered Marr and Senn's amateur attempt at cryptography and had laid an ambush.

First response. Saddle up and go for a rescue.

Stopped cold in its adrenaline rush.

Like hell. You are beyond that, now. You have had the gall to stand up and declare yourself outlaw and rebel against the Empire. Which is fine. Any being is entitled to find his own suicide.

But there are others who've joined you. You're responsible for them, aren't you? So you sure as hell can't head out on some forlorn hope, can you? You've got to worry about the bigger things.

Besides, this wouldn't be the first time that you've had to abandon a friend or even a lover to accomplish the mission, right?

Of course.

The com buzzed. Sten slugged the contact switch.

"GA."

"Mister Kilgour," the com officer reported. "Inbound. ETA one E-hour. Mission accomplished. I have him onbeam now."

Sten started to say that he would talk to Alex when he grounded, then stopped.

"Sealed?"

"Of course, sir."

"Patch it through."

The screen cleared. Onscreen was Alex; to one side of him was a demurely smiling woman. Oh yes, Sten thought.

That must be the smuggler captain who volunteered to insert Kilgour onto Earth. Sten looked at his friend.

"Welcome home," he said.

"Thanks, boss."

"No offense. But you look like slok."

"Lad, i' wae a noisesome task Ah set myself."

"You were blown?"

"Aye. But noo by th' Emp, thoo Ah hae an in'trestin' run in wi' India Sierra as we w're runnin't th' mission. An' noo on Earth. An Ah'll noo 'splain. But Ah hae traces ae whae Ah wen' lookin't for, which Ah'll noo 'splain till we face-t'-face.

"Whae's been th' haps i' m' absence?"

And Sten found himself briefing Alex. Further, telling him about the com from Ecu/Marr/Senn. He stopped short, without mentioning his decision.

"Ah." Alex nodded. "Ah ken. Y' noo hae a choice, do y'?"

Sten didn't answer.

"Ah'll hae th' *Victory* packed an' liftin' wi'in an E-day after Ah return, lad."

Sten blinked.

Alex smiled. "Y' noo thought thae was whae Ah meant, did y'? Y' were thinkin't about duty an' respons'bility, aye?"

"Something like that."

"Well . . . consider all thae lads an' lassies thae went rebel wi' y. Some went oot frae selfish reasons, some went oot frae reasons ae' aidin' th' gran' cause ae civil'zation. But more went oot 'cause they're servin't y'r wee smilin't face, lad.

"I' some ways, 'tis noo a good part ae life, wee Sten. We all should mak't decisions wi' logic an' frae th' good ae all livin't things.

"But thae's noo how it works.

"An' i' the foolish ones who're servin't you because y're one wee mon, shouldnae you be thinkin't th' same? Willin' t' spend y'rself f'r th' life ae one wee fellow rebel? 'Cause if you're noo willin't t' go doon i' flames like thae, then we're noo dif'frent thae the Emp, and p'raps should cast i' our lot immed'jately.

"Y' sh'd noo be sendi't frae which fool th' bell tolls frae, an' thae, aye?

"Ah reck y' hae noo choice othern't to gie y'self a'ter Haines an' th' two furballs."

It was completely wrong, and one of the more stupid things that Sten could do. And why he decided to go for it. What the clot, the rebellion was doomed anyway. He had zip-burp chance of toppling the Empire. So why not go down in flames on a noble gesture?

"GA," he started. Then he caught himself, and an evil smile spread across his face. He remembered a scam he had worked once before on a prison break, and thought he could ring yet another change on it.

"Negative, Mister Kilgour. I won't need the *Victory*. All I need is one Bhor robohulk and the *Aoife*. There's no reason I have to be a complete Don Quickshot. Oh yeah. And one livie crew and some actors. I want three pilot sorts, two goons, and one idiot with steel teeth. Unbathed and whacko-looking. All human. Oh yeah. I need about fifteen or so terrified cute children.

"Now, get your butt down here. I have need of your talents. And somebody to hold the fort while I'm off playing Sir Gawaine. Clear."

Sten's plan took less than half a day to accomplish.

He was still going out to his death, but at least in a sneaky, dirty, underhanded sort of way instead of the imbecilic "charge in full dress uniform waving an ivory-hilted can opener" that he had always despised.

"Soward Control, this is the transport *Juliette*. Now in normal space, coordinates transmitted . . . now. Using commercial orbit Quebec Niner Seven. Request landing instructions. Over."

And so terror came to Prime World.

"*Juliette*, this is Soward Control. Have your coordinates.

Transmitting landing data . . . now. Please enter data and activate ALS at termination of your orbit Quebec Niner Seven, over."

"Soward, this is *Juliette*. Wait one . . . uh, I've got a slight problem with your data, Control. That'll park us on the far southeast corner of the field, correct?"

"That's an affirm."

"Got a favor to ask, Soward. Any possibility of getting closer? I've got a shipload of scholarship kids aboard, and they'd get a boot out of seeing things a little closer. Plus that's a long walk to the terminal. Can we get a shuttle?"

"This is Soward. No problem. We'll tuck you right over here, near the tower. Transmitting new data . . . now. And for a shuttle . . . all we've got is commercial. Shall I notify a carrier?"

"This is *Juliette*. Thanks for the shift. And, uh, negative on that commercial carrier. My kids don't have a lot of money. This is one of those starving-students hops."

"Roger. Maybe we can—"

And the *Juliette*'s signal cut.

"*Juliette*, this is Soward Control. *Juliette*, please respond to this transmission."

Static. No response. The controller automatically hit EMERGENCY and STANDBY buttons.

"This is the tower," he said. "I've got an inbound, closing on final, and they went off the air. Info from pilot said they've got children aboard. Stand by."

Rescue crews rolled into their vehicles.

The controller fingered a touchpad, and went to both the standard landing and the Imperial Standard emergency freqs.

"*Juliette*, this is—"

"Who is this?" It was a new voice, from the *Juliette*.

"This is Soward Landing Control. Identify yourself. Is this the *Juliette*?"

A laugh.

"Yeah. Yeah. Is this the visual-transmit switch . . . yeah. Here we go."

A screen cleared, and showed an appalling scene. It was the control room of the *Juliette*. The four beings in the flight crew sprawled in bloody pools. In front of the pickup was a wild-eyed man, wearing a filthy, stained shipsuit. He held a gun.

Behind him were two equally repellent assistants. Each of them held a wriggling child in one arm—and held a knife pressed to that child's throat.

"See what you got," the man said. "Now. I want a straight patch to an Imperial livie station. Now!"

"I can't—"

The man gestured, and one of his assistants slashed a throat. Blood gouted, the other child screamed, and a body flopped on the deck.

"Get another one," the man said, and his pet goon vanished, and came back dragging another preteenager. "You see? We ain't drakhin' around. Get a—"

And the dispatcher was hitting keys.

"You better sound convincing," the hijacker said. "Because I got me another fourteen crumbsnatchers I don't mind thinslicin'. Or doin' . . . some other things to them. Stuff that's worse."

So began the drama of the *Juliette*. The feed went live on K-B-N-S-O, back on the air, but broadcasting from a temporary, planetary headquarters.

Prime World came to a stop as the battered transport orbited over Soward Spaceport. The man announced what he wanted.

"I want a link to the Eternal Emperor. Not on a clottin' com like this. But face to face. He's gotta settle something. He's gotta stop doing to my family what he done. It ain't right for nobody that big to be feuding like he was some kind of backcountry pencilneck, it ain't. And it's gonna come to an end, it is. My family's near wiped out.

"Hell, if there ain't no clottin' change, I'm subject to send this clottin' transport at full drive straight into that clottin' palace of his. You tell the Emperor that."

Hostage-rescue teams were assembled, and waited to see

if they'd be called on for the last resort of boarding the *Juliette*. The Imperial fleet patrolling offworld closed on Prime. Arundel's already alert security elements were ready with AA missiles held one count from launch, and would fire if the *Juliette* headed toward the Emperor's palace.

Of course there would be, there could be, no meeting between the Eternal Emperor and the men aboard the *Juliette*. Terror must not be surrendered to.

Negotiators began the long slow drone, trying to bore the hijackers into surrender. But the hijackers didn't respond— the only response they made was either to repeat their preposterous demand, to stare blankly at the pickup, or occasionally to shut down without a warning.

The livies ate it with a spoon. The story had everything. Crazed terrorists. The cutest on-camera kids since they caught child star Shirlee Rich in bed with her orangutan. Understanding shrinks analyzing everything endlessly. Experts trying to figure out just what world the still-unknown hijackers could have come from. Warships blasting back and forth across the sky. Unknown movement of forces that not even the biggest sleaze livie show host would speculate on, to avoid possibly exposing a secret rescue plan. Lloyds insurance executives explaining what might have happened to the transport *Juliette* since it had disappeared into Imperial Special Service all the way back during the Tahn war. Noble-looking special-weapons teams ready to sacrifice their all.

Best of all, it was *real*.

The only challenge the *Aoife* got as it closed on Prime was mechanical, perfunctory, and at least three cycles out of date. Berhal Waldman didn't even have to analyze the challenge, but found it in a standard code-fiche. Everybody was preoccupied.

The *Aoife* went straight in for a landing.

No one noticed, even in the tiny village at the far end of the narrow valley. That abominable monster aboard the *Juliette* had just butchered another child.

The destroyer may have been a tiny ship—in space, and

compared to a battlewagon/carrier like the *Victory*, or on the wide, bare tarmac of a landing field where the eye couldn't provide any scale. But it made the tower it landed beside into a toy. Waldman's fingers ran across the keys, keeping the *Aoife* hanging just clear of the ground on its McLean generators. It would not do to leave a five-meter-deep impression in the middle of the beautifully-laid-out garden. Not only for aesthetic reasons, but that might suggest to the curious what had happened.

There was no movement from the tower.

The *Aoife*'s chainguns swept the pinnacle, Honjo fingers hovering above firing keys.

The ship's ramp slid down, and Sten came out. He was wearing combat armor, and carried a willygun. But his helmet face was open.

Waldman thought that was truly insane—Internal Security could be waiting just inside. But Sten couldn't figure out any other way to let beings know they were being rescued, not attacked.

He was nearly at the door before it opened.

Marr and Senn stood there.

"I must say," Marr said. "You certainly arrive in a baroque manner, my young captain."

"Yeah. Baroque. Let's get the clot out of here before somebody baroques us in half. Later for the aphorisms, troops."

And Haines was there, in the doorway.

"Took you long enough."

"Sorry. Hadda stop and tie my bootlaces."

Behind Haines, a human male. Slender. Balding. Early middle age. Dressed about ten years out of style. Sten flashguessed that was Haines's husband. Not at all the sort of man he would have expected her to end up with.

Don't be considering that, idiot. Like you just told everybody else. Book.

Senn, Haines, and Sam'l ran for the ship. Marr hesitated for a moment, then bent and picked up a small, multihued pebble.

"There might be nothing left to come back to."

And then he, too, boarded the *Aoife*, Sten close behind him.

"Lift, sir?" Waldman asked as Sten boiled into the control room.

"Wait one."

He looked at a screen, which showed the bridge of the *Juliette*. No one was in front of the pickup, either hostage or terrorist.

"Send it."

"Yessir." The com operator next to the screen hit a button, and the *Aoife* broadcast a single letter in code to the *Juliette*.

Onscreen chaos.

Shouts. Screams. The hijackers, bellowing incomprehensibly. A young girl broke away and tried to run. She was shot down. The hijacker was shrieking in some never-to-be-translated tongue. His pistol swayed, then blasted. Straight into the pickup! Dead air.

"Oh my dear, oh my dear," Marr moaned, arms around Senn. "Those poor baby humans!"

"Yep," Sten said. "Terrible, terrible. And it's going to get worse. Berhal Waldman, take us up. About five hundred meters, please."

The *Aoife* shot skyward.

Sten was quite a prophet, as a second screen went to life, this time on a commercial station.

Blur . . . snap-focus . . . a battered spaceship . . . McLean units off . . . haze from the ship's stern as the Yukawa drive went to full . . .

Screaming incoherence from some liviecaster: "Horror . . . Horror . . . oh the horror of it all . . ."

"Full drive, if you please. Home, James."

The *Aoife* slammed into hyperspace, sonic boom as air rushed to fill the vacuum left by the destroyer.

That explosion went unheard, buried by a greater one as the *Juliette* crashed straight into the center of Soward's main landing field. There was no fire, no rubble. Just a smoking crater.

Sten turned sadly as the *Aoife*'s pickup lost the commercial 'cast.

"What an awful thing," he said. "All those beautiful little children, spread over the landscape like so much strawberry preserves. Strawberry? Tomato. Saltier-tasting.

"And *so* coincidental, too. Unfortunate for them, although they'd probably all grow up to be ax-murderers or lawyers or something, but certainly providential for us.

"As Mister Kilgour says, God never takes away with one hand but he gives with the other."

Marr and Senn uncurled from their woe and their great eyes focused on Sten. Haines verbalized it.

"You know, you're an utter bastard, Sten."

"That's what my mother always said," Sten agreed happily.

"Thanks," she said, quite seriously.

"Hey. It wasn't that much. You know me. Saint Sten. Slayer of Virtuous Maidens. Rescuer of Dragons."

Amid the banter Sten felt very, very good about himself. And very surprised they'd gotten away with it.

Officially, the *Juliette* incident remained a tragic event, another example of the growing collective psychopathology of an overcomplex civilization. Privately, though, investigators were fairly sure they had been snookered. Not that any trace of the tape Sten's actors had carefully prepared during the flight out from Vi remained. *Nothing* remained of the Bhor robohulk except a hole in the tarmac and a wisp or six of greasy smoke. But investigators knew they would have found some carbon traces of the eighteen or more beings who died before or in the crash, no matter how thorough the splatter.

When Sten heard that, as a passed-along rumor, he swore mightily. If he had given the situation one more thought, he could have scored ten or so beef carcasses from a butcher shop, and no one would *ever* have known.

Three mighty Imperial battlefleets flashed out of hyperspace in the Ystrn system, all weapons stations manned and ready to obliterate the rebellion.

Six worlds and their moons and moonlets orbited a dead star.

Nothingness.

No Sten.

No rebel fleet.

No nothing.

And as far as the most sophisticated analysis could determine, no known ship had *ever* entered this system. It had been named on a star chart and never explored. Not that there was anything worth exploring.

Sten's big con had worked. Or, rather, was working. He had never considered raiding Al-Sufi, of course, nor going anywhere that close to Prime World with his tiny battlefleet.

The deception that had been leaked through Hohne's doubled net and other agents around the Empire was just the first step.

Sten was playing liar's poker with the Emperor.

This time, there was nothing there.

Next time, in another system, there might be traces that Sten or some of his ships had recently passed through.

Not only was this game something that could be played over and over again—the Emperor could not and would not ignore any reports of Sten's presence—and burn AM2, Imperial ships and supplies, whatever faith the Imperial Navy had in its intelligence, and the Eternal Emperor's arse, but it would have a payoff.

One that would shake the Imperial forces to their souls.

CHAPTER FIFTEEN

SUBADAR-MAJOR CHETHABAHADUR SNAPPED a crisp salute. "Sah! Reporting as ordered, sah."

"Sit down, Subadar-Major," Poyndex said. "No need for formality."

Chethabahadur sat, his small, slender body stiff in the seat.

"I'm afraid I have some very bad news," Poyndex said. "I'm sorry to be the one bearing it. But there's no sense beating about the brambles and making things worse. So here it is. As you know, the Eternal Emperor holds *you* people in high esteem for your years of dedicated service."

Chethabahadur blinked. Very quickly. All other reactions were caught in time. The phrase "you people" was clearly an insult worthy of a cut throat. The "years of dedicated service" numbered in the hundreds, which meant that Poyndex should have had his throat cut a second time. As for "high esteem"—well, it was almost too much.

The subadar-major kept his expression mild, wondering at the several miracles allowing this toady to remain alive after mewling such nonsense.

"Very high esteem, indeed," Poyndex continued. "Unfortunately, he has found himself in a terrible position. Money is very tight now, you understand. Cutbacks and belt tightening has been ordered all through the services."

"Yes, sah," Chethabahadur said. "The Gurkhas have done their part, sah. But if further reductions are required, sah . . . be assured we are ready."

Poyndex smiled condescendingly. "How generous. But

that won't be necessary. Under the circumstances. You see, I have been ordered to disband your unit. As I said, I'm very sorry. But we all have to make sacrifices in times like these."

Without hesitation, Chethabahadur said, "No need to apologize, sah. Tell the Emperor the Gurkha stand ready for any command. If he needs us to disband, sah . . . and return to Nepal . . . well, it shall be done. And without complaint, sah. Assure him of that."

Another Poyndex smile. "Oh, I will. I certainly will."

The subadar-major came to his feet and snapped another salute. "Then if that is all, sah, I will depart to inform my men."

Poyndex made with a weak reply to the salute. "Yes . . . That is all . . . And thank you very much."

"It is you who are to be thanked, sah," Chethabahadur said. He spun and marched from the room.

Poyndex eased back in his chair, pleased with himself for a difficult task well done . . . although he was surprised at how easy the Gurkha major had taken the news.

Such loyalty.

Blind, ignorant loyalty.

Poyndex laughed. He keyed his com and ordered his Internal Security troops to the posts of the departing Gurkhas.

Outside, in the corridor leading away from Poyndex's office, one floor below the Emperor's private quarters, Chethabahadur had to force down the sudden desire to leap high in the air and click his heels.

For a long time now he and his men had worried over the Emperor's deteriorating personality. His actions turned their stomachs. They could not understand how a soldier they admired—Ian Mahoney—could become a traitor. And there was absolutely no way they would believe Sten, once their commander, and still, as far as anyone knew, having one platoon of Gurkhas serving under him, would turn his coat, even against the rabid beast the Emperor had become.

All of the Gurkhas had wanted to quit. The only thing that had stopped them was their sworn oath—and the certain knowledge the Emperor would consider the action a grave insult.

He would kill them all.

Worse, they feared for their people in far-off Nepal. None of the Gurkhas doubted that the Emperor would remove Nepal from the face of the planet for such a betrayal.

But now—joy, oh, joy, the heavens smiled and the Gurkha were fired. What a blessing to come from such a barbarian as that Poyndex.

Not that Chethabahadur forgave him his rude behavior Someday he would kill the man.

If this was not possible, Chethabahadur's son would kill Poyndex's son.

For the Gurkhas had very long memories.

Poyndex watched with amazement as the woman, Baseeker, abased herself before the Eternal Emperor.

"Oh, Lord, I am blinded by your exalted presence. My limbs tremble. My brain is a fever. My tongue a thick stump unable to form words befitting your full glory."

Poyndex buried a smile. He thought her tongue was working just fine. The new high priestess of the Cult of the Eternal Emperor was prostrate on her god's office floor.

"You may rise," the Emperor said solemnly. Poyndex was only mildly surprised at how seriously the Emperor seemed to be taking this interview.

Baseeker came to her knees, beat her head several times against the ground in further obeisance, then came the rest of the way to her feet. Poyndex saw the glitter of pleasure in the Emperor's eyes and congratulated himself in his choice to replace Zoran as the new high priestess. Baseeker had absorbed his coaching and then bettered it by several hundred percent.

"Please. Do sit down," the Emperor said, fussing over the woman. "May I offer you any refreshment?"

Baseeker slid into the indicated chair, poised at the edge as if relaxation would be a blasphemy. "Thank you, Lord.

But allow this humble seeker of truth to reject your kindness. I could not possibly take mortal nourishment at this time. Permit me, instead, to continue to feed my spirit upon the ethers of your holy presence."

Poyndex doubted whether Baseeker ever fed on much of anything—except personal ambition. She was all bone and gristle, wrapped tight with skin so pale it was nearly translucent. She was of indeterminate age, with a severely pinched face, sharp incisors peeking through thin lips, and eyes like small bright beads. Like a rat's, Poyndex thought.

"Whatever pleases you," the Emperor said, waving grandly.

Baseeker nodded, tucking her white robe around bony knees.

The Emperor indicated a sheaf of paper on his desk. "I've studied your proposals for reorganization quite thoroughly," he said. "An impressive job."

"Thank you, Lord," Baseeker said. "But it could not have been done without your inspiration. Frankly, the cult was left in complete disarray by my late predecessor—Zoran. Our purpose is to glorify you . . . and educate your subjects on your divine mission. But these things were left shamefully undone."

"I see you have added a new program," the Emperor said. "A proposal to build worship centers in all the major capitals of the Empire."

Baseeker bowed her head. "I'd hoped it would meet your favor."

Poyndex lifted his eyes to keep from laughing. They fell on the painting above the Emperor. It was an ultraromantic, ultramuscular portrait of the Emperor, posing heroically. The painting was in commemoration of the Battle of the Gates, which the portrait indicated he had won single-handedly. Poyndex happened to know the Emperor never was even vaguely near the fighting in question.

The painting was one of a whole gallery glorifying the Emperor. They were from the awful collection of the late Tanz Sullamora. Ordered to track them down, Poyndex's IS agents had found them rightfully discarded in a museum trash heap. Now they hung frame edge to frame edge along the office walls. The effect was unsettling, to say the least. All those saintly Imperial eyes staring down at him. It was like hallucinating on spoiled narcobeer.

He forced his attention back to the interview. He saw Baseeker's small eyes fire brighter. "This proposal is nothing, Lord, compared to my true vision," she said, full of holy fervor. "I see temples to your exalted self in every town and city of the Empire. Where your subjects can gather together and bask in your glory."

"Really?" the Emperor said. "I had no idea there were so many potential converts."

"How can it be otherwise, Lord?" Baseeker said. "For is it not written in our holy scriptures that soon your worshippers will outnumber the stars in the heavens? And that they will praise your name as the one true God of us all?"

Even the Emperor was embarrassed by this. He coughed into a closed fist. "Uh . . . Yes. The way you put it . . . I suppose it does make sense."

"We only lack funds, Lord," Baseeker said, "to put this program fully into motion."

The Emperor frowned. "I've already supplied a sufficiency of funds. Have I not?"

"Oh, but you have, Lord," Baseeker backpedaled. "And in my opinion, this has been an unfair—bordering on blasphemous—burden. In my view, those who benefit most should bear the cost. Your humble subjects, Lord, should be the ones to pay.

"I do not think it seemly for a living god to pay for his own temples. But, we—your faithful subjects—have been denied this small pleasure, Lord. And it is the fault of our political leaders, I fear. They're too busy lining their own pockets instead."

"Very well put," the Emperor said. "And refreshingly so."

He turned to Poyndex. "I'm getting tired of those penny-pinchers in the Parliament. It's time for them to put their credits where their mouths are. Get together with Avri and work up some kind of funding bill. A subject so loyal as this woman shouldn't have to go begging for funds for such a worthy proposal."

"Yes, Your Highness. I'll do it immediately."

The Emperor shifted back to Baseeker. "I have one request."

"Anything, Lord."

"I'd like you to sift through the membership. Ferret out the most ardent believers."

"We would all lay our lives down for you, Lord."

"Yes . . . But some are always going to be more willing than others. You know the type I mean."

Baseeker nodded. The word "fanatic" was the unspoken answer.

"I want them organized into a core group. I have some of special training in mind for them. Training, Poyndex's people can supply."

"Yes, Lord."

"They are to hold themselves ready. Until they hear from me. Then they are to act instantly, and without question."

"Yes, Lord. These . . . missions . . . you have in mind? I assume they will be dangerous?"

"Yes. Possibly even suicidal."

Baseeker smiled. "I know just the type of individual we'll need," she said, rat teeth snipping off each word.

Poyndex shuddered. There was nothing new about using religious fanatics as assassins. But the image of a wild-eyed cultist waving a bloody knife was decidedly unsettling. He wiped the image away. As frightening as the idea was, he could not deny its merit.

"Fine. We have an understanding, then," the Emperor said, winding things up. "Now . . . if you'll forgive me . . ."

Baseeker leaped to her feet. "Certainly, Lord. And thank you so much for gracing me with these precious moments of your time."

She dropped to her knees again and bounced her head on

the floor three times. "Praise thy name, Lord. Praise, thy name . . ."

And she was gone.

The Emperor turned to Poyndex with a huge smile. "Amazing. They really *do* believe I'm a god."

"No doubt about it, Your Majesty," Poyndex said. His survival instinct, however, kept him from smiling back. "Their beliefs may be childlike . . . but they certainly are sincere."

The Eternal Emperor looked at the door Baseeker had just exited. "Out of the mouths of babes," he murmured.

The mood broke and the Emperor slid a bottle of Scotch from his desk. He briskly poured a drink. And as briskly downed it.

"Now. From the sublime to pure damned foolishness," the Emperor said. "I have a complaint from my chamberlain involving you."

Poyndex lifted a brow. "Yes, Your Highness?"

"Apparently those honors I asked you to process have yet to reach his desk. And he has an awards ceremony to prepare for. A ceremony, I might add, scheduled for less than two weeks from now."

"I am so very sorry, sir," Poyndex said at his most humble. "It's my fault. And I have no excuses for it."

"Damned straight," the Eternal Emperor snorted. "For crying out loud, Poyndex, I know and you know these things are meaningless. But medals and honors are good public relations. Especially in these times."

"Yes, Your Highness. I'm sorry, Your Highness. I'll get on it right away."

"Never mind," the Emperor said. "Send the list to me. I'll deal with it." He shook his head. "Might as well. It seems like I have to do everything *else* myself."

"Yes, sir."

The Emperor drank more Scotch, his irritation waning. "I suppose you do have your hands full at the moment," he said.

"It's still no excuse, sir. But thank you."

"Don't thank me yet," the Emperor said. "Because I have another rather large item for your plate."

"Yes, sir?"

"I've been thinking about our problem with Sten. He's been doing us a great deal of damage. But only because he's the one with the momentum. And while we're still coming up to speed, he can continue to hit us at will. Build up his image as a bold hero of the masses and all that rot."

"He's bound to falter soon, sir," Poyndex said.

"I don't like depending on luck or another being's mistakes," the Emperor said. "We need to grab the march now. Put so much pressure on him he won't know which way is up."

"I don't mean to be negative, sir," Poyndex said, "but we've already stretched our forces to the limit. And then some. At this point, even our reserve units are strapped."

"Strap them some more," the Emperor said.

"But . . . if there should be some emergency, sir . . ."

The Emperor's eyes blazed. "Clot that! Sten's been surprising us at every turn. Hitting us from every angle. My pet news stations, to AM2 depots, to the financial market."

Poyndex puzzled. "The financial market? I assumed the economy was merely suffering because of the crisis. What could Sten have—"

The Emperor gave him a scornful look. "Don't be a fool. That had all the marks of a guerrilla action. Nothing natural about it. No. It was Sten's doing. Or one of his people."

"I see . . . Your Majesty," Poyndex said haltingly, not really seeing.

The Emperor snorted, frustrated. "Now get this through that thick skull of yours, Poyndex. This *is* the emergency. And if we don't put this fire out soon, we're going to be in even deeper drakh. Do I make myself clear?"

"Yes, sir."

"Good. Now, take a look at this." The Emperor moved aside the bottle of Scotch and spread out a map of his empire. Poyndex bent over it, noting the many circles, crosses, and arrows the Emperor had scrawled.

"These are the areas I think are the most vulnerable," the Emperor said, jabbing here and here and here. "The most likely places for him to hit next. We can cover if we move the Fifth Guard from Solfi . . . then shift the fleet at Bordbuch . . ."

Poyndex watched in amazement as the Eternal Emperor jabbed at the map, rejiggering his forces.

And every time his finger touched paper, hundreds of ships and thousands of soldiers were hurled across the stars.

In pursuit of a single man.

Much later, secure in his own small kingdom in Arundel Castle, Poyndex reflected on the state of the Empire.

He touched a sensor at his desk and the mural on the far wall of the command center shattered, and was replaced by an electronic version of the map the Emperor had shown him: the situation board. Crisis lights winking.

Poyndex scanned the bad news. Food riots. Rolling blackouts. Wildcat strikes. His eyes moved on. Money markets in disarray. Commodities seesawing. Panicked corporate reports. Appeal after appeal for more AM2.

The bad news wasn't limited to the civilian sector. Sten's attacks against the Empire were indicated all over the board. As were the declarations of war or independence from many of the Emperor's former allies.

Dead agents, blown missions, and other intelligence failures were also added to the Empire's burden.

A normal being might have despaired. Poyndex was far from normal. In each failure he saw opportunity. In each disaster, a hidden treasure trove.

Poyndex had learned much from the Eternal Emperor in a very short time. Success required perspective . . . and patience.

In this case the long view was Poyndex's—not the Emperor's.

As his black-uniformed aides hustled about the enormous

room, Poyndex once again weighed the odds. And once again he came to the conclusion that the Emperor was wrong. He was taking the threat of Sten far too seriously.

In fact, it was Poyndex's view that Sten was actually being propped up by the Emperor's attention. His antics would be seen as just that if he was officially ignored. But the more the Emperor ranted and raved and flung about ships and troops, the more attractive a figure Sten became to the Emperor's enemies.

All data suggested that the dice were loaded against Sten. His forces were puny and his resources slim, when compared to the juggernaut that was the Empire.

Sten could not afford one mistake. The Emperor could afford many.

For some reason the Emperor couldn't see this. He was completely obsessed with Sten. Very little else was getting his attention.

A large blind spot.

A small smile began to grow on Poyndex's lips. He couldn't help feeling clever for encouraging the Emperor's obsession. And slipping around that blind spot.

He'd warned the Emperor of this and that. But only to protect himself—if things went wrong. Meanwhile, he'd successfully isolated the Emperor from the outside world, moving in his own people.

The Gurkhas were the last of the old guard to go.

Now, the Emperor was totally dependent on him. It was Poyndex who had chosen Zoran's successor. Poyndex who controlled all people permitted in the Emperor's presence. And it was Poyndex who encouraged the Emperor in his madness whenever possible.

As a matter of fact, he had become so indispensable to the Emperor that he'd deliberately started making a few mistakes. Such as the mishandling of the honors-banquet nonsense.

The Emperor might be mad. But he was certainly no fool. He knew as well as Poyndex that there was nothing so dangerous as an indispensable man.

So Poyndex had to foul up once in a while. Just enough so the Emperor wouldn't resent him.

He looked up at the situation board. Not at the bad news. But at the sheer expanse of the Empire.

An Empire that in some ways bent to *his* will.

Not the Emperor's.

And as each day passed—and the Emperor deteriorated—Poyndex's influence grew.

He did not make the mistake of ever seeing himself as Emperor. At least not very often.

During the time of the privy council, Poyndex had viewed firsthand what happened to the Empire when there was no figurehead to give it form.

No. The Emperor was a necessity. At least his presence was. His legend.

There was only one large flaw. Poyndex would eventually grow old.

Weaken.

And die.

But the Emperor was immortal.

What if Poyndex could some how learn that secret?

What if he could live . . . forever?

Poyndex brushed the sensor and the situation board became a mural again.

There were more possibilities here than even Poyndex could ever dream of.

And Poyndex was a practiced dreamer.

CHAPTER SIXTEEN

"I DON'T KNOW how they discovered your whereabouts," Sr Ecu said. His holo image was shadowed on the edges from the strength of the scrambler.

"The point is, they're on their way to the Lupus Cluster right now. A 260-being delegation. Headed by the three top leaders of the Zaginows."

"Speaking as one trained diplomat to another," Sten said, "this is not what I call clottin' wonderful. I'm going to have to move our base of operations. Fast."

"I think it would be a mistake not to meet with them," Sr Ecu said, his tail agitating the Seilichi atmosphere. The flick sent him drifting across the chamber.

"I know it's dangerous to assume innocent intent." Another flick, and Sr Ecu's body steadied. "However . . . if the Zaginows do join with us . . . it will be a major blow against the Emperor. Think of it. An *entire* region—representing hundreds of clusters—defecting to our side. The propaganda value would easily equal any military venture you might be considering."

Sten tapped a nervous foot against the cold, stone floor of the Bhor com room. "I know. I know. But I still can't get past the frightening little detail that somehow the Zaginows not only connected us, but also figured out where I'm holed up."

"I was as startled as you," Sr Ecu said, "when they arrived at my front door, demanding to meet with you. My first assumption was there had been a leak. The second was the

Manabi were doomed. I had visions of an Imperial planet-buster in our immediate future.

"But after speaking with them, running all the progs through my techs, combined with my personal knowledge of the Zaginows—I see very little possibility of a trap."

"It's the *little* possibility that scares me," Sten said. "Also a largish 'howcome' . . . In other words, if they want to sign on with the revolution . . . how come they didn't do so with you? Why is it so important they have a face-to-face with me?"

"Because the Zaginows are not entirely convinced," Sr Ecu said. "They're only sure we share the same enemy. They're *not* sure we have the means to do something about said enemy."

Sr Ecu drifted closer to the camera lens. "It's up to you, Sten. They're already leaning heavily in our direction. Otherwise they wouldn't be taking such a risk."

"So, what you are advising," Sten said, "is a little diplomatic razzle-dazzle so we can reel them the rest of the way in."

"Razzle-dazzle? I don't understand this term."

"A big show."

"Oh. Very descriptive. Yes. That's precisely what I advise. A very big show."

Sten hesitated. "Did you ask how they figured it out?"

"Yes. They said they added one plus one to a great deal of wishful thinking. They used the same nonlogic to pinpoint you in the Bhor worlds. Although, I certainly didn't confirm their belief. Actually, the Zaginows didn't even ask. When they left, they just kindly asked me to notify you they were on the way."

Sten sighed. "Okay. I'll do it. What the clot? If we're wrong, I'll be too damned dead to count how many ways I was played the fool."

"You won't be alone, Sten," Sr Ecu said. Dry. "The afterlife, it is rumored, is mostly composed of fools like us."

"I feel a lot better already," Sten said with a grimace. "Thanks."

"You're quite welcome."

Sr Ecu's image was gone.

Sten began pacing to work out his thoughts. But his mind was already crammed with so many odd details of the complex war he was waging against the Emperor that he soon found himself spinning about his own fundament.

He needed advice. Badly.

"So, Sr Ecu claims it was mostly luck that led them to us?" Rykor said.

"That pretty well sums it up," Sten said.

"Ah dinnae believe i' luck," Alex said. " 'Cept when i's m' own wee hide thae's beggin' f'r it."

"Of course there's luck," Otho insisted. "The Bhor know it well. It comes in three varieties. Blind, dumb, and bad."

"We've been in kitchens," Marr said, "where we've encountered all three."

"And in one dinner rush as well," Senn said.

"I have to accept Sr Ecu's word for it," Sten said. "But I still think it was a helluva gamble for the Zaginows to take. What if they were wrong? They might as well have flung themselves into the Emperor's arms and shouted, 'Take me, I'm a traitor.'"

"Very kinky," Marr said. "I like it."

"Shush. We're being serious, here," Senn said.

"So was I, dear." He patted Senn's knee. "I'll explain it to you some night."

"When you really think about it," Rykor said, easing her bulk in the tank, "their actions make an odd sort of sense."

"Good," Sten said. "I've been short that lately. Spell it out for me. And don't use any big words. Like 'the' or 'and.'"

"I believe it's the nature of the Zaginows, Sten," Rykor said. "They are all economic refugees. Refugees have always been willing to take great risks for tenuous gain. When you have very little, the act of gambling sometimes makes you feel empowered. As if you have finally taken control of your own fate."

Sten nodded. Good sense, indeed. He had dealt with the Zaginow region before. Almost all of the many billions of beings inhabiting the area were descendants of poor working stock—human and ET alike—who had followed scarce work opportunities across the Empire. The slightest tilt in the economy impoverished them.

Like Sten's own family, they had little but dreams and strong backs to sustain them. Some ended up in slave factories like Vulcan. The lucky ones—that word, again!—drifted into the jumble of star clusters that made up the Zaginows. There the wandering ended. The refugees took root.

A strange sort of unity and common view persisted in the Zaginows. Although there was no dominant species, or race, folks were considered folks. Whether they were black, white, or green. Solid-formed, or jellied. Skin or scales.

Sten remembered the enormous gamble his father had taken in a get-rich-quick scheme involving Xypaca fights. The fact that he'd promptly lost—adding years to his work contract—had not dissuaded him from further risk. If anything, it only made his father more willing to gamble everything—anything—to escape the grind of Vulcan.

Yeah. He understood.

"P'raps i's a gamble, wee Sten," Alex said, "but thae dinnae hae much t' lose, y' ken."

This was also true. Shortly before the debacle in the Altaics, the Emperor had sent Sten to the Zaginows to do some basic diplomatic stroking. The mission had been a success, he supposed. At least he'd been able to patch some kind of agreement together without *too* much lying.

"When I saw them last," Sten said, "they were in a helluva mess. Not of their making. The Zaginows had a fairly self-sufficient and prosperous region before the Tahn war.

"They had a healthy agricultural base. Some heavy industry. Mining. Big population to do the work. And mostly well-educated."

Otho's heavy brow beetled forward. "I was unaware of

that background," he said. "I thought the Zaginows were known for their weapons industry."

"Like I said . . . that was before the Tahn war. Then old Tanz Sullamora showed up with the Emperor's money and the Emperor's clout. Before you knew it, he'd transformed the entire region into an immense defense industry."

"Then . . . when the war was over . . ."

"Ah ha," Alex said. "Th' bad luck Ah was mentionin'."

"You can't eat guns," Marr said.

"Exactly. The factories were idled and their economy collapsed."

"But . . . my mother's beard . . . Why didn't they change back?"

"It wasn't possible," Sten said. "Not without a major investment for retooling and so forth. When the money dried up, the privy council couldn't dump them off the sleigh fast enough.

"Now I can see it was even worse for them when the Emperor came back. Sure, he strung them along. Sending me, for instance. But it was easier—and cheaper—to cut them loose. And let them die quietly."

"Thae're no goin't quiet int' th' night noo," Alex said.

"Remember," Rykor warned, "Sr Ecu said this was far from a sure thing. We still have some convincing to do."

Sten nodded. "He said put on a show. A big show. Trouble is, when you look around, there isn't much to boast about. We don't have legions of troops to inspect or fleets to do flybys. Anyone with half a brain can see the Emperor only has to breathe a gentle puff and we'd be blown away."

Senn scrambled off his chair and thumped to the floor. "No difficulty at all," he said. "First off, they're here to see *you*. Not troops and fleets."

Marr dropped to the floor beside his lover. "The Emperor has all the troops and fleets that exist," he said, "Our friends *know* what that got them. A great big screwing."

"Without even a kiss first," Senn said.

Rykor heaved in her tank, water sloshing against the side.

"The furry ones are making several major points," she said to Sten. "I would listen if I were you."

"I'm listening, dammit." Sten said. He looked down at the odd little pair. "What do you have in mind?"

"If we want them to climb into bed with us," Marr said, "we're going to have to set the mood."

"In other words, a little foreplay." Senn giggled. "Which has been sadly lacking in their love lives."

"And you, Sten dear, are going to help us," Marr said.

"Me? How?"

"It's time, O Great Leader of the Revolution, to give your gray cells a rest," Senn said.

"You need to climb down from those lofty heights of leadership," Marr said in mock high drama, "and mingle with common folk."

Sten eyed them suspiciously. "Doing what?"

"Oh. Fetching and carrying," Marr said.

Senn giggled. "And scrubbing pots."

"Now, why would I volunteer to do something like that?" Sten said.

"Because in this case, Sten, dear," Marr said, "diplomacy begins in the kitchen."

"We're going to throw a little dinner party," Senn elaborated. "For two hundred and sixty plus lovelorn beings."

"By the time we're through with the Zaginows," Marr said, "they'll be down on their knees begging for your hand in matrimony."

"Or, at least in lust," Senn said.

Sten wanted to object. Not to the idea of a dinner party. That was wonderful—especially with the Empire's greatest caterers staging it. But much as he'd like to learn some of their secrets, he just wasn't into scrubbing pots to earn a look.

Then he saw the grin on Kilgour's face. Otho practically had a paw stuffed into his mouth to keep from laughing. Rykor was studiously avoiding looking at him, but the violent trembling of her girth gave her away.

Sten sighed. "Well, what are we waiting for? Let's get started."

Off he marched. Sten. The Most Wanted Being in the Empire. AKA Hero of the Revolution.

Now promoted to Chief Pot Scrubber of the Cause.

Sten wiped chicken gore on his apron and took the message from the runner. He scanned it.

"It's official," he said. "The Zaginows will be here tomorrow night."

Senn fretted. "Not much time."

"It'll do, Senn, dear," Marr soothed. "Otho's pantry is far better stocked than I imagined. We shouldn't have to cheat *too* much."

Sten hoisted a cleaver and resumed whacking chicken into parts. "Not that I doubt your abilities," he said, "but I don't see how you plan a menu for something like this."

"Well . . . We want them to be *impressed*," Marr said. "So the dinner should reflect on your success. However, we want to do business with these people . . ."

A claw taloned out of the exquisite softness of Marr's fur. It speared a tomato and plunged it into boiling water. "We want them to *like* us. We don't want them to think we believe we're better than they are, for heaven's sakes."

Marr lifted the tomato from its hot bath—spun it toward the opposite paw. Where another claw whisked away the skin. Snip. Slide. Just like that. Sten's jaw dropped.

On automatic, Marr speared another tomato and repeated the process. And another tomato was peeled. Snip. Slide. Just like that. "Haute cuisine is definitely out, out, out," he said.

"It wouldn't do," Senn agreed. "Not at all." His wickedly sharp claws were blazing through a stack of yellow onions. Skinning and chopping so deftly, Sten didn't feel the slightest sting in his eyes.

"We've decided on native dishes," Marr said. "Food one might imagine came from an ordinary being's kitchen. But still a little exotic and daring because it *is* from someplace else."

"Also, it gives us a theme," Senn said, disposing of another onion. "A Flag of All Nations sort of theme. It fits with the jumble of beings that make up the Zaginows."

"We *like* themes," Marr said.

Sten was only half-listening. He was busy gaping at the Milchens' skills. They were living kitchen machines. Full of all kinds of little tricks.

"Great. Great. Themes and all," Sten said. "But, before you go any further, I have to ask you a question."

"Question away, dear," Marr said, thunking down the last peeled tomato.

"I can't do onions like Senn . . ." he said, pointing at the furry little whirlwind, chopping up big mounds of the stuff. "I'm not built for it. But that trick with the tomatoes . . . Every time I have to peel tomatoes, I mutilate the suckers. One pound of peel for every ounce of tomato."

"Poor thing," Marr said.

"You *only* have to dip them in boiling water," Senn said in a small—I really, really, don't think you're stupid—voice.

"And he's the leader of us all," Marr said.

"I did read about it, *once*," Sten said, weak. "But I never got around to testing it out."

"There, there, dear," Senn said. "Of course you didn't."

The kitchen was filled with the delicious odor of tomatoes, garlic, and onions sizzling in olive oil. Marr tasted, adjusted the paprika, stirred some more, then nodded to Senn, who poured in fresh chicken stock.

Marr clamped a lid on the pot and set it to simmer. "When dinner is served," he told Sten, "you might want to go easy on the soup."

Sten eyed the big pot. "Sure looks like enough to go around to me."

Senn laughed. "Oh, there's plenty, all right. But this is a special recipe. A guaranteed first-course tension-breaker. For the guests, that is. Not the host. Hosts should beware of this dish."

"You see," Marr elaborated, "after we strain it through a sieve, we're going to stir in some flour and sour cream. Just enough to make it smooth.

"Then . . . a moment before we serve it . . . we add vodka. Lots of vodka! And . . . voilà," Senn said. "We give you . . . Hungarian tomato vodka soup! It's quite potent, too."

"A tongue loosener, huh?" Sten said, dry. "Did you guys ever consider a career as Mantis interrogators?"

"Amateurs," Senn sniffed.

"No challenge at all," Marr said.

"After we get the Zaginow delegation nice and soothed," Senn said, "we need to work on their courage." He was dusting chunks of meat with flour, spiked with lots of salt and pepper.

Marr was assembling chopped-up onions, bell peppers, and crushed garlic. "Build them up for a firm commitment," he said.

Senn giggled. "So to speak."

"Don't be dirty," Marr said, putting on a pan doused with olive oil to heat.

"I can't help it," Senn said, the giggles building. "My mind just *works* that way. Especially when we're cooking mountain oysters."

Sten frowned. He picked up a chunk of the floured meat. Sniffed it. "Don't smell like oysters to me."

"They're calf testicles, dear," Marr explained. "Cut from the little dickens before they're old enough to know what's missing."

"We're going to do them Basque style," Senn said. "The image is *so* sexy. Muscular brutes with large libidos."

"Makes you want to fry balls all day," Marr said.

Sten looked at the meat he held in his hand. "Sorry, boys," he said. "I hope you know they went for a good cause."

"Now, we need to engage their minds," Marr said.

Sten looked doubtfully at the large heap of bird parts he'd

carved up with his cleaver. "Brain power through a clottin' chicken? You've gotta be kidding."

"Stupid animals, yes," Senn said. "But they're so *willing*. Especially plucked and dressed out. See how patiently they await their marinade?"

"Like the Zaginows?" Sten guessed.

"Excellent, Sten, dear. You're beginning to get the idea," Marr said. "At this point we should have our new friends primed and ready for fresh approaches . . . Alert them through their taste buds there are endless possibilities once an alliance has been achieved."

"Don't be so stuffy," Senn said. He waved a spice-dusted paw at Sten. "Ignore him. The dish *is* called jerk chicken, after all," he said.

"I like it . . . mon," Sten said.

Marr set down the bunch of scallions he was dicing up. "You've heard of it?" He seemed disappointed.

"From Jamaica, right?" Sten said. "One of the old Earth islands. A place where they smoke rope fibers and drink silly fruit drinks with little parasols on top."

Marr sighed. "Aren't we running out of clean pots yet?"

"Not a chance," Sten said. "I've only heard of jerk chicken. I'm not moving until I see how this is done."

"In a kitchen," Marr said, "only the chef is permitted to be clever. Pot washers laugh at Chef's cunning jokes. Pot washers peel potatoes. Pot washers are in a constant state of awe at Chef's genius. Pot washers scrape slime from floors. Pot washers duck a lot when sharp objects are thrown at them when they make poor Chef mad. These are only some of the things pot washers do."

Marr sniffed. "What they don't do, is be clever. Pot washers are *never*, *ever* clever."

"I promise it'll never happen again," Sten said.

"He really wasn't *that* clever," Senn said.

"Very well," Marr said. "*It* can stay. But only if *It* promises to button *Its* lip."

"Mmmmph," Sten grunted, pointed at his zipped lip.

"Actually, this is a dish even a pot washer could master the first time," Marr said. "It only tastes complex."

He touched a switch under the chopping board and a metal processor revolved up. Pawfuls of chopped hot pepper and scallions went into the processor, along with a few bay leaves, some grated ginger, and diced garlic.

"Now the allspice," Marr said. "That's the anchor. You use about five tablespoons for every kilo of meat. Along with one teaspoon each of nutmeg, cinnamon, salt, and pepper."

He dumped the spices into the processor and hit the button. As it whirred, he slowly poured in oil.

"Peanut oil," Marr said. "Just enough for it all to stick together."

In two beats it was done. Sten peered at the goo.

"Another thing pot washers get to do," Marr said, "is smear goo over chicken."

"This is true. Chefs never smear goo," Senn said. "Especially when they're furry."

Sten, the comparatively hairless pot washer, began spreading the marinade over the chicken. Actually, he didn't really mind. It smelled wonderful. His mouth watered imagining what it was all going to taste like when Marr and Senn tonged the chicken off the barbecue.

In the corner, he could hear Marr and Senn arguing over the relative merits of pine nuts in Lebanese pilaf. All about him were the warm smells of a dozen dishes bubbling and simmering.

He felt relaxed . . . clear-minded.

On the whole, he thought, he'd much rather be a pot washer than a Hero of the Revolution.

Marr and Senn observed Sten's beaming face as he slathered marinade over chicken.

"Do you think he's ready?" Marr whispered.

"Absolutely," Senn said. "I don't like to pat myself on the back, but I think this is one the best jobs we've ever done."

"Beings don't realize," Marr said, "that the first—and only—

real secret of a dinner party is getting the host prepared first."

"A little kitchen magic," Senn said. "It works every time."

The Zaginow leader forked one more bite from the creamy pastry dish in front of her. She looked at it . . . as if not believing her body was capable of handling still more. The fork continued its journey and the pastry disappeared into her mouth.

She closed her eyes. Ebony features a portrait of bliss. Tasting. Mmmmm.

Her eyes snapped open to find Sten grinning at her.

"Oh, burp," she said. "Oh, heaven. But, I *just* couldn't eat anymore."

"I think the chefs will forgive you, Ms Sowazi, if you resign the field of battle," Sten said. "You've certainly given it your best."

He glanced around the banquet room. Marr and Senn had turned the drafty Bhor hall into a wonder of festooned flowers and subtle lights.

The other guests were as dazzled and replete as Sowazi.

For two hours, Marr and Senn had commanded convoy after convoy of deliciousness through the room. Whether the dish was meant for a human or an ET, each was greeted and devoured with great enthusiasm.

Beings had their elbows—or equivalent parts—on the tables now. Chatting warmly away with Sten's colleagues as if they were all long-lost friends.

As a capper, Marr and Senn had printed up souvenir menus for each member of the Zaginow delegation.

"We always do it," Marr said. "Beings like to show the folks at home what a good time they had. It's wonderful advertising for us, as well."

"Not 'advertising,' dear," Senn said. "Not in this case, at any rate. Remember, we're revolutionaries now. The military term is 'propaganda'."

"Same thing," Marr sniffed.

"True. But 'propaganda' is much more romantic."

Sten had to admit that the souvenir menus fit the bill perfectly as propaganda.

On the back was a picture of himself, flanked by the master caterers, Marr and Senn. On the front, Senn got his theme: "A FEAST FOR ALL BEINGS."

This was the menu for the humans:

SOUP
Hungarian Tomato Vodka
Miso Saki Shrimp

SALAD
Cambodian Raw Fish
Tomato Cucumber Raita

APPETIZERS
Basque Mountain Oysters
Russian Blinis and Caviar
Armenian Stuffed Mushrooms

ENTREES
Jamaican Jerk Chicken
Moroccan Roast Lamb
Broiled Salmon Steaks
Mesquite Broiled Vegetable Kabob

SIDE DISHES
Lebanese Rice Pilaf
Rosemary Potatoes
Cuban Black Beans & Rice

DESSERT
New York Style Cheesecake
Swedish Pancakes With Lingonberries

The items listed on the menus for the ETs were equally impressive.

Sten saw Marr peering from a doorway. He spotted Sten and waved. It was time.

Sten turned to Sowazi. "I think we're being called for coffee and brandy," he said.

She laughed, deep and pleasurable. "Cigars, too?"

"Cigars, too," Sten promised.

"Lead on, Sr Sten."

As he rose to do her bidding, Sten made a furtive thumbs-up motion to Marr. Everything was going according to plan.

"Here's our position," Moshi-Kamal said. He was the second member of the troika that ruled the Zaginows. "We're willing to come on board. But we need some assurances."

"I can't give you any," Sten said. "Remember, I started the conversation by saying the odds are decidedly against us. If you join us . . . it may be an act of suicide."

"But your own behavior does not bear that statement out, Sr Sten." This was from Truiz, the ET member of the troika. "You fight well. Logically. Certainly not like a suicidal being. You also have had many successes."

"They look good," Sten said, "but they're not near enough. The Emperor has had a lot of bad days. He can afford to. If I have *one* . . . it's over."

"Why are you being so candid?" Sowazi wondered. "I would think you'd be pointing up the positive. The fleets you command. The victories. The growing number of allies."

She waved at the cozy paneled den Marr and Senn had converted an old weapons room into for this conversation. "You sit here at ease, dining luxuriously, thumbing your nose at the Emperor and his hellhounds. Why aren't you boasting of these things to win us to your side?"

"I could," Sten agreed. "But the trouble is . . . Once I'd won you over, I wouldn't be able to count on you. When something terrible happened—and I promise you it will—you'd see that I'd lied. And desert me.

"There can be no mistake about this," Sten said. "This is a fight to the finish. The Emperor will never give us quarter. We lose—we die."

"I can understand this," Truiz said. The little tendrils wriggling beneath her eyes were red with frustration. "But the picture you paint is so bleak. Give us some hope."

Sten leaned forward. "Right now, I have the Emperor's forces strung across the map. What I don't have pinned down . . . I have chasing its own tail. But I can only keep this going for a little longer.

"I need two things right now. Reserves. And an opening. Without the first, it will be difficult to support the other."

"Do you think you will get this opening?" Moshi-Kamal asked.

Sten paused, as if giving serious thought. Then he nodded. "Without a doubt," he lied. "No matter how we read the progs, they keep on coming up with the same thing. The thrust of the fight is with us. Sooner or later, we're going to have a break-through."

"Then we want to be there," Sowazi said. "This . . . this . . . *being* has become unbearable."

"He is forcing us to become one of his dominions," Moshi-Kamal said. "Putting us under his heel. The beings of the Zaginows have long memories. We all come from working people. The class the bosses put in dark holes full of sharp machinery."

"This is true," Truiz said. "All of our ancestors fled from some despot or other. We can't condemn ourselves to the lives they escaped."

"Did you know," Sowazi hissed, "that he is even putting himself up as a god? He has these . . . these . . . *beings* bounding about proclaiming him a holy thing. They want to put temples up to him in our cities. It's . . . filthy!"

It wasn't necessary for Sten to comment. Instead, he looked from one to the other.

"Then you'll join us . . . even without assurances?"

"Even without assurances," Moshi-Kamal said. "We will join you."

"And we might also be able to solve your first problem," Sowazi said.

"How, so?"

"Why, the reserve forces," Truiz said. "We assume you have more beings at your disposal than ships and weapons?"

"You assumed right," Sten said.

"I'm sure you are aware that we have thousands of factories—forced on us by the Eternal Emperor—designed and tooled to build those things."

"I knew that," Sten said. "But I also know they've been shut down for some time. I figured most of the machinery had either rusted or been sold for scrap."

"Only a few," Moshi-Kamal said. "Mostly, they are in excellent condition. It's one of the benefits and curses of the Zaginows. We can't stand to see good machinery go to ruin."

"People didn't have any work to go to," Sowazi explained. "But they kept the factories up just the same."

"Are you trying to say that you've got a turnkey operation?" Sten asked. "That all you have to do is give the word and you can start building ships and weapons again?"

The little tendrils below Truiz's eyes wriggled with pleasure. "We can be up and running in one E-week," she said. "Then bring on your troops."

Now all Sten needed was the opening.

The pale, slender Grb'chev towered over Cind. The splash of red across the smooth skull throbbed with curiosity. "Your request is most unusual," he said. "Few humans have ever come to this place."

Cind looked about the small building whose mirrored walls reflected the sprawling gardens surrounding it. "I can't imagine why," she said, "it's such a lovely place."

The Grb'chev touched a switch and the door slid open.

He escorted her inside. "Sr Kyes had a love for beauty," he said. "Especially understated beauty."

Cind's smile was humble. "I've learned about that side of Sr Kyes in my studies," she said, "He was quite a complex being. Even for a Grb'chev."

"Even for a Grb'chev," her escort agreed. "But this leads me back to my first remark. In our culture, Sr Kyes is a hero. His intelligence, inventiveness, and business acumen have already taken on mythlike characteristics.

"We've converted his old headquarters into a museum. A shrine, for some." Cind and her escort were pacing through the museum's cheery foyer. "But I would think only some-one of our culture would appreciate Sr Kyes."

"Then I apologize for my species," Cind said. "After all, no one would argue that the Grb'chev are easily among the most intelligent beings in the Empire."

"This is true," her escort said. There was no modesty nec-essary.

"And Sr Kyes was arguably the most intelligent Grb'chev in this age," Cind said.

"Some say, of all time," the escort said.

"Then, how could any reasonable being—especially a stu-dent such as myself—not want to see firsthand how Sr Kyes lived and worked?"

"You are a very bright young woman," her escort said. Another switch brought another door open. They stepped into the library. Across the way, a figure worked at a monitor. A human.

"This is a most fortunate day for you and your research," her escort said as he spied the figure. "As I said before, only a few humans share your interest in Sr Kyes. One of them has a position on the museum's staff. And to my surprise, your visit happily coincides with his shift day." Her escort tapped the figure on a shoulder.

The man turned. An expectant smile on his face.

"Ms Cind, allow me to introduce you to one of our senior researchers . . . Sr Lagguth."

Lagguth rose, and put out a hand. They shook. "Pleased to meet you," he said. "It is a pleasure I almost missed. This is my normal rest day. But one of my colleagues called in ill."

"A happy coincidence," the escort said.

"Yes. A happy coincidence," Cind echoed, looking her quarry up and down.

It was no coincidence at all. And for Lagguth, it certainly wasn't going to be happy.

Lagguth had suffered through countless nights of torment, envisioning the hard-faced beings who would come to get him. They were always large. Always dressed in black. Sometimes they came with drawn guns. Sometimes with bloody fangs. But they always said the same thing: "You know too much, Lagguth. And for this, you must die."

The woman confronting him now was that nightmare, but in a disarmingly soft package. She had no visible weapon. And small, bright teeth instead of fangs.

"You know too much, Lagguth," Cind said. "And if you don't help me . . . they'll kill you for it."

"I was just a functionary," Lagguth groaned.

"I wouldn't call being the head of the privy council's AM2 bureau a mere functionary," Cind scoffed.

"I had no power. No authority. I followed orders. That's all. I did nothing to harm anyone!"

"Your very presence meant you conspired with the Emperor's assassins," Cind said. "As for authority . . . Thousands of beings whose loved ones died of cold or star-vation from lack of fuel might want to have a word with you for the authority you *did* exercise."

There was nothing Lagguth could say. He bowed his head.

"So. Speak to me, Lagguth. Or I'll drop the word. And either the Emperor's goons will get you, or the mob. I almost feel sorry for you, you poor excuse for a life-form."

"You'll speak up for me?" Lagguth begged. "You'll tell Sr Sten I cooperated?"

Cind let her voice soften. "Yes. I'll speak up for you." Then—cracking the whip: "Now. *Tell* me, Lagguth! Tell me everything!"

Lagguth talked. He told her about the strange program he'd set up for Sr Kyes. Its ostensible purpose was to search for where the Emperor hid his AM2. This was what Kyes told his fellow members of the privy council, at least.

"But I got the idea he really wasn't all that interested in AM2. His search was much deeper than that. Highly personal."

"In what way?" Cind asked.

"Well, we did gather together everything that was known about AM2. From composition, to the few known courses AM2 shipments followed before they so mysteriously stopped. We fed it into this marvel of a computer he'd developed."

He pointed to a small terminal in one corner of the library. "That's linked to it," he said. "It's still functional. But, sadly, it can only be one of a kind. I doubt any being in several lifetimes would ever be able to decipher the program he created to run it."

Cind prodded him away from reveries of Kyes's genius. "Go on. I don't have much time."

"Yes. As I said, we fed in all that data on AM2. But we also fed in everything that was known about the Emperor. We had help on this from Sr Poyndex."

Cind's eyes widened. "Poyndex. He was in on this?"

"Absolutely," Lagguth said. "He got something on Kyes. I don't know what. But, Kyes turned that knowledge back on him. Pulled him into our circle. It was he who made Poyndex a member of the privy council. So, obviously some kind of a bargain was made."

"Obviously," Cind said. The detail of the deal was interesting, but she doubted it was of any use. "Okay. So you fed all kinds of raw data into the computer. Then what? What did Kyes learn?"

"I'm not sure," Lagguth said. "But I do know he learned

something. He suddenly became very excited. He was a being, you realize, who rarely showed any kind of emotion. Anyway, he became excited. Ordered the program shut down. And then he left. In a great hurry."

"Where did he go?" Cind wanted to know.

"Again, I'm ignorant. Except that I know he left Prime. For some far place. And when he returned . . . his brain . . . had died."

Cind knew what this meant. The Grb'chev were the only known example of a higher species created by symbiosis. Their bodies—large, handsome things—originated in an exceedingly dimwitted race. Their "brains" were actually the result of a sort of virus that settled into the brute's plentiful sinus passages. And prospered into tremendous intellect.

The curse of the Grb'chev is that the "brain" had a near-absolute lifespan of 126 years. Kyes was one of the few examples on record of a Grb'chev brain that had lived a few years longer. The tragedy was the body lived happily and moronically on for at least another one hundred years.

Cind had seen many examples of this living death shambling through the streets of the Grb'chev's home world. Constant and horrifying reminders of what each member of this species faced.

Cind pointed to the terminal. "Have you tried to learn what Kyes was doing, during those final days?"

Lagguth hesitated. Then he sadly shook his head. "I'm not a very brave person," he said. He croaked laughter. "In case you haven't guessed. I've been frightened every day of my life someone—like you . . . or worse—would find me. And I'd be killed, or brain burned for the little I know.

"And so . . . although I desperately wanted to learn what Kyes was up to . . . I never could bring myself to actually do something about it."

A sound came from behind a door, just to the side of the computer terminal. Cind's hand snaked down to the place where she had hidden her weapon.

"Don't be alarmed," Lagguth said. "He just wants to be fed."

Cind's brow furrowed. "*Who* wants to be fed?"

"Sr Kyes, of course," Lagguth said. "Would you like to meet him?"

"He's here?" Cind was astounded.

"Why not? It's a good enough home for what's left of him as any. Actually, it's a damn fine home. They've put him out to pasture, so to speak. Like one would a fine racing beast. He gets everything he could possibly want. Although, to be frank, he's too stupid to really know what he wants. Sometimes . . . we have to help him with his treats."

Lagguth rose. "I really should go feed him. It's cruel to make him wait."

Cind followed him into the room.

It was a bright and cheery place, filled with toys and decorated in the bright primary colors of childhood. Kyes was perched in a vastly oversized chair, giggling at the large vid monitor. It was showing a kid livie: small things scurrying about, smacking one another.

Kyes saw Lagguth. "Hungry," he said.

"Don't worry. I've got your yummies for you," Lagguth said.

Cind shuddered as she watched Lagguth spoon-feed a being who had once ruled an empire.

Food dribbled from Kyes's mouth. He pointed at Cind. "Who, pretty?"

"A friend come to see you, Sr Kyes," Lagguth said.

Cind came out of her shock and moved to Kyes's side. She took the food from Lagguth. Kyes looked up at her. Eyes wide. Not a clue of intelligence in them. He opened his mouth. Cind fed him. He smacked his lips loudly as he ate. Belched. Then giggled.

"Make funny," he said.

"Very funny," Cind said. "Good boy."

Kyes patted her. "Happy," he said. "Like happy."

"Aren't you always happy?" Cind asked.

Kyes's head bobbed up and down. "Happy . . . Always."

Cind braced herself. Only cruelty could follow. "What if the Emperor comes?" she said. "What if he comes to take you away?"

The innocent thing that had once been Kyes reeled back in horror. "No. Not him. Not take away. Please. Not go other place!"

Cind leaped on it: "What other place?"

"Other place," Kyes moaned. "Bad place. Emperor there. Not happy me."

"Let him be," Lagguth pleaded. "He can't tell you more. Can't you see how frightened he is?"

Kyes had curled into a ball. Sobbing. The huge chair made him seem small and helpless.

Cind did not relent. "What did you find?" she gritted. "What did you find in this bad place?"

"Emperor. I say."

"What else?"

Kyes shrieked at some dim memory. A genetic haunting. "Forever," he cried. "Find forever."

"You see what I mean?" Lagguth said. "It's only nonsense you'll get. He says that all the time when he's frightened. 'Forever.' Over and over again, 'forever.'"

Kyes nodded. "Not happy, forever. Not happy."

Cind patted him. Soothing. Then turned to Lagguth. "Now, I want to see the computer," she said.

As they left the room, Kyes was beginning to recover. He squirmed upright in his seat, dried his eyes, and started tentatively giggling at the little things on the livie screen.

The moonlet was a silent wilderness of destruction. Cind moved through bomb-blasted craters and twisted, melted hulks whose designed functions were barely recognizable.

The sensors on the small device in her hand were winking frantically, as they took in data. Cind scrambled over the surface of the moonlet, pausing here and there to scan wreckage with the device. The facts were fed to the mainframe aboard her orbiting ship. The conclusions were quickly beamed back. Chirping in her helmet com.

So far, they confirmed everything she had found in the data banks of the computer in the Kyes museum.

The moonlet had been an elaborately constructed communications center. A byway on the road to the mystery that led to the Emperor's ultimate hiding place for the AM2.

But, Kyes hadn't come to this desolation with this goal. Cind was sure of that. Instead, he had come to find the Emperor. A being, most others in those days, believed dead. And he'd found him. Here on this planetoid.

She imagined Kyes, driven nearly mad by fear of his impending "death," pleading with the Emperor. Offering anything. Desperately begging him to rescue Kyes.

The gibbering hulk back at the Grb'chev museum was sufficient evidence his pleas had been rejected.

Cind worked the area for some hours. Finally she was done. It was time to tell Sten what she had learned.

The outpost was a place where the paths of two secrets had once intersected.

The first was the secret of AM2.

The second, the Emperor's apparent immortality.

Cind was weary when she messaged for pickup. Not from the work. But from the depressing thought that although she had learned a great deal in this hunt . . . the knowledge didn't necessarily add up.

And she prayed to all the beards of all the mothers of the Bhor, that she wasn't exiting the same door she'd only recently come in.

Haines rattled the papers in her hand, coldly professional. "Once we put his files in order," she said, "it became quite clear what Mahoney believed he had learned about the Eternal Emperor."

"Which was?" Sten waved impatiently at the ex-homicide detective's holo image. It was being beamed from the small Bhor resort he'd stashed her in—along with her husband and Mahoney's treasure trove.

"Don't be in such a hurry," Haines said. "Facts should be given their due."

Sten grimaced. "Sorry."

"First, I'm sending you a psychological profile of the Emperor. Mahoney drew it up as a model. My husband and I confirmed it by our own work. And double-checked with Rykor. It's absolutely dead on. Look it over when you have time."

"I'll take your word," Sten said.

"Next, I'm sending you the matches Mahoney made against that profile. He set the guide against the other times the Emperor allegedly died . . . and then returned, big as life. Each time, it was definitely the same being. There was no possibility of a surgical double. Again . . . we confirmed all Mahoney's data."

Sten groaned. "That resurrection business again. That clottin' Mahoney reached out from his grave and converted you."

"I'm no convert to anything," Haines said. "But if these facts were clues pointing to a murder suspect . . . I'd bust the son of a scrote and lead him with confidence to my prosecuting attorney. Face up to it Sten. It's a clear possibility."

"I'll face that ghost when I see it and touch it myself," Sten said. "Meanwhile . . . where does this get us?"

Haines paused, considering how she was going to put this. "What it gets us, is a far more frightening puzzle. You see, my husband and I took Mahoney's work and punted it one step forward."

"What did you do?"

"We took that profile of the Eternal Emperor—the one we all agree is a perfect match. Updated it and ran it against the man we're all ducking and dodging right now."

"And?" Sten almost didn't want to ask. "It's still the same guy, right?"

"Yeah. It's the same guy. But it isn't. The Emperor's the same overall. But when you put a closer microscope on him, he's *very* different in his behavior."

"Clottin' wonderful," Sten groaned.

"Sorry to dump it into your lap, Sten," Haines said, her voice warming in sympathy. "But, as they say in the livies, 'It's just the facts, ma'am.'"

Sten thanked her, and broke the connection.

He leaned back, letting the information churn around. They settled into this uncomfortable equation: Same but different still equalled different.

The com buzzed. The watch officer said she had Cind on the line. It was important.

As Sten leaned forward to answer, a question tingled at his back brain: If it wasn't the Eternal Emperor . . . who the clot *was* he fighting?

CHAPTER SEVENTEEN

SOLON KENNA STOOD upon the broad speaker's platform, a block of pure white marble tabernacling out from the far wall of the Hall of Parliament. Posed beside him at his handsome best was Tyrenne Walsh. Behind them was a three-story-high portrait of the Eternal Emperor.

Kenna's powerful, polished voice rolled out across the hundreds of assembled politicians: "Distinguished Representatives . . . Loyal Imperial citizens . . . Gentlebeings.

"It is with deep humility that my colleague and I stand before you on this most historic day."

Kenna's voice dipped into an oiled, humble tone. A twitch of a finger signaled the dimwitted Walsh to bow his head.

"The people of Dusable have already enjoyed vast honors from our beloved Emperor," he said.

Kenna's old-pol brain made note there was not one titter

from the group—which represented every nook and cranny of the Empire. Nor was there one whisper he could detect of the recent humiliation his people had suffered at the hands of the Emperor's enemy—Sten.

Kenna gestured to the enormous portrait of the Emperor staring out at all of them. "For reasons only our wise leader can determine, the people of Dusable have been honored once again."

Kenna's trained eyes scanned the crowd, as he spoke. Sussing out his strengths and weaknesses. Supporter and enemy. He may have been humiliated by Sten, but humiliation did not diminish his skills as a manipulator.

He and Avri had prepared well for this moment. When he was done, the Emperor's bill would be presented. A highly controversial bill, whose passage at one time had been difficult to assure.

Many favors and heaps of coin had exchanged hands in the dark corridors of the Hall of Parliament. The old mordida moved a plenitude of votes into the Emperor's column. Poyndex—for reasons Kenna chose not to ponder—had also volunteered assistance. Old files on the opposition representatives had been sifted for pressure points and blackmail. More votes were added.

Still, the matter would be close.

But, in politics, close is enough to win a kingdom.

"Gentlebeings, I am here to put before you this remarkable proposal. We are being asked to lift the veil from our eyes. To see what we have been too blind to realize for so many tragic years.

"And that is, we live in so fortunate a time that a living god walks among us. And that god is our good and holy Eternal Emperor. Whose immortality stands as an unyielding shield against the hard blows of history.

"In his sanctified embodiment, our glory goes on and on before us. Our glory. Which is his glory. And his glory, ours.

"Gentlebeings . . . I put the question to you. Let us now declare, once and forever, that the Eternal Emperor is our rightful god."

There was a stir. The gauntlet was down.

The Emperor was demanding godhood by parliamentary decree.

Kenna turned to the Speaker, an old, distinguished puppet of the Emperor. "Sr Speaker," Kenna intoned, "call the question."

The Speaker's grizzled snout pushed forward, virile tusk implants an odd vanity in an ancient, wrinkled face. "In the matter of PB 600323—titled, Declaration of the Eternal Emperor's Godhood; subtitled, Be It Resolved to Amend the Emperor's Title to Read, 'Holy,' and Any Other Word Forms Recognized As Terms of Worshipful Respect—how do you say, gentlebeings?

"All for approval . . . say Yea."

A choreographed chorus of "yeas" began to rise in the hall. Broken by loud shouts of protest. The shouts became a roar, drowning out the proceedings. One voice soared over that roar.

"Sr Speaker! Sr Speaker! Point of order, please! Point of order!"

The Speaker tried to ignore the voice. His gavel hammered down. He was particularly humiliated because the voice came from one of his own species. It was Nikolayevich, a young firebrand of a tusker.

The gavel rat-tat-tatted. Lectern pickups magnified the blows and the sound thundered through the hall. But an unruly crowd took up Nikolayevich's cry: *"Point of order! Point of Order!"* More voices were added, drowning out the thunder. *"Let him speak! Let him speak!"*

The Speaker turned helpless old eyes on Kenna. There was nothing that could be done. At least not in public. Kenna motioned: *Let him speak.* Then he slipped a hand in his pocket to trigger an alarm to Arundel.

"The chair recognizes Sr Nikolayevich, representative from the great and loyal Sverdlovsk Cluster."

The Speaker keyed the pickup that would amplify Nikolayevich's remarks.

"Sr Speaker," the young tusker shouted, "we protest these procedures in the strongest possible terms. The issue before us is an obscenity. We will not be manipulated into seeing this become law over the will of the majority."

"From where I was sitting, young man," the Speaker said with dramatic sarcasm, "the majority was quite clear. The 'yeas' were overwhelming. Now, if you will permit me, I will call for the 'nays.' And you will see how weak is your support."

"It is our right to refuse a voice vote. To demand a roll call," Nikolayevich insisted. "Let us stand up and let our peoples see how each of us votes on this matter. If the Emperor is to be a god . . . let his citizens see us declare it so. And on our heads be it."

The Speaker shot a look at Kenna for help. Kenna made stretching motions: *Delay this*.

"Very well," the Speaker said. "I will call the roll."

Nikolayevich grunted in pleasure. Sniffing victory.

The Speaker snorted. "However, since you believe this matter so sensitive—although how any of you could doubt the sanctity of our Emperor is beyond me—I will put another question to the floor first."

"Objection!" Nikolayevich shouted. "The chair may not pose another question while a previous one is still in action."

The rebel from Sverdlovsk knew his legal ground. So did the canny old Speaker. A puppet he may have been, but he was a skillful puppet.

"But the assembly *does* have the right—duty, as you are insisting—to decide the means of its voting. You say it should be by the numbers. I say it should be by vigorous acclaim."

Nikolayevich looked about him. His cronies were doing a quick count, polling their strength. The answer came back. Waverers had been heartened by Nikolayevich's boldness. For this brief moment, he had the edge.

"Call the question, Mr Speaker," he said. Flat. "And I think you'll hear the loud shouts of 'nay' put paid to this blasphemy."

He slammed back into his bench, nodding all around, pleased with himself.

The Speaker raised mild eyes. "Under the circumstances of your protest," he said, "I believe it would be unseemly to settle the matter with such dispatch. There will be no yeas, or nays, sir. No. Tit for tat, sir. I'll call the roll."

Flabbergasted, Nikolayevich popped up again. "Sr Speaker, this is incredible. You're going to call the roll to see if it is permissible to call the roll?" He turned to his fellow rebels, shoulders humped in amazement. Barking laughter. But the laughter was forced.

"Yes. That's exactly what I mean," the Speaker said. "I'm elated that my thoughts to you were so clearly expressed. Sometimes, I must confess, young representatives have me wondering if somehow senility has crept up on me."

Laughter roared out from the Emperor's allies. Nikolayevich refused to be intimidated.

"But this foolishness will take hours, Sr Speaker," he protested. "Polling us one by one on a thing so easily settled is the height of folly."

"Nevertheless," the Speaker said, "this is how we shall progress."

He turned to the master of arms. "Master of Arms, call the roll!"

The master of arms bristled forward. He opened the thick official logbook.

He began to drone them out: "Ms Dexter . . . From the great region of Cogli, how do you say?"

"I vote yea, Sr Speaker."

And so it went. One by one the representatives rose. Each vote was carefully entered in the logbook.

Kenna's forces fanned out through the great hall. With the Speaker's help, he had redrawn the battle line. If he won this vote, the second victory would be assured.

Nikolayevich's cronies worked desperately to shore up their support. But time . . . slow, dragging time . . . began to wear against it.

Still, Kenna was fuming. Yes. He would win. But now the old rule of close being good enough would be turned on its head. After Nikolayevich's outburst—loudly supported by many others—anything but total victory would appear manipulated.

This was not how the Emperor wanted to start his first day of being God.

The vote ended. Kenna had won. But the margin was slender. He could see Nikolayevich and his people out twisting appendages and shouting into hearing orifices.

And he could see that the young tusker was making progress. One of his agents on Nikolayevich's staff flashed a message to Kenna's lectern com. When the voice vote came, the message said, Nikolayevich and his cronies were planning to disrupt it with a boisterous demonstration.

Kenna wracked his brain for some other means of stalling. No matter how hard he wrung it, however, nothing came. When this was over, the Emperor would have his hide.

Where the clot was he? Some god. Not even around when you need him.

The Speaker signaled. Frantic. What should he do? Kenna had no choice. He motioned. Call the question.

"Gentlebeings," the Speaker intoned, "for the second time this day, I call the question . . . In the matter of PB 600323—titled, Declaration of the Eternal Emperor's Godhood—"

Doors boomed open. Boots hammered down.

The sergeant of arms gave the cry: "Gentlebeings, I present to you . . . the Eternal Emperor!"

Startled faces churned around.

A white-robed contingent of cultists danced through the enormous doors leading into the great main hall. Their faces beamed in ecstasy. Some swung clanging incense pots on long chains. Others strewed rose petals down the long avenue. All wore small knives in the ropes belted around their waists. The knives were sharp and festooned with streaming red ribbons.

At their head was the skeletal figure of their high priestess—Baseeker.

Behind them, boots crushing the rose petals, came a troop of black-uniformed IS officers. Their eyes sweeping the assembly of representatives for danger. Weapons at ready.

In the center was the Eternal Emperor.

When Kenna and the others saw him, they didn't notice the other little details of the entrance. The second IS troop that followed just behind the Emperor, led by Poyndex. Or the camoclad sniper teams that sprinted off to take up position. Or Avri directing nondescript figures to mingle among the representatives. When they'd been dispatched, she sighted Nikolayevich, and slipped toward him.

But these things blurred past the assembly's side vision. The Emperor commanded their full attention.

He was garbed like they had never seen him before. Long golden robes flowed over his muscular figure. The material phosphored, giving off a ghostly glow. Encircling his dark locks was a thin band of more glowing gold. In his hand, he carried a staff of yellow metal that flared at the top into a round standard. On the standard burned the symbol of AM2.

The Imperial formation swept along the avenue and wheeled onto the marble speaker's platform. The Eternal Emperor strode directly to the edge and faced Parliament. Weapons thunked and boots crashed down as the troops took position on either flank.

Baseeker and the cultists flowed around them to the Emperor. Then they lay on the platform at his feet. A nest of white-robed angels with knives.

Kenna stared. The others stared. For a moment he—and they—could almost believe. All the old myths stealthed into the room, spreading like fog among them. An ancient fog. Swept up from the cold depths of several thousand years. This was the being who had ruled them for all that time.

Perhaps he *was* a god.

"It has come to my attention," the Eternal Emperor said, "that there has been some mewling in this assembly." His voice was low. But they didn't have to strain to hear. Menace buzzed all around them.

"I don't usually pay attention to your whines," the Emperor said. "I gave you that right when I empowered this Parliament in the Imperial Constitution. It's a nuisance, I admit. But that is the nature of democracy and I have had a long time to get used to it."

In the audience, Nikolayevich barely noticed as a figure moved close to him. It was Avri.

"It is the nature of this current mewling, however, that brings me before you. I understand some honors were about to be conferred upon your Emperor. These honors, I should add, I did not seek. They were pressed on me by my subjects." The Emperor's hand flowed out to indicate the white-robed cultists.

"They say I'm a god. They have built temples to me. Temples where millions of other like-minded subjects worship. In those temples, they preach wisdom and patience and gentleness. These attributes, they believe, are at the heart of my godhood."

Nikolayevich felt a motion at his beltpak; a small lump dropped in. He brushed at it impatiently. A message from an ally, he assumed. He ignored the figure slipping away.

"I have always encouraged freedom of worship among my subjects. So, it was with some shock that I learned that these gentle folk who worship me were being brutally persecuted for their beliefs.

"In fact, I now have incontrovertible proof that this persecution was at the heart of the conspiracy launched against me by the traitor Sten. Unspeakable acts were committed by Sten against these believers because he feared their deeply felt truths stood in his way to my throne.

"For, if I am a god, who would possibly join him against me? So, you see, even my greatest enemy is a believer. A Satan set against his perfect master."

This odd dance in logic momentarily broke the spell gripping Nikolayevich. He slipped the message from his beltpak. A lump wrapped in paper. He unrolled it. The lump was a tusk, slender and finely curved—then a horror of gore at the stump. On the tusk was an ornate ring.

The ring Nikolayevich had given his lover on their first pairing day.

"This is the background to the bill your Speaker has presented on this day. A background which I kept to myself until this moment, for reasons of state security involving the traitor Sten.

"The decree will end the persecution of these innocent beings. A decree that will strike a moral blow against my greatest enemy.

"A decree that will recognize what has been so painfully obvious these many millennia. I have watched over you and your ancestors for long years. I have fed you. Clothed you. Given you the means to prosper in peace."

The Emperor's head dropped. "Ah," he said, "sometimes I am so weary . . ."

"Hail the Holy Emperor!" Baseeker shrieked. "Hail, O Great Good Lord."

The other cultists took up the cry: "Hail the Holy Emperor! Praise Him. Praise Him!"

Kenna gave Walsh an elbow poke. Then another. Walsh's eyes unglazed. "Praise Him!" shouted Kenna. Another nudge into Walsh. "Praise Him!" he shouted again.

Walsh gave him a dumb grin. "Praise Him!" he shouted. "Praise Him."

Out in the crowd of representatives, Nikolayevich and the others were suddenly very much aware that beings very close to them were watching.

Nikolayevich almost choked, knowing that his lover's tusk was not the only bloody message delivered this day.

"Hail the Holy Emperor," Nikolayevich chanted. A moment later hundreds of other voices joined in. *"Praise Him! Praise Him!"*

The Emperor smiled and spread his hands. Then he wheeled around and swept off the platform with his contingent.

He rushed down the aisle, nodding here and there as he went. Even in his speed, Poyndex could see that he was savoring the shouts of *"Hail the Holy Emperor!"*

Poyndex was the last out. He could hear the Speaker's hammer coming down. Then his cry: "In the matter of PB 600323—titled, Declaration of the Eternal Emperor's Godhood . . . how do you say, gentlebeings?

"All for approval say Yea."

And the thunder came back: *"Yea!"*

Poyndex didn't bother sticking around for the "nays."

CHAPTER EIGHTEEN

"NOTHING?" FLEET ADMIRAL Madoera glowered to the com watch officer. He refrained from adding, "Again?"

"Nossir. The *Neosho* reports no transmissions on any freq from any planet in the system. All unnatural EM bands are clean. And no sign of any ships, either, hostile or friendly.

"I had it make a double-sweep. We're picking up a lot of crap from that radio star, so I wanted to make sure before reporting."

"Right. File a preliminary report to Prime that Intel blew it again. No Sten, no nothing. We'll take the task force through on a high pass just to confirm."

"Sir . . . we won't be able to transmit until we're clear of the star ourselves. All long-range com links are blanketed."

"It doesn't matter. We'll report fully after we clear the system. Not that this'll be a surprise . . ."

He stopped before adding ". . . to those clots who think they're Intelligence."

Madoera's task force had spent too many ship-days and months chasing will-o'-the-wisp sea stories about the elusive traitor around their assigned galactic AOR to be surprised. In Madoera's estimation, this new Internal Security that'd replaced Mercury Corps wasn't capable of pouring pee out of a boot if the instructions had been printed on its heel.

None of the Alpha One-rated stories had turned out to be true. Either Sten had never been there, Sten had passed through rapidly a long time ago, or some unknown ships had been reported in a particular cluster and assumptions made they were rebel.

Why, he wondered, didn't IS realize *all* of the stories were almost certainly a crock, since every system his fleet had been punted toward was dead, abandoned, or a backwater. Just like this one. It didn't even have a name—and its only coordinates were from a charter radio pulsar, NP0406Y32.

Maybe *he* should name the damned thing. Poyndex, perhaps.

Right. And face a loyalty board when he got back to Prime. Although at the moment he didn't think he was ever going to see civilization again. He and his sailors and marine infantry would waste their substance and years pooping around the hinterlands until one day somebody discovered this Sten had died of old age and they could all go home. Or maybe they'd just lose the task force's fiches in toto, and the fleet would wander on, until the Last Donald, like some sort of *Flying Duchess*, or however the legend went.

Hell.

Madoera slammed out of the daycabin onto his flagship's bridge. He glanced at one wallscreen that showed the system, a scatter of burned worlds too close to the radio pulsar, whose image—virtual, of course, as was everything else on the screen—flashed near the screen's top. He reached over a watch officer's shoulder, and tapped three pads.

Another screen opened, this one showing just Madoera's task force. A heavy combat fleet—a tacship carrier/flagship, the *Geomys Royal*; a modern battleship, the *Parma*; two cruiser divisions, one with two heavies, the second with three light cruisers; and seven destroyers for a screen. A second crudiv was in support, with three light cruisers and four destroyers in its screen. His logistics tail was small—two supply ships and one tender, escorted by two destroyers.

A force to contend with. If he ever—and he privately thought never—could bring the rebels to battle, the action would be brief. But bloody, he was certain. Sten was misguided, but not stupid, and he and all of his fellows must know that if they surrendered they'd be merely prolonging their lifespan until a tribunal could be set up to try and execute them.

Knowing this, Madoera had issued as part of his standing orders instructions that if any rebel ships were encountered, extreme caution should be taken—they would certainly try any subterfuge or trick and fight to the last being. Certainly Madoera would do the same, if he ever slipped his shackles as badly as Sten.

Staring at the screen, Madoera wondered if there were any drills he hadn't run lately, or some highly obscure false emergency he could produce, just to keep his sailors from slacking off.

Clot it, he decided. It was bad enough they were hither-and-yonning so much. At least this time his swabs didn't need to think the old man was messing with them, as well as everyone else.

"In-system," the watch officer reported.

"Thank you, Sr One pass. Double-diamond formation."

That, at least, would be a test of how well his navigators could handle a complex formation. Especially with the real external problem of trying to keep their coms open while that pulsar sent out its tsunamis of white noise in the background. Now, just hope there's no collision while they're doing it, which probably would get me a nice reassignment to some water world with real ships. With oars.

Madoera listened with half an ear to the chatter as his flag navigator issued orders for the fleet's exercise in synchronized "flying." He yawned.

The rebels attacked.

There was no warning—the two DD's on flank security simply ceased existing. Someone shouted an alarm, and ships blinked onto the *Geomys Royal*'s screens. From "behind" the Imperial task force.

They must have known, Madoera realized, exactly what orbit the task force would set to approach this NP0406Y32, and followed them in.

The Imperial ships were at general quarters—but weapons stations were still at standby, and some missiles hadn't even been loaded in launch tubes. It had not made sense to chance damaging an expensive missile—or a more valuable crew-being—in another empty run.

A moment of panic, shouted down by Madoera and other officers throughout the task force. Steadiness returned— Madoera had turned his recruits into hardened professionals in long months of drill.

Numbers swirled across the screen showing the incoming attackers.

"Sir," a watch officer reported. "Six cruisers, estimated heavy, ten destroyers attacking."

"Thank you, Mister. I can prog that myself. What class? What origin?"

"Sir . . . the *Jane's* has no data," the woman said. "Unknown. Except—they're state-of-the-art design. *Jane's* offered the theory they're new construction."

Another wave of attackers appeared—this one from "below" the task force.

"Three battleships, seven cruisers, twenty destroyers incoming, sir. I have an ID, sir. On the battlewagons. *Jane's* has a make. All three of them were designed and built by the Cal'gata. Pre-Tahn war. *Jane's* has them as mothballed and for sale. Five of the destroyers are Honjo origin, and we have a positive ID on one. The *Aoife*."

Sten. For certain.

Now where the hell was the *Victory*? The bastard would be masterminding his ambush from its bridge. If Madoera could ID Sten's flagship, perhaps a suicide run by a couple of DD's might take out the puppetmaster. It wasn't on any screen. In some ways, that was worse. It meant the rebellion and the rebel forces had grown to the point that its leader no longer needed to accompany his beings to battle.

"All stations," an antimissile tech monotoned. "We have a multiple Kali-class launch from hostiles . . . attempting to divert . . ."

"Fox stations. Shift to local control. Acquire and launch at will."

Madoera gnawed at his lip, calculating.

"Put CruDiv One on a direct attack against the BBs," he ordered. "And punch a line through to the *Neosho*. Order it to avoid battle and break for open space and report. Captain, get your tacships out there."

"Yessir."

"Sir . . . the *Neosho* is not answering. And we have no sign of *Neosho* onscreen."

He hadn't even seen the destroyer get killed.

Madoera thought hard. "All right, then. Put CruDiv Support out, wide on a flank. Get the supply elements in with the main fleet. And tell the *Parma*—"

"Signal from *Parma*, sir. Four hits. CIC wiped out. All weapons stations under local command. Drive regulation lost. Ship being conned from engine room."

Another screen showed a third swarm coming in at the task force.

Someone shrilled, "Where'd they get—"

Snapped retort: "Silence at your station, Mister! Report as you've been trained!"

Madoera kept his calm. Closed his eyes, and let his mind battlechamber.

"Do you have contact with CruDiv Two?"

"Affirm. Staticky. A lot of interference from the pulsar."

"Order them to avoid battle. Withdraw past *Parma*, past *Geomys Royal*, and set an erratic orbit clear of action. Do not engage the rebels. Do not attempt to stay in contact with the task force."

"Message sent, sir. Will comply."

"All right. Captain. We're going to circle the wagons . . ."

Madoera ordered the remnants of his task force—a crippled battleship, his flagship, and the rest—to take a globe formation, with erratic orbiting to keep them from being targets. He issued no change in orders to the two heavy cruisers he'd sent on a flanking attack.

He'd lose them, but perhaps they might serve to confuse the rebels, at least long enough for Madoera to begin some sort of breakout.

"Sir," a talker said. "Contact from the *Aleksyev*. It reports—"

The *Geomys Royal* shuddered as a missile impacted. Metal and men screamed. Flashdark/light as primary lighting went down, and a secondary circuit cut in. Nausea swept through Madoera's guts as the McLean generators went off and he free-fell, then they came back on—but "down" was what had been to the side seconds ago.

"All stations, report damage. . . ."

The *Aoife*, at full drive, closed on the "center" of the battlefield. Berhal Waldman stood behind his deck officer, not feeling his fingers trying to dig into the steel back of the chair.

His destroyer was at the front of the vee. The other four ships were also Honjo—officers and men who had mutinied to take their ships to join the rebels. They were actually regular volunteers. And all of them had sworn to avenge the *Aisling*.

"All units, all units," Waldman ordered. "Weapons systems slaved to my ship . . . on command . . . now."

The ships obeyed. Then, "All stations, ready to launch."

"Very good. Target . . . enemy battleship. Goblin . . . half drive. Launch!"

Medium-range antiship missiles exploded from their tubes toward the *Parma*.

"Target . . . enemy battleship," Berhal Waldman said. He

ignored his weapons officer—she hadn't been on the *Aoife* when its sister ship was obliterated. This was his party. "Kali launch. One tube per ship. Kali officers . . . maintain contact with your missiles . . . launch!"

The Imperial battleship seethed flame as its antimissile batteries and lasers went after the incoming missiles from the Honjo destroyers. In the dazzle, TA systems confused the monstrous shipkilling Kalis with the smaller Goblins, and did not correctly assign priorities.

One Goblin got through and knocked out two weapons stations—and forty men—on the *Parma*. And then both Kalis struck. The *Parma* blew in half, half again, and then into fragments.

The Honjo turned for the *Geomys Royal*.

On Madoera's main screen, Imperial units were blanking—or else transmitting DAMAGE/OUT OF BATTLE signals to the *Geomys Royal*.

That was enough. Fleet Admiral Madoera lifted a mike, and broadcast *en clair*.

"All Imperial units . . . all Imperial units. This is Admiral Madoera. All units break contact. Repeat, break contact. Set individual orbits, emergency power, for base. That is an order."

He dropped the microphone.

"Captain, contact your tac squadrons. I want them to hold the rebels to the last. This is an all-units rearguard action. We must—"

"Missile closing . . . closing . . . negative diversion . . . negative acquisition . . . impact!"

The Goblin struck about two hundred meters behind the *Geomys Royal*'s bridge. Just behind the missile was a Kali. The Kali operator saw opportunity, and sent her bird directly into the fireball, counted once, and manually detonated.

Novablink . . . and there was empty space where the *Geomys Royal*—and Fleet Admiral Madoera—had been.

* * *

The survivors of the Imperial task force—one heavy cruiser, one light cruiser, three destroyers, and the fleet tender—fled at emergency drive. Their orbit would sweep them very close to the radio pulsar, then out, deep into the emptiness between the stars.

This was one sector from which the rebels had not attacked.

It was where Sten, and the *Victory*, waited.

"All tacships," Captain Freston broadcast, "we have six Imperial ships in-sector. All units, acquire data from central computer. Under squadron command: Attack. Repeat, attack."

Hannelore La Ciotat and her fellow assassins with silk scarves went in for the kill.

Sten watched from the bridge of the *Victory* until the last Imperial indicator had vanished. His face was a mask. Just as had happened with the *Caligula*, beings who wore the same uniform Sten had worn, beings he might have served with or under or drank with in gin joints, were dead.

Kilgour's face was equally blank.

"All—" Freston hesitated, then continued, "—enemy elements destroyed."

"Very well. Phase Two."

And Sten's forces would not be permitted to ride clear of the battlefield, eyes averted from the slaughter.

Forty transports, provided by the Zaginows and the Cal'gata, swept the system. Ten Bhor armed merchant ships went with them. They hunted down any fragment of any Imperial ship they could pick up onscreen. The fragments were either further destroyed by demolition teams crossing to the wreckage and setting charges, or, if they were larger, the armed auxiliaries blasted them with Goblins or lasers.

It wasn't necessary, at least, to kill any survivors they found. Not that there were many. Space war is no more merciful than naval battles far from land.

Any Imperials picked up would be given medical treatment and then transported, with uninjured survivors, to a planet at the fringes of the Lupus Cluster. Food, shelter, and continuing medical supplies and treatment would be provided on this forgotten, rather Eden-like world.

But that was all, until the war ended and either Sten or the Emperor was victorious. No mail, no notification to the survivors' families or friends.

Because the purpose of this long roundelay, back to the spoof in the dead system of Ystrn, was for an entire Imperial fleet to vanish.

Sten had deliberately chosen the area near NP0406Y32 for his plan's payoff. Any initial reports of his attack would be blocked by the pulsar. His strategy had worked perfectly.

Twenty-six warships, their admiral, and crew had disappeared.

Without a trace.

That would send a shiver through even the bravest warrior's soul.

And just as Ystrn had created the stage for this battle, NP0406Y32 would create a larger arena.

The essay purported to be a speech made by the Eternal Emperor at the graduating ceremony for one of the Empire's most prestigious naval academies, and was reprinted in *Fleet Proceedings*. In the speech the Emperor announced that these were parlous times the newly commissioned officers would face, but that they were also times of greatness. And as always, those who led from the front would be noted and rewarded.

The second item was buried near the end of the *Imperial Times*, a fiche no one in his right mind ever consulted for pleasure, but to check on the promotions, awards, and transfers of all Imperial officers.

Seven admirals had decided to take early retirement. All seven, analysts discovered, were respected—but all seven believed in the principle of leadership through battle analysis and ratiocination rather than noble posturing from the missile-torn bridge of a battleship.

The next item was the commissioning of a new super-battleship, the *Durer*. It had been especially honored by being picked by the Eternal Emperor himself as a command ship. Command ship, the analyst noted. Not yacht or personal transport.

All these smallish items were published in specialized fiches.

A larger item was the lead story in the *Imperial Times*. A mass assemblage of the Imperial battle fleets was ordered, on a most tight schedule. There would be barely six E-months for combat elements to ready themselves.

The last was big and public, however. With full fanfare, it was announced the Eternal Emperor had been requested by Fleet Admiral Anders and the rest of the Imperial General Staff to provide them with his centuries of wisdom and experience to extirpate the last, lingering traces of the bandit Sten.

The rebels had winkled the Emperor out of his bunker.

Now he was vulnerable.

Next, Sten would strike for the heart of the Empire and the Emperor himself.

CHAPTER NINETEEN

THE GREAT FLEETS of the rebellion rendezvoused in intersteller emptiness near a monstrous whirlpool galaxy. Emptiness—but emptiness very close to Prime World and the heart of the Empire.

There were thousands of ships. Zaginows. Cal'gata. Honjo. Bhor. Other ships from beings, cultures, worlds, even star clusters, Sten had never heard of. Systems' entire navies had joined the rebel forces. Squadrons had "deserted" *en masse*. Other ships, and even in some cases individual beings, had found their solitary way to the rising.

Sten sometimes wondered at their motives. Gold? Gods? Glory? Perhaps sometimes a burning, inchoate sense of injustice, a desire to end the Empire's tyranny. It had taken generations and centuries, but at last the hammer had lost its velvet padding.

The indicator lights in the battle chamber of the *Victory* now represented fleets instead of ships.

But less than one-tenth of the Empire was now in open revolt.

Sten thought that might be enough.

The orders went out. The rebellion would move into the Empire's heart, ostensibly making an attack on Prime itself. Before they could attack the Empire's capital, Imperial fleets would certainly come out to stop them.

That would be, Sten prayed, the final battle.

The real objective was not Prime at all, but the fleets themselves. Once the Empire's ability to wage war was crippled, Prime and any other world could be easily attacked, seized, isolated, or ignored.

It would be, his own sense as well as his staff's analyses, a near-run victory. Estimates were, given the present level of forces and that the rebellion had thus far maintained a tactical edge, 61 percent to 39 percent, favoring a victory for Sten. Expected casualties would be a staggering 35 percent of the rebellion's forces.

But blood was the argument, and there appeared to be no peaceful alternatives.

So be it.

"So the traitor is moving," the Eternal Emperor said. What might have been a smile moved his lips, then disappeared.

"Yessir," Admiral de Court said. "Just as your estimate and our progs said." De Court was one of the seven computer-brained admirals that the *Imperial Times* said had taken early retirement. In fact, they had been detached for special duties and were serving as a shadow general staff directly under the Eternal Emperor himself.

Their role would never be known, of course. None of the seven would be disloyal enough to mention that the final obliteration of Sten came from the brilliance of anyone besides the Emperor.

They were not disloyal . . . or suicidal.

Admiral de Court did not appear pleased that the anticipated events were, in fact, occurring.

"What are the numbers," the Eternal Emperor asked.

"Fifty-one percent chance of Imperial victory."

"That is all?" The Emperor was startled.

"Yessir. Too many Imperial elements lack real battle experience. Or else they're relatively new formations."

"I ordered the secret mobilization months ago."

De Court was silent. Not even the Eternal Emperor could create Weddigens or *Golden Hind*s simply by the laying on of hands.

"Anticipated casualties?"

"Well over 70 percent."

A long silence. Then, "Acceptable."

De Court licked dry lips. He'd been chosen, as the most diplomatically gifted of the technocrat-admirals, to handle this presentation.

"One other thing, sir. We have two single progs, not entirely quantifiable, but a probability estimation of approximately 82 percent, that the traitor Sten will be killed in this battle. And—and yourself, as well."

The Emperor was very quiet.

"Sir."

Still nothing. Then, finally, "Thank you," the Eternal Emperor said. "You're dismissed."

Scoutboats, then destroyers, then light cruisers met between the galaxies in a sudden snarl of blood. Ships swirled, launched missiles, took hits, died.

The engagement was all the bloodier because it was unexpected.

"So the bastard mousetrapped us," Sten hissed.

"I wouldn't put it that baldly," Freston said. "But the Emperor hasn't just been sitting there waiting for us."

Kilgour was in a glower of rage.

"Skip," he said. "Ah dinnae ken whae's th' matter wi' our intel. But Ah'll hae some gonads frae breakfast kippers. Later. A' th' mo, Ah dinnae hae time frae 'crim'nations. Th' sit's as follows:

"Th' Emp's got its fleets already mob'lized, aye? I's nae a total disast'r, unlike th' Emp mos' likely thinks it t' be. But it'll noo be a bonnie prog."

"GA," Sten said.

"We'll trash th' clots. Est 80 percent a' th' Imps'll nae see home again. But wi' a price. We'll take 75 percent hits ourselves. I's a Kilkenny cat's war, lad.

"But we'll mos' likely kill th' Emp i' the bloodbath. An', same prob'ility, die i' th' doin't."

Sten nodded.

He stared at, but did not see, the screens as he ran his own set of numbers.

He would probably die in this battle in the galactic dark. Very well. Sten was surprised he could accept that with a certain equanimity—or at least he had fooled his mind into thinking that.

At least the Eternal Emperor would die, as well.

And the Imperial forces would be shattered.

But a navy could be rebuilt.

Especially if—and he'd completely accepted Haines's verification of Mahoney's improbable theory—the Emperor would return. Return, and be handed the throne in exchange for the resumption of AM2.

The Emperor would be gone for at least three, possibly six, E-years. During which time the "civilized" universe would sink further into chaos. And then a madman would return, slashing out to regain his kingdom. A fifth horseman of the apocalypse.

How long would it take for another rebellion? A rebellion that wasn't aimed at the New Boss replacing the Old Boss? A rebellion unlike the Tahn war or the Mueller Rising before that?

No.

Sten issued orders, then retreated to the solitude of the *Victory*'s admiral's walk. The rebels were to take a defensive posture. He could not—would not—allow the projected orgy of mutual destruction to occur. Not when it would be unlikely to completely excise this tumor that called himself the Eternal Emperor.

No. If necessary, they could retreat. Regroup. Rethink. Or, in a worst-case scenario, follow the example of countless liberation forces through the centuries—dump arms, go to ground, and try again.

Hell, Sten thought. If this is where it ends, I can disappear into the woodwork. Change my face, change my name, and try again.

The next time, by myself.

The next time, with a bomb or a longarm.

No surrender, Sten promised himself. But now it's time to keep the beings who followed you from dying.

Inaction, his mind told him. Retreat. Passivity.

No other options occurred.

He thought of alk, or stregg. Neither was acceptable. He slumped into a chair. Stared out at the kaleidoscope that was hyperspace.

Seconds . . . minutes . . . hours . . . centuries later, the com blatted at him.

Sten slapped the switch and started to growl. Stopped himself. It was Alex onscreen, his face and voice carefully bland.

"Com 'cast frae th' Imperial forces," he said, without preamble. "Tightbeam. On a freq thae Freston says is exclusive t' th' Emperor. An' th' *Victory*'s one ae th' few ships wi' th' capability t' receive it. Y' recollect the Emp built this ship frae his own use?"

"Do you have a point of origin?"

"Ah dinnae, Sten. Noo frae any listed world. Frae a ship, Ah reck. Wi' th' Imperial forces, Ah'd guess.

"An . . . i's *en clair*. Vid an' voice. Wi' a card sayin't it's f'r y'r eyes only."

Sten started to order it to be transmitted to his com, then caught himself. No. Even at this time, at this moment before the storm, it would not be unlikely for the Eternal Emperor to transmit something meaningless—and then leak the story that the message contained private instructions from the Emperor to one of his double agents.

"Hang on," Sten ordered. "I'm on my way down. Set it up for projection on the bridge."

"Boss? Are y' sure?"

"Hell, yes. I'm getting too old to play games. Stand by."

The screen showed the Eternal Emperor. He was standing alone on the awe-inspiring bridge of a warship. The *Durer*? He wore a midnight-black uniform with his symbol in gold on his breast—the letters AM2 superimposed over the null-element's atomic structure.

"This message is intended for Sten, and only for him.

"Greetings.

"Once you were my most faithful servant. Now you have declared yourself my most deadly enemy. I do not know why. I thought you served me well, and so I made you ruler over many things, and thought that would bring you joy. Evidently it did not.

"And I have seen, to my great sorrow, that some of my subjects believe themselves to be ignored, believe they have been somehow slighted, in spite of my efforts to help them as best I can in these troubled times.

"I could reason, I could argue, I could attempt to present a larger view of the chaos that looms before all of us in the Empire.

"But I shall not. Perhaps some of my satraps *have* enforced their own immoralities under the cover of my rule, which has always been intended to provide the maximum benefit to all beings, human and otherwise, a rule of peace and justice that began before time was recorded and, with the goodwill of my fellow citizens, will continue until time itself must have a stop.

"Beings—many of them my good and faithful servants—have died. Died in this murderous squabble that history will not even dignify with a footnote. It shall not be remembered because I propose a solution, a solution that no one could argue with.

"You, Sten, say that my rule is autocratic. Dictatorial, even. Very well.

"I invite you to share that rule.

"Not as a co-ruler, because you, or those who rose in rebellion with you, could well define that as a cheap attempt at bribery. At co-option.

"No. I propose a full and complete sharing of power between myself, my Parliament, and you and your chosen representatives, in whatever form we agree to be the most representative and just.

"I further propose an immediate truce, to avoid further bloodshed. This truce will be of short duration, so that neither side can argue it is being used as a device to seek an advantageous position to destroy the other. I would accept two E-weeks as an outside figure.

"At the end of that time, you and I should meet. We should meet with our best advisers and allies, to prepare the grounds for this new and promising time for the Empire.

"I further suggest that our meeting ground be on Seilichi, the home planet of the most respected, most neutral, and most peaceful beings this universe has ever known, the Manabi. I would also ask that their most honored savant, Sr Ecu, mediate our negotiations.

"I ask you, Sten, as an honorable being, to accept my most generous offer.

"Now, only you can keep innocent blood from showering the stars."

And the screen went blank.

A blast of babble on the *Victory*'s bridge. Then silence, as everyone turned to look at Sten.

Son of a bitch, he thought.

He has us.

And there's no way out.

No way whatsoever.

CHAPTER TWENTY

STEN RUBBED TIRED eyes and tried to think. He hadn't gotten a lot of sleep in the past two weeks. What little he'd had time for had been constantly interrupted by messengers, coms, and delegations arriving from his allies. Even his thoughts, when he was alone with Cind, yammered at him.

Cind had run everyone out twenty hours ago, and forced Sten to take a sopor. He had slept hard, but not well.

Now, he was in his final briefing. His allies had presented what they wanted and expected in this Brave New World of Powersharing, a certain percentage of which was either wishful thinking or else shouldn't be mentioned until the transition was complete. And that last assumption was well up there with progging the belled cat . . .

The briefing, like everything else about Sten and the rebellion, was irregular, consisting less of those with the clout than the old guard. Himself. Kilgour. Cind. Rykor. Even Otho, who at least could be counted on to provide the nonsubtle touch.

Sten wished Sr Ecu could have been present, or could at least have monitored this session. But no one could chance even the vague possibility the Emperor would discover the Manabi and Sten were in collusion.

The *Victory*, escorted by five cruisers and eleven destroyers, was orbiting an unpopulated world less than twenty light-years from Seilichi.

Not that there was much to say in this meeting—it'd all been gone over time and again. Sten wondered about Alex, who'd been unnaturally quiet for the past few days, keeping his own counsel.

Sten poured a glass of herbal/protein drink, and sipped. He shuddered at its taste. Why were things that were supposedly good for you so frequently abominable?

"I wonder," he said, "just how long it will be before the Emperor double-crosses us?"

"It will depend," Rykor said, "on how we handle the first crisis after the Emperor grudgingly moves over on his throne to allow your presence, whatever it might be. If our solution coincides with the Emperor's, and in no way detracts from the perception that he alone really holds the reins of power . . . two E-years from that date.

"If there is a divergence of views, and ours becomes the plan operated on . . . three cycles.

"In any event, there will be an attempted counterrevolution within five E-years, either planned by the Eternal Emperor himself or, possibly, honestly mounted by his loyalists.

"But we should be, given foresight and proper planning, as well as an ocean and a half of pure luck, able to survive the first attempt to destroy the new government."

"All those estimates," Sten said dryly, "give the coalition more time than we would have if we'd accepted battle. Time enough to figure how we're going to RF the Emperor before he does it to us."

Kilgour shook his head. "Ah'll noo be rain't on th' march-past, but Ah'm sittin' here rec'lectin' a place called Glencoe, a clan called Campbell, an' a pol named Dalrymple."

"Which means?" Otho rumbled.

"Naethin' 'cept m' own buddin't fears, lad. Whae deal-in't wi' a madman, y' cannae use logic."

"We've gone through this before," Sten said. "The Emperor is hardly going to try a double cross now. He proposed the meet in the first place, so it'd be his flag of truce that'd be dishonored. Of course he's mad, and of course he wants my skin for his drumhead—but he certainly would not try anything while we're all under the protection of the Manabi."

A com whispered, and Alex crossed to it and read the message onscreen. He keyed an answer and blanked it.

"Ver' well," he said. "Y'r ride t' th' conference's inbound."

"And why will we not descend from the *Victory*?" Otho asked. "Should Sten arrive like a beardless one? Perhaps on a trading ship?"

"Close," Alex agreed. "He'll be usin't a transport. Ah' borrow'd a liner frae th' Zaginows. An' dinnae be sayin't 'we,' less y' think Sten hae a mousie i' his pocket. Sten'll be descendin' ae a man of peace, which i' whae we want ae th' perception frae all. Aye, Rykor?"

Rykor wallowed in her vat, considering.

"How dimwitted of me," she said. "And I am the being who prides herself on not automatically making assumptions. Yet I've always taken for granted Sten would land from the *Victory*, properly escorted by his allies.

"However . . . what exactly do you propose, Sr Kilgour?"

"Sten arrives on Seilichi wi' but one aide. M'self. We'll hae a tightbeam frae th' liner t' the *Vick*, which we'll hae off-world, an' well awa' frae th' Emp's fleets.

"We'll nae look like bloody-handed rebels, but ae wee an' Ah do mean wee, peacelovers, i' y' ken. Dav'd agin' th' Phar'ses, or howe'er thae tale goes.

"It'll make a braw point, frae th' livie crews, Ah wager."

Rykor closed her eyes and ran the visuals. Yes. It would look impressive. Sten, one small man standing victoriously against the Emperor.

"Rykor, we'll hae y'rself oop here, listenin't t' all thae haps, an' keepin't ae clear mind."

Cind was on her feet. "Sten isn't going down there without any escort."

"Well spok't," Alex said. "But he will. Y'r Bhor an' th' Gurks cannae stand up t' a laserblast frae a battlewagon. An' thae's noo point i' a martial show, solely t' be showin't th' size ae our claymores, noo is there, lass?"

Cind was about to go on—but Alex moved his head slightly to the side. She stopped cold.

Sten, too, was looking at Kilgour. Alex just stared back, expressionless. Ah, Sten, thought. And is there any harm if he's right?

"We'll do it Alex's way," Sten said, before Otho could come in with a bellowed rejoinder.

"The Emperor wears plain dress whites when everybody else is in full dress uniform. We'll play another version of the same card.

"Somebody grab one of my dogsbodies, and make sure I've got a Boy Virgin Outfit. Now, I'm going to run everyone out. I want something disgustingly dull to eat and some more sleep. We're ready."

Sr Ecu hovered in the center of the huge landing field within the "crater" of the Guesting Center. His senses were at their finest tune. This meeting, and the subsequent series of conferences, could be not just the culmination of his own life, but that of the Manabi as well.

His race had always viewed the Emperor, and Empire, with skepticism and a measure of dislike. His authoritarianism brought continuity, a degree of peace, and a degree of plentitude, to worlds beyond worlds. But at a price. The price of tyranny. Sometimes it had been somewhat benevolent, sometimes it had been otherwise, such as the terrible conflicts like the Mueller Rising and the Tahn war, which, when all the rhetoric died, had been only fought to guarantee the rule of the Emperor. Ecu had long wondered whether it could be possible to correct the Eternal Emperor's excesses and still maintain the benefits.

Could this be the chance?

How romantic, his brain said. This, from a being whose life has been spent in the labyrinth of diplomacy, trying to ferret out true meaning from babble.

You expect Eternal Peace to come from a meeting between a being you believe to be quite mad and a young rebel who not many years ago was that madman's assassin? Who—knowing the nature of humanity and its lust for power—will take only a short time before he sees himself as the Emperor?

But still.

The livie cameras scattered along the "rim" of the Guesting Center had gotten tired of the nearly dead air—motionless footage of the Manabi's red-and-black bulk hovering over bare tarmac—and had returned to a pursuit they seemingly never tire of—interviewing themselves as to what anything and everything meant.

A sonic lash broke into their circle game, and, overhead, the Eternal Emperor's ship lowered toward a landing, with a small scoutboat as its landing guide. Ecu recognized the *Normandie*—the Emperor's old, heavily armed secret transport. How odd. Ecu would have expected him to make as impressive an appearance as possible, and arrive aboard his new super-battleship, the *Durer*. He knew that overhead, just offplanet in a geosynchronous orbit, hung a full Imperial battlefleet as cover.

Ecu felt a flicker of hope. Perhaps the Emperor didn't want to present a warlike image.

But that was not the case, he realized seconds later, as a landing ramp sliced out and heavily armed Internal Security humans in their black uniforms doubled out in squad formation and took up position around the ship.

No one else came down the ramp.

Overhead, a whine, and Sten's ship—the civilian liner Ecu had been told to expect—lowered down toward the field. It shifted from Yukawa drive to its McLean generators, and grounded on its sponsons.

A wide portal yawned in one of them, and two beings stepped out. Sten and Alex Kilgour.

Kilgour wore the full regalia of an Earth Scots laird, from bonnet to cloak to kilt to sporran. But there was no *sgean dubh* in his stocking, no daggersheath at his belt, and the scabbard for his great broadsword was empty. Kilgour did not even have a pistol concealed in the sporran worn over his crotch.

Sten wore a pale blue tunic that buttoned to his neck, and trousers of the same color. He was bareheaded and wore no decorations.

No security beings followed them. The two walked out into the soft sunlight and waited.

Across the field, bootheels clashed and weapons crashed as the IS troops came to attention.

The Eternal Emperor and his entourage came down the ramp. As expected, he wore a plain black uniform with the Imperial Emblem on its breast. Around his neck was one decoration—one of the liviecasters correctly identified it, in a hushed voice, as the Giver of Peace decoration that he'd received at the conclusion of the Mueller Rising.

The 'caster went on to identify the Imperial dignitaries: Avri, his political chief of staff. Tyrenne Walsh, figurehead ruler of Dusable and the Eternal Emperor's usual stalking-horse in Parliament. And so on down, from Count This to Secretary of Protocol That. The liviecaster misidentified one being, but Ecu knew him well: Solon Kenna. The Eternal Emperor was bringing his sharpest political minds to this meeting. Ecu felt that horrible stir called hope move in his soul once more.

Best of all, Poyndex was not part of the throng. Once more, a favorable sign that perhaps this conference was intended to bring a measure of peace to the Empire.

Sten and Alex moved to greet the Imperial troupe. The entourage stopped, and the Eternal Emperor walked forward alone.

"Sten." It was a completely neutral acknowledgment.

Sten, foolishly, had to stop himself from saluting. The habit of years died very hard.

"Your Highness."

"Shall we begin?"

Sten forced a smile to his lips and nodded.

Sten and the Eternal Emperor were alone on a balcony near the crest of the Guesting Center. The balcony appeared to be just a ledge on the outer near-vertical slope of the volcano-styled Center.

After the conferees had been shown to their quarters, the Emperor had asked Ecu if he might have the pleasure of talking to Sten alone for a few moments. The meeting was not to be recorded.

Ecu asked Sten, who hesitated, then agreed.

It was just twilight, and purple drifted across the sky above them, coloring the wide valley around the Center. The young Manabi who escorted them to the balcony told them it was screened against anyone, especially a liviecaster, who might be indiscreet enough to focus a parabolic microphone on the two of them. Sten and the Emperor looked at each other, and Sten half smiled. No one would be *that* indiscreet, he knew.

There were two chairs and a large cart equipped with a McLean generator at the rear of the balcony. The Emperor walked to it and opened the doors.

"Scotch. Stregg. Alk. Pure quill. Beer. Teas. Even water. The Manabi certainly worry over dry throats."

He turned to Sten. "Would you like a drink?"

"No," Sten said. "But thank you."

The Emperor picked up the flask of stregg. Turned it back and forth. "I used to drink this," he mused. "But I found I've lost my taste for it. Isn't that unusual?"

He looked directly at Sten, then his eyes shifted back and forth. Sten found the gaze uncomfortable, but did not allow himself to look away. After a few seconds, the Emperor looked elsewhere.

He walked to the edge of the balcony and sat on the low railing, looking out at the valley.

"Unusual beings, the Manabi," he mused. "The only real trace of their civilization is underground. I would feel unsettled, bothered, that if I vanished in the night, there would be no sign whatsoever that I had ever existed . . . no mark of my own on the face of the planet."

Sten had no answer. Again, the Emperor looked at him, his eyes doing that mad dance.

"Do you recall our first meeting?"

"Formally, sir?"

"No. I meant the night of Empire Day. When you were head of my bodyguards. I assume you have heard that I dismissed the Gurkhas. Romantic as they are, I found their capabilities limited. Anyway, that night was when I asked to see your knife. Do you still have it, by the way?"

"I do."

"May I see it again?"

Now Sten smiled. "I hope there are no security types out there who might misunderstand," he said. He curled his fingers and let the weapon slip down into his fingers. He passed it across to the Eternal Emperor, who looked at it curiously and handed it back.

"Just as I remembered it. You know, I have dreamed about this knife from time to time. But I don't remember the circumstances of the dream. Yes. I should have realized its symbolism to you back then."

It took a moment for Sten to understand what the Emperor meant. Before he could protest, the Emperor went on: "That was an interesting night. You introduced me to stregg, as I recall. And I cooked. I don't remember—"

"It was something you called Angelo stew."

"Oh yes." The Emperor was silent for a moment. "That's something else I find I don't have much time for any more. Cooking. But now that this . . . disagreement . . . will be cleared up, I'll be able to return to my old ways. Who knows? Maybe even think about trying to build a guitar again." His expression hardened. "It's good to have a hobby in your twilight years, isn't it?"

Sten thought it best to remain silent.

"Empire Day. That, I suppose, is where the dry rot set in. Hakone. The Tahn. Mahoney. The Altaics . . . Christ!"

The Emperor peered intently at Sten. "You don't know what you have asked for, Sten. How all this goes on, and on, and it never slows and no one ever is grateful."

"Sir. I did not ask for anything. This powersharing is—"

"Of course you didn't ask," the Emperor said, a note of pettishness in his voice. "But after all these centuries, don't you think I know? Give me credit, at least, for not being a fool."

"That is something I have *never* thought, Your Majesty."

"No?" The flickering gaze turned away, back to the darkening landscape far below. "How bare," the Emperor mused. "How barren."

He rose. "I plan on eating in my quarters," he said, and smiled. "I would think that any banquets or public feastings might well wait until we have reached an arrangement. Don't you?"

"It doesn't matter to me," Sten said. "But I'm not particularly inclined to ten courses and having to come up with polite toasts."

The Emperor's smile became larger. "That was one of the reasons I respected you at one time. Even, perhaps, liked you. You had no truckle for pretense. I sometimes wonder how you found yourself capable of *this*."

He nodded, and, still smiling, went inside.

Alex Kilgour saw Sten to his chambers, and, yawning mightily, went to his own rooms.

Once inside, he doffed the outfit he mentally referred to as th' Laird Kilgour drag and shrugged off the pretense of exhaustion. He took from the lining of his valise a phototropic camouflage suit and zipped it on. The valise's straps became a swiss seat, and he took a small can of climbing thread from his sporran.

An' noo, he thought, we'll ken i' th' luck ae th' spidgers appliet t' all Scots, or solely t' Bobbie th' Brucie.

The problem was that he was not sure exactly what luck would be defined as.

The IS technician ran and reran his tapes. He was trying to figure out just where an annoying buzz on a low freq was coming from. Not from the *Normandie*, nor from any of the Imperial staff. Nor from any of the liviecasters' equipment.

He had tracked the static to the Guesting Center itself, but it wasn't from any of the Manabi's electronics.

The tech had finally nailed it. The buzz was coming from the portable com that the rebel's aide was carrying. Typical, he thought. Can't even use a handitalki without mucking it up.

But it was annoying. Sometime, during this conference, he would ask one of his superiors to talk to the clot and tell him to get a new chatterbox.

He went back to his main task, ensuring that the link between the picketboat and the newly installed apparatus aboard the *Normandie* was functioning perfectly.

The Eternal Emperor took Avri twice, in the manner that pleased him most. The woman bit hard into the pillow. A scream at midnight would be ignored by sensible beings if it came from the Imperial quarters in Arundel, but here on Seilichi an unnecessary and foolish alarm might be raised.

The Emperor went to the fresher, then stopped by a case and took a tiny object from it. He returned to the bed, ran his hand down Avri's close-cropped hair in what might have been a caress, and, as the injector's tip touched the woman's medulla oblongata, he pressed the bulb.

Avri slumped into deep unconsciousness.

It would be her last sleep.

The Emperor rose and put on a black coverall from his baggage, a coverall that had built-in climbing harness bonded into it, and thin, rigid-sole rock-climbing shoes. He pulled a mesh vest over it and closed its fastenings. He wished again for a pistol, but he knew that there had been little chance of getting a firearm through the Manabi's automatic security devices. This would be enough.

He flexed his knees. He pushed the double windows onto the balcony open. Far below him, in the crater's center, was Sten's ship, his own *Normandie*, and the picketboat. It was very dark, and very quiet. He thought he saw the single sentry posted at the *Normandie*'s ramp walk out into the open, about-face, and pace back. He didn't matter. The day the Emperor could not slip past a gate guard was the day he was ready to admit to being the fool that Sten, and it seemed the rest of the Empire, considered him.

To either side of this apartment his aides and supposed confidantes slept. Dream on, my servants, he thought. For now you are performing the finest duty to the Empire you could dream of. And your sacrifice will not have been in vain.

He looked at the naked sleekness of Avri. A slight feeling of pity crossed his mind. But not for long. The only way for a sacrifice to be convincing is when something important is really given away.

Besides, she had started to bore him.

He had already begun to consider other, more skilled women who had drawn his eye.

He unclipped a can of climbing thread from the vest, touched its nozzle, and the end of the single-molecule chain bonded to the edge of the balcony. The Emperor slipped his hands into special jumars—trying to climb down the thread barehanded would be exactly like trying to climb down a flexible razorblade.

The Eternal Emperor slid over the edge of the balcony and, nerves thrilling and blood singing as had not happened in years, went down into the night.

Kilgour was quite comfortable. He had one toe on a firm stance almost three centimeters wide, a safety loop around an outcropping, and one arm around it as well.

He could have danced.

He kept watch, a great spider, invisible, as his phototropic uniform was now on exactly the color and pattern of the false rock the Manabi had built the Guesting Center from.

A bit below him, halfway across the crater, he saw movement. He focused the night glasses more exactly and zoomed in.

Th' Emp's apartment, aye. And one lad comin' oot.

Luck, eh? P'raps th' worst. Good luck—an impossibility—would have been Alex spending a cramped night out here with nothing happening, and the conference beginning as expected.

Noo. Who's th' wee lad danglin' frae th' rope o'er there? Th' Emp his own self?

Alex frowned, reanalyzing his various progs of possible Imperial blackguarding.

He had anticipated some kind of double-dealing here on Seilichi, but none of his plans matched what seemed to be occurring.

Back aboard the *Victory*, following the final briefing with Sten, Alex had led Cind and Otho to his own quarters. That was the only place on the *Victory* that he knew was unbugged by anyone, not Freston, not Sten. Especially not Sten. Although, from the look the boss had given him, Kilgour was pretty sure Sten knew what was going on.

"Whae we're on th' ground," he'd started, "Ah'll wan' you t' be standin't by. On command frae me, or frae Sten, or i' th' event com is lost wi' us, y're t' take th' bridge, an' read an' follow th' orders Ah'll hae gie'en y' afore we depart. E'en i' thae means relievin' Cap' Freston i' he gets arg'ment'ive.

"Ah knoo 'tis a hard thing t' ask, but Ah'll hae t' request y' to oath me thae y'll follow th' 'structions wi'oot fail. Trustin' me thae Ah hae noo but th' best ae intentions frae Sten, an' frae this clottin' rebellion thae's likely t' cause th' death ae us all.

"I' y' trust me, I' y' trust Sten . . . y'll do as Ah'm desirin't."

Cind and Otho had considered. Cind had been the first to nod. Besides, she had suspected that Alex was planning for what had become Cind's worst nightmare—a nightmare she saw herself not being able to end, save in a suicidal battle royal. Then Otho had grunted. He, too, would obey.

Kilgour expressed pleasure in their confidence. Sent them out.

He had reflected . . . Glencoe . . . An eerie, narrow, rain-dripping desolate valley on old Earth, whose laird had delayed taking an oath of allegiance to the usurper king until the last minute, and then had been further prevented from an unpleasant if necessary duty by winter storms.

The laird had not considered that the usurper would have a pol named Dalrymple who wanted to make an example of someone who'd failed to sign, nor that there was a treacherous clan named the Campbells, all too willing to garner favor from the sassenach William.

Campbell soldiers appeared in the glen, and were given traditional Highland hospitality. Treachery was in their heart, treachery they did not wait to implement. That night, fire and the ax came to Glencoe, and women and children went howling into the snow and ice and frozen death.

Glencoe, Alex had thought. Aye. Sometimes, contrary to whae all th' finest planners think, treachery dinnae wait till th' perfect mo, i' th' dark ae th' moon whae th' raven rattles its deathcry.

And so he came to Seilichi prepared for the Emperor to double-cross them, from the moment the liner he'd cozened from the Zaginaws landed, till now, when he saw that man in black, who appeared to be the Eternal Emperor himself, abseil out the window.

He already had the corridor outside the Imperial apartments covered with a mechanical sensor, and Alex knew any movement from any of the Emperor's retinue would be met with alarms from the Manabi who, though no warriors, kept a cautious watch through the night.

Alex puzzled one more moment, wishing desperately he

had somehow been able to wangle a sniper rifle onto Seilichi—an' then we'd ken whae a *real* expert ae duplic'ty's capable of, aye?

Then he thought he had figured the Emperor's scheme and touched a switch at his wrist. Then Alex went back up his own climbing thread like a spider fleeing the flame, a flame Kilgour knew would be real in moments.

The Internal Security technician was sound asleep, far from his instruments. He never knew that the annoying static, that buzz, stopped the instant Alex touched his handitalki. The static was a deliberate broadcast.

There are at least two ways to broadcast a warning. The first and most common, is to start a commotion when trouble threatens. The second, and sneakier, is to have a commotion *stop* at the sign of danger.

Like Sherlock Holmes's famous dog, which did nothing in the nighttime, the end of the deliberately generated static from Kilgour's com was a tightbeam alarm linked to two spaceships.

The GQ alarms yammered aboard the *Victory*. The ship, already at standby, went to full combat readiness.

Cind, Otho, Freston, and Lalbahadur had not been asleep, nor had they intended to go offshift until Sten returned, even if they'd had to progress to stimulants and cold showers.

"All stations ready, sir," the officer of the watch reported. "No external signs of GQ readiness apparent."

"Very good," Freston said. He turned to Cind. "My orders from Mister Kilgour in the event of alarm were to place myself under your command, and obey your instructions absolutely. Take over."

"Thank you." Cind took a deep breath, and keyed her pore pattern into the small fiche holder Alex had given her when they left the *Victory*.

The instructions were simple:

WAIT IN PRESENT ORBIT UNTIL THREATENED. DO NOT, REPEAT DO NOT, ATTEMPT OFFENSIVE MOVES AGAINST EMPIRE. DO NOT, REPEAT, DO NOT ATTEMPT TO CLOSE PLANET OR MAKE PLANETFALL. MAINTAIN WATCH ON FREQ QUEBEC THIRTY-FOUR ALPHA. IN THE EVENT IMPERIAL COMBAT ELEMENTS ATTEMPT TO ENGAGE, BREAK CONTACT, MOVE COVERTLY TO [a set of coordinates]. THIS WILL BE RENDEZVOUS POINT. IF NO CONTACT MADE AT SECONDARY RV, VICTORY IS TO REVERT TO INDEPENDENT COMMAND AND TAKE WHATEVER ACTION OR ACTIONS IS DEEMED CORRECT AT THE TIME. GOOD LUCK.

. . . and the squiggle that was Kilgour's signature.

"We just wait," Otho interpreted.

Cind growled—a noise that dignified her Bhor training—and then gritted, "We wait."

The Emperor's feet touched down, and he slid down to his knees. He broke the climbing thread off and discarded the jumars.

A few guardspots glared around the three ships on the landing field. Once again, there was no movement except for the single sentry at the *Normandie*'s ramp.

Crouching, he made for the picketboat.

The broken static-buzz signaled to yet another ship.

Hannelore La Ciotat was awake, feet out of her bunk and on the tacship's deck. Her tacship's GQ alarm was a civi-lized *bong*ing, the synthesized sound of a bell. It was more than loud enough to cover the cramped crew area.

La Ciotat sealed the front of her shipsuit and damned near physically threw her onwatch weapons officer/XO out of the command seat.

"I relieve you, Mister." Her fingers were like fluid across the panel. POWER . . . UP . . . SYSTEMS STANDBY . . . CREW READY . . . WEAPONS READY . . .

She touched keys, and the tacship lifted clear of the ground on McLean drive, ripping away from the camouflage net that

La Ciotat and her crew had staked over the tiny ship a day earlier.

The tacship was hidden just inside the first twist of one of the canyons leading to the great valley the Guesting Center was in the middle of.

La Ciotat ghosted the ship around the bend.

"I have the center on visual," she told her XO.

"Roger. All screens show same."

"Drive status?"

"Drakh-hot, Hannelore."

And she, too, waited.

"Up, lad! Th' Emp's movin'!"

Sten's mind groped out of a disremembered, terrible dream, and Kilgour was pulling him up.

"What's the—"

"Shut up!"

Alex tossed him a phototropic suit, and Sten pulled it on. He looked around for some boots.

"No time, Sten! Move!"

Kilgour shoved him toward the door that yawned into a deserted open corridor, light glaring, and Sten was in a stumbling, nightmare run, not sure if he was still asleep and dreaming, but the rough carpet hurt his feet, and Alex slung him around a corner and up a ramp, toward the top of the crater.

"Which way—"

"'I' y' speaki't again, Ah'll coldcock y', Ah swear! We're i' th' eye ae th' storm!"

A great door, barred, that led out onto a balcony on the outer wall of the crater. Alex, without slowing, crashed into the door and sent it pinwheeling away. Some sort of alarm—fire, intrusion, it didn't matter—began sounding.

The Eternal Emperor came in the picketboat's port. The duty officer jerked in surprise, even though he'd been briefed.

"Lift ship," the Emperor snapped, as he turned and slapped the PORT CLOSE switch.

"Broadcast as ordered!"

"Yessir."

The officer lifted a security cover, and slid the port of the recently installed control across, and the machine across the field, in the *Normandie*, began ticking seconds.

Overhead, in space, the signal yammered the *Durer* and its escorts and sailors into combat alert.

The McLean drive brought the tiny picketboat clear of the ground.

Across the landing field, the sentry at the *Normandie*'s portal came fully awake, his willygun coming up in his hands. What the clot was going on? Nobody told him anything? Clottin' corp of the guard hadn't said anything—

A predawn wind whistled across the balcony, a wind Sten never felt. Alex had his com up.

"Pickup! On this station!"

"Got you," came a calm, unhurried woman's voice that Sten thought he recognized. "On the way."

"So you were right," Sten recovered.

"Aye. The bastard's ducking out the back door. Solo."

"Oh, Christ. We've got to alert the Manabi," Sten said, knowing futility.

"What can they—" Kilgour winced as the com screamed at him, as a transmitter aboard the *Normandie* obediently began jamming cast on all freqs.

Across the valley, they saw a tiny miniature sun. La Ciotat's tacship, blazing toward them.

The Imperial picketboat's commander lifted his ship onto its tail, and kicked in full Yukawa drive, shooting the craft straight toward the stars. Barely clear of the crater, he went to stardrive, and the picketboat vanished into space.

A relay closed aboard the *Normandie*.

The whine/roar of the picketboat shattered Ecu's sleep. His sensors came instantly aware, forcing him from that other universe he inhabited in times of differing consciousness, a universe of soft-chiming crystal in mild winds where thought itself was sentient, beautiful and visible, a universe of non-flesh and forever widening horizons.

He had drifted toward one clear panel in his alternate state, a panel looking out on the center of the Guesting Center. His sensors picked up the flash as the Imperial picketboat went into space.

Ecu felt the wings of his mind spread, spread like his own great lifting sails, and that other universe open to him, welcoming him, like a silken bridge.

La Ciotat bashed the com into silence when the jamming started its screech.

"Ma'am, I lost—"

"Shut it!" She had the balcony on visual. La Ciotat brought the tacship screaming toward the Guesting Center, flipped it end for end, McLean antigrav lagging far behind trying to define down, braked on Yukawa drive, and skidded down on the balcony, backward, fins grinding at the synthetic stone.

Her bosun had the port open, just as Sten came through it—in the air. Alex had picked him up and hurled him five meters as the port opened. A second later, the bosun was ground zero as Kilgour impacted on her. The woman wheezed, sure that ribs were broken. Kilgour rolled off, not noticing, hit the port-closing switch, shouting, "Get out of it!"

La Ciotat hit the Yukawa switch, spitting the tacship off, into the air. Her thumb was stretching for the STARDRIVE panel when

The final switch closed.

The Emperor had chosen the *Normandie* not only because he was reluctant to sacrifice the *Durer*, but because the yacht/liner had great galleries and banqueting rooms.

Great rooms that had been stripped and filled with AM2. And now, on command, they detonated.

* * *

An unanswerable question: Was Sr Ecu "dead"—by conventional beings' definition of the word—before the blast, or when the kilotons of Anti-Matter Two, the single mightiest power known, were detonated?

When the Emperor's bomb went off, it would have looked from deep space, for nanoseconds, as if the Guesting Center were a real volcano that had erupted.

Then the valley itself vanished in a sympathetic explosion, a blast moving faster than the eye could see, catching and obliterating its own debris.

Perhaps half of the Manabi died in that instant holocaust, as a quarter of their planet ripped and tore in a quake beyond all measurement.

And then, from the *Durer*, a planetbuster was launched, a nearly destroyer-sized missile, or rather two-stage missile, given a stardrive generator, Imperium X armor, and more tons of AM2 as a warhead. The first stage impacted directly where the Guesting Center had been, and the second stage was set off, driving at full power, toward the planet's core.

It did not need to break through the mantle before the main charge detonated to function, but, given the head start of the Anti-Matter Two blast from the *Normandie*, nearly did.

For a moment the Manabi home world looked like a holiday lantern, as if its landmass were clear and a viewer could see directly to the planet's molten core. It bulged . . . grew . . . and exploded.

Seilichi rocked and shattered, pitching its land, its oceans, and its atmosphere up, out into space, and then the planet itself broke, magma spilling like the liquid center of a child's candy.

In space, battlescreens blanked, then secondary power went on.

The Eternal Emperor looked at the boil that had been Seilichi without expression. "Do you have contact with the *Durer*?"

"Affirm."

The Emperor took the proffered microphone.

"This is the Emperor," he said without preamble. "Were any transmissions or ships picked up from Seilichi after we lifted?"

"One moment, sir . . . No sir. One minor transmission, intended receiver unknown, no response found, from the Center itself. Nothing else."

The Emperor gave the microphone back to the picketboat officer.

Very well, he thought. It is over. There will be a certain amount of housecleaning and damage control necessary. But the problem has been solved.

It was almost a pity Sten hadn't had a chance to know he'd never been a serious threat to the Empire or the Eternal Emperor. No one had, really. Not ever.

Not from the beginning.

And when, his mind rambled, *was* the beginning?

Perhaps . . .

Perhaps on the island of Maui.

Thousands of years ago. When time's measurement dated from the birth of a dead god.

Maui . . .

And a shatter of broken glass . . .

BOOK THREE

DRAGON VARIATION

CHAPTER TWENTY-ONE

Maui, A.D. **2174**

THE BOY HURTLED across the sagging plank onto the next hulk, arrowing across its foredeck. He saw the tarred cable anchoring the scow to its brother just in time, and jumped— foot skittering on the gunwale—then he was in the air, the muck and slime of Moaloea Bay below him, sullen tide splashing the polluted water against the black hulls. He landed, almost falling, and darted around the high-piled scrap on the bow's deck and flattened.

Behind him yelps turned to shouts. There were six of them. All of them older, all of them bigger.

All they had wanted, they said, was to see what the boy had in his ragged military-surplus knapsack. What they said, what they wanted, did not matter. Their intent was clear. The boy had taken a new way across the bay, moving through the maze of grounded ships, half-sunk hovercraft, trawlers of the fisher families, and oared houseboats that might have belonged to the rich two generations ago. He slipped past the tiny junks of the Chinese boat families, unchanged for thousands of years, working steadily toward the ship channel. Across the channel was the far shore and Kahanamoku City.

The boy knew that when the six found him, they would not kill him. Probably not, at any rate. But he would certainly be beaten. That was not a problem. He'd taken beatings before, and would take them again. And those who would thrash him would have bruises of their own for mementos.

It was what was in the knapsack that had made him run, and would make him fight.

Because they would take the pack from him, and open it. The treasures inside would be mocked, ripped, and tossed into the murky waters. Three books. Real books. Books the old man who owned the pierside junkshop had not wanted. One fat book. Two slender. The fat one was very old, had small type, and was called *The Thousand Nights and a Night*. He knew nothing of what it was about, but a glance inside promised adventures with strange beings in strange places, with creatures called rocs and djinn. The second book looked equally impenetrable, but was equally promising: *Freedom From Gravity, The Equations and Early Experiments of Lord Archibald McLean*. Perhaps he could understand just how those great landbarges could fill themselves with cargo, and then effortlessly lift into the sky and float over the watery slum of the bay, out past the barriers to where the great torchships berthed. The last volume was medium-sized: *Starchild. Growing Up in Deep Space*. The holo of the author inside the front cover made her look a proper dwonk, but what did that matter? She'd at least gotten off this planet, and she looked to be not much older than the boy.

Thumps. Now they were on this barge. Gleam of violet, gleam of yellow. No. Leong Suk would be shamed. A thought crossed his mind—a thought far older than the boy's years. There's nothing wrong with being ashamed of yourself—if you're alive to feel that way later.

A howl. He'd been seen! A hand clawed down at him, to drag him up to meet a balled fist or a stick. The boy grabbed the long-abandoned glass vase and slapped it across the stanchion next to him. The glass shattered, and the boy bounded up, whipping the vase like a saber across the face of the older boy.

Blood. A scream. Another scream, from the boy himself, as the older one fell away, and the boy leapt toward the second of his pursuers. Again he slashed, and blood spurted from the second one's arm. Then there were shouts, clattering, and five teenagers ran like a demon of the sea was behind them. One lay writhing on the barge, hands covering the ruins of what had been a face.

The boy came back to himself. He twisted sideways and pelted down the deck of a dredger, ignoring the shouts of the crewmen cleaning the chains and buckets, jumped over its stern, onto a small boat, then another leap . . . and he disappeared. He did not stop his flight until he'd scrambled onto the stern of a just-departing crosschannel towboat. He slumped against its wire railing, panting. He still held the broken vase in one hand. Now it was violet, yellow . . . and scarlet. The boy dropped it into the water.

He thought about what had happened. He did not feel as if he'd won a victory or something. He didn't feel proud. But the three books were still safe in his knapsack. He decided he knew something he hadn't known before. You had to know what you might encounter. And you always should give yourself an edge. More than anyone knew you had. Maybe a weapon . . . maybe . . . maybe just knowing something. He shook his head. He was not sure where this thought was taking him, but he would return to it later. He had learned something valuable this day.

The boy's name was Kea Richards. He was eight years old.

By the twenty-first century, Hawaii was a rotting slum. Its few natives were living on reservations, supported by government guilt checks. Its native flora and fauna were nearly extinct outside of a few botanical gardens and zoos. And its population was close to twenty million humans. As always, world events had not been kind to the islands, from the Chinese descent into barbarism before they once more closed the bamboo curtain at the end of the twentieth century, to the anarchy that disrupted Japan, the religious wars that turned Indonesia into an illiterate theocracy, and the earthquakes and exclusionary (anti-Asian) laws passed by the government of North America in the opening decades of the century, before its collapse and takeover when Earth finally achieved a single government.

Of the islands, Kaui and Oahu were the least spoiled, since they had the greatest wealth. Least spoiled from original paradise in the same sense that Manhattan Island of the twentieth century was identical with the rock Peter Minuit purchased in the seventeenth century. The Big Island of Hawaii was not rural, not urban, but dirt-poor, serving as a labor pool for cheap manual workers.

The center of Hawaii was now Maui/Molokai/Lanai/ Kahoolawe/Molokini. In the dim past, they had been a single island, and Man was now in the process of making them one again, with floating barricades and causeways. The reason was Space. Hawaii was the perfect midpoint launch station for torchships headed offplanet to the terraformed worlds of Mars and some of the Jovian/Saturnian moons. Or else, less frequently, to where the great sailships waited to build their crews for the generations-long journey to the stars. And Hawaii had been the launch point for two of the five true starships Earth had been able to build and send out on their government-bankrupting explorations.

Businesses blanketed Maui, from bars to machine shops to import/export to who-really-knew. The sea itself was covered with ships, anchored or tied one to another, from skiffs to huge restaurant boats. The islands were encircled with huge floating Hamilton barriers, patterned after the Thames tidal palisades that required only a few minutes to automatically lift into floating breakwaters, in the event of hurricanes or tsunamis. There were even larger breakwaters circling the deeps—what had been Kealaikahiki Channel—where the torchships ported.

When Kea Richards was born, his family ran a small diner on Big Island, in the city of Hilo. Kea vaguely remembered his father and grandmother talking about the old days back on the mainland. The diner served anything and everything, and Kea remembered his father boasting they could make anything anybody wanted, given a recipe and the ingredients. He even thought they'd been challenged a few times, and, he dimly remembered, had been victorious making some strangely named and even-more-strange-tasting dishes. He himself was thrilled when his father would pile a box on a chair near the grill and put his infant son atop it, and pretend to consult him as he cooked. To this day, he still remembered recipes or parts of recipes.

He had trouble remembering his mother, except that she was very pretty. Or maybe he remembered her beauty because Leong Suk would talk about it. But not in a complimentary way. She was half-Thai, half-Irish, which is where Kea got his eyes, as blue as the skies above in the winter, when the trade winds blew away the pollution. Kea was her only child and that was just as she wanted. The boy never knew why his father would sometimes sing a song, which Kea couldn't remember any of the words to except "Oblahdee/Oblahdah/Life goes on . . ." but it would instantly spark a blazing row.

When Kea was only five, his mother disappeared. His father searched, fearing the worst, not sure what the worst meant. And he found his wife—or, rather, found what had happened to her. She had volunteered for a longliner. The elder Richards shuddered, a reaction Kea did not understand for years, until he was able to find some of the declassified accounts of the misery, murder, and insanity that happened on the monstrous sailing ships, even before they were beyond contact in their reach for the stars.

Kea Richards cried a little. Then they told the boy that it did not matter. His mother would be happier, somewhere out there. And they could be happier here. Just the three of them. Two years later, the tsunami struck.

Kea was climbing a tree when the ocean left. A girl had said that the tree had a coconut, and Kea wanted to see what the fruit looked like. Pollution had killed the native coconut palms decades earlier. He had looped rope between his feet, put a single safety line around the tree trunk, and was shinnying up the palm when he chanced a look out to sea. He gaped. It was as if the tide was going out, except going out in a roar, receding far into Hilo Bay. He had never seen such a sight. There were fish, stranded and flopping in the exposed bottom mire. A wreck of a boat was being turned over and over as the Pacific was sucked away, just as if someone had pulled the plug from a washtub.

Two thousand kilometers at sea, there had been a suboceanic earthquake. The quake set three waves in motion toward the Hawaiian Islands. Each of them was only half a meter in height—but there were a hundred kilometers between wave crests. Instruments sensed the quake. They should have sparked alarms. But there were none shrilling across the city of Hilo when the tsunami struck. The great barriers protecting the Maui Complex and the torchship port slid smoothly into position. There were none around Hilo.

Kea heard screams. Saw people running. Some were running for the waterfront in curiosity, others were running away. Down the street he saw his father. He was shouting for Kea. Kea whistled, and saw his father gesture frantically. Kea obediently started to slide down the tree.

He heard the roar. And the sea returned to Hilo as it had four times in a little more than a century. The ocean floor had slowed the base of the seismic waves and now, as the water shallowed before land, the waves crested. The first wave was not the biggest Kea had seen—his father had taken him to Oahu and shown him the North Shore during a winter storm, and he'd shuddered as the great breakers, as high as ten meters, thundered against the land. This wave was only five meters tall, they said later. But it traveled at a speed of almost eight hundred kilometers per hour.

The first wave shattered the great breakwater as if it had never existed and rolled on, breaking, foaming, destroying. It ripped apart buildings, ships, houses, groundcars, hovercraft, men and women. Ripped them apart and used them as battering rams. The front of the wave was a solid wall of debris. Kea thought he remembered seeing his father try to run, and the wave catch him and their tiny home and diner. But perhaps not.

He woke, a day and a half later, in a charity hospital ward. He had been found by a fishing boat, still lashed to that tree, floating nearly a kilometer out to sea.

No one ever found the bodies of his father and grandmother.

Kea did not end up in an orphanage. An elderly woman appeared at the hospital. Leong Suk. She told the officials that she had once worked for the Richards family, and they had treated her well. Kea did not remember her. Kea went home with Leong Suk that day. She had a small shop on a back street in Kahanamoku City, selling nonperishable groceries and sundries. She and Kea lived upstairs. That first day, she informed Kea what the rules were. He was to be a good boy. That meant he was to keep certain hours and help in the store when she needed him. He was not to give her trouble. She said she was too old to be able to raise a hellion. She did not know what she would do if he was bad. And one more thing. Kea was to learn. That would be the only path out of the slum. She did not care what he became, but he was not going to spend his life in Kahanamoku City. Kea nodded solemnly. He knew she was right. This place had already cost him his entire family. He felt it was trying to kill him, as well.

Kea, already a well-behaved child, gave Leong Suk little trouble—except when it came to school. He came home after two weeks at the local grammar. He was not learning anything. Leong Suk was skeptical. The boy proved it by reciting, chapter by chapter, what his class was supposed to learn during the next quarter. She wondered whom they could find for a tutor. Kea soon ferreted out a likely candidate.

Three streets away was the Lane of the Godmen. Tiny storefronts, each one with a different shaman or priest, each one looking for converts and acolytes. Kea came dashing home, shouting about one. The Temple of Universal Knowledge. A bit bigger than the other hovels—and filled with fiches, microfiches, and piles and piles of books. It even had a battered computer link to the university library.

Leong Suk told the boy they would go to this temple. Inside, it smelled a little musty, a little bad, as did the "priest," a balding, obsequious man who called himself Tompkins. Yes, he meant what he said. No one could know too much. Only when a being knew All Things could he achieve perfection, and he must study all his life and, if blessed, other lives to come. Then would come translation. He listened to Kea read aloud. Asked him some questions—questions that might have puzzled a secondary-school graduate. Tompkins beamed. Yes, he would happily take Kea as a student. His fee would be . . . it was astonishingly cheap. Leong Suk saw the way Tompkins was looking at the boy, and told Kea to go outside. She told the man that he was not to preach his religion to the boy. If Kea decided to become a believer . . . that was as it would be. That was not a problem, the little man smoothed.

One more thing, the old woman said . . . and Tompkins shrieked slightly, as mother-of-pearl blurred around Leong Suk's wrinkled hand, and the point of a double-edged butterfly knife touched his chest. "You will never touch the boy," she said, nearly in a whisper. "You will never *think* about touching the boy. Because if you do . . . you will wonder why your friend, death, took so long to find you." Tompkins shuddered . . . and the knife vanished.

Whether Leong Suk was correct or not, the man was never anything other than a perfectly correct teacher to Kea. In fact, whatever Tompkins's private desires might have been vanished in his awe, as the boy seemed to effortlessly inhale anything that was put in front of him. He particularly throve on mathematics. Engineering. Physics. All practical, though. He seemed to have little interest in pursuing theories. When he was twelve, Tompkins asked Kea why he seemed less interested—even though he read voluminously—in the social sciences. Kea looked at Tompkins seriously, as if not sure whether to trust the man.

"Hard science is what will get me out of here, mister. Out of here . . . and up there." He gestured upward—and it took Tompkins a moment to realize that the gesture swept out, out to the stars themselves.

Richards learned other things. How to make change quickly and efficiently. How to spot snide, and refuse it without making a bother. To speak four, and get along in three others, of the more than twelve languages spoken in his neighborhood. He grew tall, strong, and handsome. His smile, and his blue eyes, brought him other teachers, in other subjects. Some were the giggling girls his own age. Some were young and teenaged. And some had husbands. He learned to look behind all curtains in a bedroom before he took off his pants. He learned how to jump from a second-story balcony and roll-land on the mucky street below without breaking something.

He learned where to hit someone and hurt them worse than you hurt yourself. And, more importantly, he learned when to hit and when not to. Sometimes he needed more than a fist. Sometimes he needed an edge. He learned how to use those things, too. He did not lack teachers. The riot police found it necessary to patrol Kahanamoku City in squads, with gravsleds overhead for backup.

When he was fourteen, Tompkins gave him a series of examinations. He passed them, handily. Tompkins did not tell Kea what they were—but he did inform Leong Suk that the boy had just passed the standard entrance examinations for the Academy of Space on the mainland.

"Should he go there?" Leong Suk wondered. Tompkins shook his head. Even though Kea wanted to go into space, that was not the way. The Academy would fit Richards for the military—and that would be not enough for what he thought Kea was capable of. But he refused to tell her more.

The spaceship was tiny—at least compared to pictures Kea had seen of the longliners that hung off Earth, or the torchships that sat like so many oranges, torches underwater, out beyond the barrier. There was no sign on the ship, nor a special marking on the berth. But Kea knew the *Discovery* was a starship. It was one of the five true starships, and the only one still on Earth. Two others had been scrapped: the others were in mothball orbits off Mars.

The ship's stardrive was simple. Idiot-proof. A blink—Alpha Centauri. A word—Luyten 726-B. A full sentence—Epsilon Indi. Half a cup of caff—Arcturus. The problem was fuel for that engine. It had made two voyages and was unlikely to make a third. The fuel for each voyage, an exotic synthetic, had taken five full years, a manhattanproject commitment, and the resources of an entire government to synthesize. Even so, the synthetic only let the engine develop half-power. The ship was a freak, like Leonardo's tank, Lilienthal's airplane, the *Great Eastern*, or the *Savannah*.

Kea stared, hypnotized at its sleekness, dreaming of where it had gone and where it might go again. He left the port at dusk. But he came back again. And again.

Kea was sixteen when Tompkins died. After the morgue crew had left, he and Leong Suk looked at each other. "We must find," she said firmly, "if he had a family, and communicate with them." They searched through the ruins and baled papers of a failed man's life. They found no sign that Tompkins had any friend or loved one anywhere on Earth or the planets. But they found a small antique safe. Leong Suk agonized, but eventually told Kea that perhaps they should open it. Perhaps he knew someone with that skill?

Kea did: himself. An older boy had once shown him. Kea twisted the dial, ear pressed against the door, listening. And he could hear the tumblers fall, just as the other boy had told him he would. Inside, there were two envelopes. One of them contained almost two thousand dollars in new credits, and a will. The money was for Kea. The other contained forms, and exact instructions on how they were to be filled out and who they were to be sent to. The old woman and the boy stared, in that reeking, moldy store. But the instructions were clear.

Kea filled out the forms and sent them off to the named person on the mainland. Within a week, a thick letter came back to him. He was to contact a certain person in Oahu. That person would have him take some tests. Kea followed those orders, too. They waited.

Six weeks after they had decided the whole matter was either a joke or complete madness, another letter came to him. This one was from the Director of Admissions, California Institute of Technology, Pasadena City, Province of California. He was welcomed to the Entering Freshman Class, Fall, A.D. 2182. Kea Richards had won. He would not live, or die, in Kahanamoku City. Now he would be free.

CHAPTER TWENTY-TWO

Pasadena, A.D. 2183

KEA SAT ON the edge of Millikan's Pot, waiting to meet the smart guys. So far, there hadn't been any. Cal Tech was a rather large disappointment, which he was just now realizing at the beginning of his sophomore year. His freshman year had been a blur of auditorium-sized classes, expensive fiches, loneliness, and work. He'd had little chance to evaluate the world he was now in. The blur had probably been increased by Leong Suk's death, just before Christmas of 2182. Kea hadn't been notified of her death until after the funeral.

Cal Tech was just as much a fraud as any of the faiths on Godmen Lane. And like all good swindles, it looked great from the outside. It had more Nobel laureates than even Houston or Luanda—but most of them taught one or two survey courses and perhaps a doctoral-level program with a handful of specially chosen disciples. The school, with more than 25,000 students, was approaching its three hundredth anniversary, and was a soar of the most modern architecture and imagination. About the only buildings left from the "olden days"—before the institute had begun its cancerous expansion, devouring not just a nearby city college but the city's main center as well—was the fountain he was sitting on, and the nearby Spanish-style Kerkhoff Hall, now used for freshman orientations.

The work, while hard, largely consisted of swotting: rote memorization and regurgitation at periodic examinations. Both of the Theory courses he had qualified for this semester seemed to preach enhancement/modification of the past's breakthroughs rather than instilling any truly original thought in the students.

He wasn't so cork-topped that he had expected Cal Tech to be perfect, that it would give him the Secrets of the Ancients. But he had thought the school would have *some* original thinkers, scientists who were looking beyond this system/time's moil of rote repetition of the past's errors. Maybe there were sages, he thought, and he was just too damned young and dumb to know who, or where, they were. Yeah. Or maybe the original thinkers had gotten fed up and were teaching offplanet on Ganymede or Mars. If so, why were there so many offworlders going to Cal Tech?

Not that any of Kea's doubts had shown up in his work—he was holding a flat 4.0 average and had been on the Founder's List both semesters of the previous year. He was set. All he had to do was keep his grades, smile, morale, and genitalia up, and he would be a Twenty-second Century Surefire Success. Which meant, he thought wryly, he would be sucked into one of the super design-plants like Wozniak City and, eventually, if he behaved properly, allowed to put his name on a "particularly elegant" computer path. Or, even more dizzyingly, to have a tertiary process in some synthetic industrial plant named after him. Perhaps they would reward him with a two-week, all-expense-paid trip to Nix Olympica. On one of the lesser peaks, of course.

Kea suddenly grinned. You're right, my lad, he thought. There's no option but suicide. Lie down in front of the next railbus as it passes, baby blue. Speaking of which . . . He looked at his watch—this year the fashion was to wear a timepiece on the wrist—and realized he'd best bust buns, or he was going to be late for work. He'd have just time to drop off his fichecase at his far off-campus rooming house, where he paid far too much for a tiny attic room, and change clothes.

Now forget all that crap you were thinking. You will not end up a cog in somebody else's machine. Hell, you can go back to Maui and start all over again as a gangster before you allow them to do that to you. Or you could volunteer for a longliner . . .

He shivered, and ran a thumb up the fastener of his jacket. He felt suddenly cold. The fall sun, no doubt, wasn't as warming as it appeared.

The hashhouse/ginjoint Kea worked in was in the middle of a bad district. About a million or so years ago, Kea had discovered after he peeled through geological layers of wallboard, paint, and flocked wallpaper, the place had been named the Gay Cantina. Now it had no name as far as anyone knew— it was just the dive over there. All the licenses were in the name of the owner, a glowering goon named Buno, and everything was paid in cash.

Buno hadn't believed anybody as good-looking—i.e., without any of the district's *de rigueur* face scars—as Richards, let alone anybody who was attending Cal Tech, would want a job in his dive. But Kea, who had spent a lot of time remembering his father's cooking and over the past several years had done the meals for Leong Suk and himself, persisted. Besides, he thought, it'd be a hoot seein' what happened the first time a yayhoo decided to hurrah the kid. Buno tried him out.

Now there was a smallish vee-notch in the countertop— and a wide dark stain around it. After that the district left Richards alone, especially when they noted that after he'd taken the chef's knife out of the counter—and the thug's hand—he hadn't called the police.

Kea worked from sixteen hundred hours until some vague time called closing, which meant when the last drunk had stumbled out and no more were reeling in. Mostly the dive was pretty quiet and Kea could get his studying done. But not this night. The house was very busy, with a steady stream of hungry and even partially sober customers. About 2100, ten very unhappy drunks fell in. It was just another night. And then Austin Bargeta showed up. Kea, putting together a fried-egg-and-ham-and-cheese sandwich for one of the boozers, didn't see him when he entered. But he did recognize Bargeta's rather remarkable voice when he asked for a menu. Kea had heard it several times before—he and Bargeta were both suffering through Particle Theory and its Immediate Application in Common Yukawa Drive Situations.

The Bargetas were richrich. The family had been founded four generations before when a brilliant designer had made his trillions, building among other things one of the first portable triple-lobe astrographic instruments. Then he had married the daughter of one of Japan's most respected *yakuza*/bankers and the dynasty had begun. The family was very old-money now, with most of the wealth in holding companies. The rest was in interplanetary building/transport. Each Bargeta generation was presented with a choice—a child could become either family head or else a trust baby. The family head would prove himself by running the high-risk building/transport division, and the behind-the-scenes bankers would take care of the rest of the nearly automatic money machine. Being the Chosen One meant wealth and power beyond comprehension.

Austin Bargeta was making a run at being the heir apparent, or so Kea had heard. The problem and the gossiped wonderment was how long the family name would carry him before he was punted into the outer darkness, a failed heir apparent.

"Austin."

It took three blinks for Bargeta to sort of recognize Richards. He wasn't being a snob, Kea realized. He was not much more sober than the ten drunks behind him.

"Oh, it's Richards," he said. "You're in one of my classes. *What* are you doing *here*?"

"Some of us," Kea said, "have to work. You've heard of work, haven't you? What most people do? For money?"

"Oh. Oh, yes. I'm sorry. Didn't mean, and all . . . don't mean to sound like . . . been gazing on the wine while it was red, you know."

"Yeah. Austin, I've got to tab you to something. This isn't exactly your kind of place."

"Why not?" Bargeta turned and looked around, and nothing, from the graffiti on the wall to the stained ceiling to the clientele, seemed to register. "Seems quite . . . you know, authentic."

"It's that. Okay." Kea shrugged. Feed the kid—which Richards thought of Bargeta, even though Bargeta was a year and a class senior to him—and slick him out of here. "Can I get you something to eat?"

Bargeta focused on the menu. He was studying it when one of the drunks shouted, "Hey, cookie, if you're through blowin' in y'r bitch's ear, I'd like to order m' eats." Kea ignored the shout. Bargeta did not. He swiveled off the counter stool, face turning red, as if he were in a vid. Wonderful, Kea thought.

"I understand," Austin said with great clarity, "that you call your mother Piles, because she is such a bleeding ass. Or am I mistaken?"

The drunk came up in several waves. Kea noticed, as he slid unobtrusively to the cashbox, that the man was a Samoan. There weren't that many humans wandering around Pasadena measuring two meters in any direction. Kea also knew that the Samoan culture is maternal, and that, very shortly, Bargeta was going to be steamrolled. Bargeta took on some kind of half-assed martial arts stance as the Samoan juggernauted toward him.

Kea took a wrapped roll of quarter-credit coins from the cashbox. Bargeta hit the Samoan with a snap-punch. The man grunted, but did not otherwise move or react. Then he swung. His punch took Austin in the shoulder and sent him spinning back, to sprawl across the counter. Kea slid the roll of coins into Bargeta's hand. Austin's fingers kinesthesiaed over the roll, told his brain what he was holding, and he came back up, whatever too-doo-woo self-defense system he'd been practicing forgotten. He swung a roundhouse punch, quite wildly.

The Samoan didn't bother moving aside. Austin's punch

caught the man on the side of the jaw, and Richards could hear bone break and cartilage crunch. The Samoan shouted pain as blood spattered, and he slumped to a sitting position. His jaw hung slack and to the side. His friends were on their feet—and Kea had his cleaver out and had fingered the memory code for the cops before they could close on Bargeta. It was perfectly all right to call for heat in this instance—none of the drunks were local lads.

By the time the riot squad materialized, Kea had unobtrusively gotten the roll of coins from Austin's fist and busted it into the appropriate change drawer. They tucked the brokenfaced Samoan into a meatwagon and told his friends to haul butt out of there. Then they turned to deal with Austin. Kea, again impulsively, said he would take care of him. Kea called a cab, made sure Bargeta had enough credits to pay for the ride to wherever he lived, and started shutting down the kitchen. A thought crossed his mind that he would *never* make a good Machiavellian.

Three days later, when Particle Boredom Etc. met, Kea checked the results of a particularly bastardly verbal they'd had at the last class. What the course lacked in interest, the instructor made up for in severity. Second from the top. Not bad, Kea thought. He would've maxed it, but he had gone home the night before with one of the waitresses, who wanted to show him her new flat and other things of possible interest, and had been more than a little hungover. Austin's voice gloomed over his shoulder. "Oh crap. And I actually *studied* for the brute." Kea spotted Bargeta's name. In the subbasement. As usual.

Kea turned. Bargeta looked about him. No one else was near the bulletin board. "You know," Bargeta said, slightly lowering his voice, "I was not *that* drunk. And I never forget anything. You would appear to have prevented me from being mashed across one of your restaurant's walls."

Kea grinned—Bargeta, if one disregarded that voice and his born-to-the-manor manner, wasn't unlikable. "You weren't in any trouble. Clean-living sort of aluno like yourself . . . you would've beanoed him, easy. Or, anyway, a bolt of lightning would've come through the roof and saved your butt when Vishnu decided to jump in."

"He was *that* big?"

"Bigger."

Austin laughed. "As I said, I owe you. When—or rather if—this class comes to an end, lemme buy you a sudser. Not that I'm what I think that railbus was accusing me of being. Unless," he said with mock alarm that became real as his mind considered that once again he might have inadvertently offended, "you're a pledger? And not that I have anything against, uh, well, if you're the kind of man who, well, you know, doesn't really, well; like women all that much."

Kea shook his head. "Nope. I'm a normal red-blooded lusher."

"Good. Good. And now the thought occurs that perhaps we could talk about some other things. About some other difficulties I seem to have stumbled into that you could advise me on."

Over several beers, Austin made his proposal. He wasn't exactly the shining star of Cal Tech, he freely admitted. And a GPA of 1.5 was *not* gentlemanly enough to keep him at the institute, which would seriously displease some people. Some people, Kea was sure, were the decision-makers in the Bargeta family. Austin wanted to hire Kea as a tutor. Richards started to take a pass, and then, in one frozen instant, caught himself. Go ahead. Somebody's trying to give you the edge, just like that broken vase. Just like that roll of coins you passed this kid. Don't turn it down. He accepted.

Tutoring wasn't hard—Austin was a quick study. Admittedly, whatever Kea'd crammed in one ear slipped out the other within a week, but what of it? There didn't seem to be any professors interested in anything more than a proper regurgitation of their own magnificence. And it wasn't as if Austin would ever have to *use* any of the knowledge he supposedly had. At that point, Kea became fascinated as to just how smart he could make Bargeta. Assuming he was willing to play any angle—just as he'd been willing to play any angle to get away from Kahanamoku City. The answer was, very smart indeed, as Richards discovered the university had its own underworld, just as crooked as anything on Maui. Exams could be purchased. TAs could be bribed to write papers. Or to mark someone in attendance. In some cases, where the instructor was a complete mountebank, even change grades. By the end of the semester, Austin was scoring honorable 2.5's–3.0's in all his courses, and in one massive six-credit lab course that was in reality a gut run, an amazing 3.5. "And," Austin marveled, "it's all because you showed me how to focus on what's important."

Austin asked Kea if he wanted to move in with him before the next semester started. Richards jumped at the invite. It wasn't as if they would get in each other's way—Bargeta actually had a *house*, sitting on an open lot by itself. Six bedrooms. A maid, a cook, and a yeeves to take care of the details. Austin took his new friend around to meet *his* friends. Kea, tall, rugged, with a strange and colorful background, was at first the latest wonder in Bargeta's circle. It was assumed that sooner or later he'd pass on, as did all of Austin's new best friends, male or female. But Kea did not. And he became an accepted part of their gatherings.

Kea studied these rich young people and their mannerisms carefully. He learned, in fact, all that the upper crust could teach. It was fascinating. The rules were as exact as any of the triads back on Maui would require from a member. And the penalties for error, even if they weren't as physically fatal, appeared to be almost as damaging. At times he felt he saw Austin Bargeta for what he was—a shallow, superficially charming user, who in fact was playing Kea like a marionette. And he saw the Bargeta family, even though he had only met one member, as part of a great conspiracy of the status quo, a status quo that was keeping mankind from its real destiny.

Of course, that immediately produced a question from within: What destiny, Kea? He did not have an answer to that, only the feeling that mankind was holding itself back from some great goal, a goal out among the stars, a goal that would be shared by other beings as intelligent or more so than mankind.

Space travel was more than two centuries old now, and what had been accomplished? The Solar System was explored and a few worlds terraformed. Fifty or so longliners had set sail into the unknown, and those who had managed to message back reported emptiness beyond, and horror and degeneracy within. A few stars had been touched by the astronomically expensive starships. One extraterrestrial race had been contacted. What an accomplishment, he jeered.

Austin's senior and Kea's junior term passed smoothly as well. Bargeta graduated. Not with honors—no amount of cheating and bribery could have managed that—but comfortably in the upper third of his class. Kea was First Junior. Next year he knew he would be the Prime graduate of the institute. With that degree, Kea would have little trouble finding a suitable position. Perhaps with Bargeta Shipping. Perhaps elsewhere. Soon—perhaps in only three or four years—Kea would go into space. The future looked quite bright. It became dazzling on that long, celebratory weekend after Bargeta had received his diploma and sprang the great surprise. He felt he owed Kea, and he wanted everyone to know it, especially his family. He wanted Kea to be his guest for the summer—or at least part of it, since this summer would last twice as long as any Kea had known. Kea would also have to make minor alterations in his own plans—he wouldn't be able to start his final year at Cal Tech until the first semester of '85.

Austin's smile grew as he saw Kea frown at the proposed changes to his life. Then he paid off the buildup. The reason Kea would have to start school late was passage time. Come September, he'd still be at the Bargeta family's vacation compound, the one they called Yarmouth. Near Ophir Chasm, now a freshwater ocean.

On Mars.

Kea felt, as Austin beamed, as if he'd suddenly entered freefall aboard one of the early spaceships. School could wait, his career could wait. Space. It was the beginning of the end.

* * *

Mars, A.D. 2184

Her name was Tamara. She was seventeen. Tall. Dark-haired. A lean curving body. Pert breasts. Eyes that dared, and told Kea no dare was forbidden—if he had the courage to follow through. She was also Austin's sister.

She did not look more than passingly like him. She was perfect. Perhaps Kea realized that what the gods had failed to give Tamara, the finest plas surgeons had. But he probably would not have cared. It was a measure of Kea's intoxication with other things that it took some time before he became aware of her.

His brain-drunk had begun as soon as the ship had lifted. A Mars trip was still a rich man's pleasure, costing, in real credits, about what a first cabin on an Earth ocean liner would have cost during the days of the Cunards. The suite he shared with Austin, and one of the family factotums burdened with reports, was one of the largest on the transport. It measured four meters wide by seven meters long. Austin told Kea that this was always the worst part of the passage—he felt trapped.

Kea never noticed. For one thing, the suite was not much larger than the cramped apartment he and Leong Suk had shared. And for another, the suite had a "port"—actually a vid screen linked to through-hull pickups mounted at various places around the transport. Mars grew in the forward pickup. As the transport closed on the wargod's world, Kea could pick out details. Valles Marineris. Tharsis. Olympus Mons. All spectacular—but what most riveted Kea's attention were the works of man. Not just the haze of Mars's new atmosphere, or the oceans and lakes, or the twinkled lights of the new cities, but the offplanet marvels, some of which had been allowed to remain, as reminders and memorials. A space station. The First Base on Deimos. One of the great mirrors, in a geosynchronous orbit over the north pole, that had helped melt Mars's ice caps.

That, he realized, wasn't a deliberate monument. It was the centerpiece of a junk heap. He cozened his way to the bridge, learned how to use the pickup's controls, and scanned the orbiting scrap, for reasons he was never sure of. There were dead deep-space ships he recognized from books, museums, or models he'd never been able to afford as a boy. A longliner that had never been completed or launched. A space station, peeled and shattered—Kea remembered reading about that disaster of a hundred years earlier.

And, to one side, by itself, a tiny ship. Another one of the starships. The second one he'd seen. He wondered why he seemed to be the only one who saw them as a mingle of triumph and defeat. Promise and tragedy. For want of a nail. Hell, for want of a goddamned energy source . . .

Kea went back to the "suite" and prepared for landing. Bargeta senior, Austin's father, was waiting for them. He was frightening. Kea wondered if he would have felt the same about the older man if he didn't know how much power he wielded. He decided yes, he would. It was Bargeta's face. Hard, measuring eyes. The thin lips of a martinet. And yet the jowls of a sybarite and the body of someone kept in shape only by highly paid trainers, not from physical labor. It was, Kea realized, the same face Austin would wear, if he was chosen to replace Bargeta, in forty years or so.

Mr Bargeta was very friendly to Kea. He was grateful to the man who'd helped his boy out of that imbecilic school slump he'd fallen into. In his letters, Austin had mentioned Richards frequently, he said. Kea knew this to be a lie—Austin never communicated with his family except to plea, directly and briefly, for an advance on next period's allowance. The older man said that before Kea returned to Earth, they would have to talk. About the future. Kea's future.

Kea felt as if he were in the middle of a twentieth-century mafia vid and about to be made a member of a crime family. Perhaps, he thought, that wasn't just a piece of romantic foolishness. He put the thought aside.

There were ten or fifteen Bargetas—including cousins and relatives-by-marriage—resident in the compound. And the family retainers. He asked—and was told that thirty men or women were required for each "guest." More, for "special occasions." Kea was reminded that, truly, the very rich were not as common folk.

The Bargeta compound was only a hundred meters from the near-vertical cliff that led down to the sea that had been the Ophir Chasm. The compound had originally been one of the earliest bubbles; it had been acquired by the Bargetas and truly turned into a pleasure dome, even after the no-longer-needed plas was stripped away. There were main buildings and outcabins. Halls for drinking or playing tennis—even Kea became fascinated with what a ball could do in a low-g world. Lawns. Heated pools. A cabana had been recently built on the cliff-edge. From it, a round clear elevator shaft, with McLean plates, dropped down to a floating dock and the effervescent ocean.

That was where Tamara swam into his consciousness. Literally. He was perplexing over the sails and rigging of a trimaran tied up to the dock. Kea had done some sailing on Earth, but only on a monohull. He was trying to figure out, if he tacked sharply, whether the boat would spin out, a wing would shatter and he'd be trying to navigate a catamaran, or if the craft would just go into irons, when Tamara sealed out of the ocean onto the deck.

At first he thought she wasn't wearing anything—and then realized the color of the small one-piece suit was exactly matched to her deeply tanned skin. He wondered—after he'd begun recovering from the basic arrival, why she wasn't shivering. He himself was wearing a one-piece shorty wetsuit against the chilly breeze and cold water. Then he noticed the tiny heatpak in the suit, tucked at the base of her spine. Tamara padded forward, without saying anything. She eyed Kea intently. Kea turned slightly to the side. His suit was tight, and he would rather not embarrass himself.

"You are Austin's Saint George." Her voice was a purr.

"I am. I left my card in my other armor. Dragons rescued, virgins slain, my specialty."

Tamara laughed. "Well, there certainly aren't any dragons on Mars, either. So you can relax." She introduced herself, curled down beside him, shoulder touching his. "I guess the family owes you for helping my brother," she said.

Kea shrugged. "Not by my calcs. The scale's zeroed."

"Perhaps. You'll be staying with us all summer?"

"Right. My return ticket's an open booking. But Austin said we'd best take the . . . what is it, *Copernicus*. It's set to lift on . . . hell, I still haven't figured out the months here . . . Earthdate in the first week of September." Kea dimly realized he was babbling.

"A long time," she said. "We'll have to make sure you aren't bored. Won't we?"

"I, uh, don't think that—I mean, how can you be bored on *Mars*?"

"That is not," Tamara announced conclusively, "the sort of boredom I was talking about." She ran her fingernail down Kea's arm, and it seared like a branding iron. Then she was standing. "You know," she said, "moonrise is special on Mars. The best place to see it is from the cabana. It's away from the compound so there's no lightspill."

She walked to the edge of the trimaran. "Far enough," she went on, "for as much privacy . . . as anyone could ever need." She smiled as if at a secret memory or thought, and then flatdove into the bubbling, CO_2-charged water. Kea's mouth was dry.

The cabana had four bedrooms, each of them made up. It was staffed by four blank-faced men. They asked if Kea wished anything, or any service. Showed him where drinks were iced and snacks were kept. Told him he had but to touch the com and someone would be there within minutes. Then they disappeared. The cabana's main room was circular, with glass walls that would opaque at the touch of a switch. In its center, a huge sunken sofa was around a hooded fireplace, with wooden logs arranged to roar into flames at the touch of a match. A fireplace? On Mars? Not likely, between pollution laws and the incredible permits required to do anything to a tree. It was, of course, false, as Kea discovered.

After a few moments, he found the correct setting, so that the logs were guttering down, flames flickering shadows against the walls. Now, for the drinks.

And Tamara was there. She wore a teal-green pair of flaring pants, and a matching sleeveless top. The pants were scooped far below her navel, and the top ended approximately at Tamara's rib cage. Approximately. Tamara picked up two already-filled glasses she must have poured from the cloth-wrapped bottle that sat in a bucket beside her.

"To . . . to the night," she said. They drank. And they refilled their glasses, and went back to the couch. They talked. Kea could never remember the exact conversation. But he had told her his life story—and Tamara listened, completely fascinated, sitting very close to him. He ran out of words.

Tamara put her glass down. Somehow they'd emptied that bottle of sparkling wine. She reached out, and touched his lips.

"Soft," she murmured. She leaned closer, and her tongue flicked across Kea's lips. He started to kiss her—and she pulled back. She unfolded, and walked away from him—hips swaying. There must have been some sort of hidden fastener on the halter top, because it was suddenly gone. Tamara flipped it over her shoulder. Turned back and looked at him. Her face serious.

She touched her midriff, and the pants fell into a silk pool about her ankles. Tamara stepped clear of them. She stretched, long and lingeringly. Kea stared, unable to speak or move. She walked slowly into a darkened room. She looked back at him and smiled. Then she disappeared into the bedroom. Light flared, as a mock candle was lit.

Kea was free. Free to follow her.

"No," Tamara said. "This time . . . this time you'll just watch." She unwound the scarf, and began knotting it at intervals. "Next time . . . *that's* yours."

Mars became a shadow, a blur. The center of the world was Tamara's body. Nights were a swirl of movement, ecstasy, a sudden flash of sweet torture. Days were exploration and daring, making love anywhere and everywhere. Tamara's passion seemed to increase the greater the risk of discovery or embarrassment. Particularly if the discovery might be made by a member of the family. Not that Kea came to Tamara's bed as an innocent. She learned from him, as well. She wanted something new. And so, reluctantly, he showed her some of the techniques he'd heard of or even, once or twice, had demonstrated in the cribs of Maui.

She learned well and then eagerly practiced those dexterities. She combined them with other skills she was already familiar with. The style of lovemaking she preferred was prolonged, exotic, and would have a lightning-shock of pain/pleasure at the climax. Kea felt as if he were a bit of wood, floating at the edge of a maelstrom, and then being drawn down, deep into its center.

He was in love with Tamara. That could mean disaster. Ruin. But it was a fact. What made it worse—or, perhaps, better—was that Tamara seemed to be as besotted, as passionate and overwhelmed, as Kea. Kea allowed himself to dream of a future—a very different future than he had conceived of before. One which would be for two people.

Kea was amazed. Anything he wanted to do, Tamara seemed delighted to oblige him in. It was as if he were the ruler, instead of . . . His mind shied away from the rest. Once, they went to the dockyards at Capen City. He was fascinated by the array of ships of varying types. Here, torchships were landed in great aboveground cradles rather than ported in water, and Kea could even walk under their bulging enormity and fully realize just how huge they were. Tamara, not terribly interested in the ships themselves— "Darling, we *own* half of them"—was fascinated by the color, squalor, and lurking danger. Several times she told him how safe she felt with him.

Something was bothering Kea. Why were the spacecrews dressed in such a slovenly manner—very different from the heroic posturing of the vid that still occasionally dealt with space travel? Why were there so many notices tagged outside the local hiring hall? And why were the notices so weathered, as if they'd been posted for a long time, with no one desperate enough to answer them?

Tamara and Richards found seats in a crowded dive that called itself a cafe, drinking some terribly sweet concoction Tamara'd ordered from the barkeep, and he tried to think it out. Ignoring the groundpounders, almost everyone they had seen was a spaceman(woman). High vacuum and all that. So, why were all of the conversations he overheard about drink or drugs and how iced they had been the previous night. Or else how terrible the conditions were aboard ship, and which was the least ghastly hellship to sign aboard on. Their language wasn't that of science or engineering, but the lazy-palated monotones or drunken sudden rage of the poor and desperate. It sounded like Wino Row. Why were the eyes of these brave space pioneers so dull? So dead?

He heard, for the first time, of Barrier Thirty-three, the term used as if it were some sort of gateway to Hades. He asked—and found it was the standard bulkhead division between the crew/engine spaces and the cargo/passengers. Something was very wrong. But he didn't know what. He drained his glass and took Tamara's hand. She was staring, entranced, at a woman down the bar whose tattoos covered every inch of skin that could be seen outside the stained cut-down shipsuit. The woman seemed as interested in Bargeta.

Tamara frowned when Kea said he wanted to hat up—but didn't say anything. She gave the tattooed spacewoman a long smile—and Kea remembered that smile from other, private times—as they left the bar. That night, he slept alone, not wanting to disturb Tamara with his dark mood, still disturbed by what he had seen and still wondering what it meant. She laughed away his apologies the next day. She had gone back into Capen City. And looked up some "old friends."

The end came in bright sunlight, on the deck of the trimaran where it had begun, about an Earth-week later. Kea had spent the morning preparing himself. Making sure he had the correct words. Then he was ready—as prepared, he hoped, in this matter of the heart as if it were the most important examination he would ever take. Which it was.

Tamara listened quietly to his stammer that grew into fluency. Then he was finished. Kea waited for her response. It came as a giggle. Then a full laugh. "Kea," she said, when the laugh died away. "Let me understand. You're saying that you think the two of us should . . . be together? When this summer is over? Back on Earth, even?" Kea, feeling his guts writhe, as if he'd just stepped into a gravshaft and the McLean power was off, nodded.

"*Live* together? Or—do you mean like a covenant? Kea, darl', you sound like an oldie, talking about *marriage*! Oh dear. This is delicious. *You?* With me? Oh, my, my." And she dissolved into laughter. Kea got up, and walked numbly across the dock, and found the elevator up to the clifftop.

Sometime later, he found himself in the main house. It was dark. Kea had not eaten, nor gone back to his room. He had tried to be invisible, especially to any of the Bargetas. A couple of the retainers asked if he needed anything. Kea shook his head. He saw one woman's eyes soften. She started to say something, but just put her hand on his arm. Then she looked frightened and hurried away.

He didn't know what he would do next. How could he stay out of Tamara's way for the rest of the summer, a summer that had gone from paradise to purgatory? He couldn't just leave. Austin was his friend. All he wanted was a secret, hidden place, to crawl into and lick the gaping tear Tamara had ripped.

He heard laughter. Austin. "Oh dear, oh dear," he said. "Was he *serious*?"

"If not, he's the best japer on Mars." Tamara.

"I guess it shouldn't be unexpected," another voice said thoughtfully. Bargeta senior.

"I'm sorry, Father," Tamara said. "But I thought—"

"You needn't bother with an apology," her father interrupted. "I'm hardly concerned that you found the rustic to be handsome. Nor how you chose to scratch an itch. It would be most hypocritical for me to suggest my daughter behave as if she were a Renunciant, when we know the family has always had a taste for the . . . rawer side of life, eh?"

There was laughter. Shared laughter. Family laughter at the casual mention of a minor secret.

"So it's my fault." Austin.

"Not really," his father explained. "You've just been reminded of a lesson you perhaps let slip from your mind, when you rewarded this young man's assistance by letting him into your life. But it's not a new lesson. Remember how hard it was when you realized your nannies weren't Bargetas and had to be treated a certain way? Or the children we allowed the servants to have, so you'd have playmates, and how you cried when it was time for them to be sent away? So don't chastise yourself, Austin. It's a lesson we have to learn and relearn."

"So what do we do?" Tamara. "I mean, I can see that letting Kea sulk around for the rest of the summer like some moonstruck swain out of a poem will be really dullity."

"Don't worry," Bargeta senior said. "Perhaps he'll simply vanish. Or jump off a cliff. Or sail off into the sunset. Moonstruck yokels do things like that."

The clink of glasses as someone poured a drink. Then, Austin's voice: "Actually, Father, when you stop to think about it, this whole thing is *very* funny. Isn't it?"

Tamara's titter. A chuckle from Bargeta. And then all three of them were laughing very hard. Harsh, unrelenting laughter. Kea heard no more. Their mirth vanished. As did the Bargetas and Yarmouth itself. The only thing in the entire universe was a tattered, yellowing PLACES AVAILABLE notice, on a spacecrew hiring hall.

CHAPTER TWENTY-THREE

Alva Sector, A.D. 2193

THE PINLIGHT WAS a frantic red pulse on the monitor. "There it is again, Murph!" Vasoovan twittered. "At one o'clock."

Captain Murphy "Murph" Selfridge squeezed into the navigation cubicle. He was a big, formerly athletic man, gone to seed. He bent over his first officer. The light pulsed back at him. Kea Richards watched his commander's broad features take on an oxlike look of puzzlement as he studied the winking light. "I don't get it," the captain finally said. "Same damn coordinates?"

"Same damn coordinates, Murph," Vasoovan said.

"Sure you didn't make some kinda screwup?" Murph asked. "Maybe you better run it through again."

The Osiran sighed the martyred sigh of the constantly incompetent. "If *you* say so, Captain," she twittered. Slender pink tendrils moved swiftly over the com unit. Touching sensor pads. Spinning dials.

Richards and the two scientists kept silent. Their card hands forgotten on the tiny rec table of the cramped instant-bucket-of-bolts some corporate sales veep had misnamed *Destiny I*. There was no *Destiny II*. The first model was so poorly designed and built that only the ten ships had been completed. And those had been sold for kiloweight. Richards's skinflint company had bought two and put them into service. For the past five E-months, it had taken all of Richards's skills as chief engineer to keep the *Destiny I* in

one piece and headed for the mysterious signals emanating
from Alva Sector.

Vasoovan rebooted. The monitor blanked, then came back
on. The light was still blinking. But this time at six o'clock.
"What the hell's goin' on, Vasoovan?" Murph demanded.
"How come the sucker keeps movin' around on us?"

"Don't blame me," Vasoovan protested, anger building. "I
just do my job. Same as anybody else." She turned her large
oval face full on the captain. Vasoovan had the permanent
grin of a carnivore. Even after five months in close proxim-
ity with the ET, Richards found the face unsettling. He
watched two of Vasoovan's eyestalks check out Murph for
signs of argument. The other two craned over Murph's head
to study Richards and the scientists.

One scientist pretended not to notice. She stroked a straying dark curl from her eyes. The other—the man—turned his
handsome profile away. But Kea stared back. He knew better
than to give the Osiran an edge. "What're you looking at,
Richards?" Vasoovan's twittering was shrill.

"Apparently not very much," Kea said. "In my book,
watching my captain and his first officer doing tight twirls
around their backsides hardly qualifies as entertainment."

"You've got no cause to gripe," Murph said. "You're getting triple time for this trip, with some pretty hefty bonuses
all around if we come up with something."

Richards pointed at the wandering light on the nav board.
"If that's our bonus, Captain," he said, "I wouldn't be making
plans for any big spending when we get back. From where
I sit, the company's money is pretty damn safe."

"Come on, Kea," the captain urged. "Let's not be negative. We got a good team, here. And, by god, we're gonna
take this thing all the way over the top."

Kea shrugged. "Sure, Murph. Whatever you say."

"It's *their* fault," Vasoovan said, indicating the scientists.
"This whole thing was their idea. Know what I think? I'll
tell you what I think—"

Dr Castro Fazlur—chief scientist of the expedition—broke

in: "It actually believes it has a thought process, Ruth. Amusing, isn't it?" He crooked his lips into a smile of non-amusement.

Dr Ruth Yuen, Fazlur's assistant and lover, ducked her pretty head. Trying to stay out of the line of fire. "Oh, come now, Ruth. Be honest," Fazlur pressed. Handsome gray-fox features pushed forward. "Don't you find it tragic that the only sign of allegedly intelligent life mankind has found is this tentacled thing?"

"Watch it, Fazlur," Vasoovan hissed.

The scientist ignored the warning. "I'd say it was the eye-stalks," Fazlur said. "What IQ exists in an Osiran is mostly consumed controlling that primitive biological function. This would explain its limited language capabilities. You will note, Ruth, dear, that it speaks the argot of a common ship rat. Obviously, its mental powers are too taxed to achieve a civ-ilized person's vocabulary."

Vasoovan's features turned from pink to parboiled. A pow-erfully muscled tentacle reeled out, searching for a heavy object to hurl. Then snatched back as the captain slapped at it. "Come on, guys. Lighten up. I got enough problems with-out you piling on more." Murph pleaded.

It was at this point that Kea felt a warm, shapely foot press against his calf. It rose up his leg, caressing higher . . . higher. Ruth's dark eyes flashed. A red tongue tip licked an upper lip. It was that Tamara kind of look. Suddenly, the already-cramped world of *Destiny I* slammed around him. He tossed in his cards. "I'm going to catch up on some sleep," he said. "When you figure out where we're going . . . be sure to wake me." He rose, avoiding Ruth's hurt look, and stalked out. The too-familiar sound of quarreling voices faded as he made his way down the corridor.

Surprisingly, he found the fresher room unoccupied. The rest of the crew, fifteen in all, was either at work or bunked down. This was a rare opportunity to scrape off some of the grime the overtaxed atmosphere system aboard the *Destiny I* kept spewing out. He peeled coveralls from his greasy body, then groaned as hot spray needled his flesh. No one ever got really clean aboard *Destiny I*. For months, they had all been walking around in the thickening miasma of their own smells. Eating stale packets of heavily manufactured chow, since scarce water also meant a crimped supply of fresh vegetables from hydroponics.

The needle spray cut off as his hot water allotment was used up. Kea suffered zed guilt as he punched the button and the shower resumed. Crap on those company pinchcredits. A delicious fog filled the room. He spread the soap on thick and lathered up.

The expedition to the Alva Sector had been a bust from the get-go. Kea had signed on against his own good sense. Being chief engineer of a bucket of bolts had never been his idea of a life's work. He'd had big dreams, once. Dreams that seemed to be worth achieving. Then he had thrown it all away over that inbred, high-society woman. If it had happened to somebody else, the situation would be laughable. But the memory of the other, harsh laughter on Mars would be with him for years. He was so young and dumb he didn't ask why the first deep-space company he had hit up leaped on him as if he were solid gold. Sure, he had aced their aptitude test. And gone through the exams in a third the allotted time. Kea had half expected to be rejected, despite his high test scores. After all, he had no experience. He had also assumed the competition would be fierce for something so exotic as career in deep space. Especially now that private companies—sniffing fat profits and guaranteed monopolies—were venturing out on the few bridges to the stars that had been built with government money.

He started getting an idea how wrong he was in his first job as a wiper aboard a cargo hauler making the jump out to Epsilon Indi. His fellow crew members were as stupid as his chief engineer. And *his* brain cells numbered fewer than the fingers on his mangled left hand. What the crew members lacked in intelligence, they made up for in greed and sloth. Any time the ship ported, it was all the captain could do to rouse them from the drinking and narco dens to make the next flight.

His next job—a long jump out of Arcturus—proved the first ship was no exception to the rule. If anything, the feebles making up that crew and officer staff were *less* competent. That journey had ended in near disaster when the captain ignored the clearly charted meteor belt and wound up hulling his ship. Four crew members had died before Kea had jockeyed a patch into position and sealed the hole. His knowledge of Yukawa drive had been tested when it was discovered the engine was damaged. And no one aboard had the skills to repair it. There had been a lot of praying for the next seventy-two E-hours as Kea jury-rigged the stardrive into some kind of working order. The jump home went without incident.

It was then he had been recruited by his present company—Galiot Inc., a division of the megagiant SpaceWays. "Galiot's a brand spankin' new division, son," the recruiter had boasted. "You'll be seein' places and doin' things folks are just startin' to dream about. Our mission's to come up with new ways and ideas for SpaceWays to make money. They're puttin' big credits behind us. If you join, son, you'll be joinin' quality. Nothin' but the best for Galiot Inc. Cuttin' edge all the way." Kea had hired on at a two-grade jump in position. And it wasn't long before he'd worked his way up to chief engineer.

Yeah, he thought, as the needle spray soothed tension-knotted muscles, the road might not have been long, but it sure was torturous. It wasn't the risk that made it so. Hell, risk was spice. Here he was getting his chance to act out his boyhood dreams. Starships bound for adventure in the beyond. But the company did its best to spoil all sense of wonder. They hired and bought cheap, making intellectual companionship minimal and turning the most routine labor into knuckle-busting frustration for lack of quality machines and tools. The company had a knack for turning any assignment into boredom—interspersed with fear of a pointless death as shoddy equipment failed at a touch.

What the bejesus are you doing here, Richards? Stuck on a one-E-year-minimum expedition. Surrounded by the sorriest, most cantankerous, ill-mannered employees of Galiot Inc. You could have stayed at Base Ten. Waited for another contract. Okay, you were bored out of your skull. So, what's new about that when you work for Galiot Inc? You could have guessed. Hell, you *knew*, Richards. Knew at the time you had best tell them to put that contract where the sun doesn't shine.

He heard the fresher door open. Through the clouds of steam he saw a lush, female form slip out of tight-fitting coveralls. The warning bells hammered. Dr. Ruth Yuen smiled through the mist, then slowly lay down, on the fresher's small changing bench. "Mmmm," she said. "I *like* my men nice and clean."

The last time she had left his bunk, Richards had sworn to himself that was it. The end. The woman was more dangerous than anything aboard the ship or outside in cold, cold space. A guaranteed knife in the back. So, tell her no, Richards. Tell her no. Send her back to her full-time lover and boss, Dr Castro Fazlur.

Go ahead, Richards.

But his feet were moving forward, taking him out of the shower. Ruth's smile grew broader. She looked up at him, eyes half-closed. Her hand reached up. Caressed Kea's stomach. Slid downward. Her left leg lifted off the deck, knee bending, and she put her foot on the bench. She let her leg fall open, then reached down and touched herself, stroking.

"What're you waiting for, Richards? Do you need a written invitation?" As he knelt over her, her legs came up, locking around his waist.

Sure, Richards. Tell her no.

Just like you told the company no.

He had heard the rumors about Operation Alva even before he had been approached by Captain Selfridge to join the crew. Word was that a routine scan of the remote Alva

Sector had come up with a strong but intermittent disturbance in the normal background radiation. The pulse came from an area no known body existed. It was not a black hole. Or any of the theoretical formations posed by twenty-second-century physicists to explain the newly unexplainable. Also, as far as anyone could tell, the blips or buzzes showing up against the radiation background charts came from a "natural" source.

Kea was oddly stirred by rumors of the unexplained phenomenon. The small-boy/adventurer in him wanted badly to see for himself. To be the first to know a thing before anyone else. To rediscover his sense of wonder. Then his hard-won cynicism reasserted itself. Unless there was proven money in it, the company would ignore the whole thing. The required government report would eventually be drawn up, filed, and forgotten in a bureaucratic black hole. So, he'd returned to the room the company provided 'tween-contract workers and buried himself in his steadily growing collection of historical works. Then he had gotten the news of Dr Fazlur's arrival. The scientist was reportedly an expert on alternate-universe theory. Kea had nearly dismissed this news outright. He had met too many of the company's pet experts. They always proved to be nothing more than PhDs for hire, with no qualms about bending fact to meet an employer's expectations. He had figured Fazlur was there merely to draw up the report, to maintain the company's license requirements with the government. This guess had been reinforced when he heard about Fazlur's gorgeous "assistant"—Dr Ruth Yuen—and how he liked to nuzzle and paw at her in public. The man was obviously more playboy than scientist. Then he'd heard about the many metric tons of equipment being unloaded from the ship that had borne Fazlur and Yuen to Base Ten.

"Company's turned on the money machine," an old space jock had said at one of Kea's favorite dives. "Somethin's gotta be up!"

A small forest of special antennas had been erected on Base Ten's exterior skin by around-the-clock crews. Kea had

seen it for himself upon his return from a quick, one-week
hop. As his ship had floated toward Base Ten's docking bay,
he had noted the odd configuration Fazlur had ordered constructed: wires knitted together and strung from towers until
they formed an immense gill-net receiver. The old space jock
had not exaggerated when he talked about the money machine
going full bore. Something was up, indeed.

Kea had paced his room. Picked up Gibbon. Tossed it.
Flipped through the *Anabasis*. Tossed it, too. Ditto *Plutarch's
Lives*. And Churchill. Too many hours dragged by. When he
had gotten the message from Captain Selfridge that he was
putting together a crew for an expedition to the Alva Sector,
he had bounded to the meeting as fast as a strong young man
can bound in three-quarters gravity.

"Company thinks real well of you, Richards," Selfridge
had said.

"Thanks, Captain."

"Hey, none of that captain business," the man had
protested. "I like my ship loosey-goosey. Informal. Makes
for a better team. That way we all pull together when you-
know-what hits the fan . . . Call me Murph."

"Sure . . . Murph," Kea had said, thinking then and there
he ought to blow out. Only a fool would sign on a ship run
by a captain who said, "Call me Murph."

"That's right, Richards. Loosey-goosey. And we'll get on
fine. Anyway. Company put you top of my list for the chief
engineer's slot. Now that I metcha, and we talked . . . I can
see why."

Kea hadn't responded. He would have blown the deal. He
had spoken maybe fifteen words since he had arrived at the
captain's temporary HQ. If old Murph spent an equivalent
time checking out the others, they'd wind up with a crew
that would give Long John Silver the heebie-jeebies. "One
thing I oughta mention," Murph had continued. "I gotta
Osiran for my new first officer. Name's Vasoovan. Any problem with that?"

Murph had instantly misunderstood Kea's raised eyebrow.

"Now, I won't blame you if you're sorta prejudiced against Osirans. Taken a good man's job, and all. But this Vasoovan comes highly recommended. Even if she is a bug."

"No. I've got no problems with Osirans . . . Murph," Kea had finally said. This was no lie. He was too much a mongrel himself to be prejudiced. He had heard fine things about Osirans in general. But not as company employees. Osirans were a pretty proud group. Hated the idea of being beholden to humans because they'd been the ones to make first contact. The only ones who would work for humans, Kea knew very well, were mal-contents and incompetents. Which meant Murph's first officer was a likely loser with an attitude. Another bad sign. So, if his own name was on the recommended list, what did that make him?

"Now, this is a real ticklish mission we got here," Murph said. "So you get hazardous-duty pay. And that's triple time, friend. One year guaranteed."

Kea had smiled, acting pleased. So that explains it, he had thought. As one of the company's youngest chief engineers in grade, triple time would be pretty cheap. Which explained the Osiran. Rock-bottom wages there. And good old Murph looked like the sort of guy who had to work cheap. "Plus bonuses if we bring home the bacon," Murph had said.

"What exactly are we after?"

"You probably heard the scuttlebutt in the bars about the weird readings they're gettin' out of Alva Sector, right?"

"Yeah. *Everybody* heard."

Laughter. "Figured that. No secrets on Base Ten. Anyway, they got the readings. Clerk drew up a filing, like we're supposed to. Law says the company's gotta report unexplained stuff like that. Part of the license with the Powers That Be. Public duty, and all that BS."

Public duty, meaning pure research and intellectual development, was a sop the big companies threw the opposition when they won the right to commercialize space. Little money was actually spent. SpaceWays and its fellow franchisees met only the vaguest spirit of the law.

"The report got punted forward," Murph continued, "and everybody figured that was that. It'd get buried along with all the other jerkoff stuff. Which is where Fazlur comes into the story. The doc's an expert on alternate-universe theory. Don't ask me to explain it, I'm a space jockey, not a dome-head."

"I promise I won't," Kea had said.

"So Fazlur sees the report. Gets all excited. Runs it through the computers, and bingo, it comes up three cherries. Proof there's an alternate universe, he says. A leak in space."

"Why is the company listening?" Kea had kept his features bland. Inside, his heart was hammering. "What do they care? Unless there's money it in for them."

"No money," Murph had said. "Not a chance. This expedition is, and I quote, 'purely in the interest of the advancement of science,' end BS quote."

Kea had just stared at him—a working stiff's Don't Con Me stare. Murph had laughed. "Yeah. Right. Actually, what's goin' on is that our fearless parent company—SpaceWays—has got its tit in a political wringer. Some government types say they're skinnin' the research credits too fine."

"So they're looking for a nice bone to throw to the dogs, right?" Kea had guessed.

"You got it. And so did Fazlur. He may be a domehead, but he's got a good business nose. He pulls some strings. A junior veep sees a chance to make senior. And son of a gun, all of a sudden, we got us a scientific mission."

So, that's all it was, Kea had thought. A little cheapie non-effort to spread oil on troubled political waters. This thing was bound to be screwed from the get-go.

"So, Richards. I did my dance. Give you my best dog-and-pony show. What do you say? You with me?"

Kea had rolled it over. And over again. It still didn't look good. However . . . An alternate universe? The other side of God's coin? And there was a measurable leak . . . A door. Into . . .

What?

Richards had to know. "Yeah," he'd said. "I'm with you."

Kea watched Ruth ankle down the corridor. She paused at the door, turned, flashed that wicked grin, then the door hissed open. She disappeared inside. He waited a few moments. It wouldn't do for them to arrive together.

Murph's call for a meeting had caught them in the middle of another wild session of lovemaking. The voice on Kea's room speaker had barely died away, before they were pulling on their clothes. Now he was cooling his heels to allay any suspicions Fazlur might have. Kea cursed himself for getting into the predicament. The woman had come on from the start. She had a body and look that dared you to find out what she knew. Which was a helluva lot. She had told him Fazlur was a pig. She put up with his demands because it was the only way she could keep her job. Otherwise she would be just another scientist with a sheepskin for hire.

"I have to use what nature gave me," she'd said, tracing a shapely finger along even more shapely naked flesh. But Kea had noted that for her the danger of getting caught— and the ensuing trouble it would cause—lent heavy spice to sex. Again, like Tamara. Don't point fingers, Richards, he thought. It gets to you, too. Every time she comes knocking . . . you open the door.

The most maddening thing about it, Kea realized, was that the situation was right out of a basic frosh psych text. An obsession directly related to his failure with Tamara. It helped that the sex was absolutely fabulous. Feeling far younger than twenty-eight and ashamed of his addiction, Kea decided enough time had passed. He paced down the corridor and entered the bridge. They were all waiting. Murph and Vasoovan and Fazlur. Behind them, Ruth threw him a kiss.

"What kept you, Richards?" came Vasoovan's irritating twitter.

Fazlur looked at him. Did he suspect?

"A little trouble in the engine room," Kea said.

"Leak in the seals again?" Murph misguessed.

"Yeah, Murph. Trouble in the seals again." Kea watched Fazlur turn away . . . satisfied? "What's going on?" Kea asked.

Murph thumbed at Fazlur. "Doc's got some kinda answer." He turned to Fazlur. "Why don't you run it down?"

"Yeah, Fazlur," Vasoovan prodded. "Tell us why you've had us chasing a big fat zero for five months."

"It is not a phantom, my dimwitted companion. Of this I assure you. When we started out, the signal we were picking up from the apparent discontinuity in the Alva Sector was certainly steady and strong enough. Our dilemma came only when we grew close. The steady pulse we were receiving appeared to shatter."

"I think your equipment is all screwed up, is what I think," Vasoovan said. "You were seein' something that wasn't there."

"Then what, you fool, do you think those blinking lights were on the monitor? That's not *my* equipment." Vasoovan was silent. Eyestalks astir. Wandering or not, the blips on the screen did indicate *some* kind of presence. Fazlur smirked at Vasoovan, then turned serious. "What I did was gather up all the recordings of Vasoovan's sightings. Then I crunched the data. To see if there was some sort of pattern."

"Which there was," Kea guessed. Otherwise they wouldn't be here talking about it.

"Which there was," Fazlur confirmed with relish. "Viewed in isolation, it appeared the signal was wandering all over the clock. One o'clock to six o'clock. To nine . . . When one steps back for perspective, however, one would observe that it repeats the nine, then six, and on to one, again." He sketched as he talked. The result looked a bit like a tilted *U*.

"What's causing it?" Richards asked.

"Some of it is due to the presence of black matter," Fazlur said. "No doubt about it. A very strong gravitational force is at work here, and I'll be the first to admit I hadn't considered it. But that's not the whole answer. I think what's really happening is that we're viewing an alternate universe bleeding through the discontinuity. It's well known that early in the life of our own universe, positive ions were so compressed that no light could escape. As the ions separated—we now imagine—light began to burst out of that dense ionic fog. I believe something similar is going on in our not-so-theoretical alternate universe. Dense ionic fog—or its equivalent in that universe. Light pushing to get through. And finding the path of least resistance through the discontinuity and into our own universe."

"Good work, Doc," Murph said. "I guess. But I'll leave that to our bosses. Tell the truth, though, what you're tellin' me may be *the* answer. But that answer don't have the ring of Bonus City. Hope you can punch it up better'n that when we get back to Base Ten."

"Oh, I can do *far* better," Fazlur said, preening. "I can take us there . . . and prove it!"

"Hey, come on, Fazlur!" Vasoovan protested, predator's grin stretched wide on her long face. "Let's not get stupid about this. I'll buy your theory. I'll even back your act with the company to earn my share of the bonus. But, we gotta face facts, here. Which is—ion fog or no ion fog—we don't know how to get from *here* to *there*."

"Yes we do," Fazlur said. He drew a line straight through the tilted *U*. Made a circle at eleven o'clock. "This is our course for the next jump." Silence all around. Kea saw Ruth puzzling. Judging. Then he saw her nod. She believed he was right.

Murph finally broke the silence. "Gee, Doc. That's good crap, and all. But I think we got enough. The politicos will be happy we really *did* something. Which means the company'll be happy. End story."

"Don't be a fool," Fazlur said. "If I'm right, we're talking about the greatest discovery since Galileo. Redefining reality itself. Forget the fame. Although every member of the crew will go down in history. Think of the fortune, man. The fortune."

Murph turned to Kea. "What's our status?"

"Engine's in okay shape. Everything else is so-so. Including fuel." Kea had no choice but to be honest.

"I don't know," Murph said. "I just don't feel right making this kind of decision myself."

"Can't buzz the Powers That Be," Vasoovan said. "We're way out of range."

"If you turn back now," Fazlur warned, "I swear I'll see you fired and blackballed for life."

"Come on, Doc," Murph said. "Don't be like that. I'm just sayin' I feel real uncomfortable decidin' this whole thing solo."

"I'll take responsibility," Fazlur said.

"That wouldn't be right," Murph said. All he meant was it wouldn't be enough to protect his big-hammed behind. "How about we vote on it? Just the officers and you two. We don't need to ask the crew anything."

Kea almost laughed aloud. A ship's captain calling for a vote. Instead, he said, "Why not?" He raised a hand. "Start with me. I say we go."

"Crap on you!" Vasoovan said. "I vote for home."

Fazlur and Ruth joined Kea. Murph could see which way the land lay now. "Okay. I'll go along with the majority. Sorry, Vasoovan, but I gotta keep the peace. It's my job."

And so the last stage of Operation Alva was launched as cynically and halfheartedly as the first. Kea didn't care. He was determined to see the other side of God's big coin. An old line crawled into his brain: "This is the stuff dreams are made of."

A fine rain of fire curtained across space. And that curtain seemed to swirl and billow against a gentle cosmic wind. It was a place where two universes touched . . . and bled through.

Kea peered at the image on the ship's main screen and watched birth and death enacted instantly as small particles from one universe touched one from another and exploded in pinprick bursts of light. Pinbursts that played up and down

the shuddering curtain that Fazlur called a "discontinuity."
Kea thought, Discontinuity? No. More like the Gate to
Paradise. Or Hell.

Fazlur's voice came from behind him: "Now, Richards
. . . if you could take sweep in a bit farther . . ."

Kea worked the joystick. Onscreen, the sweep he'd helped
Fazlur and Ruth deploy swooped into view. It consisted of
a small cylindrical unit designed for use as a 'tween-ship
shortrange courier, now pushing a net made of specially
treated plas wires. On a bar across the bottom of the screen,
numbers jumped and played.

"Just a little more . . ." Fazlur's voice coaxed. "A little
more . . ."

Suddenly the sweep's net was alive with pinbursts.
Antiparticles colliding against particles. A small drama being
played out against the plas wires of the net. Kea kept the
sweep steady on its dip-in-and-out course. It wasn't hard.
The joystick's sensors showed no interference. Then the pinbursts stopped abruptly as the sweep completed its journey
and returned to normal space.

Fazlur's voice gloated behind him. "I've done it! Done
it!" Kea knew Fazlur was seeing his name in history books.
The first scientist to explore another universe—albeit by
remote. He punched in a command putting the sweep on
autoreturn and swiveled in his chair.

"Done what?" came Vasoovan's annoying twitter. "We're
in on this same as you, buster. It's a team. Right, Murph?
We all get equal shares."

"Uh . . . Gotta get back to you on that," Murph hemmed.
"See what the book says."

Kea could tell that good old team player Murph would
like the bonus cut in the rank-share system. He could see
those crafty old eyes in that disarming hail-fellow face buzz
in calculation. Let's see, now, he'd be thinking . . . That way
me and Fazlur split fifty percent . . . That'd be . . . Uh see
. . . what's the biggest bonus the company ever put out?

"I don't gotta read the book, Murph," Vasoovan shrilled.

"This is expedition rules, fella. Fazlur as team leader gets twenty. We all split the rest. Equals."

"Will you all just stop it," Fazlur stormed. "Who cares about the company bonus? Put it in a glass, swallow, and urinate."

"Say . . ." Murph said. "If you don't want any part of your bonus, we'll be glad to split up your share. Won't we, Vasoovan?"

"You got it, Murph."

Kea broke in. "Why don't you explain it to them, Fazlur?" This was the third time he'd taken the sweep through. And he'd watched over Fazlur's and Ruth's shoulders as they figured and refigured. He had a faint idea what Fazlur had discovered. But it was very faint.

Fazlur nodded. He turned his craggy, handsome face to its best profile. "It's as simple as this," he said. "We have just reached into another universe—and brought back evidence of its most basic material. This material—in our own universe—would become the source of unlimited power. A small flask of it, my friends, might supply all the wants and needs of a city and its inhabitants for a hundred years." Fazlur giggled. The giggle turned to laughter. The cabin was silent until he stopped. "So much for your damn bonus," he said.

The faint idea bloomed to understanding in Kea's head. Power . . . Fuel. Wars had been fought over it. Hundreds of thousands had died on oil fields. Power . . . Weapons. Hundreds of thousands more had died in the nuclear fires of the past. Power. Wealth. The greatest fortunes—and families—had been founded on its gold. He looked around the room at the others. Each in his or her own way understood. Even the lowliest grease monkey would have understood. You did not come to space . . . and stay . . . and not understand these things. Kea looked at Murph: Jock's face. Clown face. But somehow oddly solemn. Vasoovan: Pink features paler than he'd ever seen. Big predator's grin. Tentacle curling and uncurling. Ruth: Eyes alight. Red tongue-tip flicking out. And himself.

He wished he could see himself.

"Uh . . . Doc . . ." came Murph's voice. Throaty. "What do you call this . . . uh . . . stuff?"

"A good question, Murph," Fazlur said. Kea didn't blame him for sounding so pedantic. "It's the opposite of matter in our universe. But we can't call it anti-matter. Because we already have anti-matter in this universe. Perhaps we should express it in its simplest terms." He turned to Ruth. "Something commercial. Recognizable even to the ignorant. I find it always helps when I make my presentations to funding boards."

"Easy." She shrugged. "If it isn't anti-matter, exactly . . . then it's new anti-matter. Stress the newness, somehow."

"How about Anti-Matter Two?" Kea suggested.

"I like it," Ruth said. "Simple."

"Anti-Matter Two . . . Yes. That'll do. Very very well. The heading will get their attention." Fazlur was satisfied.

"What I like," Murph said, "is it fits real nice on the side of a building. AM2." He drew the symbols in the air: AM2.

"How sure are you about this, Doc?" Vasoovan twittered. "You got proof?"

Fazlur rose, turned from them, and looked up on the screen at the curtain of fire. "I'm sure. Very sure. And I have the proof. But it is not absolute. And in this, my friends, we must be absolute. Otherwise . . ." He turned back, the fire raining on the screen behind him. "There are those who would kill to control this. You *must* realize this."

Fazlur stared at them hard. One by one. He came to Kea. Richards thought of the Bargetas. The other great families— and fortunes. And the opportunity *and* threat they would see in AM2. The issue was control. The Haves against the Have Nots. The man was right. The Haves would attack with lawyers, writs—and assassins. Kea nodded. He knew. As did the others.

"If we want any rights—bound-in-steel guarantee rights— to our discovery," Fazlur said, "we must make that proof patentable. A patent so strong that no one can question our rights."

"How do we get proof, Doc?" Murph asked.

Fazlur pointed at the screen. "We have to go in there to get it," he said. "And come back again."

Kea had never heard silence to thick. There was no argument. No heated questions: Can it be done? . . . Are you sure? . . . What if? . . . The struggle was within each of them. They all knew Fazlur would answer; Yes. I am. I don't know . . . I've never been there before. Kea swallowed. He looked at the screen. He saw the gentle fire rain, the billow and curl of space, as alluring as any woman he'd ever known.

He . . . Just . . . Had . . . To . . . See.

That line again: "The stuff dreams are made of."

Kea cleared his throat, startling the others to life.

"I think we should go," he said.

it was a place like the other.
but not familiar.
it was . . .
not.
I don't like it.
why?
i don't know.
is it colder?
no. but i'm . . . cold.
is it darker?
no. but i can't . . . see.
what's wrong, then?
i'm . . .
lost.

A juddering into normalcy. They all looked at each other, dazed. Ruth's hand crept toward Kea's. Fazlur saw it. An odd light came to his eye. Then the screen caught his attention. "We're on the other side," he said quietly.

Kea looked up. The remotes were panning along the rear of the ship. The curtain of fire was behind them.

Destiny I was through.

* * *

"Reckoning by the discontinuity," Murph said. Voice crisp and professional. "On time-tick . . ."

Vasoovan's twitter was modulated: "Check. Coordinates . . . x350 . . . Proceeding . . ."

"Half power . . ." Kea broke in. "Drive steady. All functions normal."

"Readings . . . positive on the port sensors, Doctor," Ruth said. Calm.

"Course starboard nine now . . . Thank you, Ruth. A little less on the data stream, please . . . There you go."

Fazlur's fingers flew across his key unit, monitoring the incoming data. He nodded. Yes. Yes. And yes. Then he keyed out. "I think we can go home now, Captain," he said. Formal.

Murph nodded to him. Stiff. "Thank you, Doctor." Then; "Vasoovan. Set the course for XO . . . We're going home."

It came as a spot on the screen that blazed the colors/no colors of this strange universe.

An infinitesminal spot.

"Murph! Eleven o'clock!"

"What the crap is it?"

"Dunno. Pint-sized moon, maybe."

"Don't look too close."

"Naw. Not real close. But maybe we oughta—"

Two bodies approached in space. Composed of mass. Potential of that mass. And gravitational displacement.

But one was the stuff of one reality.

One another.

Opposites attract.

What do double opposites do?

The explosion took *Destiny I* midships, cutting it like a shark ripping into fat-bellied tuna.

Fifteen died.

Five survived.

The gods of this place were kind to the fifteen.

Kea came awake. It was dark and bloody. Acrid.

There was no pain.

Numbness.

He heard voices.

"All dead." A wail.

"There's us, Murph! There's us. We're alive."

Me too, Kea wanted to say. I'm alive, too.

Not even a groan escaped.

"What'll we do? Oh, God, what'll we do."

"I'd kill you, Murph. I'd kill you if it wouldn't leave me all alone."

"Gotta think. Gotta think."

"It's your fault, Murph. We never shoulda come, damn you!"

Check the damage, Kea wanted to say. The urge was desperate . . . Check the damage.

He felt his lips tighten to speak.

A wave washed in and took him away.

He was thirsty.

God he was thirsty.

A voice. Ruth's.

"Hell, I don't know. He's broken up, or something. Inside. I'm no physician."

"What about Fazlur?" Murph's voice.

"Who cares?" came the twitter—Vasoovan. "He got us into this."

"Castro's worse," he heard Ruth say. "I followed the directions in the medkit best I could. The stump stopped bleeding, if that's any consolation." Her voice was cold.

"Still out?"

"Still out. Thank God. Those screams were awful."

Water, Kea thought. I'm so thirsty.

"We've got practically no rations," Vasoovan shrilled. "And very little water."

"I say we put them both out of their misery. And we can live a little longer."

"That wouldn't be right," Ruth said. Perfunctory.

"Naw," Murph said. "Guess it wouldn't . . . Besides, long

as they're out, they ain't costin' us anything. Except air. And we've plenty of that."

The tide lifted Kea up again and carried him off.

Pain. Waves and jabs of it.

But it was bearable pain. And there was no numbness.

There was still no light. Eyes . . . felt . . . crusted shut. Dried . . . What? . . . Blood? Yes, blood.

"Jeez, this suit stinks," he heard Murph say.

There were sounds of fastenings being opened. The clank of equipment falling.

"Did you get back as far as the drive unit this time?" Ruth asked.

"Yeah. Wasn't hit too hard, either. And the input to the controls checks out."

"Can we run it?" Came the twitter.

Kea heard Murph sigh. "I *said* it wasn't hit too hard. Meaning . . . it's fixable. But not by me. And not by anyone else here."

Kea struggled the word out. "Water."

"Hey, it's Richards." Murph said.

"What's he want?" Vasoovan asked.

"Water. He said water," Ruth said. "I'll get it for him."

"Hey, Murph," Vasoovan said. "We didn't talk about *this*, Murph. Last we talked, you said they ain't costin' us anything. Remember?"

"I remember."

Kea was suddenly frightened that a decision was being reached. And even more frightened how it would come out. Where was Ruth? Why wasn't she speaking up for him?

Don't wait for Ruth!

"I can fix it," Kea croaked.

"He *really* is awake," Ruth said. Meaning: he heard us talking.

"What's that you say, partner?" It was Murph. Jovial. Kea felt him move close. Imagined him peering down. "You say you can fix it? Fix the drive?"

Kea wanted to say more. A lot more. But he hadn't the strength. So there was only one response. "Water," he croaked. Then he fell back. It was his first and final offer.

A rustling. Then cool water touched his lips. He lapped it until he'd had enough. Perfume floated down to him, along with a voice. "Oh, darling," Ruth said. "I'm so very happy you're alive." A kiss brushed his cheek.

He slept.

Kea hoisted himself on his good arm to get a better view. The other was strapped tight to his body. "That's a good seal," he said. "That's a keeper. Now . . . lift it up and you'll see a Y-shaped impression."

On the screen he saw Murph's suited hands do his bidding. He was crammed into a space between the drive unit and a bulk-head. "Got it," Murph said.

"Good. You'll find a tool that matches in your beltpack. But before you open the cover . . . make sure you set up the shield."

"Damn straight," Murph said as he went to work.

"No sense worrying about cancer," Vasoovan twittered. "None of us are going to live that long."

"Humorous," Ruth said. "*How* jolly you keep us all."

Kea ignored the start-up of another bickering match. He fell back into the cot. "Get me some soup," he said. Ruth turned a deadly look on him.

"You had your ration," Vasoovan said.

"Soup." Kea said. He was sick. He needed more. End discussion. Kea looked up at Murph working in the drive room. When the cover was off, the next step should go pretty easy. Hunger knotted under his ribs again. As sharp as if they were broken clean. Instead of cracked.

He lifted himself up to look for Ruth, his back barely supporting him. She was still sitting in the chair. Vasoovan was watching, enjoying herself. "Who are you to give people orders?" Ruth snarled. "Who are you to break rules and eat and drink more than the rest of us?"

"Doesn't matter," Kea said. "Do it—or they'll make you."

Hysterical twitter. "No eat. No work. Guy drives a hard bargain."

All four of Vasoovan's eyestalks turned on Ruth. "Get him what he wants," she said. "Or we'll put you in the soup with Fazlur." Ruth did as she was told.

Kea settled in to wait. Murph should be ready for the next little step in about four hours. Then Kea would trade yet another bit of knowledge for nourishment. And another. Until it was done. Two more weeks, he thought. And then we shall see what we shall see.

Fazlur had died three days earlier. He'd tossed and groaned for an eternity, never quite conscious, nor quite out enough to not feel pain. No one had moved to help him, much less feed him or bring him drink. Kea hadn't spoken up for Fazlur. Why bother? They would have refused him help. Kea's bargain would not be stretched to include Fazlur. Murph, Vasoovan, and Ruth were the strong here. Kea was helpless until his injuries healed.

Besides, in Vasoovan's predator logic of survival, Fazlur was the most expendable. "We get lucky and make it," Vasoovan had said, "we don't need him. Not alive. We got his proof. His absolute proof. All in his data file."

"I just wish he would get it over with," Ruth had said. "I can't stand his infernal groaning. He used to sound like that sometimes when we made love. A pig." Kea had turned away from them. To his own thoughts. And sleep.

Sometime later, Kea had come to semiconsciousness. Fazlur was groaning. The others made the noises of sleep. Then he heard movement. A softer patter of feet. The smell of sweet perfume. The groaning stopped. Abrupt. Then the soft pad of feet.

They found Fazlur dead the next day.

"Run him through the reclaimer," Vasoovan had twittered. "Add him to the soup." He was referring to the sort of nutrition stew produced by their own waste and the dwindling supply of plant protein being produced in the damaged hydroponic room.

"Why not?" Ruth had said. "Make some use out of him. It seems so fitting, somehow."

Kea had watched them lug the corpse out of the room. Hunger gnawed at him again. He heard light footsteps. Ruth's perfume. He took the mug from her without looking up. He drank. There was no taste at all.

Poor Fazlur.

The curtain between universes hung before them, beckoning. If things had worked out differently, Kea supposed it would have been called Fazlur's Discontinuity. He looked about the room. Vasoovan. Murph. Ruth. No one here would give Fazlur a drop of the credit. As for himself . . . well, he had ideas of his own. Just formulating.

"We're ready," Vasoovan said.

Kea struggled up. Some life was returning to his bound-up arm. He was getting stronger. Barely. "One thing more," Kea announced, "before we go through."

They turned to him, alarmed.

"Don't worry. The drive unit's fine," he said. "But what I want you all to remember when we get to the other side is that it's five months home."

"Yeah? So?" From Murph.

"So now that everything's working okay, some of you might get the idea you don't need me anymore. That the chief engineer is expendable—like the chief scientist." No protests. No offended denials. Only silence. "I took out insurance to keep us friends," Kea continued. "I fixed the drive unit, okay. But I slipped Murph a little extra task to do. An extra step."

"Like what?" Murph demanded angrily.

"Like I rigged the unit to go down in a couple of months. And when it goes busto, my dear companions in adversity . . . you're going to need me again. I guarantee it."

Kea fell back into the cot. "Now, go, dammit!"

They went.

* * *

They found the air leak a week later.

"It's not my fault, Murph!"

"You were supposed to check, dammit!"

"I checked. Not my fault, if I missed something. I'm no engineer." Two of her eyestalks turned to peer at Kea's figure, prone on the cot. His duties had been shared out among them. Kea stayed silent.

"Let's not get into this bickering again," Ruth said. "The leak's plugged. Fine. Now, the question is, Do we have enough?"

"Not a chance," Murph said. "Not with most of the five months to go. And—" He broke off. A long silence.

Then Vasoovan finished it: "And four of us breathing."

There it was. Kea had been waiting.

"Yeah," Murph said.

"Yes . . . I can see that," Ruth said.

They all turned to look at Kea. Eight eyes upon three living forms peering at his own, air-consuming self.

"It'd be close," Murph said. "Still be maybe a month short."

"By then," Ruth said, "we might find other means . . ."

"What about the drive unit?" Murph said. "The little trick he played on me?"

"I think he lied," Ruth said.

Kea smiled at them. A big, broad smile. A smile right up from the warrens of Maui.

"Yeah, and maybe he didn't," Vasoovan said. The eight eyes turned away. But Kea remained watchful.

"What'll we do?" Murph asked.

"Simple," Vasoovan said. "We gotta have Kea. We gotta have you. And we gotta have me. I'm the nav—"

Kea didn't know where the hatchet came from. It was painted the slick red of emergency tool gear. The handle was short. The blade blunt. Ruth brought it down between the four eyestalks. She was a small woman, barely coming to Kea's chin. But she swung with the force of survival. The hatchet buried itself in the Osiran's brain globe. The haft protruded back—giving Vasoovan a protuberance that looked like a long human nose. Pink goo blobbed out and dripped to the floor. The tentacles shuddered, then were still.

Ruth stepped back. She looked Murph full-on. "Well?" she said.

"She kinda got on my nerves, anyway," Murph said. "All that twittering."

"The rations are getting low," Ruth said.

"I noticed. Let's make some soup."

He dreamed of kings. Of empires.

Menes was the first. A crafty old devil who welded upper and lower Egypt into the first empire. He ruled for sixty years. And was killed by a hippopotamus.

The Persians bowed before Alexander's sword. He died in a swamp. Kublai Khan got it right. He quelled the mighty Chinese. And died of old age.

The Romans pushed the bounds of the known world and beyond. They fell to thieves on horseback.

Elizabeth was fine. The best of them all. She was the dazzling acrobat of the monarchs. Kea sometimes wondered why she hadn't killed her sister sooner. Instead she bore the threat of deadly plot after deadly plot. The romantics said it was deep, sisterly feeling. Kea believed it was simply because Elizabeth hadn't thought it was time.

He had learned much from these people during those long hours of offwatch reading. His interest was not casual. The nature of the powerful had confounded him. He had been smacked on his ignorant blind side. Kea was determined to understand. So he had gone at it like an engineer. Taking each monarch and his kingdom apart. Putting it back together again. Piece by piece. Sometimes rearranging those pieces to see how it might have turned out. An empire, he had discovered, could take several forms. It could be crown and throne. Altar and blood sacrifice. An army standard with its accompanying secret police. A presidential seal resting on stolen votes. A company logo above a penthouse suite. But they all had one thing in common: an idea. An idea of a perfect life. Real, or promised. And for the idea to work, it had to satisfy from top to bottom. Starving masses do not praise their monarch's name on Feast Day.

In one of the folktales he had read, one of the ancient kings went among his subjects in disguise so he could learn firsthand how to sweeten their disposition. The king's name was Raschid. In the real world, the ward bosses, commissars, and priests fetched food and comfort up tenement stairs to sell for votes. The Robin Hoods—Huey Long, Jess Unruh, Boris Yeltsin—stole from weakened kings to create their own power bases.

Dictators preferred triage. Kea thought of it as rule by the three G's: genocide, gulags, and gendarmes.

Still . . . No matter the form of the empire, or the means to maintain its rule, all of it circled back to the idea that was in the heart of the king who founded the empire.

And Kea had AM2.

His arm hurt. This was good. Like the pain before. He would be able to use it soon—though he had kept this from Murph and Ruth. He had a fever. An infection. A boil on his belly the size of a saucer. He'd have to hide that, too.

Kea heard whispers in the darkened room:

"C'mon, honey. I'm hurtin'."

"Get away from me."

"We done it before. What's another hunk?"

"You reneged on your bargain. You lied."

"I couldn't help it, honey. I was hungry. Real bad hungry. I'll give you halvsies in the morning. Swear it."

"Get it now," Ruth said. "Give it to me, now."

Silence.

Ruth laughed. "What's the matter . . . Daddy doesn't want to play slap-belly anymore. What's this. *Tsk tsk. It's* hungry. But Daddy's going to be selfish, isn't he?"

Murph made no response.

Then Kea heard Ruth gasp. And for one . . . two . . . three

heartbeats, a violent, muffled struggle. Then a distinctive crack.

Kea felt a knot in his gut untighten. A sudden release of pressure. A terrible odor rose up from the burst boil. Then sudden chills. And sweat. Good.

The fever had broken . . .

He awoke with Murph standing over him. "You're lookin' better," he said.

Kea didn't answer. And he didn't look around the room for Ruth.

Murph stretched. "I'm hungry," he said. "Want some soup?"

"Yeah," Kea said. "I'm hungry, too."

"It's gonna take longer than we thought," Murph said.

"I can see that," Kea answered. He was looking at the latest computations on the screen.

"Damned Vasoovan," Murph said. "Lousy nav officer. Good thing you spotted her screwup and set us right."

"Real lucky," Kea said. He hobbled back to his cot and eased himself down.

"Maybe it won't be so bad," Murph said. "Maybe we'll get picked up when we first get inta range and they hear our SOS."

"That could happen," Kea said.

"Only one bug in that chowpak," Murph said. "And that's if we lose a buncha time puttin' that little trick of yours straight. When it blows." He grinned. "How long did you say it would take to fix again?"

"I didn't," Kea said.

Murph looked at him. "Naw. You didn't . . . did you?"

Kea clamped his bound arm tighter and felt the edge of the filed-down plas spoon. An old, familiar boyhood friend. Murph came closer to him peering down with bloodshot eyes. Flesh hung loosely from his big jock's frame. His cheeks were hollow, face pale as death. "You don't look too worried," he said. "About the delay and all. 'Specially with your delay on top."

"We'll make it," Kea said.

"I'm not what you call clever," Murph said. "I know that about myself. And it don't bother me. I leave clever to guys like you. More power to ya, I say."

He moved to the edge of the cot. Kea could see roped muscles play through the sagging flesh of his neck. He scratched his bound arm. Slipped the knots free.

"'Course I woulda thought of lyin'," Murph said. "I'm clever enough for that. Don't make captain in this man's company if you ain't quick on your feet."

"I guess you don't," Kea said. He scratched again. The spoon slipped upward.

"Naw. You don't," Murph repeated. Kea saw Murph make the decision. Saw the click in those cunning eyes.

Kea came off the cot, right hand striking up to the chin, left hand—the bound arm—free, the spoon thrusting. It took Murph in the windpipe. Kea saw the eyes widen. Felt the flesh give. The sharp rush of air. He collapsed back as Murph flopped to the floor. A hand beat against his leg. He heard the whistling horror of Murph expelling his life.

Stillness.

Kea moved his foot. It thumped against Murph's body. There was no reaction. Kea let the weakness take him. All tension drained away. He would rest now. Later, he could get up and recheck the course. Let his eyes run over the readings of happy machinery at work.

Then he would make some soup.

There was plenty to eat and drink, now. Plenty of air to breathe. It would have been a lot closer, though, if Murph hadn't figured out that he had lied.

CHAPTER TWENTY-FOUR

New York City, A.D. 2194

MANKIND WAS A little low on heroes when Kea Richards, sole survivor of the *Destiny I*, returned from Base Ten to Earth. Kea was not sure how the hero card would help him with this ultimate edge he had happened on, but he was canny enough to not let it go unplayed. He had worked out the tale he would spin on the long journey home. He told the truth about the cause of the disaster. A collision with a meteorite. He merely left out it had occurred in another universe. And he certainly didn't tell them about the AM2.

Richards came on humble. He played up the image of an ordinary, hardworking space engineer who had been able to snatch victory from the jaws. He also made much of the "fact" that when those fearless scientists and self-sacrificing space crew members around him died, generally with Expressed Noble Sentiments As Their Last, it was his great good fortune that his formal education at Cal Tech, even though it had been interrupted by financial problems, was remembered and applied directly to the various emergencies.

He took an enormous advance and cooperated cheerfully with the ghost preparing his autobiographical fiche. He went to the banquets and lectures, charging whatever his newly hired agent could cozen. And he was delighted to attend the parties and presentations afterward. He smiled, listened intently to the men and women he met, the ones with power, who glorified in their ability to attract the latest hero. He lied, and lied again.

Sometimes he wondered what the old Kea Richards would have thought, the Richards of Kahanamoku and the first two years in California. The Richards before the Bargetas or long hard years in space, on the far side of Barrier Thirty-three. Shaft him, he decided. A man had to grow up sometime and get over the idea that life was a pretty pink wonderland full of bunnies and lambiekins.

Besides, now there was Anti-Matter Two. The key to personal power, he was honest enough to admit to himself. But it was also the ultimate gift for man, and any other species he would encounter in his explosion out into the universe. Richards could not afford the luxury of an Ethics 101 debate, even within himself.

He was undecided as to what to do next. Anti-Matter Two. Whole galaxies of cheap, raw energy. As Fazlur had said, it would change everything, creating a civilization—or barbarism—unlike whatever had gone before. Richards was determined the vast changes would be for the better. *He* would make damned sure it was properly directed to the benefit of all. Neither fuhrers nor premiers, doges nor rockefellers, would batten from what he already thought of as his discovery. Nor the Bargetas. And this energy wouldn't be diverted to evil, as most everything from gunpowder to petroleum to the atom had been.

Consider the immediate problems you have. The first and most important, he thought, is to stay alive, and always guard your back. This secret has already cost lives—and is worth the death of entire worlds. Richards knew any hint of the secret of Anti-Matter Two and the Alva Sector would also be enough to put kidnappers with mind-draining tools and assassins on his trail, hired by those who stood to gain/lose the most from AM2. At the very least, charges might be trumped up against him by planetary governments.

Very well, then. So he would need to treat the Alva Sector as if it were some kind of hidden mine, deep in a jungle, that only he knew the directions to. He must not return to the Alva Sector, and that discontinuity in N-space, unless he

knew he was not being tracked. Nor was it worthwhile returning to in the immediate future, his mind ran on. Before Anti-
Matter Two could be developed, someone must create a
handle. A shield. Some substance, synthetic or natural, that
was a solid, that was malleable, and that was absolutely neutral to both matter and anti-matter.

Richards gnawed his lip. That was a real problem. He
grinned—as if the thought of assassins and brainburners was
gathering nuts in May. He continued analyzing and thinking,
and came to the wonderful catch-22—except this was a triple
whammy: To utilize Power (AM2), he would have to achieve
Power (wealth/clout). Which could most easily and safely be
accomplished by cultivating Power. Catch-222.

That third Power was the men and women whose egos he
was stroking as he toured his saga. And they were the beings
he was determined to transform or destroy as he helped the
human race achieve its destiny. He remembered the ancient
saying, If you are not part of the solution, you are part of
the problem. But this suggested his next move.

A job. He had no intention of renewing his contract with
Space Ways/Galiot. Not with all these other offers that were
coming in. Corporations wanted him solely for the Hero
Factor, just as they hired gravball stars for the same reasons.
Richards would be expected to continue pressing the flesh,
except this time for the benefit of whoever was paying him.
That would give him a chance to travel the halls of power.
He carefully examined the various letters, verbals, and mes-
sages he'd gotten—glork that he'd more or less ignored.

One was from Austin Bargeta. Call him, anytime, day or
night, on a private line. The message slip was balled up and
hurled into the trash can in a reflex. Kea caught himself.
Bargeta? A known entity. Someone he'd had unlikely dreams
of encountering—on Richards's terms and turf—someyear.
This could be someyear. He'd heard, in spite of his mind's
promise to never concern himself with the Bargetas unless
he found them in some sort of gunsights, Austin had ful-
filled his early promise and become The Man—replacing

his father at the head of the Bargeta octopus.

Bargeta senior had suicided three years after Kea's life had been shattered—or at least changed inalterably—on Mars. Suicided under conditions the tabs could only hint at being unthinkably disgusting.

He smoothed the slip out and stared at it, thinking. Possibly. He made his way to a library and did some research. Very possibly.

Bargeta Ltd. still was one of the colossi of the twenty-second century. But it was tottering. Bad investments had been made. Bargeta Transport, the tree all the lovely money-bearing branches grew from, was blighted. The old man had ordered new plants built, plants that never came up to full production. He'd commissioned new-model spacecraft, models that were offered on an already-saturated market, and craft that seemed to offer no more than a new crew/compartment/drive configuration rather than any real engineering improvements. And then he'd "passed on," and Austin had been given the scepter.

Austin had done no better than the previous generation, the business rags told Kea. He had been reluctant to newbroom the greedheads out of the holding corporations until almost too late. Then he had decided there was a far brighter future transporting people instead of commerce from world to world, and had a quarter of the Bargeta fleet converted to liners, just as a medium-size recession had cycled through the Solar System. Austin had proudly and personally bid on new transport routes, routes that thus far had failed to be profitable. Kea laughed quietly then, a sort of laugh Bargeta senior would have found familiar.

Now, as to Austin himself. Covenanted, naturally. To an ex-poser, Ms Smiling Breasts of a few years back. Two children. Mansions. Travel. Philanthropy. Ratchetaratcheta, Kea thought. Where's the dirt. Ah. Austin travels alone a lot. With his staff. Richards squinted at the holo showing Bargeta and staff boarding a spaceship. Even with the retouch, it appeared that Austin considered eye appeal a definite factor in his choice of advisers. There was more explicit gossip, and even some holos, in the sleazier and less controllable tabs.

That was enough. Kea placed the call. Austin was thrilled. Delighted his old friend, his roommate, the man who had taught him everything, would take the time. They must get together. What's the matter with tomorrow? Kea wondered, deliberately pushing it. Oh, well, there was this meeting. Stuffy, dull, but you know, I must wave the banner and look concerned, make a couple of real Decisions. Take all day. Ah, Kea said. I understand. Let me check the old logbook here (Kea had found that the execs he socialized with loved it when he used nautical terms, terms that no self-respecting swab back of Barrier Thirty-three would have recognized unless he heard them in dialogue on a vid). Oh. Hell, you can't believe how tied up I am, Richards said. He was scheduled, pretty close to fourblocked himself. Let's see here. McLean Institute next week . . . that thing in New Delhi . . . plus you know I've been talking to some people about some interesting things I've considered, things that directly came out of what happened Out There. There were some interesting commercial possibilities I'd discussed with the late Doctor Fazlur that seem to be worth developing. But we'll get together. Sometime. Maybe after I put together some venture capital.

Suddenly Austin's meeting was unimportant. Tomorrow it was! Smiling, Kea clicked off, and the smile vanished as quickly as Bargeta's image. All right, you bastard. On my terms this time. And we'll talk about me becoming your Pet Adventurer.

In fact, they talked about a lot of things, over three days, several meals, and many bottles. Everything except Mars. Austin tentatively mentioned Tamara once. She was now married—how old-fashioned—to some transoceanic hovercraft racer five years younger than she was. They were living in the new offshore resort near the Seychelles.

Kea nodded. Hoped that she was quite happy. Be sure and say hello, if you happen to talk to her. And remember the time you got blasted, and we sprayed CALTECH with acid across the Rose Bowl's synthturf just before that stupid groundball match they used to play every Newyear's? Ah yes. Those were the days.

By the end of the marathon session, which Kea's always-sober backbrain labeled as mental coitus interruptus, Richards had a job. The amount, terms, and exact definition of which were undefined. "You know," Austin went on, still in that nasal tone and collegiate slang that Kea had almost forgotten, "we'll let the suits finagle everything after the decimal."

That wasn't exactly how it worked. Two mornings later, Kea showed up at Bargeta Corporate, ready to work. The press, mysteriously tipped the wink, arrived about an hour later for the announcement and a press conference. The negotiations began. They were handled by the same legals who had gotten Kea the sizable advance on his memoirs. Kea had told them to shoot for the stars, and they did. One of the Bargeta Ltd. negotiators had gone, in outrage, to Austin's office. Bargeta wasn't interested in tiddly little numbers and clauses. Make the damned deal. This man is my friend. Besides, he said, after a pause, the media's been talking about how we stole a march on everyone getting him to work for us. Do you want to be the one to say that Bargeta could not afford the universe's biggest hero? Do you? I certainly won't. He stared at the negotiator. The negotiator returned to his office, contacted Richards's attorneys, closed the deal, and sent out his résumé.

At first, Austin and Kea traveled together a lot. Austin never got tired of saying that it was just like the old days, and Kea never missed a chance to agree with him. It was going very well, Kea thought after half a year. He was meeting the real movers and shakers.

Plus, he had been able to offer a few real suggestions to Bargeta. Suggestions that were obvious to anyone who didn't live with a solid gold suppository up his bum. Suggestions that'd made Bargeta Ltd a few million credits. Bargeta was starting to think that he'd made a real bargain adding Kea to his staff—and boasted to his mate that he had always been able to fit the right person for the right peg, and he had seen the worth in Richards years and years ago, back as far as Cal Tech. Now it was time for the next stage. A good swindler always salts the mine with a little real gold. Gold, or whatever valuable the mark will easily recognize. Cal Tech was the salt this time.

Kea hunted down the most respected, most recondite professor on the campus. A double Nobelist. Kea had conned his way into one of the woman's seminars when he was a freshman, and suffered mightily. Dr Feehely remembered Richards. What had he been doing since he'd taken her class? Well, she hoped. She remembered him as not being gifted in theory, but showing great practical promise. Was he well? Was he happy? Had he perhaps achieved some post at a university somewhere? Kea, trying to keep from laughing, came up with some plausible story about labwork and study. The reason he had wanted to consult with this woman, whose mark had been made in microanalysis, was that someone had presented Kea with a particle concept. He did not understand anything on the fiche, and, remembering Doctor Feehely, had sought her out. Could she take a few minutes? And would she mind if Richards recorded her?

She normally did not take consulting jobs . . . but for an old student . . . Feehely scanned the fiche. Raised eyebrows. Snorted. Raised eyebrows. Snorted. Raised eyebrows, and shut off the reader. "If this particle existed," she said, "it would be quite interesting. Your friend did not present an adequate synth, and the only way I could see this model existing mathematically is if one posited it were some sort of nonconventional matter. I would hate to use a popular term such as 'anti-matter,' because that would be a misnomer."

"How would this particle . . . if it could exist, work as a tappable source of energy?"

Eyebrows. Snort. The doctor chose her words. "Again, this is an incorrectness. But I will take an analogy from ancient history. Assuming—and this is also an impossibility—

this particle could be handled safely, the effect would be that of using nitroglycerine . . . you know what nitroglycerine was?"

"No. But I'll learn."

"As I said, using nitroglycerine as fuel in an internal-combustion engine. An enormous amount of energy, but one that the engine could never handle. Of course, all this is mere amusement. Fairly puerile, I might add. Such a particle could not exist in any sane universe."

"Thank you, Doctor. I have won my bet. Would you mind giving me the mathematics on that?"

"Well . . . all right. But I am afraid I will have to charge you for that, so I hope your bet is of a consequential nature. Perhaps . . . a lunch?"

The description, of course, was an abstract of the AM2 particle. Kea had laboriously taught himself how to write the description of the last six months. And Kea knew of an engine that could handle that power. Stardrive. Again, all he lacked was a "handle." And the bet *was* of a consequential nature: The Universe.

Richards would have liked to have bought Doctor Feehely more than a meal. Hell, he would have purchased a restaurant, dedicated to making only Feehely's favorite meals and delivering them to her study for the rest of her life. But he didn't—he bought her lunch at the faculty dining room. And he could reward her no further. When business progressed further, any link with Richards or AM2 could well be lethal to her. And beyond that, she could be in even greater danger—from Kea himself. Kea Richards knew once he came close to achieving power for himself, some beings would have to die. Another saying he took as gospel: Three beings can keep a secret, if two of them are dead . . .

With the doctor's mathematics in hand and a copy of his original abstract, he sought out Austin. He told him he had something of the greatest importance to show him. But privately. This was far, far too big. He began with a story. The story of how, just before catastrophe struck on the *Destiny I*,

Doctor Fazlur had been analyzing some observed phenomena taken off a darkstar they'd made close passage by. And he had been coming up with some remarkable equations. Equations that suggested a certain substance could be synthesized. A substance a bit like something he had observed off that pulsar. If his suggestions were correct, the substance could be synthesized, and modified into . . .

At that point, he gave Austin Doctor Feehely's equations. He scanned the first page on the screen, frowning. "Kea, old sock," he protested. "You, better than anyone, know how easily I parse numbers. Can't you give it to me straight?"

"I just wanted to make sure you'd believe me. Because otherwise you'd think I was completely gonkers." Kea had found it useful to sometimes use the old Cal Tech slang that Austin was so fond of. Then he played the abstract. Austin sat in silence, thinking. Then he managed an "Oh."

Kea watched closely—did he really track?

After a moment, Bargeta said, in a small voice, "If this particle, this substance, you know, could be synthesized . . . Oh. Kea, I see why you sought me out. I see why you were so mysterioso about some things that you planned to develop. You know, Kea, I feel like . . . who was that person? Speechless on a peak in Darien? Although what could be so impressive about Connecticut, I've never known. This is very big, Kea. Very, very big.

"I . . . I could be Rutherford. Better. I could be a Doctor McLean. Bigger than him, even, because this is more than just dinky little antigravity. This is everything. Stardrive first, then I am sure there will be some way to modify the substance to power anything. Everything. I feel like the first man who pumped gasoline out of the ground, whatever his name was. Oh my. Kea, this is not some kind of wicked joke, is it?"

It took almost a week of vacillating—this was too big, too important, it couldn't happen, there would have to be some government notification, perhaps a consortium of transport corporations, we could at least mount a feasibility study, actually, this would make us all richer than whoever that old Greek was, are you sure, Kea, that we should be doing something, I mean, you know, there are things that man simply wasn't meant to know, although I don't have much truck with tract-thumpers, and Christ, you know they say that genius deteriorates generation by generation, and this would certainly prove that a canard, you know, I'd be thought bigger than Father, bigger even than the first Austin, the one I'm named after, you know, the one who started this company . . .

Finally, "We'll do it."

A special team of lawyers and accountants were set up. They were to be firmly under Kea's direction. As was the lab he would build under supersecrecy. This might be expensive, Kea warned. Austin was willing to commit up to 10 percent of Bargeta Ltd.'s pretax resources per annum. The lab was built and top-line scientists hired for the project. Deep-space test and research ships were planned. Everyone in the corporate world knew Bargeta Ltd. was R&Ding something spectacular. Fortunately—for Kea's purposes—Austin had such a reputation as a lightweight the project was an instant joke, thought of in scientific slang as an edsel, whatever that might've been. Kea told no one why he had dubbed the operation Project Suk.

All of the hardware, and all of the personnel, were real. But it was a complete tissue. Kea knew AM2 could never be synthesized—or if it could, it would be even more gawdawfully expensive than the present fuel for stardrive. He caught himself. Never say never, he thought. Anti-Matter Two couldn't be synthesized at this moment in history, nor, most likely, at any other. Leave it at that. Besides, who would bother—once we find a way to shield the particles, which will also mean that we'll have a way to shield mining/processing ships, AM2 would be dirtcheap. For me, at least, he thought.

There were three reasons for this elaborate charade. First, it would provide an acceptable screen for where the substance really came from one of these years. Not that important.

Second, it would provide exploration ships, who were sent out with explicit instructions. The instructions were known but to those crews. They would search for an element that could be used, modified to create this shielding, which Kea had dubbed X. The exploration reports were also carefully studied, in the event they could produce a line of thought that would justify research that might lead to the synthesis of this shielding.

Yet another benefit Project Suk provided was a very quiet recruiting station. Richards sought out the best researchers on the project, which meant some of the best workers mankind could produce. The best—with two additional requirements. The first was that each person was either unattached, their family could travel with them, or they were estranged from any relatives. And the second was that each of them had some secret. An unpunished crime. Their sexual habits. Unpopular political or social theories in their home provinces/planets. Alk. Drugs. Or, best of all, that they were simply misanthropic. These people, if Richards's efforts produced anything, would be used to finish the development of AM2. Richards bought First Base on Deimos for a lab. He told Austin this was where the core research for the X particle would be conducted. There would be no possibility of leaks to business rivals—because no one except cleared Bargeta personnel would be allowed on Deimos, and all of the ancillary laboratories would be limited to a segment of the overall problem.

Finally, and most importantly, Operation Suk was Kea's cash cow. Of course there were comptrollers and such. But the day an experienced spaceship engineer couldn't steal the company's shirt, while it yet thought it was wearing a formal, was the day the sun would die. Especially when Operation Suk was run in such extreme secrecy.

Six years passed. Kea was, as one of his better-liked, less-reputable, and richer mining-ship friends put it, busier'n a onelegged man at a butt-kicking contest. Colorful, but accurate.

First, there was Operation Suk to run. Since he was the only one who really knew what the project was supposed to produce, he was required to go through all lab and operational summaries each reporting period and, frequently, call for the raw data. It gave him the reputation of being a very hands-on manager, as well as someone who was grudgingly respected because you couldn't slip one past *him*. But respect did not replace enough sleep, or personal relaxation.

Second, he was busy "helping" Austin run Bargeta Ltd. In fact—and Kea made sure that all of the people he was meeting found this out, subtly—he was running the dynasty. Austin was now regarded as even more of a numbnuts, to one level of the work force, and a dilettante, to their superiors. And Kea encouraged Austin to get out more. Travel. Get away from the job. Stay fresh. Stay active. If you bury yourself with all this little crud like I'm doing, who's going to make sure we don't stumble into a manhole?

He was careful to let Austin make the decisions, and let him make some that were very poor without protest. Kea could have done a more exact job of stage-managing, but he knew just how sensitive and paranoiac the incompetent were. The last thing he needed was to be fired. Except, at his level, being canned would be phrased as "resigned to pursue exciting interests of a personal nature."

He also traveled extensively incognito. There were people he needed to meet and industries to research that had nothing to do with Bargeta Ltd. Sometimes he traveled under a false name, with false papers. One of his favorites was H. E. Raschid, in tribute to Burton and Scheherazade. Now and again people grinned—and Richards made a mental note of the person as worth cultivation.

His new contacts and friends extended far beyond the business world. Politicians. Some people who had interesting trades, some of them quite beyond the law. He spent money lavishly, but cannily. He was always willing to contribute to a pol's coffers, without regard to the man or woman's party. Eventually he controlled a significant number of Ganymede's traditionally available estates general. He also owned about a quarter of the moon itself. The estate he had constructed was more a small, ultra-secure industrial park than the sprawling demesne of a rich man.

Which is just what Kea was now. Not only was he lavishly paid by Bargeta, with his own keys to the vault with Project Suk, but his new friends offered tips and suggestions. Kea played the market in every legal and illegal manner possible, so long as it was fairly subtle. Eventually there might be an investigation and an accounting—but when or if that day came, he would either be dead, have disappeared, or have made himself beyond the law.

Then came the breakthrough, a few months into the new century. An expedition returned. Not from the stars—Kea had chanced gross amounts of Bargeta's capital to fund two stardrive expeditions—but from the Solar System's backyard. Just beyond Pluto, just beyond the shatter that had once been thought to be an eleventh planet of the system. A meteorite, almost a quarter kilometer in diameter, had been found, tested, and brought back. The ships' captain reported more drifting bodies out there that spectroed as being the same matter.

It was the X material. Nonreactive to anything that the Bargeta labs could come up with. Hard to work, but not impossible. It would not retain radiation or anything else it was bombarded with. It even failed to react to a small bit of laboratory-produced "conventional" anti-matter.

It had a melting point high enough on the Kelvin scale to be suitable for ship armor, but low enough to be workable in a high-tech foundry.

Sensing victory, and allowing himself a flash of arrogance, Richards named the X substance. Imperium X. And he ordered a certain, very unusual ship to be moved from its parking orbit around Mars to the secret lab on Deimos. There it was given a plating from bow to stern, just a few molecules thick, of the new element. The ship was that old starship he'd seen drifting in a junkyard above Mars's polar regions years ago, which he'd purchased earlier and had modified in several ways, among them so one man and several computers could run it. It was already fueled—a good segment of Project Suk's resources had gone just to power the ship. Now for the Alva Sector, the discontinuity, and the final test.

The company announced Richards was finally going to take some time off. Kea told Austin that he would be absent for a minimum of three Earth-months. He was going somewhere, somewhere he wouldn't even tell his best friend about. Just as Austin had told him to do, a year or so ago.

"I did?"

"You did. We were fairly gassed at the time. Remember? Hey, you're the one who forgets nothing, right?"

Austin didn't laugh. Lately he had been wondering about Kea. He seemed . . . sometimes . . . as if he were setting his own course. Or, at least, behaving as if Bargeta's knowledge of the dynasty weren't that important. Perhaps, he thought, he'd have to talk to Kea. He *was* his friend, of course. But Austin remembered Mars, and remembered his father's reminder that the lesson of proper place must be learned and relearned, taught and retaught. There was no such thing as an irreplaceable man at Bargeta Ltd. That applied even to family members—Austin had sacked a couple of cousins just this year. No one was that vital—except, of course, Austin himself.

Two days before his planned disappearance, Richards was working out—on his private, single-station, no-links computer—the erratic series of orbits he would take to the Alva Sector. He was buzzed. His receptionist—Kea quite deliberately hired men or women for their competency and, preferably, homeliness, in deliberate contrast to Austin's office harem—said he had a visitor. She refused to announce herself. What should the receptionist do?

As she spoke, appearing to be puzzled, she kicked a pickup under her desk in the outer chamber, and a screen lit up, as instructed. This would not be the first person who preferred not to give a name to arrive at the boss's sanctum. Kea stared at the image. He was quite proud that he took less than two seconds, by his count, before he said, in a clear, normal voice, "Ah yes. Show her in."

Tamara. Still lovely. She wore a business suit that appeared to be styled for a man—once again, androgyny was the in cycle—but with a silken-looking blouse underneath, a blouse whose colors shifted and changed as sunlight and shadow crossed it. Under the suit, she would have nothing on, Kea knew. She still had that look. You may take me, any way you wish. If you can. He swam weightless for an instant. But he did not show it. He would be damned if he did.

He was delighted to see her. Embraced Tamara like a long-fondly-thought-of friend. He refused to let his mind tell him he felt her erecting nipples under the coat against his chest. Hold all calls. A drink. He seated her on his office couch, and sat close to her. But not that close. He had dreamed of seeing her again, all these years, he said. What was she doing in town? Recovering, Tamara said, her voice still sending chills, chills to match the time she'd showed him what could be done with nothing more than a few ice cubes and a leather strap. Recovering from what?

"My husband and I . . . are no more." She shrugged. "He's obsessed with his racing, although he certainly hasn't won anything of late. Boys and their toys, and that. I guess he never grew, and I did."

Well. Sorry, and that.

"I've been thinking about you a lot. For a lot of years. And I thought . . ." She stopped, waiting for Kea to pick up on the signal.

Richards waited, his expression patient, interested. Perhaps this old, respected friend was about to present an entirely new idea? Tamara tried again.

"You know, there are a *lot* of things I remember very, very well. Fireplaces. Silk. Laughing a lot. A hard-to-explain windburn." She forced a giggle, and Kea frowned for a moment, then visibly "remembered" the circumstances.

Tamara's brows furrowed for an instant. This was not going as she'd planned . . .

"But mostly, I remember mistakes. Especially one."

"Yes. I do, too."

"I think," Tamara said, her eyes now humbly down, on her hands clasped in her lap, "that all I can say is that I was a little shit in those days. And it took me a while to grow up. And that you'll never know how sorry I am, and how much I want to make it up to you."

She managed a tear. Kea found her a handkerchief. He shrugged. "Neither one of us," he said, "was exactly an adult in those days. One mistake balances another."

Tamara started to say something, then stopped. She puzzled, unsure of what Kea had meant by his last. Then she went on. "At least," she said, "Austin wasn't as stupid as I was. So it's not like you vanished, and it's not like life only gives you . . . I mean, we're in the real world. And people get a second chance, don't they?"

He took her in his arms. Kissed her. Not in a brotherly manner—but not with any marked passion. "Of course they do. And . . . you know, I've never forgotten you."

Kea stood and gently lifted her with a genteel hand under the elbow. "Now we have the time to get to know each other properly. Look. As soon as I'm back from this . . . business trip, I'll give you a call. Maybe have dinner or something. We have a *lot* to talk about."

He walked back to his desk. Tamara stared at him. She painted a smile across her face. He responded. She slowly went to the outer door, and opened it. She looked back at him. He was still smiling. Tamara stepped outside, and the door hissed closed. Just before it shut, and just before the insulation cut sound, Kea laughed.

Loudly. A harsh, unrelenting laugh. A Martian laugh. Then he forgot her.

Kea Richards vanished from man's haunts. He and the starship he had never bothered to name. He zigged his way

across the galaxy toward the Alva Cluster. He tracked toward
the discontinuity. Against interstellar blackness, he saw once
again the sparklers flashing, an independence fireworks
against the moonless night as tiny bits of normal matter col-
lided with AM2 particles.

He set his course. Through the discontinuity, and into that
other universe, the universe of black and all colors. He navigated, at quarter-drive, by the blind-flying system he had
developed after years of hard thought, a sophisticated evo-
lution of the navigational system Murph and Doctor Fazlur
had improvised.

He had a prox detector mounted in the ship's nose. It signaled. He was closing on some interstellar debris. Perhaps
no more than half a meter in size. But it would be Anti-
Matter Two, more than enough to shatter this tiny ship he
was aboard. He killed stardrive, went to secondary Yukawa
drive, then cut all power, braked, and let inertia close him
on the chunk of Anti-Matter Two.

He looked at another instrument and felt hope. This registered any object impacting on the ship's skin and was sensitive enough to go off if an Earth raindrop landed on it, when
the ship was parked. Or less, actually. The readout showed
his starship had been hit by particles after entering this mad
universe. AM2 particles. With no adverse effect to the ship.

The prox detector's signaling was a continuous *bong*ing.
Richards moved to another workstation. He fitted his hands
into waldos and concentrated on instruments. From a bay
just below the ship's nose, a probe extended. A claw. Another
modification of Kea's. A scoop. Plated with Imperium X. He
worked for long minutes with the unfamiliar controls. Sweat
spattered on the controls in front of him. If he had been
wrong, not only would all these years have been wasted, but
he would be very dead as well, if Imperium X was not the
perfect shield he had thought it to be, and the AM2 detonated in its beyond-nuclear hell.

The probe's instruments said the chunk was inside the
claw. Eyes involuntarily closed, brain expecting mindshatter

explosion, he closed the waldos. And again, nothing happened.

He was the proud possessor of a chunk of Anti-Matter Two. He moved the long arm back inside the ship and the bay hatches closed. The inside of the bay was also plated with Imperium X. He touched controls, and the ship went to lightspeed, on an orbit out of the discontinuity. This was the moment of real victory. Right now, even before the research, development, mining, and rest, Kea Richards had just made himself lord of the universe.

The world ended less than a year later, in two cataclysms. The catastrophes occurred a month apart. The first bannered every liviecast throughout the Solar System and to the scatter of settled worlds beyond. Deimos had blown up. The moon was now a blasted irregular asteroid like Phobos. An impossibility. Moons do not self-destruct. Deimos was uninhabited, except for three or four caretakers at the old First Base. More facts surfaced. In fact, Deimos had been well-populated. Several hundred men and women had been working in a secret complex of laboratories around the old First Base. The development belonged to Bargeta Industries. The screamers grew larger. Five—no, six—no, four hundred and fifty beings had vanished. Someone must pay.

The livie and newscasters stalked Bargeta Ltd. headquarters. Its CEO, a white and shaken man, stumbled through a prepared statement. Yes, the laboratory was a project center for his corporation. No, he would not say what it had been developing, except that it pertained to spaceship development. No, Austin did not know what happened. Bargeta scientific investigators were already trying to determine the cause of the disaster. No . . . no further comment. The 'casters found Kea Richards. He had no statement. No ideas. And absolutely no comment.

"What the blazes happened?" Bargeta screamed.

"I don't know," Richards said. "I had a com two E-days before, from Doctor Masterson, the director. He said that one of the exploratory teams had a new and fascinating lead, but it was so out of the ordinary he declined to be specific, for fear of embarrassment until further tests were made. Maybe something went wrong with those tests."

"Christ," Austin moaned. "All those people. The best scientists we could find. It wasn't like they were worker bees or anything. My God, my God. Do you realize what they're going to say at the annual meeting? How am I going to explain this to the stockholders?" Kea didn't know.

The second disaster was internal. Auditors had prepared a final report on Operation Suk. It was like some kind of financial black hole, Austin thought as he scanned the fiche. Thirty-eight percent of all convertible assets of Bargeta Ltd.—not just the transport company, but some of the holding company's assets as well—had vanished into the project. Worse was the classified scientific report attached—it appeared that the attempts to synthesize Kea's X substance had not only failed, and in the failing destroyed Deimos, but the entire idea had been proven absolutely fallacious. The Philosopher's Stone. A pollution-free oxygen-combinant combustion engine. Cold fusion. Bargeta was . . . if not bankrupt, lurching toward it. The huge conglomerate was broken now. It would be lucky to survive two more fiscal years, unless some kind of miracle happened, a miracle no one could see on any horizon.

Austin scrolled through the last page, and went looking for Kea. He found him in his office. The chamber was stripped bare. Travel boxes were stacked in one corner.

"What—"

Kea indicated an envelope, hand-addressed to Austin, on his desk. Bargeta read it. It was Richards's resignation. "All this," Kea said, in what appeared to be a shell-shocked monotone, "was my fault. I . . . I was wrong. No gold, no rainbow."

Bargeta looked for words and didn't find any. Kea started to say something, but merely put his hand on Austin's shoulder. Then he left.

Bargeta walked to the window and stared out and down the two hundred stories to Madison Avenue. The world had just ended for him, for his family, and for Bargeta Ltd. What next? What now?

Next was Bargeta and allied stocks plummeting even before the emergency stockholders meeting was called. Somebody had leaked the report to the Street—and Wall Street had divisions on every continent and planet. Investigators later found someone had also dumped Bargeta stock a day or so before the report had been released internally by the audit department. They could never determine just who'd been the original holder of the stock, since the certificates had traveled through a dizzying number of hands before being sold.

Kea Richards was gone, abandoning his Earth estates, his friends, his women, and his possessions. It was odd, and showed a previously unknown Spartan side, that in fact he didn't own that much. His mansions were only half-furnished, the half that someone on the outside might happen on. Or else they were leased furnished. The same with his yacht and his gravcars.

Austin Bargeta stammered through the emergency meeting. The corporate shareholders were as shocked after they had read the report as Austin had been. They adjourned, to meet again on the morrow. Austin was not there for the meeting. Immediately after the adjournment, he had taken a pistol from his private wallsafe. It was an antique 13mm caseless automatic, firing gunpowder-charged rounds, that had been in the family since the beginning. He had recently had shells custom-made. Now he pulled the slide back, and let it go forward, chambering a round. Turned the large pistol awkwardly, held it against his temple, thought at least the Bargetas had some honor, and pressed the trigger. The bullet blew most of the frontal half of his brain away. Unfortunately, it did not turn him into a corpse. Austin Bargeta, blind, mute, brain capable of only providing motor responses, lived on.

Kea Richards, from his self-exile on Ganymede, sent a

shocked com. Could he help? He had some personal credits, and if they could be used to keep Austin from becoming a public ward, the family had but to ask. The family declined. Bankrupt they might have been—but they were not reduced to charity. Kea felt a flicker of regret—the bastard should have been a better shot.

Kea was revenged. As, he felt, were many, many others. His unknown mother, driven to the horrors of a longliner. His father and grandmother and the other citizens of Hilo, drowned because most likely whichever fat-cat company had been supposed to maintain the tidal barriers had cut corners on maintenance to fatten their coffers. Leong Suk, who had never had a chance to know anything but poverty, from her native Korea to Maui. Hell, even that poor sad bastard Tompkins, who surely deserved better than to spend his life as a crackpot down a filthy alley. All the bluecollars he had grown and lived with, who sweated, worked, and died, so that people named Bargeta could have trimarans on Mars. The spacemen who killed themselves with alk or died in industrial "accidents" because shipline owners had little interest in safety standards beyond the letter of the law. The Bargetas and their gutted conglomerate were on the first. There would be more. Many more.

Kea was ready to build his "weapons" for the takeover. Only one man had died when Deimos blew up. He was one of the blasters Richards had hired from Mars's underworld, a demo expert who evidently hadn't been as expert as he had bragged. All the others, scientists, machinists, support people, and their mates, had been evacked days earlier to Ganymede, where the real task would begin. Kea Richards was ready for his "wilderness years."

CHAPTER TWENTY-FIVE

Ganymede, A.D. **2202**

KEA HAD GIVEN himself twenty years to reach a throne—a throne that he would have to create. But it didn't take him that long—everything went to lightspeed. Some of the acceleration was deliberate. Richards knew he had only so much time to establish a completely secure physical, moral, and economic stronghold before They would try to take it away from him. The "They" would include not just business tycoons and supercorporations, but planetary governments as well. So he moved very fast. What little personal life and recreational time he'd had as Bargeta's troubleshooter appeared like a lifetime of idle luxury now.

At first, it seemed to everyone Kea Richards really had retired to piddle about on his vast Ganymede estates with scientific toys. What actually happened was that his starship was modified to accept AM2 for fuel. The "fuel tank" was no bigger than Richards's torso and was made of Imperium X, as were the feed lines and chambers in the engine itself. There had been a seemingly insurmountable problem keeping the engine lubricant from ever contacting Anti-Matter Two, but eventually the problem had been solved.

When all ground tests were completed satisfactorily, Richards and Doctor Masterson quietly boarded ship. Overhead, filling the sky, was the reddish bulk of Jupiter. Kea lifted the ship on McLean power, then went to Yukawa drive. Offworld, he checked the ship's ultrasensitive receptors. The ship was not being monitored. And then the ship went to stardrive. AM2 stardrive.

Nothing spectacular happened. Stardrive was stardrive was hyperspace was boring. Nothing was exciting about this test flight—except that the drive-activation control was closed, and drive automatically cut before Richards could take his hand from it. Arcturus's red-yellow bulk and its twelve worlds hung onscreen. Three other star systems were reached that E-night. And on return to Ganymede the fuel "tank" appeared to be as "full" as on departure.

Cost? Not calculable. The fuel was a bit of the small chunk "mined" by Kea beyond the Alva Sector. There was still three quarters of the debris left, held in an Imperium X vault on Ganymede. Now the dream was a reality. The ship was further modified, its hold gutted and lined with Imperium X.

Again, Kea vanished. Three E-months later he returned with a full cargo of AM2. That was enough Anti-Matter Two to provide energy, he calculated, for the entire career of every space-ship ever built, with enough left over—but this was on fairly shaky mathematics—to run all of Mars's power plants for three E-years. Sooner or later Kea knew he would have to build roboticized mining ships, everything in them either made of or plated with Imperium X, move them through the discontinuity into the other universe, and set them to work. He would also have to come up with some kind of long-distance on/off switch, a com whose signals would have to be at least as eccentrically targeted as Richards's chosen orbits to the Alva Sector.

Kea had studied, with some amusement, the attempts of the so-called oil sheikhs to use their control of the petroleum resource to reshape the culture of Earth. Perhaps admirable in its appalling egocentricity, the plan had of course failed in unreality, greed, and hypocrisy. If Kea had to play that card, however, he was determined it would be the highest of trumps. But the on/off power switch could wait. Now it was time to start rattling some cages.

Kea stepped out of retirement and announced plans to

build luxury ships—spaceyachts, really—and run them from Earth to Mars as a first-class service. At a rumored price three times that of conventional passage. There was some quiet scoffing in the resorts, bars, and clubs catering to the gigawealthy. Nice thought, but there weren't that many super-rich fools. Not enough to support Kea's scheme. Oh well. He would go bankrupt, and come looking to them for a position, which any of them would be happy to provide.

The ships were built. They looked to be more medium-size freighters than luxury carriers. And back of Barrier Thirty-three, some compartments were left empty. Modifications would be made on Ganymede. Kea had some odd ideas of his own, which would be made at the small port on his estates. On Ganymede, the ships were fitted with stardrive engines. Fueled. And crewed.

Since no one gave a diddly damn about spacemen, no one had noticed that recruiters had been filtering through space-ports. Looking for the best, those who hadn't lost their illusions and those who looked to the stars as a challenge, not a swamper's scut job. Those who passed the amazingly stringent tests were brought to Ganymede and trained. Surprisingly, about 15 percent were paid off and regretfully returned to their home worlds—psychologists discovered that even a spaceman might be afraid of the stars beyond the "known" worlds. Eventually the men and women were shown the new ships. Taught to navigate, pilot, and service them. And sent out. To the stars. Looking. For valuables. And for extraterrestrials.

Two years after Kea had launched the first starship, *seven* intelligent—human or near-human equivalent as a minimum—extraterrestrial races had been found. Three of them were evolved enough to have interplanetary travel. None had stardrive. They would. On Kea Richard's terms.

Kea's espionage reported, a little worriedly, that there were some amazing rumors about what Richards was doing out on Ganymede. Kea sighed—the secret couldn't have been kept forever. Too many people on Ganymede, in spite of precautions, had seen starships lift from Richards's port and simply vanish. And spacemen/women tell bar tales. It was time for the next stage.

A new corporation was chartered in the no-questions-asked, flag/bank-of-convenience Province of Livonia. Clive, Anon. The charter was carefully written to be so vague that the new company could do anything from painting itself blue and dancing widdershins to terraforming the sun. Livonia's laws being what they were, the only person whose name appeared on the charter was a local, one Yaakob Courland, as Livonian law required. He was paid, in cash, for the use of his name when the papers were filed, and promptly forgot about the event, since it was the fifth set of papers he had signed that day. But that was the last time the company was anonymous.

Earth vid/livie crews were asked if they would be interested in attending a press conference, in which Kea Richards would make a major announcement. It was to be held at New York's near-abandoned Long Island spaceport, at a certain time. Another conference was announced. On Mars, at Capen City's port. Kea Richards would appear, to make a major announcement. Both conferences were on the same day, two E-hours apart. No one noticed the apparent error. Both conferences were moderately well attended—although not one-tenth as many journalists actually showed up as later claimed to have been present.

Because Kea *did* attend both events. In fact, having gotten lucky with takeoff clearance, he had to waste almost a full E-hour on the ground at Capen City, waiting for the press. His announcement was simple. His research company had made certain major improvements in the stardrive engine, improvements which, attorneys said, in fact, qualified the engine as an entirely new invention. Some thousand patents were being filed in The Hague, on Mars, and on Earth. Any infringement on these patents, once they were granted, would be met with the most severe legal penalties. Kea figured the crockola of Superengine would satisfactorily murk up the cesspool for a while, anyway.

On Mars, after he had made his announcement, some fifteen starships that had been waiting offworld landed. Each of them carried a cargo like man had never seen before. Unknown minerals. Gemstones. Sealed "plants" from beyond the stars. In two cases, extraterrestrials landed with the humans, ETs previously unknown.

Kea offered man the stars. But at a price. The new, improved engines would *not* be offered for sale, nor would they be licensed. All transport with the new engines would be the sole province of the Clive, Anon., starships. The little corner of creation man thought of as his universe went insane. And everyone went after Kea Richards.

He retired to Ganymede and went deep into his bunker. Quite literally—he'd had many levels excavated below his mansion. He could take anything up to and including a nuke with zero damage—at least to himself and his immediate staffers. And he watched the fun. Everyone wanted to ship aboard his craft. There was a monstrous waiting list, a waiting list that almost made it practical to ship or travel conventionally. Almost, but not quite. And Richards had set his rates to be exactly what they should be—he allowed a 30 percent markup for profit and, for the moment, another 20 percent for risk.

His fellow capitalists were frothing, lawyers charging back and forth from court to suite to corporate headquarters. The situation was quite simple—Richards had just announced the steamship to his friends, who were sitting, paddles in hand, on their floating logs. This sounded like Kea Richards had a monopoly. Incredibly illegal. Civil and criminal charges were made.

Richards, through his lawyers, had but one standard announcement. He was innocent. But he firmly believed in justice, and had full faith in the wisdom of the courts. Unfortunately, though, he had been advised that he would have to cease shipping to any city, province, country, or world where such charges pended.

That immediately brought battalions of new heavyweights onscene, filing *amicus curiae* briefs on behalf of Clive, Anon. Their companies were as varied as mankind's choice of trades, but all of them had one thing in common—they wanted/needed to be able to ship/receive something from Point A to Point B in less than a lifetime. The shipping companies, and their hastily if massive filings, vanished.

Still heavier guns rolled up. Governments themselves. Kea Richards was seen as a Threat. He should share this miracle engine with everyone, for the Good of Mankind. Richards declined. Mankind would benefit quite well, thank you, through Clive, Anon. Orders were issued for his arrest. One came from the tiny province of Rus, the other from Sinaloa, both traditional places where influence and credit could purchase anything. Kea's lawyers informed the courts that under no circumstances, being in fear of his life, would Kea surrender to these warrants.

Very well, he would be arrested on Ganymede and extradited. Armed forces would be provided by the as-yet-unnamed men who'd charged Kea with crimes. The furies after Kea next discovered that all the credits invested in Ganymede's politicians had been well spent. The pols were honest—that is, they stayed bought—and Richards remained free and unextraditable. "Trapped," at least for the moment, on Ganymede. But what of it—he had access to any ship he wanted and any destination that could be navigated. With galaxies opening in front of him, Kea imagined he could live without caviar or cabrito for a spell.

Eminent domain was suggested next. His ships would be seized. It was pointed out it might be a little difficult to "stop" a spacecraft that would outperform, at quarter-drive, any conventional starship. And how, exactly, did any government propose to do this, in deep space? Eventually even the bureaucrats were convinced that Halt in the Name of the Law was a little ludicrous between planets, let alone between stars. It was rumored someone had laboriously defined inertia to them.

Government ships could be armed, came the bumble. That brought a stinging release from Richards's headquarters. First, all basic interplanetary treaties had banned military development in space. Second, and more to the point, Kea's ships were armed. This was a fact—Kea had purchased some tiny lunar lighters, given them AM2 stardrive, put in a prox detonator in the nose next to a warhead—also AM2, of course—and adapted a standard commercial robot piloting system to the lighters. Each starship had been given a missile. Now each looked like a chubby shark with a remora. The ships themselves were also equipped with remote-controlled chainguns mounted inside each ship's cargo port.

Very well, the pols floundered. His ships would be arrested—seized for an Admiralty court—when they made planetfall. Kea's main lawyer announced quite coolly that, first, if Clive, Anon., became aware of any warrant being issued, the firm's craft would blacklist the city, province, etc., as before. If force was used, that would be regrettable. Any such country attempting this deviousness would be considered as beyond the law. No better than a corsair nation. And not only would charges be filed in the still-extant if ludicrous World Court, but force would be met with force. The uneasy peace continued. It was prolonged by the rumor—never verified— that all of the new starships were booby-trapped, so that any intrusion beyond Barrier Thirty-three would be a disaster.

Evidently there were disbelievers. Because, quite suddenly, as one of Richards's ships were clearing for lift from Ixion Port—Alpha Centauri's most developed world—the ship, most of the port, and some of the city's industrial section vanished in hellflame. Richards's enemies seized on this—the new engines were unsafe, and should be banned, and Richards himself prosecuted. Kea was worried—and then an amateur shipfreak surfaced with an amazing audio track. He had been recording ship-tower chatter, and, quite clearly, any listener could hear the takeoff drone being interrupted by shouts, the clanging of a hatchway out of crewspace, gunfire, and then silence. The critics were not only answered, but somewhat discredited. But that was too close for Kea.

He had been carefully winnowing through the personnel roster of his retained spookshop, and hiring away the absolutely loyal, and those who were qualified in certain irregular areas.

The truehearts he used for personal and estate security. The others made up a very specialized hunter-killer team. They went looking for whoever had hired the hijackers. And they found them—the woman and her son who headed SpaceWays/Galiot. Somehow a commercial gravlighter went out of control and crashed into a mansion on a tiny, private Aegean island. Without any surviving heirs, SpaceWays went into receivership until the situation could be sorted out. Just to make sure that the robber barons and their thugs got the message, Kea hired more security people. These had a new task—to baby-sit, unobtrusively, his spacemen. Anyone interfering with one of his crew members, whether it was pumping for info in a barroom or trying a backalley snatch for interrogation, was intercepted and "handled roughly."

Kea bought more shipyards and commissioned more ships, and they went out to the stars. For deployment around the worlds of man, he had a different class of ship built. These were AM2 warships, missile/rocket/laser/chaingun—armed partrol craft, which escorted the liners and freighters safely away from the dangerous—i.e., inhabited—worlds. Governments may have been banned from building warships, but no one had mentioned private enterprise, for the simple reason that before AM2 drive, a spaceship/starship built for combat was absurdly wasteful. Kea was spending a fair amount of his time thinking about weaponry. One of his technicians, a Robert Willy, had pointed out that there was no particular reason a tiny particle of AM2 could not be given a shroud of Imperium X and made into an explosive bullet, if the shielding was cast with a deliberate, high-impact-sensitive fault. He also believed that, if this "bullet" was made small enough, and the latest generation of hyperpowerful portable lasers was used, that the AM2 bullet could not be "fired" by laser. Kea Richards, thinking grimly of Alfred Nobel, his invention that was intended for the benefit of all mankind, and the effective if terribly dangerous "dynamite guns" that were produced, gave Willy his own research team and access to Anti-Matter Two.

The vids and the livies, reflecting public perceptions and

feelings as the media have always done instead of creating it as too many fools believe, were beginning to banner Kea as a liberator. Greater than Edison, greater than Ford, greater than McLean, even. Kea knew they weren't even close, although the thought sounded like it came from a megalomaniac. They still didn't understand, any more than someone in the middle of massive change ever does, the total revolution that was going on. But they would.

Everything was running at full drive. Kea was worried, because he knew what would come next and wasn't sure that he would be able to block the next attempt to deny man the stars.

Perhaps the assault team had forgotten about Jupiter light and thought they would have complete night for their cover. Or perhaps they didn't care. But it was no more than three-quarters dark when they attacked, Jove hanging overhead like the largest color-streaked party light ever built. They were well-trained commandos and must have practiced on full-scale models or at the least livie-simulations of Richards's estate.

Alarms screamed, and Kea rolled out of the bed he had slumped into, exhausted, less than an hour before. Not awake, he stumbled to a closet and pulled on a dark coverall. Hanging nearby was an LBE harness with a pistol and ammo belt. A machine carbine dangled next to it. Wishing that he'd had more time, and Willy'd been able to perfect his AM2 weapon, he jacked a round into the carbine's chamber, tugged on zip-closure boots, and headed down the hall. The ground roiled beneath him, and Kea tumbled down. He didn't find out until later that was a small picketboat, under robot control, that had been sent smashing into one of his compound's perimeter labs as a diversion to attract emergency crews. Kea came up, ran on. Into one of the mansion's lobbies.

"Mr Richards! The bunker!" Security's watch commander was waving at him. Then a crash, and supposedly impact-proof plas and reinforcing alloy fell into the chamber. The officer spun, shouted, died, as two black-dressed men dropped into the room, weapons firing. One of them saw Richards, gun came up, recognized their target, the gun was knocked away, and they dove toward him. Kea held the trigger full back and three rounds on full auto/control shattered the pair. So they were under explicit orders, he thought. I'm not to be killed. That'll slow 'em down a little.

Richards's security men swarmed into the lobby. One of them flipped a blast grenade up, through where the skylight had been blown away. Another explosion, and screams. The hell with the bunker, Richards thought. If the bastards know enough about this mansion to hit close to my bedroom, they've probably got that targeted as well. Gunfire chattered from outside the main entrance and lasers flashed seen/never-seen red eye-memory. Shouts.

"Let's go," he yelled, and ran toward the main door. Absurd, absurd, he thought. Are you leading from the front, or are you playing Roland? You are an engineer and maybe a back-alley brawler. You've never been a combat soldier, nor been much interested in being one, or even watching the livies that glorify their slaughter.

The mansion's main anteroom was a haze of smoke and gunfire. Kea watched his "soldiers"—and most of them had been trained in one or another of the various armed forces of the Solar System—fire, cover, and maneuver forward. Amazing, he thought. Just like the vids. Just like the livies. Another thought came: Did the livies reflect reality, or are all of us aping what we've seen done by actors? Come on, man! You don't have time for this slok! There were four attackers left, crouched behind the solid planters, containing now-bullet-shattered ferns. More grenades rained—never liked the ferns anyway, and there'll sure be a redecorating bill after this, amazing how the mind can spin all these stupid things out—and the first wave was obliterated.

Kea's security may have been surprised by the first assault— but now their training and constant practice took over. Great doors that appeared to be part of the three-story walls slid open, and wheeled autocannons were rolled out. They were set up—

as intended—behind those planters that had been designed to double as a firing point, and ammo drums slammed home.

Outside, on the vast reaches of the grounds, Kea counted three, no four, small ships. This was not a small-time operation, he realized. The second wave rose from cover and charged. The front of Kea's near-palace had been laid out with graceful, flowing, low, close-barred railings that swept the viewer's eye toward the splendor of the house itself. It was considered part of the magnificence that had made the house a prizewinner in architectural circles. In fact, the flowing walls had been drawn up by Kea himself, working with his head security man, and were intended to channel not the viewer's eye, but an attacker's charge.

The railings were just high enough to be hard to hurdle, and the bars were far enough apart so they offered neither cover nor concealment. Now, they worked as intended, channeling the attackers directly toward the main entrance. Directly into the killing zone of the autocannon.

Guns yammered again, and blasts fragmented the night, and men and women shouted and died. A wounded, bloodied man stumbled through the smoke, gun hanging down, and was shot down. He was the last. Without a pause, the autocannon were pushed out into the open, and opened up on the four spacecraft. Two of the ships blew apart, the other smoked menacingly, and the last gouted flames.

Kea's security split into three elements. One group took up a defensive perimeter around Kea, a second charged the ships, their task to make sure all the attackers were down. The third element quickly, skillfully, began searching the bodies and, after making sure the wounded were disarmed, dragging them toward a common collecting point. Kea watched, his mind suddenly dulled. After some time, his Head of Security approached. "Sir, I have a report."

"Go ahead."

"There were at least seventy-three invaders, possibly more. We don't know how many were aboard the ship. Twelve are still alive."

"Who are they?"

"No IDs on any of the bodies. The two that're talking claim they're indies, hired out of Pretoria by freelancers they'd worked with before. Neither of them know who's the original hire. Assuming that this *was* a for-hire hit, which I don't."

"Keep looking. Will your two injured stand up to interrogation?"

"Negative, sir. Not now, maybe not ever. Those thirty-mill rounds tear hell out of everything."

"Do you have a prog?"

"Not really," the security commander said slowly. "Maybe mercs, working for one of your enemies. Maybe coverts that got sheep-dipped and this is a deniable black." Kea nodded. It could have been the Federation, Earthgov, Mars Council, or any of the supercorporations.

"What about the wounded, sir? I mean, after we've gotten whatever we can?" Kea hesitated, as an aide approached.

"Sir, we have a com from NewsTeam Eleven. Leda. They say they've gotten six calls reporting gunshots and explosions, and want to know what happened. They'd like to talk to you . . . and they want to dispatch a team."

Kea thought quickly. At first his reaction was to welcome the newsies. He'd have time to change into a bathrobe and bewildered expression, and throw a conference on the basis of Who Would Dare, Why Would Anyone Attack an Innocent? and so on and so forth. He reconsidered. "You can tell them that my security was conducting an extremely realistic exercise. They're welcome to send a newsteam—Ganymede is a free world—but they are not welcome to land on my property. As for me—I'm offplanet. Testing a new ship. You have no contact with me at the moment. You can tell them that when I return, you imagine, I would be willing to talk to them, although about what, you have no idea."

The aide blinked—a thickie, Richards thought—frowned, then scurried away. Kea turned back to his security commander. "Does that answer your question?"

"Yessir." The officer took his pistol from its holder, chambered a round, and walked toward the enemy-casualty collection point.

Kea walked out of the shambles and looked up, beyond the sky-filling bulk of Jupiter, his eyes going beyond, toward the settled worlds. Now we'll wait. Until someone whines. And then we'll know who my biggest enemy is.

But he never found out. There were not even rumors in the grayworld of the mercenaries.

Kea grew even more concerned. This attempt could have worked. And it wouldn't be the only one or the biggest. It had been handicapped because "They" wanted Richards alive. But sooner or later someone would determine that at least the status quo must be maintained—and surely one of Kea's people knew the secret of stardrive.

No one did, of course. But that would not bring Kea Richards back from the grave. He needed a miracle.

CHAPTER TWENTY-SIX

Clarke Central, Luna, A.D. 2211

THE MIRACLE ARRIVED in late spring. It was first observed and tracked by a Callisto-Mars Yukawa drive ship. It was an irregular chunk of rock not much more than a kilometer in diameter. It might have been considered a small asteroid, but its characteristics showed no semblance to the rocks tumbling beyond Mars. The navigator noted the orbit and roughly calculated the meteor's speed. He reported and forgot it. The report was logged, and the navigator's figures checked, rechecked, and extrapolated. The tech at MarsNavCentral blinked, swore, and ran the problem again.

The figures indicated that this chunk of interplanetary/stellar debris was on a collision track with Earth's moon, plus-minus 15 percent probability. The tech told his supervisor. His supervisor, realizing the navigation center's annual budget was up for review, commed the existence of this hurtling rock to a local vid science-news reporter. And the reporter's editor knew what built ratings and sold ads: FLASH: Scientists Report a New Interstellar Meteor on a Collision Course with Luna! Superspeed Asteroid to Crash into Moon in 158 E-Days! Mars Entire Population in Jeopardy! Earth Itself Endangered!

Chaos and craziness, from scientists to the media to the public. Early on, a literate antiquarian named the rock Wanderer. The name was seized on as the only thing everyone agreed about as the Solar System's sanity level dropped like the long-ago ocean in Hilo Bay. Kea, from Ganymede, watched and read in growing amazement and concern.

Theories were offered. Studied. The Solar Federation set up an emergency headquarters on Mars, in the central Clarke complex. It took a week or so, but eventually enough pols had been reassured there'd be more than enough time and ships to evac them before Wanderer impacted. And then the speeches and the "viewing with concern" went on. A state of emergency was declared. But nothing was *done*. Worse, as the probable impact time grew closer, nothing was even suggested.

Should the Moon be evacuated? How? There were almost two million people living under its cratered desolation. And what about Earth's population? Should everyone move to high ground, in the assumption Earth would experience the most erratic and deadly tides in humankind's history? Words, words. No actions.

Kea had thought his cynicism to be unshakable in his belief that society, as presently constituted, could muck up a rock fight. He should have been unsurprised as the media hollered, the pols debated, the scientists chased ever-receding decimal points, and the people clamored. The clamor included new prophets preaching that the sins of the past were about to be paid for. Mobs who knew that the world was coming to an end, and therefore utter license should be the order of the day. Cops and soldiery who seemed more worried about the possibility of riots than what response they would have to the catastrophe.

Words, and more words, as Doomsday grew nearer and nearer. There were even some utter stiffs who suggested *nothing* should be done. This was part of nature, was it not? Man had evolved through catastrophe. This was Intended to Happen. This would usher in the Next Level of Being. Intended by Whom varied from fruitbar to fruitbar.

Seventy-three days.

Kea sent for Doctor Masterson, his head scientist. He respected the man, as much for his pragmatism as for his ability to keep secrets and administer equally individualistic and iconoclastic scientists and technicians. Masterson ran his own prognoses: Prog: that Wanderer would collide with the Moon. 85 percent. Prog: that Wanderer would bankshot and crash Earth. 11 percent. Prog: that the Moon will shift its orbit closer to Earth. 67 percent. Prog: that the impact would be great enough to shatter Luna completely. 13 percent. Prog: that Wanderer would knock some fairly impressive chunks off the Moon. 54 percent. Prog: that one or more of those moonlets could impact Earth. 81 percent.

The effects . . .

Kea did not need to listen. He was enough of a scientist to envision the radioactivity that would be produced if a decent-sized chunk of Luna, say about the size of Wanderer hit land. And to consider the likelihood of great earthquakes and even the slight possibility of tectonic plateshift? Wanderer promised the cataclysm—but still no one proposed any action as a rushed onward. Pols were besieged with solutions, it was true, from using all the Solar System's rockets to push the Moon out of the way to building a great cannon that would blast Wanderer out of its lethal orbit. But none of them, even those that might be possible, were implemented. Studies were authorized. Military and police forces were put on alert.

Forty-one days.

Kea thought there were only two alternatives. First was that he was living in a completely mad universe. The second was that he was mad himself. Because a solution seemed quite obvious. But no one had taken it. At least yet.

Kea moved. First was to punch a com through to Earth. He snarled at the time it took to get through, and then at the fuzziness of the hyperspace link. Someday, he thought, he would have to find himself an R&D dwonk, give him assistants, a few million credits, some AM2, and tell him to come up with some kind of system that'd enable one being to talk to another across a distance without both of them sounding like they're sitting in barrels and looking like so many triple-imaged blurs. Someday.

He eventually got through to his target—Jon Nance, the highest-rated liviecaster going. Nance was busy. The world was coming to an end, or so everyone said, and he was occupied being Chicken Little. Kea said very well. He would go to the competition. What did Kea have? He would not say. But it was big. And it involved Wanderer. Nance was very interested—there had to be something new to the story besides reporting the latest hysteria or drone of inaction. Richards told Nance to pack. Stand by with a full crew. A complete recording setup, plus two remotes. And a link to go live to Terra. A ship was on its way to pick them up.

"O Joy," Nance said sourly. "I'm going to have to unfasten an entire crew. Walk away from the desk, and put in my summerman to anchor. And just a smile for the cheeses and the producers. You've got to give me more than that."

"Never mind," Kea said. "This link isn't secure, and I don't always trust you, anyway. I'll still have the ship at Kennedyport in . . . two E-hours."

"Christ, it'll take me longer'n that to get a gravcar out to the port!"

"Sounds like a personal problem. Two E-hours. Or else

I'll rent a doculivie crew and your net can bargain for their reels. Along with everybody else." He shut off. Then he let himself grin. Masterson may have been the prog specialist in some areas, but Kea wasn't that bad himself. Prog: that Nance would be there with bells and recorders? 79 percent. Minimum.

He ordered the ship that was on standby at his own field to lift for New York. That was one ship. He needed two more. One of his newer transports would serve. He ordered Masterson and the best sober pilot he could winkle up to get ready. He sent for his own ship, the starship he had seen so many aeons before in its junk orbit off Mars. The ship that had been the first fitted for AM2. So what?—he had avoided sentimentality when it came to objects. He had never even given the ship a name beyond its registry numbers. It was time to get rid of the starship—increasingly he'd wondered, if the ship ever fell into the wrong hands, if it might some-how provide a clue to the Alva Sector. This would be a fit-ting way—if Kea was correct—for its end.

He had a pilot lift it to a clear area outside one of his experimental workshops. One minor modification was made to the controls. Starships are not normally fitted with timers. Then he himself lifted the ship, and hovered it into the super-secure AM2 storage areas. A remotely controlled, Imperium-sheathed cargoloader took a chunk of Anti-Matter Two from a vault. Kea, as he delicately took it in his own ship's grab-claw, thought the less-than-500-kilogram-in-weight block might even be what was left of that first chunk of AM2 he'd grabbed on this ship's maiden voyage into the alternate uni-verse. He was ready to roll.

The two ships cleared Ganymede and set an orbit to inter-sect Wanderer. Waiting for them was the third ship. And, as Richards had known, a grumpy, evil-tempered Nance was aboard. Evil-tempered, until Richards told him what he pro-posed. And then he melted.

Kea had one remote set up in the control room of his own ship, the second in the port of the ship Masterson was aboard.

The three ships were powered into Wanderer's path. Richards fancied he could feel the whirling chunk of rock moving toward him, like a railbound train in a tunnel. Enough. He told Nance he had better patch down to New York, to his net. There wasn't much time left.

Nance's ship hung about fifty kilometers from the other two. Richards thought it was far too close, but Nance said uh-uh. He had to get his "picture," and little dots of dark against a greater dark wouldn't cut it. Kea shuddered again, thinking about the nature of livies. How could anyone allow— let alone spend a career lifetime ensuring—other beings to gather in his mind, smelling what the liviecaster smelled, seeing what he saw, and even experiencing the 'caster's conscious, controlled thoughts? Masterson's ship was less than fifty meters from Richards's. Kea donned a spacesuit and dumped ship atmosphere, leaving both lock doors open. A line linked the two ships.

Nance was 'casting. Inside Mars's orbit, he said, in his calm-but-excited patented manner. About to witness what might well be the most spectacular feat in man's history. Kea Richards was about to attempt to destroy Wanderer, using a new and unspecified method, but one that involved his secret engine. And as coached by Kea, Nance wondered why the Federation hadn't even *tried* anything, but were still sitting on the Moon, jacking their jaws . . . (though he worded it far more politely than that).

Kea was ready. The remote—a vid, of course—showed a spacesuited man moving around a control room. What was not shown was the outside bay port opening and the ship's grabclaw extending that huge chunk of Anti-Matter Two in front of it, exactly like a fearful peasant trying to ward off the evil eye.

For melodramatic effect, Richards had told Nance to begin a countdown when signaled. It started. There wasn't much to do—the trajectory was set, and the controls were linked to the downcounting timer. At three minutes thirty seconds, Kea headed out. He swarmed across the rope, severed its

connection to his doomed starship, and closed the lock door,
his every action recorded by that second remote. He shut the
vid off—Masterson had been emphatic that he never wanted
to be seen on vid or livie—and went into the other ship's
control room.

One minute, he heard Nance cadence. Twenty-seven seconds. And ten . . .

And zero . . . the timer closed, and the ship across the
way vanished. Vanished into full-power stardrive. Not even
a second later, it impacted into Wanderer.

The livie-recorder that Nance wore like some great helmet,
and the accompanying vid camera aboard his ship, overloaded
into the ultra and burnt out. Kea had warned him. But the
audio pickup was still active, and Nance's voice continued,
live, straight to the net headquarters in New York, and from
there to man's worlds.

Kea barely noticed the 'caster's excitement. He was busy.
He'd taken the ship controls and sent the transport, under
half Yukawa drive, toward the meteor. What meteor? A collection of gravel in loose formation. Of Kea's ship, there was
nothing whatever remaining.

Kea listened to the broadcast, still live, coming from
Nance's ship. He had not known there were so many syn-
onyms for "hero." Richards smiled. Actually, this time, he
was a bit of a hero. He was surprised he felt a shade embarrassed. Hero, eh? Kea the Galactic Hero, he thought in amusement. Now Kea had the name. The tools. Wanderer had given
him the stage and the floodlights for his grand entrance. All
he needed was the fanfare. And he was fairly certain what it
would be, even if he didn't know who'd show up to blow in
his ear.

CHAPTER TWENTY-SEVEN

Ganymede—A.D. 2212

ONE WAS THE prime minister of a commonwealth. He represented the big families. One was a businesswoman, a member of the board on two thousand blue-chip firms. Another represented Big Money. He controlled the skim on two-thirds of all electronically transmitted cash. The last was labor chieftain of three continents.

"Most of the military is behind us," Labor said. "The rest will follow if we do a deal."

"Amazing how timid generals can be," Kea said.

"They would have come," the prime minister said, "but they were worried—despite our assurances to the contrary—that they might be spotted . . . They send, however, their humblest apologies and warmest greetings."

Kea snorted. "Like I said . . . timid."

Big Money cut to the bottom line. "But still with us," he said. "You know we wouldn't be here, Mr Richards, if we didn't have all our i's dotted and t's crossed."

"The point is," the businesswoman said, "the Federation's presidential election is upon us. Time is short. We need to know *now* if you'll be our nominee."

"I'll have to be honest with you," Kea said. "The other side has come to see me as well."

Labor laughed. "if you didn't figure we already knew that, Mr Richards," he said, "you wouldn't have let our shadows fall upon your doorstep."

"We're not amateurs," Big Money said. "We came prepared to substantially increase the offer."

"I think we had better stop right here," Kea said, "while I explain my position."

"Explain away," Labor said.

"I'll tell you the same thing I told them. I don't need this. I'm richer than anyone has a right to be. I'm forty-seven years old. I was thinking of taking it easy for a while. Resting on my laurels, as it were."

The businesswoman clapped. "Lovely speech. We'll see the spin doctors use it."

"The think-piece writers will devour it with relish," the prime minister said. "I can see the Op Ed headline now: 'Hero who saved civilization spurns all offers from grateful public.'"

"We let that kinda thing bounce around for a week or so," Labor cut in. "Then play up the mess the fat cats and backroom boys have got the Federation into. Before you know it, folks will be beggin' you to save 'em again."

"Then you reluctantly . . . and humbly . . . agree to a draft," the prime minister said.

The businesswoman graced him with her most charming smile. "Is that what you had in mind, Mr Richards? More or less?"

Kea laughed. "The others believed me just a little longer than you people," he said.

"That's why we're number one," Big Money responded.

"Number one . . . but without a candidate," Kea said. "Which is the same boat your competition is in. At this rate, both parties will wind up in a tie out of sheer electoral boredom. And even if you win . . . The Federation is in a mess. You guys have put it in the crap house. What are you going to do about it? What are your big ideas?"

Dead silence greeted this. But Kea believed it necessary to drive his point home. "The current state of the Federation is no fantasy, my friends," he said. "The economy is in shambles. You've got twenty wars of various sizes. Famine.

Drought. Industry is stalled. Inflation running amok. Interest rates sky-high . . . if there was anyone with money to borrow. Besides that, lady . . . and gentlemen, you look in fine shape to me."

"You must be interested," Labor said, "or you wouldn't have bothered to fill up your stone bucket before we got here. If you get my point."

"I got it," Kea said.

"Which brings us back to the price," Big Money said.

"What *could* I want?" Kea asked. "I've got AM2. Which means I already control everything—from the stars on down."

"You tell us, Mr Richards," Labor said. "What *do* you want?"

Kea told them. Unlike the first group, there was no quibbling. No negotiation.

The deal was cut right there.

Port Richards, Tau Ceti—A.D. 2222

It was a gentle sloping hill, carpeted with a thick lichen-like plant—purple with green pinhead buds—that released a heady perfume every day at dusk. Kea breathed in the scent as he strolled up the hill—alone, except for the ever-present security screen spread out around him. He stopped to rest just before he reached the summit, puffing with effort.

Kea turned back to view his vacation campsite. The cynical street kid in him laughed. The encampment consisted of his personal tent—a two-story-high gold fabric pavilion, really—and more than sixty smaller tents to house staff, security, and other bits of his entourage. Kea snorted. Publicity had billed the trip as a simple camping vacation. A well-deserved rest from the awesome burdens of his office as President of the Federation. The fact that he had chosen to take his vacation upon a newly opened world—named in his honor—in the Tau Ceti system, was given much significance by his pet livie commentators.

"Is it not fitting," one commentator had said, "that this

simple man . . . this ordinary man of the people . . . President Kea Richards . . . should seek to refresh his spirits in the stars?"

"Most analysts see this journey as symbolic," another said. "Through Kea Richards, civilization has pushed its boundaries into the great beyond. Now, President Richards is reminding us that there are many more worlds to conquer. That our future is a never-ending frontier."

This trip to the frontier was just another stone mortared into the legend Kea had been building for ten years. The legend of the common man. A self-made man. A man who remembered well the plight of the poor from whose ranks he had emerged. A genius in the rough, continually seeking new ways to better life for all.

Some of that was even true.

In ten years he had created a commercial empire greater than anything before. New ideas and renewed vigor had birthed industries that churned out goods—priced within easy reach of all. Food flooded out of giant agricultural combines in unprecedented volumes. Science and invention had exploded. Star probes were bridging vast distances. Terraforming engineers were at work on scores of worlds like Port Richards—adding territory to the Federation. Even the arts flourished in an atmosphere of free-flowing money and ideas. There was no denying Kea Richards was the engine that had made all those things possible. And AM2 was the fuel powering that engine. The robot delivery system had been tested and perfected. AM2 was being shipped regularly, and in large quantities—with zero chance of anyone learning the source.

Naturally, he had enemies. Many enemies. Kea watched one of his guards aim a sniffer at the path ahead, checking for booby traps. He divided his enemies into three groups: the idealists, the covetous, and the insane. The idealists he nurtured. Especially the weak. Free expression and open debate gave such a wonderful patina of democracy. The covetous he co-opted, or crushed. As for the insane . . . Kea saw two other guards swing to the top of the hill, weapons ready . . . well, there was not much you could do about them. Except take care.

Kea's intellectual side insisted he'd accomplished a miracle in ten years—two terms in office. Fazlur had been a pessimist when he had predicted AM2 would turn the known world upside down. With Richards controlling it, Anti-Matter Two had also turned it inside out. But his gut twisted in revolt. Beware, it said. If you stop now, all will be lost. All will be reversed. The Bargetas and their ilk will be running things again. And all will return to inbred stagnation. Some of the old families were still holding out on Earth. These were a few of the covetous ones Kea had allowed their head. Let them have their outmoded factories. Let them continue spewing their pollutants across the planet. Let them break the back of the Earthbound poor. Each day hundreds were joining the migration off Earth. Climbing aboard ships powered by AM2 supplied by Kea Richards. Fleeing the chaos and misery Kea's enemies had created to new worlds their president was opening up.

It's going so fast, Kea thought. So fast and so well. In ten years, what I've built will easily double again. In fifty more . . . who knows? Pity I won't live to see it. A great yearning pit opened in Kea's stomach. A yearning as deep as the one that had clutched at him when Fazlur first proposed that they enter another universe. God, he wished he could see how it would all play out.

He heard a thundering from the far side of the hill. Kea hurried to the hilltop. He saw an official Federation ship settle into its berth. Around it was the enormous raw wound of the new spaceport being hurled up on Port Richards. It was the official delegation from the Federation's electoral college. Come to tell him that the people had begged him to stay on as president. Not just for a third term. Not for another five years.

Kea Richards had been elected President For Life.
Surprise.

The boys in the back room had come through.

But that had been the deal.

On Ganymede—ten years before—the guy from labor had gawped. "Whaddya mean, for life?"

The businesswoman had hissed at him. "Until he's dead, stupid. Or wants to retire." She had turned to Kea. "Right?"

"That's the deal," Kea had said. "If I'm going to run it . . . I want to run it like my own company. Elections every five years will tie my hands. I'll always be forced to take the short view."

"What'd the other side say?" Big Money had asked.

"They weren't happy," Kea had answered.

"Because they couldn't swing it?" Labor'd guessed.

"Yeah," Kea had said. "They said they couldn't swing it."

"I don't see the problem," the businesswoman had said. "Not for us, anyway."

"We couldn't do it all at once," the prime minister had said. "We would have to smooth the way. Prepare the groundwork."

"We could do it by the end of his second term for sure," Labor had said. "He's pretty damned popular. If you get my drift."

"If we agreed to this . . ." Big Money had ventured. "As your loyal supporters . . . and dearest friends . . ."

Kea had bowed . . . almost kingly . . . "and soon to be trusted advisers . . ." he had added.

Big Money had smiled . . . acknowledging . . . "Yes. We would. And as your advisers, could we presume you would listen if we had a word or two about your policies on AM2?"

"Absolutely," Kea had said. "As a matter of fact, I have been discussing my long-range strategy with my managers. It has become time for what people have termed a monopoly to end. We're presently arranging a plan to license sales of AM2, Imperium X, and the modified drive engines to . . . the proper concerns." He'd given them a meaningful look. "I'd be happy to listen to your suggestions . . . for individual cases."

The room had brightened immensely. Aglow in the vision of new private fortunes to be won.

"Let me be the first to call you Mister President," Labor had said. He stuck out a hand. Kea shook it.

That had been it. A presidency conferred with a handshake. Details to be filled in later by constitutional lawyers. It was the first time Kea had really tugged on the AM2 line and reeled in the fish. And as time had gone by, he had gotten better and better at it.

Kea watched the delegation descend from the ship. A gravlighter was waiting to take them to his encampment with formal word of his new title. Tonight they would all celebrate. Tomorrow he would pay off a few more IOUs.

Then it would all be his.

It was like an old-fashioned marriage, really. The monarchs of old had understood. A kingdom was the source of your greatest grief and happiness. You were wedded to it. For life. Kea was Emperor, now, in all but name. He didn't have even a niggling of guilt for having bought and paid for it by keeping one of the greatest discoveries in history to himself. The Chinese emperors had kept the secret of the workings of time for centuries. What would the people do with it? they asked their court scholars. They do not have the skills or fortitude to take responsibility for its appointment. This should be left for us to decide. This should be our burden, and our burden alone.

Kea remembered a line from his early childhood. "What's time to a damned hog?"

He thought of the piggish greed aboard *Destiny I*. Ruth murdering Fazlur and the Osiran. Her murder at Murph's hands. Murph's intentions on his own life. Kea had vastly refigured his concept of evil since that time. He had drawn up his own scale, and found civilization wanting. But shouldn't these things be left to a Higher Authority? To God? Maybe. But Kea had been to another universe . . . and returned. And found no god in either place. Perhaps there was Something. A god on his throne far beyond the stars.

But until that god was found, this world would have to make do with Kea Richards.

He started back down the hill. If he hurried, he would have time to change before he greeted the delegation. Kea picked up the pace. The guard beside him looked surprised. And began to lope. Kea ran faster. Feeling young . . . and lightheaded.

Suddenly, there was a sound in his ear of a thunderclap. Distant, but somehow very close. A red haze fell before his eyes.

His mind shouted, "Not yet! I'm not . . . done."

Kea was unconscious before he hit the ground.

A panicked guard knelt beside him. Tumbled him over. Clumsily felt for signs of life. Found the faint hammer of the pulse. Frantically she keyed her com unit. In moments, the hillside was thick with frantically rushing vehicles and people—fighting to save the life of their new President For Life.

Ganymede—A.D. 2222

"Your doctors made no mistake," the great physician said. "It was a stroke." Her name was Imbrociano. In the field of anatomical damage and regeneration, she had no peers.

Kea unconsciously gripped the numbness that was his left arm. Remembered his helplessness on *Destiny I* when it had been bound to him. This time, however, it was his whole left side that was useless. Imbrociano nodded at his arm. "We can get that going again," she said. "Nerve implants will do the trick. Some rather complicated rewiring should take care of the rest. Although I should warn . . . you will be definitely weakened."

Kea steadied himself. He needed courage now. "That was not my greatest concern," he said. "What about the remainder of their diagnosis?"

The physician sighed. "Unfortunately for you, I have no quarrel with that either," she said. "There is a good chance it will happen again. There's no telling when. A week? A year? More? I can't say. But I *can* say . . . it is unlikely you will survive a second attack."

Kea laughed. Harsh. "You're not much on bedside manner," he said.

Imbrociano shrugged. "Lies are time consuming," she said. "And time is something you are definitely lacking."

Kea laughed again. This time, it was a full-bodied chortle. The joke was on him. Hadn't one of his last thoughts been about the emperors who held dominance over time? But not all time, he thought. Not biological time.

Imbrociano peered at him, then nodded, satisfied. "You're taking it well," she said. "No hysteria."

"I'm not the type," Kea answered.

"No. I guess you wouldn't be . . . Mr President." She rose to go. Kea raised a hand to stop her. "My staff spoke to you about the need for secrecy?"

Imbrociano shuddered. "They stressed it . . . quite intensely. Really, sir. There was no need for threats. President or not, you are my patient. I have my oath."

"Forgive their enthusiasm," Kea said. Dry. Thinking that if his enemies got wind of Kea's illness, they could soon change her mind. "I'd be in your debt," he said, "if you stayed on . . . until I decide what to do next."

"You're still considering surgery," she asked, "even though the ordeal is most likely to be pointless?"

"I'll let you know," Kea said.

She left, a puzzled woman. But no more puzzled than Kea. What *was* he thinking? What could he do? The best physician in the Federation had just told him he was doomed. His advisers were urging him to choose a successor. Meaning one of them. Unspoken—but implicit—in their constant hammering was that it was also time to reveal the source of Anti-Matter Two.

If I die now, he thought, the system—that perfect system—he had designed would automatically shut down. All traces wiped. And the secret of AM2 would die with him. The system had been the only *real* protection against his enemies.

A shield of knowledge against their assassins. But what was the point of it now? Without AM2, the Federation would collapse. All his work for nothing.

So? Giving them the secret would be worse, wouldn't it? There would be terrible wars over control of AM2. He'd run the progs countless times. Each time the death toll burst through the top of the scale.

It was too late to produce an heir. Besides, he had dismissed that prospect from the beginning. He knew too much about kings and their children. They lived miserable lives waiting to succeed. Sometimes plotting against their parent. Almost always overseeing the death of the kingdom that parent had built. You had to look no further than the Bargetas to see the deterioration from generation to generation.

Enough wandering. He had to make up his mind. Who should succeed him? Who could he trust with the secret of AM2?

The answer came back: No one.

I *must* decide, he argued. I have no other choice.

There must be another option, came the insistent voice. There must be.

But . . . everyone has to die . . . Eventually.

But we're different, the voice said. Special. We know a thing no one else knows. A great pure thing that sets us apart from anyone who lives now . . . or has ever lived before.

Kea wrestled with this insanity—for he thought he must have gone insane—for a long time. Finally, he slept. Floating. Dreamless. Aides and nurses monitored him. Noted the peacefulness of the bio charts.

He awakened. Refreshed. Alert. Ravenous.

He sent for his breakfast.

And he sent for Imbrociano.

She answered all his questions, then listened closely as he outlined his proposal. Calmly. Dispassionately. "Yes. I could do it," she finally said. "I could build a living body . . . a human form . . . exactly like yours. There are theoretical obstacles, to be certain. But with the right team and sufficient funds . . . it could be done."

"Then you'll do it?" Kea asked.

"No. I won't."

"Why not, for godsakes?"

"You can't deny death, Mr President," she said. "And that's what you're doing. You must see this whole thing is highly irrational. I can make a copy of you. Duplicate you. But . . . I can't make that new organism be *you*!"

"What would be the difference?" Kea pressed. "If it had all my thoughts . . . my knowledge . . . my motivations . . . identical cells . . . all the stuff that makes me . . . then it would be me. Wouldn't it?"

Imbrociano sighed. "I'm a doctor. Not a philosopher. A philosopher could better explain the difference."

"I can make you very rich," Kea said. "Bestow many honors."

"I know," Imbrociano said. "Enough to overcome even my ethics. But if I participated in such an endeavor—and succeeded—I can't help but think I would more likely be signing my own death warrant. It would be dangerous knowledge, you must admit."

"I thought of that," Kea said. "However, for you to accomplish what I have in mind will most likely take the rest of your professional life. It will be a very secure, very lavish life. This I guarantee."

Imbrociano thought for a long time. Then she said, "If I don't do this, you'll find someone else. Albeit not as skilled."

"Yes, I will," Kea said.

"Which would once again leave me in jeopardy. For knowing too much."

"This is true," Kea said. Flat.

"We'd better get to work, then," Imbrociano said. "We might not have much time."

Ganymede—A.D. 2224

His luck returned. Along with health, bestowed by Imbrociano's talents. The nerve rewiring was simple. The rehabilitation exercises torture. But it was worth it.

Richards rose from his chair and walked to the far end of his office. He was alone. He watched his progress in a mirror. Approved. Now, only a slight limp betrayed the lingering traces of his paralysis from the stroke. It had been easy to hide this from the public. Politics has long experience keeping those kinds of things hushed up. In FDR's time, Kea recalled, few people were even aware he was bound to a wheelchair for life. He walked back to his desk. Eased his fifty-nine-year-old bones into the soft chair. And poured himself a drink from a decanter on his desk.

It was Scotch.

He savored it. Just as he savored a few moments' peace from the breakneck pace of his duties. Then he tensed as a headache twinged. His heart fluttered—was this it? But the pain fled along with fear. Thank God, he thought, that worry will be over soon. One way or the other.

Imbrociano was almost ready. Everything was in place. He only had to say the word and great, shadowy forces would be put in motion. Kea had worked feverishly to reach this point. Shifting staff. Pulling strings. Creating and collapsing whole bureaucracies. Covering his tracks in a hailstorm of governmental actions and decrees. Vast industries were at his disposal, with no one manager aware of what the other was doing. Starships had been flung here and there at his bidding. He had spun an elaborate, supersecret network, with cutouts and switchbacks and complex electronic mazes created by canny old spies. During that time Imbrociano and her team had worked at equally as furious a pace. With the entire Federation's treasury at their disposal as a budget.

Kea sipped his Scotch, letting the warmth tease the kinks in his side.

The first part of his plan to cheat death had been relatively simple. Imbrociano would build a walking, talking, thinking duplicate of Kea Richards. The second part—yet to be put into motion—was simpler still. Horrifically so.

He steered his mind away from yowling terror. He'd have to deal with it when the moment came.

The third part of his plan was vastly complex. To begin with, he'd had new improvements of the old model in mind. Tinkering with several genes to make his alter ego invulnerable to disease and aging. When the organism was in place, the aging process would be gradually reversed. He had picked thirty-five as the place to stop. Kea thought that had been the best time for him. His peak in many ways. With the process spread out over many years, his people would barely notice their President For Life shedding middle age like a snake its skin. In theory, the new Kea Richards would be able to go on and on throughout the centuries without wearing out. Virtual immortality.

"In practice," Imbrociano had said, "I doubt very much this is possible. An organism—especially a thinking organism—is too complex. Vulnerable to many things we are ignorant of. Not just physically vulnerable, either. There is the psychological to consider."

"I could go mad," Kea had said. With no emotion. Imbrociano had only nodded.

"I could also be assassinated," Kea had said. "Or, held against my will. Forced to do and reveal things."

"There is that, too," Imbrociano had said.

These problems had led to the key part of the grand scheme. An engineer at heart, Kea had started with a machine. A judgment machine. Fitted with powerful reasoning programs. Remote sensors to monitor the alter ego. Judging mental and physical conditions, as well as outward threats. The organism itself would have a bomb implanted in its gut. Threatened by torture, brainscan, or fatal attack, the bomb would blow with an enormous force. Killing all within its range. The same would happen if the judgment machine decided he was no longer mentally fit to rule the Federation. Kea called it the Caligula Factor. He had no wish to become a tyrant who ruled over an endless hell.

He had been proud of himself for thinking of that. Proud of it still, he thought, touching up his glass with Scotch. It was his own secret gift to his forever kingdom. If he was absolutely honest with himself, however, he would have to admit he was a little broad in his definitions of mental disturbance. But during these fits of honesty, he had rationalized that his future self might require some leeway to survive. It was impossible to imagine all the circumstances he might face over the centuries. What seemed insane today might be expeditious in the far tomorrow.

The machine orchestrating all of this was contained in a completely automated hospital ship; a ship not only built with redundancy on redundancy, constructed with bus bars a meter thick when a centimeter would give a lifespan of decades, but given complete self-analyzing and repair capabilities.

He had hidden it where no enemy could ever find it—the alternate universe. The source of his AM2 operation.

He thought of it as N-space.

And just in case his enemies ever tracked the ship down, it was defended by the best weapons of this age. It was unlikely anyone who attacked would survive. The hospital ship would sit in readiness, waiting for the signal to call it into full life. At that signal, the ship's robotic staff would build yet another Kea Richards—to replace the one that had just been . . . removed. The flesh would be grown from the genes Imbrociano was even now stockpiling from frequent biopsies. The mind—the id of Kea Richards—would be perfectly reconstructed as well. Right up to the final thoughts before . . . death.

"This will take time," Imbrociano had warned him. "A little more than three years before the duplicate is constructed. You'll have to be aware of these gaps."

He had overcome the problem by having an elaborate library computer installed. It would constantly monitor every newsfeed and knowledge resource in the Federation. All this data would be fed to the new organism after the awakening—during tutorials. But he must be wary. The organism would be new. Untried. Imbrociano's psych techs told him too much pure knowledge without practical experience could doom it before it started.

The return to power would be gradual. A ladder of experience. With awareness fed in along with each step upward. And at any point, the judgment machine could decide the new organism was lacking in some way and destroy it . . . to start again.

Oddly enough, the easiest of all his tasks in preparing for immortality had involved the political.

Because his hole card was AM2.

When he died, the AM2 shipments would automatically halt. There would be no more for a usurper until Kea's rebirth and return. Economic chaos would result. A three-year power drought. The throne stealer would be so weakened, he would topple at a touch when Kea Richards rose from the dead.

A hero reborn.

It was a powerful legend to build on.

Kea looked up at the antique clock on the mantel. It was time to start.

Imbrociano was waiting.

He finished his drink. Replaced the glass on the tray and pushed the whole thing away. And he buzzed for Kemper—his chief of staff. They went over the things to be done in his absence. Last-minute legislative details. Appointments to higher office. That sort of thing. His staff was grudgingly getting used to his mysterious absences. He had slipped away regularly to add to that tolerance. Sometimes in his guise as the common engineer—Raschid. Sometimes with a few chosen people for a little stealth diplomacy.

"What if there is an emergency, Mr President?" Kemper said dutifully. He knew the answer, but thought he'd be remiss if he didn't ask. "How can we reach you?"

Richards gave him the usual response: "Don't worry. I won't be gone long."

After Kemper departed, Richards pulled a bulky travel kit from a drawer. Then he pressed a stud beneath his desk. A panel swung away in the wall. Kea plunged into the dark passage. The panel closed behind him. A short time later he was aboard a small spaceyacht, listening to the captain chatter with the first officer—waiting for tower clearance. He turned in his seat to see if Imbrociano and her people were comfortable. Imbrociano waved to him. Smiled. A sad smile. Kea waved back. Settled in for takeoff.

There was the shock of the thrust . . . a roaring in his ears . . . then weightlessness. Kea savored every sensation of the flight. As if it were to be his last.

Imbrociano's voice came in his ear: "Would you like a sedative?"

He turned to her. Motioned for her to sit next to him. She did. Her eyes were hollowed from lack of sleep. "I'd rather not," Kea said. "Somehow . . . I don't know . . . I want to be aware."

"I understand," Imbrociano said. "But we won't reach our destination until tomorrow. Why not get some rest?"

"If this doesn't work," Kea said, "I'll have a lot of time for that. Permanent rest."

"You can still call this off," Imbrociano said. "Really. I urge you to."

"I've made up my mind," Kea said. "There's no need for you to feel guilt."

Imbrociano grew silent. Picked at her sleeve. Then she said, "If it eases your mind any, there will be no pain tomorrow. No sensation. I'll inject you with trancs first. So there will be no fear. The lethal dose will come next. You'll inhale . . . and by the time you fully exhale, you'll be . . . dead."

"Reborn, actually," Kea said with forced lightness. "Or, as some might say, exchanging one vessel for another."

"But it can't be really *you*!" she exploded. "Perhaps by casual definition, yes. It will talk, walk, and think like you in all matters. But it still can't be you. The essence in each of us. That makes us individual. The soul."

"You sound like a preacher," Kea said. "I'm an engineer. A pragmatist. If it walks like a duck . . . talks like a duck . . . it must be Kea Richards."

Imbrociano put her head back. Tired. Defeated. Then she patted his arm. Rose. And returned to her seat.

Kea felt genuinely sorry about what had to happen next. He fished out the travel case. Peeled away a small panel of material to reveal a depression. A heat-sensitive switch. He *liked* Imbrociano. Despite her stiff manner, she was genuinely human: afflicted with the curse of empathy.

His affection for her was the second reason he had chosen to alter the plan. The first reason was pragmatic. It was best to begin with maximum impact. A suspicious accident. Triggering finger pointing and political purges. Government in disarray. The cheers at his miraculous return would drown out many questions. Some of those he would get around with obscure hints of enemies in hiding. The rest he would erase by simply rewriting history.

He would have a long time to do it.

The second reason was pity. For Imbrociano. He could not bear to think how hurt she would be that he had lied to her. It was a terrible emotion for a person to be confronted with at the moment of his death. Even worse than the betrayal itself.

He trusted her.

But he couldn't take the chance.

Trust no one, an old king had once advised another. Not even me, your friend . . . *Especially* me!

Ah, well. The decision had been difficult. But deadly necessity had won the hand. But he knew he would always mourn Imbrociano. Just as he would mourn others. It was a king's burden. One he would have to bear.

He moved his finger to the depression in the case. When he touched it, the bomb would destroy the ship. Everyone would die. Instantly. Except for . . .

. . . Him?

He was suddenly sweat-soaked. His heart bruising his ribs with its hammering.

What if Imbrociano was right?

About what?

My soul?

Yes . . . Your soul. Goddamned y—

Kea shuddered in a long breath. Blew it out. Drew another. He closed his eyes. And thought of the gentle curtain of fire billowing in the cosmic winds. He was floating through it now. Saw the particles leaping about as if they were alive.

Now? Should he do it now?

No.

One more moment.

One more thought.

Kea sucked in stale cabin air. It tasted sweet.

I will be the forever king, he thought.

The Eternal Emperor.

He pressed the switch.

CHAPTER TWENTY-EIGHT

N-Space—Year One

THE MAN SAT quietly in his seat, watching the color/noncolor through what appeared to be the ship's port. He was dark and muscular with startling blue eyes. He wore a white form-fitting tunic and soft white slippers. He'd been watching dazzling lights for many . . . days . . . weeks . . . months? The terms made only vague sense.

He never tired of the view, even though it hurt his eyes. It was always the same. But different. Shifting shapes and patterns. Bursting bits of color. It had always been so soothing. But not today. It made him tense. Yearning. The cabin's womblike coziness felt smothering.

A thought came to him. He peered through the port. The Voice said it was the place where two universes touched. A gateway. Yes, he knew that. But, what was it called? An answer crawled into his brain: . . . Discontinuity.

Fazlur's Discontinuity.

He snapped up. Felt the hair on his arms prickle up. Where did that come from? The Voice? No. It came from . . .

Within!

The man rose and padded to the far end of the cabin. There was a mirror on that wall. He peered into it. Saw the face. For the first time, it seemed . . . familiar. As if it didn't belong to . . . someone else? Yes. That was it. He rusked a hand across the cheek. Again . . . the sensation was so . . . deeply . . . familiar. He looked into the eyes. Saw the sardonic creases at the edges. The blue that could turn so quickly gray and cold. He laughed. Heard the echo of that laugh collide around the room.

God. The sound of it was so wonderful.

He touched the surface of the mirror, trembling fingers outlining the reflection.

He nearly wept to find himself there.

Then he pulled himself together. He stood back from the mirror. Put his hands on his hips . . . posing for his own benefit. He looked long and hard at the image of himself. Measuring for any sign of weakness. Finding none. He nodded. Satisfied.

A thought jumped up: The forever king.

He frowned. What was the rest? Back there, when . . .

He remembered.

"I am the Emperor," he said aloud.

He grinned at his image in the mirror.

"The Eternal Emperor."

BOOK FOUR

KING IN DANGER

CHAPTER TWENTY-NINE

BLURRY. VERY BLURRY. Worse . . . then better as the rangefinder autoadjusted.

A rolling mountain meadow. A series of hillocks around it. The hillocks pocked with cave mouths. Adjustment, Sten's mind told him. You are in the middle of a city. The meadow's turf was artificial. As were the hillocks. The cave mouths were doorways leading down into huge caverns.

Near the end of the meadow, the ruins of what had been a low building with arched openings. Deliberately smashed when a huge Imperial battleship smashed in for a landing atop it.

In front of the building, a platform.

Correction. A scaffold.

Standing on it, a man dressed in black and half-hooded. Holding a pistol.

In front of him, two Imperial soldiers in battledress. Between them, held firmly, a large golden-furred being.

Blur-around: the "meadow" packed with other golden ones. Between them and the scaffold, more Imperial troops in the mottled-brown combat uniform of the Guards. Their weapons were leveled at the crowd.

A furred out-of-focus head blurred across his vision.

Movement, and Sten was looking again at the scaffold.

Sounds: drumroll.

Sounds: earshattering whistles.

"Th' lad thae's aboot t' gie hieself lopped is Sr Tangeri," Alex's voice explained. "I' y' ken th' Cal'gata hae a whistlin't

frae speech, y' perhaps sense thae dinnae be fond ae th' notion
thae leader's aboot f'r th' high jump. We're i' th' place th'
Cal'gata call their Gatherhome. I's th' equivalent ae
Parliament. Or was, at any rate."

A hailer voice boomed and echoed from the battleship.

"Y' noo c'n make oot th' words. Th' lad wi' th' pickup
hae antique gear. But th' Cal'gata're being tol' thae this i'
th' penalty frae high treason, an' thae'll be more penalties t'
follow."

The echoes stopped, and Tangeri was turned to face the
crowd. Instantly the executioner's hand came up, and the pistol
fired. The front of Tangeri's skull exploded, and the body
slumped.

The soldiers heaved the corpse forward, off the scaffold.

"An' noo," Kilgour's voice went on, "i' gie's interestin'."

Whistles louder, louder, damped by the pickup's controls.
Blackness.

"Th' lad wearin' th' 'corder's movin't closer."

Blur motion. Running. Moving with the crowd. Guns
firing. Screams. Human screams. Running forward. A squeal-
ing Tangeri, fur blood-soaked, waving an Imperial willygun.

Perspective jolting. Moving over something. Something
soft. A body. A torn-apart Imperial soldier.

Dragonroar.

Blackness.

"Th' battlewagon opened up wi' a chaingun."

Vision. The sky. A dot an object a diving hawk explosion
SOUNDBLANK . . . groundjar . . . blackness.

"Ev'dently," Kilgour's voice explained, "thae wae a wee
Cal'gata who got airborne wi' some sort ae spitkit, an' the'
Emp's destroyer screen didnae stop him. An' he calc'lated a
fair trade wae a battleship frae his life.

"Ah reck th' lad wae right."

Vision. Flames gouting from the Imperial battleship, from
a great hole just behind the bridge.

Blurmotion again. Running. More shots. Then sky, and
Sten gasped as pain racked him. Blackblank.

He could see. Somebody else could see.

Now he was a long way away from Gatherhome. It was far below him. The battleship was walled in flames, and the square appeared deserted. A mill of Imperial destroyers filled the air above the wreckage. Suddenly one destroyer was a ball of greasy flame, and again the pickup blanked.

Sten lifted the livie helmet away.

"What happened to the first Cal'gata? The one who started recording?"

A grim-faced Alex shrugged.

"Thae, Ah dinnae know. Killed, Ah reck. Else why w'd another pick up th' gear? But frae y'r info, th' battlewagon wae th' *Odessa*, an' the Imperials lost twa battalions ae th' Second Guards. Th' rumble Ah heard frae th' smuggler wi' Wild who brought th' tape wae that near ten thousan' Cal'gata went doon ae well. Needless t'say, th' Offic'l Emp News dinnae hae ought ae th' matter."

"So that's what they're calling a drum patrol," Cind snarled. "I guess murderers like the Guard look hard for some kind of label that doesn't say what they're really doing."

"The Guard may be bad, following orders like they are. What's worse," Otho rumbled, "is that's what the Emperor is calling justice."

Sten got up, walked to a screen, and stared out, thinking. The *Victory* and her escorts hung in deep interstellar space, far from the haunts of man.

"So I'm dead," he mused aloud, "but the rebellion continues."

"Like a summer fire in an ice oasis, one that's been knocked down but not extinguished and can flare up at any time," Otho confirmed. "Burning down here, flickering up there. Here they'll chance a battle, there they'll peg an Imperial sentry at his post with a rock."

"An'," Alex added, "th' Cal'gata, ae y' saw, are holdin' firm. As are th' Zaginows. Eventually, th' Emp'll hae th' forces t' move in an' level 'em. But nae frae ae least three, four E-years is m' prog.

"While thae's some ae y'r allies thae hae sued frae peace, thae's others that hae gone oot t' th' barricades or are just practicin' noncoop'ration frae reasons ae their own.

"Plus thae's purges i' Prime, i' the Guard, across th' armed forces, i' th' rubberstamp Parliament, e'en.

"Th' Emp hae biggish problems, puir lad."

The Eternal Emperor did. He may have killed Sten, but the price had been far greater than he'd calculated. The obliteration of the peaceful Manabi, a race respected and admired if only as an ideal, sent a low boil of anger through civilization.

None of the propaganda played, all of which centered around the story that Sten had set a trap for the Eternal Emperor, who had barely escaped after killing the rebel leader in hand-to-hand combat.

Sten was dead, the Emperor lived, was the comeback. Peddle y'r p'raties i' another town.

And it was clear to many beings that the Emperor's offer of a truce and powersharing was exactly what it had been— bait for the Emperor's own trap.

Rebellion roared, died down, rose again, flickered on, stretching the already-strained forces and assets of the Empire.

Sten had wasted no time mourning the Manabi, nor cursing himself for not allowing that final battle to be fought, damn the consequences. He couldn't. He had been betrayed. What of it? The war had just begun.

He didn't realize he'd spoken aloud, until he heard Otho's rumble of approval. He turned.

"It does," Otho said. "Now is the time for you to reveal yourself. You did not die. Now is the time for your forces to rally and strike again."

Both Alex and Cind were shaking their heads. Alex started to say something, then deferred to Cind.

"If we do," she asked, "and we get the battlefleets to reassemble, those that haven't been destroyed by the Imperial forces or fled into unknown parts of the universe, what's to say we won't end up where we were? Facing another Asculum, where everybody dies and nobody wins?

"That's the way my ancestors the Jann used to fight. And there's great tales and ballads of how we stood to the last man or woman.

"Very impressive," she said, her voice oozing sarcasm, "and inspirational for young heroes. But it didn't play very well for me later, when I grew up, and also when I found out that not only did we lose those battles—but pretty often the war, as well.

"Like Alex might say, clot that for a lark."

Kilgour nodded.

"Th' lass put i' better'n Ah c'd. Ah'll but mention Culloden, which'll gie wee Otho some'at t' look up a'ter th' meet."

Sten nodded agreement with Alex and Cind, remembering something his first drill sergeant, a combat veteran named Lanzotta, had told the assembled formation of recruits on their first day of training:

"Some general or other said a soldier's job is not to fight, but to die. If any of you fungus scrapings live to graduate, you'll be ready to help the soldier on the other side die for his country . . . We build killers, not losers . . ."

"Rykor," Sten said. "Logic check."

The psychologist waved a flipper from her tank. She mourned the Manabi, especially Sr Ecu, more than any of the others. Or perhaps, she thought, trying to lift herself from the grief that sent a constant well of tears down her leathery cheeks, these others have lost more friends and loved ones, being experienced soldiers, than I have.

All these years, all these decades, she thought on. Doing the Emperor's frequently bloody work, and because there was seldom a body in front of me—flashremembering a small-time criminal's body flopping into death on the brainscan—I thought I knew how to deal with loss.

Learn from this, Rykor. Learn that all that you preach may be logical and practical. But the next patient who seems

unable to accept the truth of your comforting or logic—don't
think them to be thick or obstinate.

"Go ahead, Sten," she said, forcing attention.

"If I suddenly rise from the dead, I assume I could attract
a fair number of allies—old ones, new ones—to my flag.
Ignore that. Now, if I stay dead, will the Emperor's persecution of my ex-friends be any worse—will any more beings
die—than if I rolled away the stone?"

Rykor thought hard.

"No," she said finally. "Your logic is acceptable.
Persecution . . . irrational revenge such as the Emperor is
practicing right now . . . is terrible. But open war kills far
more, including the innocent."

"As I thought," Sten said.

"Okay, troops. Here's the plan," he said. "We tried the
wide-open frontal-charge approach, and it didn't work real
well. Maybe it's my fault—I never was the kind of warrior
who liked the noonday sun. Reflections off the armor are a
pain in the butt, if nothing else."

Sten was surprised at his mild joke. All right. He was
relearning the harsh lesson of war—mourn for your casualties overlong and you will certainly join them.

"This time, we'll do it right. In the dark, in the fog, from
behind with a stiletto. And I think staying dead will be part
of that.

"No more battles unless we have to, people. Now we're
going after the Emperor. And this time we'll take him or
we'll kill him. Any way we can."

He looked around. Rykor was silent. Otho frowned, then
grudged agreement. Cind and Alex nodded, as did Captain
Freston.

"Ah'm glad t'hear thae, lad. Long live Mantis an' thae,"
Alex said. "I' fits right in wi' m' own plans. Ah'd like permission t' run a wee solo shot ae m' own. Ah wan' Poyndex."

Alex explained. He had been analyzing these new purges.
Some of them were public or secret allies of Sten. Others
had obviously offended the Eternal Emperor. But other

deaths or imprisonment had no obvious explanation.

"Ah tried runnin' th' basic ineptness ae any tyrant," Alex continued. "But th' computer upchucked on m' thinkin't an' sayit try again, goon."

He did. An answer was Poyndex. The man was clever, Kilgour conceded. Again, he had first thought that Poyndex was adding to the purge list to take care of his own enemies—the head of a secret police normally did that every time his ruler needed some heads rolled. But Poyndex was far brighter than that—he had no problems disposing of his enemies as he encountered them. The Emperor had given him a great deal of authority—and the sanction to kill his own snakes without need to use the Emperor as a cover.

The eventual explanation was simpler. Alex believed that Poyndex was trying to make himself the one indispensable man.

"Wi'oot," Alex added, "gie'in th' Emp thoughts thae Poyndex harbors gran' ambitions ae th' throne f'r himself, although thae'll come, thae'll come."

The Gurkhas had been discharged, Alex learned. At one time he thought it was out of Imperial Irk because a platoon or so of them had volunteered to serve under Sten, before he declared the rebellion. Then he thought they'd been removed to allow Poyndex's own creation, Internal Security, to move in. That was part of the explanation, which also accounted for Poyndex's replacement of Mercury Corps and Mantis Section with IS.

But there was more to Poyndex's maneuvering than just that, Alex believed. Poyndex intended to be the only conduit the Emperor had to anyone—his officers, his military, his Parliament, his people.

"A course, th' mon's dinkydow," Alex said. "Afore he gies t' be th' only channel t' th' Emperor on his throne, th' Emp'll roll his wee head. Consider some lads ae th' past. Bismarck. Yezov. Himmler. Kissinger. Johnes.

"Th' only one gray em'nence whae dinnae fall i' Rich'lieu. Poyndex i' a cap'ble lad, but he's noo a Rich'lieu."

But all that would lie in the future. At present, he'd been fairly effective in isolating the Eternal Emperor. Now, considering that Poyndex was already a turncoat, having headed Mercury Corps during the Interregnum and then lifted to the privy council by the conspirators before he double-crossed them to the Emperor . . .

"Ah hae plans," Alex finished, "t' mess wi' th' heads ae both Poyndex an' m' frien', th' Emp.

"I' th' lines ae th' poem, 'They hunted till darkness coom on, but thae foun'/Nae a button, or feather, or mark,/By which thae c'd tell that thae stood i' th' groun'/Whae th' Baker had met wi' th' Snark.'"

Sten eyed his friend. He knew that Alex would only get more specific if directly ordered to. Let Kilgour run his own mission.

"How'll you get to him?" Sten said. "As far as I know, the bastard barely budges out of Arundel, unless he's traveling with the Emperor."

Alex grinned.

"Ah hae made tight frien's wi' wee Marr an' Senn. E'en though they're retired, an' on th' oots wi' th' Emp, thae still hae been t' Arundel a bit. Th' *new* Arundel. Which they say, knowin' th' architect i' charge, was built *exact* like th' old one. An' they knew e'ery crook an' nanny ae th' braw stonepile long afore you wandered i' th' scene wi' y'r wee maps an' overlays."

Sten frowned. Arundel was the Emperor's citadel on Prime, styled like a triple-scale copy of the Earth castle, and with extensive works and gardens added around it and command bunkers and living quarters tunneled far underneath. It had been destroyed as one of the opening shots of the Tahn war, in a futile attempt to kill the Emperor. After the Emperor's return, it had been rebuilt.

Then he got it, remembering that layered map and his own term as conscientious head of the Imperial bodyguard. And he remembered a certain prison break some months afterward, a prison break from Arundel's dungeons.

Sten nodded.

"Take it away, Alex," he said. "What kind of backup do you need?"

"Ah dinnae need but whae Ah hae. M' ship thae Wild's loaned me. M' pilot. Ah'll hae transport waitin' ae Prime. Frae there, it'll be one in, twa oot i' th' motto."

Alex saluted, quite precisely, as if he and Sten were back in the service. Sten puzzled, stood, came to attention, and returned it. It was a very crisp, very military farewell.

And Kilgour was gone.

Alex was telling only some of the truth. He had considered that his scheme against Poyndex could succeed best as a solo run. But there was more to it than that.

The back of his neck still crawled.

He savored each day, each minute, because he had the feeling it could well be the last. He had put his house—his huge estates and castles on Edinburgh, assuming they were yet unburnt by the Emperor's revenge—in order.

Now he was ready.

At least, he thought, i' Ah'm answerin't m' weird, Ah'll noo take wee Sten wi' me.

He shut the mood and the thought off.

Dinnae be gloomin't aroun' ae i' y'r some braw Norsemen. Back on Earth, aeons gone, we listen't t' their keenin' an' slipped behind 'em an' slit their weasands.

Go oot wi' a smile, lad.

He was at the door to his own compartments. As he palmed the doorswitch and it slid open, he heard a giggle.

The first woman he saw was Marl.

Oh dear, he thought. Ah'd recked th' lass was gie'in' me th' look back whae Ah wae trainin' her, an' th' Laird knows she's a fine woman, haein' strength i' her bones an' a brain i' her skull. M' type, exactly, an' Ah did hae plans f'r th' twa ae us.

But wee Hotsco made her moves first, and Alex, kind-hearted thug that he was, hadn't quite known what, if anything, to say to Marl, assuming he'd been right about the mutual attraction, not egotistical, and so he'd sort of stayed clear of the Counterintelligence Division he'd setup.

Marl, he noted, as the door slid shut behind him, was looking especially gorgeous, in a sleek wrap of a skirt, a frothed blouse, and a wrap laid to one side.

As was Hotsco, who was wearing one of Alex's shirts and a dab of perfume behind each ear.

Oh dear, he thought. This'll noo be splendifer'us.

"Ladies," he managed.

Marl and Hotsco looked at each other and laughed. Alex noted an empty bottle in an ice bucket nearby.

"I would guess," Hotsco said, "that our hero there is wondering what he should be doing."

"Ah'm thinkint," Alex managed, "Ah'll be needin't a wee drink."

Hotsco got up and got him a drink from the compartment's bar. Stregg. Iced.

"Your friend Marl showed up a couple of hours ago. She's been telling me stories about spying and that. And we've been . . . talking."

Hotsco's tongue came out . . . moistened her lips.

"It turns out . . . that we have some common interests," she said. "Besides you, I mean."

"Oh dear."

It was Marl's turn to laugh.

"With Sten dead," she said, "there's not much in the way of CI to do. The Bhor have everything well in hand. And since I'm Head of Section, I gave myself a talking-to. Told myself I was working too hard, and deserved a break."

Alex shot back the stregg and, while his esophagus returned from hyperspace, poured himself another.

"Marl came here," Hotsco said. "And I invited her in. She's quite a woman, you know."

"Ah ken," Alex said, now with a note of suspicion.

"Her world has some . . . interesting social customs. Very interesting," Hotsco purred. "Ones that *both* of us would be intrigued with."

"Oh dear."

"You're repeating yourself, Alex."

Marl and Hotsco were both trying—with little success—to keep straight faces.

"I thought that she might want to come with us to Prime," Hotsco said. "It's a very long passage, you know. She thought that was a wonderful idea. So I helped her pack. She's ready to travel. Isn't that exciting?"

Alex recovered.

"Aye. Aye. Y're welcome t' go, wee Marl. Ah think y're daft, thinkin' goin' int' th' belly ae th' beast is a holiday, but y're welcome."

Marl walked up, and sedately kissed him on the cheek, in thanks.

"When's the ETD?"

"Ah thought," Alex said, "we'll lift ae once. Hotsco's ship's fueled an' ready."

"Do we have to leave now?" Hotsco wondered. "I talked to Marr and Senn . . . and they're sending in a wonderful farewell meal. Perhaps in the morning shift?"

"Why then?" Alex asked.

Hotsco walked to the huge, circular bed and sprawled across it. It had been originally built, it was surmised, for one of the Emperor's favorite's pleasure. She stretched and rolled, a smooth, lithe kitten.

"Why," she purred, "there's so much more *room* here. A lot more than on my ship. Even if we put the bunks together in my cabin. Isn't there, Marl?"

And all Alex could manage was yet another "Oh dear."

CHAPTER THIRTY

"DOWN WITH THE Emperor!" the woman screamed, her mouth ragged with hate.

"Death to the slayer of the Manabi!" another being shouted—its display organ swollen to bursting.

"Kill the great blasphemer!" a huge bear of a man bellowed. "Kill him."

The three were among fifty agitators working the crowd to a fever pitch. Not that it needed it. Some twenty thousand angry beings were spread out in front of the Parliament building.

They were being held back by a wavering line of black-uniformed Internal Security storm troops.

Banners the size of small buildings jutted from the crowd of demonstrators. The largest one—in the center—was a huge blowup of the Emperor's face. Splashed in blood-red paint across the face was the word MURDERER.

The crowd started chanting in unison: "*Down with the Emperor! Down with the Emperor!*"

Poyndex's gravcar swooped over the crowd. He keyed his mike: "Move in the tracks," he said, calm. "Then activate Alpha and Delta companies."

"Yessir," crackled the voice of his aide.

Poyndex watched with professional interest as nine enormous personnel carriers burst into view. They struck from three sides, boxing the crowd against the front of the Parliament building. Thick clouds of pepper gas spewed from their turrets. As the crowd screamed and pulled back in shock, hundreds of IS troops exploded out of hiding and attacked with clubs and stun rods.

A com shrilled at Poyndex's belt. He glanced down. Irritated. Then he saw the winking red light. It was the Emperor.

Poyndex sighed. Even in the middle of a riot, the Emperor came first.

He patched into his aide and turned over command. Then swung the gravcar around and headed for Arundel.

Poyndex was definitely not looking forward to the meeting. With a full-blown riot in his own backyard, the Emperor was not likely to be the happiest of supreme rulers.

He braced for the worst.

"I'm sick of this nonsense," the Eternal Emperor roared. "Don't they know they've lost? Sten is dead. The head has been cut off. There is nothing left for them to do but bleed to death and die, dammit."

He pointed an accusing finger at Poyndex. "You're not keeping the pressure on. You're just sitting back and resting on *my* laurels. *My* victory."

"The rebels can't persist much longer, Your Highness," Poyndex said. "It's only a matter of time."

The Emperor's first slammed down on the desk. A mass of reports spilled to the floor. "Time? Don't speak to me about time!

"My fleets are still spread out over two-thirds of the Empire. A day doesn't go by that the Zaginows or the Honjo or the Bhor—or some such group of malcontents—find a new and interesting way to embarrass me.

"What's more . . . this madness is costing me. I'm bleeding cash like a pricked pig. And every week these fools oppose me adds at least a year to our eventual recovery."

The Emperor glared at Poyndex—as if he were the source of all his woes. "They think we're weak, Poyndex," he said. "Even after the Manabi, they don't think we have the nerve to hold the course."

"A few more victories, Your Majesty," Poyndex said, "and the opposition will collapse. All the progs will bear this out."

"Drakh on the progs," the Emperor said. "My gut says different. My gut says this has taken on a life of its own. That bloody mess outside the Parliament building is just one example. No one would have ever dared it, before. And how the hell did they get onto the palace grounds, anyway?"

Poyndex grimaced. "We should have that mopped up shortly, Your Majesty," he said. "And the ringleaders brought to justice."

"Be damned to justice," the Emperor said. "I'm the judge. I'm the jury."

He grew silent a moment. Lost in thought. Then he looked up at Poyndex. He spoke. So soft Poyndex had to strain to hear.

"Why do they make me angry?" he said. "I can be kind. Generous. Ask any of my friends." The Emperor looked around the empty room as if to seek them out. Unconsciously his hand moved forward—reaching for the com unit. Then stopped. There was no one to call. The hand snatched back.

Poyndex remained quite still. It was no time to draw notice. He watched emotion play across the Emperor's features. Then they became stone.

He turned to Poyndex. "I must secure my godhead now," he said. "Crush this thing once and for all."

"Yes, Your Majesty," Poyndex said, ready for orders.

"They shall go the way of the Manabi," the Emperor said. "I want their home worlds destroyed. So when their ships and troops return, they find nothing but dust."

"Yes, Your Highness," Poyndex said, already thinking of how to put the order into motion. Choosing the ships, the teams, and the trusted officers who would lead.

"It is not necessary for the explosions to go off simultaneously," the Emperor said. "There should be just enough delay—a few hours at most—between each planetbuster for the reality to sink in.

"And by god, when I'm done, they'll know what terror is. They'll know my wrath. They want a better life? Fine. Let them look for it in the hereafter."

He glared at Poyndex. "Why are you still here?" he snarled. "You heard what I want. Do it."

"Immediately, Your Highness," Poyndex said. He came quickly to his feet, saluted, and moved to the door.

"One more thing, Poyndex," the Eternal Emperor said.

"Yes, Your Majesty."

"Next time there's a riot . . . Clot the gas. Use guns. You hear me?"

"Absolutely, Your Highness," Poyndex said.

The Emperor stared at the door as it hissed closed behind Poyndex. Perhaps he had given the man too much leeway. Lately he'd begun to notice all the Internal Security forces around him. Forces Poyndex commanded.

He realized that he had become isolated. Cut off from all opinion. And everyone about him was a stranger. This was not healthy.

Why had he allowed this to happen? The answer came to him, grudgingly. Fear. Of dying. Clot the duplicate who would replace him. It really wouldn't be *him*, would it? Freedom from the judgment machine came with a curse. The curse of mortality.

So he needed Poyndex and his guards to keep him safe. He required a ring of security so tight, no one could possibly penetrate it.

Yes. But what if Poyndex turns on you? Like he turned on the privy council.

The Emperor didn't think this would happen. Poyndex was ambitious. Supremely so. But he wasn't the kind who desired the spotlight. He'd prefer to rule from the shadows. From behind the throne.

Still . . . his goal *is* to rule, isn't it? To make the Emperor his helpless puppet?

The Emperor decided then what Poyndex's fate would be. But he would wait just a little longer.

A great deal more blood needed to be shed. And when it was done, he would need a fall guy.

To the Eternal Emperor, Poyndex looked like the perfect Judas goat.

CHAPTER THIRTY-ONE

"EACH TIME I pick up a new trail," Cind said, "I think, This is it. Now I've finally got the SOB."

Cind picked up beach sand and then let it fall in a gentle stream. "But then I hit a dead end and that bastard wins again. I can almost hear him laughing at me."

"You're not alone," Haines said. "I've fine-toothed Mahoney's files and come up with a lot of great leads. But they all peter out before I'm barely started. Makes me feel like a clottin' rookie."

"I still think this is the right way to go," Sten insisted. "I'm convinced this is the quickest—and least bloody—way to defeat him. Once we learn where the Emperor gets his AM2, then we can go for his throat."

"No one's ever done it before," Cind said. "Imperial history's littered with failures. Look what happened to Kyes."

Silence overcame the small group. They were sprawled on one of Nebta's gentle beaches. The day was cozy. The waves lapped softly at the shore. Flying creatures soared above the water, crying their lonely cries.

But the beauty of the day was lost to the conspirators.

Except for one. The gentle giant who was Haines's husband—Sam'l. He was listening to their talk with interest, but a part of his mind kept free. To soar with the flying creatures.

"Discovery is a remarkable thing," he said, a little dreamily. "There are stirring tales of beings who have dared and suffered much to succeed in their quest. I read those tales when I was a boy. It's probably why I became an archaeologist. So I could have adventures of my own."

Sten smiled. He quite liked this big, shambling man. And he had learned to listen with patience. Because Sam'l always had a point.

"And did you?" Sten asked.

"Oh, yes. Many. I shall bore you with them some night over more wine than is good for me. Because that's all they are good for . . . polite conversation.

"In fact, some of the greatest discoveries are found in museum basements. Incredible things. Astounding thoughts. Dumped in a heap to wait for several centuries until some bored student happens to paw through the mess."

"You're saying the answer is probably right in front of us," Sten said.

"Something like that," Sam'l answered. "Perhaps we just have to hold up what we already know. Turn it this way and that. Until we find the proper light to view it in."

"Where should we start?" Cind asked.

"Why not start with the element itself?" Sam'l said. "Anti-Matter Two."

"If it were gold, or iron, or even Imperium X," Cind said, "we'd have a pretty good idea where to look. We'd have the laws of planetary geology and three or four other sciences to go by."

"That's interesting all by itself," Haines said. "In other words—Anti-Matter Two has no counterpart in nature."

"Possibility one," Cind said, "is that AM2 comes from someplace in the universe that has yet to be found. By anyone except for the Emperor, that is. But that's sort of the assumption I've been going on. And that hasn't gotten me anywhere except very old, very cold trails."

"What about another universe?" Sam'l the dreamer suggested. "An alternate universe? That would explain why its structure has no counterparts in nature as we know it."

"I don't mean to be a wet blanket," Sten said, "but it was my impression that everyone who's dabbled in alternate-universe theory was pretty much of a strange-o. And that modern science agrees no such thing exists."

Haines stirred. "Mahoney had something in his files about that," she said. "I didn't pay much attention at the time."

"What did he have to say?" Sten asked.

"Nothing specific," Haines said. "Except he thought it was pretty interesting that the Emperor has always seemed to go out of his way to quash any research on alternate-universe theory. According to Mahoney, some very prominent scientists had their wings clipped for venturing into that area."

"Maybe I'd better wake up," Sten said, "and start paying more attention to some of Ian's weirder ideas."

"Like the immortality business?" Haines laughed.

"Yeah. Exactly like that. Maybe one has something to do with the other."

"I like it," Sam'l said. "One answer for two. That always makes for an elegant solution."

"That's what Kyes was after," Cind said. "And he came pretty close."

"I don't know what hat the Emperor pulls his rabbit out of," Sten said. "He dies. He comes back. I'll ignore Haines's bit of intelligence that this time around maybe we're not dealing with exactly the same person. Just for a time, we'll put that aside, and stick to what we know.

"One . . . Each time he disappears, according to Mahoney, he's gone for about three years. It was six this last time, but I think we should put that aside as a one-time break in the record.

"Anyway, for three years no one hears or sees anything of him. Which means he must have a hideout. A hideout so secure that no one has found it for—I hate to say this—a couple of thousand years.

"Two . . . Anti-Matter Two comes from a place equally secure. Equally hidden. The privy council found out how well hidden it was, to their extreme bad luck."

"It would be stupid to use two different places to accomplish pretty much the same thing," Cind said.

"One thing the Emperor isn't," Haines said, "is stupid."

"So if we find one," Sten said, "then that should give us the other."

"Are we still considering the possibility of an alternate universe?" Sam'l asked.

Sten shrugged. "Good as anything else."

"Actually, for our purposes it's far better than most things," Sam'l said. "The Emperor would need an entrance and an egress. A door, so to speak. A gateway between universes."

"Yeah?" Sten looked at him. Blank.

"If I recall my undergraduate physics," Sam'l said, "the kind of gateway we are discussing would cause a disturbance in the cosmic background. A discontinuity, I believe it is called."

Sten got it. He said, "Finally, we're talking about something you can measure. Instead of never-never lands and spooky supposition. If there's a blip in the cosmic background, we have a chance of finding it."

"Except, we don't know which way to look," Haines pointed out. "It's a big sky. We could spend a lot of forevers checking it out, bit by bit."

"I'm not so sure about that," Cind said.

They all looked at her. Praying for a break.

"There were several places Kyes was interested in he hadn't checked out yet," she said. "They were areas Kyes suspected might be safehouses on the path the Emperor takes when he returns. All my own progs confirm he was correct to suspect them. They fit the profile."

"I think we should correlate your stuff with Mahoney's," Haines told Cind. "Ian was working a lot of the same angles."

"Good idea," Cind said. She smiled at Haines. She quite liked her. And as Sten's former lover, Haines reflected well on Cind's own good taste.

"If this were a homicide case," Haines continued, "which

this is, in an awful sort of way—once I figured out where the crime was plotted, I'd tie into the com lines. Bug the clot out of the place. And wait for the suspect to call. When he did, all I'd have to do is trace it."

"Sticking to your analogy, my love," Sam'l said, stroking his wife's hand, "I'd guess you wouldn't have to wait. The line would be continuously open, assuming that everyone's theories dovetail. The Emperor would need to maintain communication with his hideout . . . and, Darling, have you ever noticed you've now got me talking like some kind of livie cop? Also, wouldn't there be some kind of open link to a relay station, like the one Kyes evidently came to grief at? There must be more than one of those—the Emperor doesn't depend on chance any more than, say, Schliemann did."

Sten forced calm. He didn't want to jinx the moment. "It's at least worth checking out," he said.

"It's better than that," Cind said. "All my instincts are ringing bells that this is the way to go."

"Go with them, then," Haines said. "Instinct is what separates the rookies from the pros."

Sam'l broke into the flow in his hazy, dreamy way. "I keep wondering," he said, "what our lives would be like if AM2 could be copied and manufactured—like many of the common elements. How different things might have turned out, if you could brew it up as easily as our hosts, the Bhor, brew stregg."

His lips curved into irony. "But I suppose it's highly unlikely such a thing is possible. To actually synthesize AM2, I mean. My college text, if I recall correctly, said even if this were a possibility, the expense would make the whole thing an exercise in futility."

"Mahoney didn't think so," Haines said.

Sten jumped. "What?"

"I said, Mahoney didn't think so. He had a lot of stuff in his files on synthetic AM2. Under the heading of Disinformation. I've only just started to go through them."

She tapped her head, shaking her memory. "There was

something in particular in one of the files. Something
Mahoney wanted to bring to your attention."

Sten nodded. She had shown him several items already
that Mahoney had marked with an *S* so Sten would pay particular mind.

Haines smiled, remembering. "Oh, yeah. Something about
a 'Bravo Project.'" She looked at Sten. "Do you know what
that means?"

Cind saw Sten draw back in shock. Saw his face drain of
color. What was wrong? She reached over to touch his hand.
It was cold.

"Yes," Sten said. Grim. "I know what Bravo Project
means."

Then he saw the worry on Cind's face. And Haines's. Even
the unflappable Sam'l's brow was furrowed.

He forced cheer into his voice. "But I'll have to do some
double-checking on my memory," he said. "With Rykor."

His insides were far from casual—Yeah, he had to see
Rykor, all right.

About a nightmare.

He was back on Vulcan.

Karl Sten. A Mig kid turned Delinq with only hours to
live before Thoresen's exterminators tracked him down.

Bet was with him. So lovely. So young. And Oron. That
odd, brainburned genius who knew only the present.

Mahoney loomed up at him. A much younger Mahoney.
Strong and confident. But the adolescent Sten wasn't sure he
was to be trusted.

"I must have confirmation of Thoresen's plan," Mahoney
said. "I've blue-boxed into the exec and central computers,
and there was nothing on Bravo Project except inquiry-
warning triggers."

Bravo Project! There it was again. Sten felt a wrenching
at his chest. A sob bubbled up, and broke.

Easy, Sten, came Rykor's voice . . . It's past. It's over. It's
all been mourned . . . He felt a faint sting. Then calmness

as the tranquil took affect. He heard faint scratching sounds. Rykor manipulating the keyboard. Coaxing up images. And Mahoney's big, cheerful face was torn away . . .

One of Thoresen's guards paced along his beat. Sten floated in behind him. His hand circled the man's throat. His knife lunged forward. And he heard the gasp and felt life draining away. There was no remorse in him. Only an odd flicker of joy.

. . . Self-disgust welled. And then flooded over . . . So many deaths by his hand. Murders. Rykor's soothing voice crept in: Let it go, my friend. Let it go.

But he couldn't. The man was dead. Snuffed out. No better than an insect. Sten moaned—God, forgive me . . . and there was another sting . . . and the tranquil lies spread through his veins . . . And the image flipped to—

They were inside the Eye. Thoresen's hidden safe revealed. Sten sprayed the touch lock. Liquid at Kelvin-Zero crystallized the steel. Bet stepped forward with a hammer and tapped. The metal shattered. The door came open. They were in! Sten felt the long-ago thrill. Looked up at Bet and Oron. Grinning like maniacs for beating Thoresen at his own game.

. . . Again, the sting of tranquil. Sten struggled against the terror that would follow. Shouted away the bat wings rustling in his darkest memories. The hammering of his heart eased. He took comfort in the sensation of the hard table under his body. The electrodes attached to his head, arms, and legs. He heard the splash of liquid. It was Rykor, shifting in her tank. No. There was nothing to fear. Trust Rykor. With Rykor operating the brainscan, he was safe. Sten let the images move on . . .

Flip. Flip.

Sten reached into Thoresen's safe. Found the file amid the jumble of paper and bundles of Imperial credits. The folder. Thick and red. Titled: Bravo Project.

The images came slower now. Flip. Flip. Flip . . . Oron taking the folder. Flip! The papers spilling to the floor. Flip!

And Sten was scrabbling for the papers. Stuffing them into the folder. No particular order . . . And he saw . . . Flip! Oh, jesus, one of the Delinqs was falling . . . chest blasted away . . . And . . .

The image froze. Sten felt vomit rise. Heard Rykor mutter, Too far . . . reverse . . . Sten shuddered at the sting of the tranquil and . . .

Flip!

Back to the papers . . . scrabbling for them . . . slower . . . Flip! Slower . . . And he could see them, now. A page at a time. Flip! A title leaping up—RECREATIONAL AREA 26: A SUMMARY OF ACTIONS . . . Flip!

. . . Wait. Have to stop. Have to see. Go back . . . And Rykor's voice called to him, It's no good, Sten. Put it behind you. Go on . . . Sten refused. He fought the voice. The kind coaxing voice. A stinging sensation. And now there was the tranquil to fight.

Sten pushed the veil away. Forced the image forward. *He* was in control, dammit!

And the agony of Recreational Area 26 came tumbling back.

The Row.

Riotous voices. Barkers and shills plying their trade. Joyboys and joygirls out in force, emptying Mig pockets for Thoresen's coffers. And there was more. Gambling machines hooting enticements. Drunks brawling. Sociopatrolmen charging into the melee, clubs swinging.

There were 1,385 beings on the Row that day.

Among them—

Sten felt a cry of joy burst from his lips. There was his father, Amos. His mother, Freed. And his brother and sister, Johs and Ahd. He shouted. But they didn't hear him.

Stop this, Sten, Rykor hissed. But he wouldn't listen. Couldn't listen . . . because he knew what was going to happen next . . .

Sten tried to shout for his family again. Fear clutched hard as his voice feathered into a whisper. He saw them enter the Row. Saw the big lobby doors shut tight behind them.

He stood there. Frozen. Waiting.

More voices.

"Then dump Twenty-six," Thoresen said.

The tech protested, "But we've got almost fourteen hundred people—"

"You have your orders."

Explosive bolts fired around the dome panels.

In sympthetic reaction, Sten's body flailed against the operating table. At the brainscan's controls, Rykor watched, helpless. If she interfered now, the damage would be so severe Sten would be fortunate to merely die.

Sten jumped again as he heard the typhoon roar of air blasting into space. And he was a forced witness—trapped by his own fool self—as . . .

Almost in slow motion, the escaping hurricane caught the shanty cubicles of the Row—and the people in them—and spat them through the holes into blackness.

He heard a tech's voice: "Come on. They were only Migs."

Then the chief tech: "Yeah. You're right. That's all they were."

Sten wept.

Rykor worked over him for hours, using all her psychiatric skills as well as her vast pharmacopoeia to bring him back into something vaguely approaching normalcy.

Then she took him back. Past the nightmare of the Row. Back to Bravo Project.

And the secret Thoresen himself later died for.

The secret of synthetic AM2.

Sten huddled in a blanket. Sweat streamed from him, but he was cold. He felt as if he had been pried open, emptied out and discarded.

He took the mug Rykor offered, and sipped at thick, hot, nourishing broth. Rykor's flipper brushed a control panel and soft music swelled. Cleansing music. He closed his eyes and let it wash over him for a long time.

Then he opened his eyes and took another drink. He saw Rykor's large, empathetic eyes studying him.

Sten made a face. "Never again," he croaked.

"I am very sorry, my dear friend," Rykor said. Her rich voice gave meaning to empty words.

"Me, too," Sten said. "At least . . . now we know. Not only is it possible to make AM2 . . . but, we have the formula and procedure. I'm not a chemist, and it sounds like the process is a pain, and expensive as hell. But so what? Production cuts prices."

He stopped, thinking.

"And this just turns the whole clotting universe around and around, doesn't it? Or does it?"

"What do you intend to do with the knowledge?" Rykor asked.

"I'm not sure," Sten said. "This changes a great many things."

He lifted weary eyes to plead with Rykor. "Don't say anything," he said. "I need time to think."

Rykor studied him. Thinking, He's my friend. A trusted friend. But some secrets are worms that probe and spoil all goodness.

"If something happens to me," Sten said, "you've got all the information. Do with it as you please."

"Very well," Rykor said. "I'll wait."

"Thanks," Sten said, weak. Then his head slumped. Rykor's flipper came out and lifted the mug away before it spilled.

He slept for many hours. It was a dreamless sleep.

CHAPTER THIRTY-TWO

HOTSCO LET HER number two run her ship and the surreptitious movements toward Prime World. She had smuggled things on and off Prime so many times it wasn't a challenge anymore. And her exec had already been making noises about getting her own ship, once this absurd commitment Jon Wild had made to social justice and drakh like that was over.

The third reason was, Hotsco had better things to do. As did Marl. As did Alex. He was most glad, by the time they closed on the Empire's capital, that he stayed in something near shape, and that he was a heavy-worlder.

Hotsco had been right—Marl's culture had some *very*, sometimes even excessively, interesting customs. She was a beaut, he thought fondly. As was Hotsco. He wondered what his wee mum would think if he brought them home and introduced them to her. Hmm. That might require some preparation.

Besides, he was going to die on Prime, he reminded himself.

When Hotsco's ship, the *Rum Row*, closed on the first of Prime's elaborate screens, Hotsco took the bridge.

Sten may have needed an elaborate diversion to slither the *Victory* onto Prime to rescue Haines and the others. Hotsco did not. She ghosted down, past mechanicals that seemed rusted solid, past patrol patterns that seemed loose-weave, even once past a patrolling Imperial destroyer within visual range.

She brought the ship down in atmosphere, and slipped

toward a midnight landing, in one of the deepest spots of the River Wye that ran through the center of the green, protected Valley Wye. If the landing had been witnessed by one of the fanatic fishermen who considered the River Wye as their Mecca, Sten and his minions would have been considered fiends incarnate, and the worst punishment the Eternal Emperor could wreak on them considered corporal. Kilgour—who'd been known to cast a bit of feather and fur to assuage the savage salmon gods without ever landing one of the three-meter monsters—felt a little ashamed. But only a little.

He slid out of the ship's airlock in a spacesuit and swam to the bank. The *Rum Row* was under about seven meters of water, resting on the bottom. Not very much, but the dark anodizing would hopefully camouflage the ship against the river's bottom. Of course, if the Wye was overflown by a patrolcraft with sensors, the quality of the camouflage or the depth of the water wouldn't matter.

But why think about trouble?

He buried the suit under a layer of turf for quick retrieval, and headed directly for Ashley-on-Wye, the small town in the valley's center, where he hoped to set up his RV/safehouse. The town appeared abandoned. Quiet, deserted cobbled streets. There was a sign of life in one bar, where, long past closing, songs were being sung, barmaids being pinched and pints poured. Kilgour ignored his thirst and moved on.

The Blue Bhor was dark.

Kilgour settled down to wait for dawn, unobtrusively, under a bush. Either his friend was gone, bankrupt, or conceivably arrested for past sins by IS or the gamekeepers; was out poaching; or else would be out . . .

Just at dawn Chris Frye, ex-Mantis, proprietor of the Blue Bhor Inn, fanatic fisherman and skilled cook and drinker, came out the side door of his inn carrying a rod and creel.

He strolled past a bush, and stiffened. He stopped. Puzzled a bit, then dug into his creel as if to make sure he had not forgotten something.

"Y' c'n drop th' charade," Alex advised. "Ah wonder'd i' y' still hae y'r moves, an w'd spot m' marker."

Frye took the tiny colored metal clip that could've been a flower from a twig and pocketed it as Alex stepped out.

"Sod off, Kilgour. I had those reflexes as a poacher long before I took the clottin' Emp's shilling. What're you doing on Prime? You and your traitorous friend're supposed to be dead, according to the lies I've heard from the drakh-for-brains propaganda mill."

"Rumors ae m' passin' bein't overrated an' thae. Din't figure you'd put up wi' the drakh comin't doon ae late. How bad is it?"

"Clottin' clotted," Frye said quietly. "Anybody who had anything to do with Mercury or Mantis, even way back then, isn't exactly thought of as the best citizen. Nobody's gotten boxed yet, but you're watched pretty close.

"Or so I've heard from friends who drop by. Most folks here in the valley don't remember what kind of sojering I did, and wouldn't cough if they did. Gotta tell you, Alex, I don't know what the hell happened to the Emperor, when he wasn't around—but something sure as hell did.

"Tell you the truth, when they shot Mahoney, and then Sten ran up the black flag, I clotting near nailed the door shut and took off to join you clowns. Only thing that stopped me was a strong feeling of cowardice and old age."

The two eyed each other. It had been a lot of years, indeed, since Mantis, and almost as many since Frye's Blue Bhor had been used as a safehouse when Sten was investigating the attempted murder of the Eternal Emperor.

"You look a bit older, a bit fatter, and a bit grayer," Frye observed.

"Dinnae we all, mate," Alex said. "An' how's th' life ae a publican?"

"The doors stay open," Frey's business, offering meals, beds, packed lunches, ghillie-ing, and alk to the dedicated rod-wranglers who came to the Blue Bhor, brought credits in—and Frye's love of good food, drink, and not letting friends pay for anything poured them out just as rapidly.

"I assume you want something?"

"Not much. Just a place for some friends of mine to stay."

"How many?"

"Twelve."

"About the crew size of a small spaceship," Frye said. "I thought I heard something around midnight. Well, welcome to the king's enemies and all that. Clottin' Emperor. Just one question, so I can shriek quietly and wake up the whole clotting town. Is Sten one of them?"

"No. Ah'm th' hottest ae th' lot, an' Ah'll noo be stayin't."

"Well, bring 'em in, then. I knew there was something lacking in my life lately. Listenin' for the tread of the hangman, the knock on the door, and the clap on the shoulder. Damn, but I love getting back into harness, particularly if it's something that sounds a lot like high treason. I can't say how *nice* it is to see you, Sergeant Kilgour."

Since the citizens of Ashley-on-Wye slept late as a habit, there was no problem moving Marl, Hotsco, and the rest of the smugglers into the inn without notice.

Then they waited until nightfall. Frye fed them sumptuously and kept asking if there wasn't something he could help with. Transport? Credits? Frye had some interesting things that went bang buried around somewhere. Phony ID? Hell, did Alex need backup?

No to all of them. What Alex didn't have, he could steal.

He kissed Hotsco and Marl good-bye.

"Y' hae th' orders, noo? I' y' dinnae hear frae me wi'in th' week, or i' y' hae reason to suss thae Ah'm blown or y're under s'picion, y' promise t' haul oot like y' hae a Campbell a'ter y'r skirts?"

The two women promised.

They watched Alex disappear into the darkness, just another casual laborer headed for towncenter and transport to somewhere on Prime.

They looked at each other.

"How long?" Marl asked.

"We'll wait till there's frost on Sheol," Hotsco said.

"Good. And if Alex gets nailed?"

"We'll go in after him," Hotsco said softly. "If we have to take him out of Arundel itself."

They touched palms. The compact was made.

CHAPTER THIRTY-THREE

THIS IS ANOTHER fine fix you've gotten me into, Sten. Here I was, Cind thought, a nice, innocent young sniper. All I ever needed was a bit of adrenaline every now and then when a bullet came too close, a chance to prove I could outsneak whoever sent that bullet in my general direction, and perhaps a small medal and a bonus for encouraging that being on to the next metensomatosis.

But no. Sten had to come along and encourage me to larger endeavors. Shouting charge, and letting *other* people go out there and find out if the enemy believes in reincarnation. Sneak down dark alleys that have an absence of the rules of land warfare but a strong presence of thuggery. Declare intent of treason to history's most powerful ruler. Spy, cheat, steal, and assassinate, down in the muck and the mire.

Tsk, she thought.

All because you looked at that reputed demigod of a war chief and thought he looked lonely and had a nice butt.

However, there were, she realized, preening slightly in the mirror, *some* compensatory factors in irregular warfare.

Such as the way she looked at the moment. Nose to toes, she oozed wealth from every centimeter. All her clothes and accessories had been custom-made after her surreptitious landing in a city halfway across the world of Prestonpas.

Kilgour had told her, when you're playing a role, become it, from the mind out. So I settled for the skin out, she thought. Four months' pay for what Sten would, being a man, probably admire as a nice, simple little outfit and pay little real attention to. And as far as the skin? She'd indulged herself with a complete derm treatment, massage, and hairstyling. She noted with amusement that even though her military close-crop didn't give the stylist much room to create, it hadn't affected the size of his bill. But that was one of the prices of being a richbitch.

Cind lifted her rented Stewart/Henry sporter from where it'd been parked out of the mansion's line of sight, and headed for the entrance to the gates.

This being rich, she thought—smelling the sporter's creature-hide seats and admiring the hand-rubbed interior of what appeared to be real wood—could become addictive.

Although there were drawbacks, she admitted. Such as the tiny purse beside her. Once you put in your com, some necessary tools, a recorder, and a handgun, there wasn't room for anything else, really. She guessed one reason the very rich surrounded themselves with retainers was to have someone carry the makeup kit and the gravcar keys.

She grounded the gravcar in front of the mansion's closed gates. Heavy steel, with stone portals. The annunciator on the post beside it lit.

"May we be of assistance?"

"Brett of Mowatt," she said. "Plath Architectural Society. I am expected."

"We welcome you," the voice smoothed. "Please proceed directly to the main entrance. Someone will be waiting."

The gates opened, and she sent the gravcar down the long, winding gravelled road, past the freshly polished sign that read SHAHRYAR, past manicured lawns, past perfect topiary, past stone fountains, to the great rearing mansion in the middle of the estate.

She marveled.

Not the least of her marvel was the knowledge that this was one of the Eternal Emperor's connecting points. Kyes's computer data, and Mahoney's limited information, said this mansion, and others like it, were dotted around the universe, to serve one purpose and only one:

When the Eternal Emperor "rose from the dead"—and she shivered slightly, not believing in but still remembering Bhor legends of those who'd passed beyond life—this mansion would be his first stop. Here, assuming Kyes's analysis was correct, he would be brought current with whatever had happened in the Empire during the years since his death/assassination.

A further marvel to her, and this one in anger, was that once the Emperor felt himself properly briefed, he would leave the mansion—and it would be razed to the ground. What a bastard, she thought. So what if the grounds would be donated to the locals as a park? Sarla, it's just like what Sten told me the clot's done to the province of Oregon on Earth. Okay, everybody away from the river. Abandon your homes, your businesses, your lives. Here. Take money, and don't bother the Emperor. He wants to go fishing.

She turned her mind back to the task at hand.

Finding this station, given the initial data, had not been that difficult. Profile: a constantly staffed mansion or its equivalent that purportedly belonged to a family/someone who seldom used it. Yet the mansion would be equipped with a state-of-the-art library computer and personnel, and would receive almost every techno/military/scientific publication.

Interesting, Cind thought, and the basic thinking is worth study. This is an almost-totally-secure path he's designed. Secure because, just as Alex has said, no one looks at the rich too closely. He said that Ian Mahoney had put it best: "You want to run a safehouse, run a drop, have a team on standby—or anything else nefarious? You don't find a warehouse in the slum, unless you're an amateur or a criminal.

Find yourself a nice, rich, bohemian, if possible, neighborhood, where nobody knows or cares who's coming or going . . ."

That gave total security. It was totally secure because, to consider the possibility of something like this mansion even existing, you have to accept the premise that a dead man can come back.

This was only the third mansion that had come close to Cind's profile, and, whereas the first two had a prob of less than 50 percent, this one touched 93 percent. The cover story was—and it was a curiosa item every now and then on the Prestonpas livies—the Shahryar family were ex-traders, who were eccentrically devoted to wandering ways. They would buy an estate on some world they had only heard about, fully equip it, and maybe not visit it for a generation or even longer. And when—or if—they visited it, they would demand complete secrecy.

A woman was waiting for Cind outside the huge entrance to the central house. Either the portal was counterbalanced or else the woman had a Bhor or a heavy-worlder on standby just to open and shut the clotting thing, Cind thought. The woman, Ms Analiza Ochio, as expected from Kyes's analysis, was the estate's librarian. She would be an innocent, absolutely believing the Shahryar cover story, and had been recruited for her technical skills, her liking for a semisolitary life, and probably a certain naïveté.

She was familiar with the Plath Institute and its fiches. Would, umm, what is the correct way to refer to you, m'lady?

"Just Brett." Cind smiled. "Titles are something that get you a better table at an overpriced restaurant, and that's it. Sometimes."

Ms Ochio asked her in. Refreshments? Of course. We have almost everything. It may be a solitary life, but it's a very comfortable one. Perhaps some caff. No, I had lunch before I left my hotel. They chatted for a while, then:

Now, if you'll give me the details, Brett? I'm very curious as to what your interest is in this estate.

Cind explained. The newest series Plath was publishing was to be on the residents of the fabulously wealthy. Not just the flash and filigree of how large the dining hall is, or how many worlds the crystalline chandelier came from, or what rare mineral the swimming pool is surfaced with—although that will be in them, and probably what will make the hoi polloi buy the fiches—but how practical are these grand palaces? Each fiche would contain not only a full floor plan, but livie-portrayals of each room. On a B-track, the occupants or staff of the mansion would discuss how well planned and laid out the mansion was, and on a C-track, one of Plath's resident architects would provide an analysis.

Ms Ochio's smile had vanished.

"*Every* room?"

"Well," Cind said, "I don't think we would be interested in all the bathrooms, unless they're something unique."

"Sorrow," the woman said. "That just won't be possible. The grounds . . . some of the outbuildings . . . the first and most of the second floor, and the library are quite open. We had one of the local garden societies tour a portion of the house just three weeks gone. You would be welcome to record them.

"But the rest of the building, particularly the residential areas upstairs? No. The Shahryar family is very protective of their privacy, I was told when I accepted my contract, and was given quite explicit instructions. So . . . if those are your plans, I fear you may have wasted your trip."

"Could you communicate with the family? To make sure?" Cind asked. "Oh yes. I forgot. Most reclusive. Oh well. Thank the powers I'm not working on piece rates."

She stood.

"Might I refresh myself? Then, perhaps, you'll show me, just for my own personal curiosity, the parts of the house that the public is allowed to see?"

"Pleasure. The facilities are just beyond the library doors," Ms Ochio said.

Cind opened the door and stepped through. As she did,

she flicked a small object back, onto the table, in front of the librarian, closed her eyes, and ducked, shielding her face against the blueflash.

Ochio had time to puzzle at the tiny ovoid—and then the bester grenade went off. She slumped. Two E-hours would pass before she came back to the world, completely unaware of the time loss.

Cind patted the woman down. No vital-signs indicator that would set off an alarm—she had bumped Ochio a couple of times entering the room and had been pretty sure she was clean. No com, no panic button, no nothing. Cind dragged her behind one of the sitting room's small couches.

Two hours . . .

Gun out, but half-concealed, she slipped out the door into the great house.

She looked at the library's doors. Maybe. According to the input on Kyes's computer, gotten from the debriefing of another of the Emperor's librarians, there'd be two sysop stations for it. One would be the central station for the library, the other was code-sealed and could access certain unknown files. Files privy to the Emperor-to-be.

If she had time, and wasn't blown by then, she would take a stab at a little intrusion. But that wasn't the intent of her mission.

She went up the stairs, ignoring a gravlift for fear it'd alert someone there was an interloper loose in the house, and headed for the top floor. From what Ochio had said, that would be the most likely place for what she wanted.

There had been nothing on the roof her preliminary overflight suggested might be a 'cast antenna. so it would either be in a room or—she grimaced—tucked away somewhere under the mansion's eaves. Oh well. It would not be the first set of creepy attic critters she'd crawled through. If she still struck out, she would have to chance combing through the outbuildings. Which would mean a good shot at encountering security—in her overflight she'd seen uniformed guards walking the grounds.

She went through the mansion's top floor in a blur—checking/cover/checking in the blur of a highly trained security specialist. Clear . . . clear . . . clear . . .

All the rooms appeared quite innocent—furnished as if expecting the momentary arrival of the obviously extended Shahryar family and their equally huge staff of retainers.

Clean. Bright. Sparkling.

Cind went in a door, next to a stairwell curve, glanced around—Kholeric, this bedroom's got to be for the third-ranking apprentice scullery maid, and she'd have to be a little person, nothing interesting—and back out . . .

She stopped before the door could close.

Looked up and down the hall. At the stairs. Either whoever had laid this floor out was drunk, or else incompetent. Or else I did even worse at geometry than I thought. Back inside. No—the room was still too tiny for the amount of space it evidently occupied. Or maybe, she thought, this room's intended for somebody with a *major* anal fixation, because nobody needs a fresher that big.

The bathroom door was locked. Cind took two of the "necessary tools" from her purse. With the first, she swept the door and jamb. The little "bugeater" told her there appeared to be no security monitors on the other side. The second tool went against the pore-pattern "lock"—odd thing to lock the *outside* of a bathroom. The slimjim hummed, analyzed, and the lock clicked open. Cind pushed the door open. Y-reķa.

The com station was elaborate, and automated. Cind ran through the checklist Freston had dummied up for her and, recorder humming, set to work. Not being a commo specialist, she wasn't sure she was getting what she came for—but the registry/control/tracker for the antenna array, evidently secreted in another part of the house or estate, surely looked as if the com was "aimed" to receive a tight-beam signal from somewhere.

A somewhere that might be the Emperor's sanctuary.

She checked the transmitter nearby. It was completely

automated, and she was afraid to mess with it. Most likely the transmitter was intended to send out a "Don't come here" to the Emperor-in-transit if the mansion's purpose was exposed.

She had—she hoped—what she came after. And she'd left no trace, having plas-coated her fingertips and palms so that any dusting would produce no identifiable prints on the few things that she'd actually touched. She relocked the door behind her.

Now for some cake icing.

She still had just under an hour, and so far had heard no alarums and excursions from downstairs. If necessary, she could always drop back into the sitting room and blank Ochio for another two hours.

The antechamber was still deserted. Cind cracked the library doors. The huge gallery rose to an arched, clear skylight/ceiling. Fiches/reels/files and even books were stacked on the shelves that ran from the floor up ten meters to the ceiling. Now this, she thought, is the kind of library Sten would like to have. When this is all over. If this is ever over.

She looked for life. Nothing.

Cind went in. Near the door was one sysop station. Ochio's. Now where was the other? The one with all those interesting eyes-only files.

She spotted cables—cables, which meant someone was very worried about transmission security—that ran out through one wall.

Cind exited the library and found another unobtrusive room, this one with its wall in common with the library. She popped the door and went in.

Joy, joy, joy, she thought, looking at the computer station. I don't know what I am doing. *When in question/Or in doubt/Run in circles/Hack and shout*, and she sat down at the keyboard. A keyboard, for heaven's sakes. And the computer will be coal-fired, and the screen will be monochromatic. They laughed when I . . .

She touched a blank key. The screen lit.

RECEIVING. ENTER CURRENT DATE AND STATION.

Cind guessed as to the last, and hit keys.

The date, and SHAHRYAR.

SYSOP LOGGED ON. ENTER CLEARANCE.

Oh clot.

Uh . . . Emperor. No. Empire. No. Oh. Wait a minute.

ENTER CLEARANCE. YOU HAVE THIRTY SECONDS BEFORE ALARM.

The name bubbled up in her mind. Saying a small prayer, she keyed . . . RASCHID.

CLEAR. SYSTEM PRIVILEGE GRANTED.

No way. It could not be this easy. But:

REQUEST COORDS, TRANSMITTER TO SHAHRYAR RECEIVER.

PLEASE WAIT.

A light began blinking.

I'm in, she exulted, then, hearing the scuffle of feet outside, rolled out of the chair, and the two security techs burst through the door. They wore gas masks and body armor, and it mattered little as Cind snap-shot them both below their faceplates, and sent two rounds into the lying computer screen, and then dived out the door, bellyfirst.

She hit, skidded, rolled, and dropped the covering guard beside the door, and shot twice at another one coming down a stairway—dammit, I missed, but I sure whitened your hair, woman.

Cind, wanting heavier artillery, shoved her pistol in her suit's waistband, grabbed the dead guards' rifle—an Imperial-issue willygun, she noted, and shame on breaking your cover—thumbed the safety down to autofire, and sent a burst shattering the doors into the library.

And now the alarms were howlingroaringscreaming, and there were shouts, and Cind saw a face peering around a corner. She sent a burst in its general direction, another burst blowing out a huge window, grating, alarm wires and glass and all, and dived through her newly created exit.

Hell, just like a clotting infil course, she thought, turfing down across a bush, feeling that ultraexpensive suit rip and tear, siderolling down to the ground, burst . . . burst . . . burst . . .

There, that's got them pinned down or at least thinking for a minute; after all, they may be Imperial-trained, but their reflexes are a little slow, and why the clot can't I find the car key.

She found it, as she slid behind the controls of the Stewart/Henry . . . POWER ON . . . GENERATOR TO SPEED . . . WAITING COOLANT FLOW . . . Come on, I really don't give a damn if your luxury handbuilt engine cooks off like a teakettle . . . READY . . . READY . . .

Full lift, full drive, and the passenger door and some of that hand-rubbed dashboard exploded, and the gravcar was airborne, straight ahead, screw the twisty path, for those gates, and she rolled out of the gravcar, three meters in the air, hit turf at twenty kph, rolled a PLF, and was behind some stupid bush carved to look like some clotting animal, and then running, scuttling low, unseen, using every bit of cover.

The Stewart/Henry flamed, ten meters short of the gate, and about fifteen in the air—bastards must've had some kind of antiaircraft capability in that goddammed gate—and plowed into the manicured lawn.

The fence . . . not yet . . . wait a second, woman . . .

Come on, you stupid gravcar . . .

The demo charges she had thoughtfully left in the sporter's trunk blew up, sending the stone portals and metal gates pinwheeling up, around, and then down in a ball of fire.

Cind blasted the fence's alarm system and the jagged glass it was topped with in an obvious distrust of anything electronic. They'll think it's part of the general defunct-o as everything's hemorrhaging.

I hope. Up, up, and away.

Exactly like an infil course, she thought, rifle across the walltop, slither on side, roll down, hit in firing position.

Nothing to shoot at.

She doubled away, into the surrounding brushland, grateful that the Emperor not only secured his mansions with a lot of grounds, but had them built way out in the country.

It would be a three-klick cross-country run to where she had her backup hidden—a bottom-of-the-line utility gravsled bought on the local graymarket.

She surveyed damage—mission, not costume or scrapes. Negligible, she decided. Since the Emperor and his people were operating on the basis that Sten was dead, and she herself wasn't a known entity to the Empire, or so rebel intelligence indicated, the most logical interpretation was that some high-credit computer criminal had tried a speculative B&Eing. And if someone in Internal Security added things together, and got a worst-case explanation—well, she'd asked Sten about that, and he said it was all to the good if the Eternal Emperor got the idea that some unknown hellhound is on his trail.

At least I got to try flashin' and prancin', Cind thought. For an amateur, I didn't do badly, richbitching.

And I think I'm one step closer to the Emperor.

CHAPTER THIRTY-FOUR

THE ETERNAL EMPEROR would not have been pleased to see the use Sten and Cind were putting to his former suite aboard the *Victory*. The luxurious sleeping area—with its athletic-field-sized bed—was littered with fiches and printouts and wads of scrawled notes.

Sten and Cind were perched on the bed itself, plotting the Emperor's demise.

They went over all the information Cind had gleaned. And then checked it again. Finally they were done. There was only one more piece missing.

"I don't see any other way to look at it," Sten said. "That tightbeam antenna has to be the key."

"Which gives us one directional leg," Cind said.

Sten grimaced. "Yeah. But to get a fix we're still going to have to come up with another. A second leg. Right now all we know is that the Emperor's hideout is somewhere between Point A and infinity."

Cind nodded, gave a weary sigh, and lay back on the bed. As one side of Sten's mind worried at the problem, the other noted the slender form of his lover. She was gloved into a black skintight jumpsuit that covered her from neck to heel. It had been a long time since they'd had many hours together.

A small part of him wished the impossible. That their existence could be different. That he and Cind could be normal beings with normal problems. Instead, the course he was on required him to continually risk the life of the person who was closest to him.

"Well, I'll be a beardless mother," the woman of his dreams suddenly exclaimed. She sat up in the bed. Abrupt. "Wait just a clottin' minute, here!"

"What do you have?"

Cind shook her head, impatient. Started burrowing through notes. "I'm not sure . . . but if you will button your lip for a second, my love, I'll . . ."

Her voice trailed off as she grabbed a handheld and began punching in data. Sten did as he was told, watching with growing interest as she muttered to herself and pawed about for more bits of information.

She finally looked up at him, eyes bright with excitement. "I think I've got it," she said. "The other leg, I mean. Or how to find it."

Cind scooted closer to Sten, so he could see the handheld's small screen. "See . . . That little factor that kept messing us up before. We thought it might be static. Or, maybe even a screwy secondary from all that security apparatus. But look. That wasn't the explanation at all."

She watched anxiously as Sten weighed the information

on the screen. "Maybe I'm full of it," she said, beginning to doubt herself. "Maybe my brain has turned to something like one of Kilgour's pet haggises."

"No," Sten said, hastily running a recheck program. "I'm pretty sure your mind is functioning perfectly."

A grin split his face from ear to ear. "It's a second beam, all right. It's gotta be. On a different freq and aimed in a completely different direction!"

Sten quickly patched into the *Victory*'s main logic banks and ran the data. In a few moments the answer came back. "That's it," he said. "There's no other possibility."

Cind chortled in triumph. "Now all we have to do is track that bearded wonder down . . . and locate Point B. Which should be . . . I'm hoping . . . one of the relay stations like Kyes found. Except that it hopefully won't have done a melt-down. Run a fix from there, and that should give us the other leg—straight into the Emp's scrotum."

She knelt on the bed. Hoisted a lovely hand to give Sten a salute. Looking sexier than hell. "Sir! I respectfully request permission to investigate."

Sten hated what he had to say next. He would have to tell her no. His rejection would take a great deal of explanation. None of which Cind would buy.

This time, he would be the one to go. Alone.

Not out of love. Or fear of losing her. Well . . . not really, he rationalized, steering to the cold facts of the matter.

When Kyes had confronted the Emperor on that burned-out AM2 station, he had come supported by an entire team of former Mantis operatives. Yet there'd been some kind of mistake made—and the station had self-destructed.

As skilled a soldier as Cind was, she was certainly not as experienced as any member of that grizzled team of stealth warriors. And he assumed the relay station had far more devices for self-protection than just autodestruct.

Sten had spent a small lifetime in Mantis. It was not ego that told him he was the best of the very best. His built-in Mantis calculator delivered this up as solid truth.

He was the only logical choice for the mission.

But how could he say all this to Cind and get her to understand? To see the situation clearly, and unemotionally. With no rationalizations of her own to spare her lover from danger?

He saw the flushed excitement on her face. The dancing lights in her eyes. He hated to kill that look.

Sten told her. She raged at him. She reasoned with him. She pleaded with him. But he held his ground.

Finally the matter was settled. Or at least they'd declared a truce and had agreed not to discuss it for a while.

On the shaky theory that one couldn't eat and be angry at the same time, he rang the mess to serve dinner in the suite.

They spent the first half of the meal in near silence. The second in light chatter. By the time they got to the snifters of crusty old port, the chatter had turned to serious talk.

Sten told her about Rykor and the brainscan and Bravo Project.

"I still don't know what to do about it," he said.

"Some people would wrap it in suit-proof patents," Cind said, "and then sit back and rake in several large fortunes."

"I know I won't do that," Sten said.

"I figured as much," Cind said, with a small smile.

"Besides," Sten said, "the ability to manufacture AM2 really doesn't have much to do with the problem we have right now. I suppose one reason I've put off a decision is because I'm not sure how this is going to turn out."

"I've thought of that, as well," Cind said. "I wake up with the cold sweats sometimes, wondering . . . What if the Emperor wins?"

Sten said nothing. He refilled the snifters.

"But that sort of thinking is pointless," Cind said. "He either will or he won't. Sometimes Bhor fatalism can save a lot of agonizing."

She swirled the port in her glass. Thinking. Sten could see she was hesitating to ask a question. Then she spoke, without lifting her eyes.

"What happens if *we* win?" she asked. "Who—or what—is going to replace the Emperor?"

Sten shook his head. "It isn't up to me," he said. "As far as I'm concerned, this is a revolution. Not a coup. Other beings are going to have to make those kinds of decisions. It's their future. Their choice."

"I think you're being a little romantic," Cind said, "if you think it's going to be that simple. You'll be the man of the hour. The rescuer. More to the point, there's the AM2. Whether it's natural or synthetic. From an alternate universe or a processing plant. You'll be the one holding the keys . . . the keys to the Emperor's kingdom."

"I'm not much enamored of that thought," Sten said. Flat.

Cind put a hand on his. "I know," she said. "And that's why I love you. It's also why I want you to think about it. Because when the moment comes, there won't be much time to decide."

"I notice you didn't offer your opinion on what I ought to do," Sten said.

"I'm the last person who should say," Cind answered. "Do I think you'd make a good ruler? Clot, yes. Would I rather have you to myself? Double clot, yes."

She squeezed his hand. "I'm prejudiced, remember?"

Sten flushed, embarrassed. Cind giggled. "How cute," she said. "You're blushing. Now, I've got something on you. The great rebel leader, blushing like a boy."

"Blackmail," Sten said.

"Absolutely," Cind replied.

She slid out of her seat and slipped into his lap. Sten found his arms full of a wriggling, willing woman. Kissing at his neck. Nipping at his earlobes.

"What'll you give me if I don't tell?" she whispered. Naughty.

Sten's hands were busy moving over the form-fitting jumpsuit. Outlining curves. Exploring hollows.

"I'll tell you in a minute," he said. "But first, you tell me. How the hell do you get this thing off?"

She took his hand . . . and showed him.

The whisper came hot in his ear: "There," she said. "Press . . . right . . . there!"

CHAPTER THIRTY-FIVE

THE GUARDS' BOOTHEELS crashed louder and closer. Alex hung like a spider in his web just above the great blast doors that led from the huge parade-ground/bailey into Arundel Castle. Waited patiently, eye on his timer, trying to ignore the skin-crawl.

It had grown worse the closer he got to the Emperor's castle. Not that he had encountered any concrete reasons for this death-tick. Kilgour's self-insertion had been a piece of cake. Thus far. And by his own self-deprecating definition.

He had ridden public trans from Ashley-on-Wye to the nearest decent-sized city. Then he had checked to make sure there had been no recent changes to the ID required on Prime World, and that his own fake cards were correct. Then he found a bad section of town, and bought a currently-in-register gravcar at one of the town's graymarket hurleyburleys. None of the unpleasant questions such as Place of Residence, Place of Work, Reason for Cash Purchase, References, or the rest that might have concerned a conventional dealer were asked.

The sled may have been registered, but its drive was in unspeakable shape—the McLean generator would only lift the gravcar three meters, at max, and held the car at a 15-degree angle to the side. Top speed was no more than 55 kph.

Alex dropped another hundred credits to the seller's purported brother, to get it running right. He knew the "brother" would jury-rig the repairs, and probably fill the lubricant reserve chambers with something on the specific gravity of molasses—frozen. But what of it? The craft was intended for only a one-way trip.

Twenty klicks outside Fowler, the city closest to the Imperial grounds, Alex found a litter-filled field just beyond one of Prime's omnipresent parks. Clottin' gorgeous, he thought. Put i' a park, w' penalties f'r trash, an' thae'll still be clots thae'll dump their slok ten meters beyon' the gate. Exact whae Ah been seekin', however. He lifted the gravsled into the middle of the lot, grounded it, smashed the ignition and choice parts of the drive, stripped its registry off and buried it, and abandoned the wreck.

He hitched into the city and disappeared into its high-rise slums.

Step One, Two, and Three were accomplished successfully—getting onto Prime, setting up a secure base, and infiltrating into Fowler. Now for a cooling-off period. There was just a possibility he'd been tracked from his arrival, and the Emperor's Internal Security was giving him rope, to see what mischief he had in mind. I' dinnae be likely, he thought. But why chance m' neck i' th' noose? I's th' only one Ah hae.

He had rented the room because it had two separate "back doors"—one out onto a rusty, abandoned fire ladder that Alex had secretly reinforced, and the second from the other side of the corner room onto some rooftops just made for a rapid departure. Plus it had a half-arsed kitchen, so he wouldn't be forced out into public view.

After a week of laying low and eating packaged food not much better than military rats, he concluded he had dragged no tail with him. On to the next part.

He treated himself to a bottle of expensive brandy, remembering he would have to dump the flask somewhere else to avoid suspicion, since people in the district he had taken lodgings in seemed addicted to simpler pleasures, such as filtered industrial alk or home brew. And he plotted.

Stage Four would be getting himself as close as possible to Arundel. Stage Five would be getting into the Emperor's castle. Stage Six would be out and gone for home, hopefully in one flat-out run.

Alex's plan—one in, twa oot—was that he'd have a partner when he left.

Poyndex. He was fairly sure the man might have some objections to being snatched, and might become violent, or at the very least vocal.

Neither of which was in Kilgour's scheme, especially since a brouhaha would produce an uncomfortable feeling for him, such as death. And for his overall plan to work, Poyndex would have to vanish silently and completely. The Snark would have to be a Boojum. But he didn't want the distinction to be made positively until it suited Alex, Sten, and the rebellion's plans.

Alex's ambitious plan was to vanish Poyndex straight to the brig of the *Victory*. There he would be offered the same choice his agent on Vi, Hohne, had been given: double or be brainscanned.

Alex cynically figured that Poyndex, being a purported professional, and having turned his coat once, wouldn't even hesitate as long as Hohne had.

All of Alex's sources on Prime said Poyndex was the Emperor's cat's-paw in everything. His knowledge of the Emperor's closely held secrets would help in the final days.

At that point, Alex planned to have Poyndex surface, publicly. *That* would be yet another blow to the Empire.

All he had to do was bell his pussycat . . .

He forced himself to pay no attention to that little backbrain chant saying, "And lang lang may the maidens sit/Wi' their goud kaims in their hair, A'waiting for their ain dear love/For him they'll see nae mair . . ."

Maybe he *would* be killed this time. He felt it likely. Maybe this was his last run—but what of it? He had never had the idea he was either immortal or that he would die in a silken bed of old age. But he was determined that at the least, his run on Poyndex would succeed before he would consider taking the journey to the Isle of the Blessed.

He muttered as he finished the bottle. He was going on like a creaking seer, mewling around a cauldron on a blasted heath, thinking naught but wrack and ruin. Stick to bus'ness, lad. But if he *was* a seer, and his plan held up in the sober morn, Alex foresaw a minor crime wave in Fowler's future. At that point, he shut off the single light in the shabby room and rolled over to sleep.

He slept. If he dreamed, he did not remember them when he awoke. He ignored the hangover and reconsidered his drunken plans of the night before. They still made sense. Alex went out for one beer and a plate of greasy eggs and settled down for a nap until night.

The first theft was from an ambulance, parked at the back of an emergency ward. Kilgour, cross-trained as a medic in Mantis, knew just what he needed to clip from the gravsled's kit. He got what he needed, muttered at one object's unwieldiness, and left, relocking the ambulance's door behind him.

He stashed his loot, and checked the time. Ver' good, he thought. Ah still hae time, i' Ah hurry. Th' bistros'll nae be closin't frae another three hours. Back out into the night he went, headed crosstown to another part of Fowler, where an ungrated window didn't immediately suggest a brick and an eyeball-calculated trajectory.

The joint wae jumpin', he thought, looking through the mesh fence at the luxury gravcars parked behind the exclusive boîte. One . . . two security bein's, a couple of carparks. Nae problem.

He used a small laser to cut a Kilgour-sized hole in the fence and went into the lot. He stole the registration plates from six gravcars—and put five of them back. On different craft than the ones they had been taken from. He replaced the fence grating and, with the sixth plate, went back to his tenement. Clean and simple. Kilgour rewarded himself with a couple of beers in an after-hours dive. He bought some rounds, and made some friends.

The next day, he lazed around, after doing minor stretch exercises, only going out for a meal and a shopping expedition. He bought three days' worth of dried rations, a pack, a canteen, a flash, a set of camouflaged coveralls, and a cammie groundsheet. He wished the Mantis phototropic camouflage was available on the open market, which it of course was not. He couldn't have brought a set with him, since he had carried nothing that would even lift an eyebrow in the event of a stripsearch. The birdwatcher's gear would have to do. His final purchase was a small but heavy-bladed "survival" knife. His next stop was at an electronic hobbyist's center, where he bought some innocuous devices and the tools and circuitry necessary to modify them.

Then he allowed himself one of the two indulgences he had promised himself for the mission. He found a grocer's and bought three kilos of inexpensive, thin-sliced lean beef, salt, fresh parsley, and a collection of dried spices. Back at his tenement, he strip-cut the beef, about three centimeters wide. The strips went into a marinade of soy sauce, water, some cheap red wine, some hot sauce, and spices—garlic, a handful of juniper berries, summer savory, pepper. The garlic, berries, and spices were sautéed a bit, and then dumped, hissing hot, into the rest of the marinade. The strips of beef went in to soak for a day.

About midnight, he went back to the dive he had scouted the night before. One of his new friends was waiting. He had secured what Kilgour had expressed interest in. Actually, he had an assortment. Kilgour sneered audibly at the mini-willygun, although that was the weapon he would have preferred. But, as he told the fence, "I' Ah gie nabbed, wi' one ae th' Eternal Emperor's owene pieces ae AM2 artillery, Ah'm f'r th' high jump, an' Ah dinnae wan' t' revisit m' old haunts, f'r a while yet." Also that'd keep the fence from thinking Kilgour had major mayhem in mind, and possibly keep him from singing to the local constabulary about the gun-buying stranger to whom he owed nothing in the way of a buttoned lip.

For similar reasons he rejected a large-caliber handgun, and a folding-stock carbine, even though they were conventional projectile weapons. He chose—and then bargained for half an hour over the price of—a smallbore targetshooter. "Ah dinnae wan' t' be doin't more'n bluffin'," he lied.

Happy he had convinced the fence he was no more than a lightweight mugger, he trundled home and to bed.

Early the next day he finished off the first indulgence. The strips of beef were drained and laid on the counter. Over them Alex sprinkled salt—at least a pinch per slice. After that, chopped parsley. Then *very* generous pinches of a potpourri of the spices he'd bought. Thyme. More savory. Sweet basil. Pepper. Garlic pepper. Herb pepper. Marjoram. Some cumin, just for the hell of it. He pressed the spices into the meat with the flat of his knife, then flipped the slices over and repeated the seasoning. The meat went into the tenement's dilapidated oven, set at its absolute lowest, and with a cork holding the oven door open a centimeter or two.

While the beef dried, he went to work on the electronic devices, turning them from innocent gimmicks into proper burglar's tools.

He took a long nap, storing energy for the future. When he awoke, just before dusk, the slices of beef were dry, twisted, black, thoroughly nasty, and no more than a kilo in total weight. He admired his jerky. Ah'm noo th' cook th' Emp, Marr, Senn, or e'en m' wee Sten is. But this'll chew easy, i' th' woods i' th' rain. He sealed the jerky in a water-resistant pack. Then he packed and cleaned house. If Security was able to find the tenement, all of their most clever sweeps would yield them nothing, except that the slum had been rented by someone who was compulsively neat.

He went looking for his second indulgence. Taking all of his debris, from that brandy bottle to the electronics tools he'd purchased with him, and leaving them in an industrial dumper.

He found a restaurant big enough so he wouldn't be remembered, and savory-smelling from the outside. And he ate. First he protein-packed, even though he knew that wasn't the best way to prep himself for the run, but clot th' nutritionists, he thought. Ah'll hae someat t' think aboot, eatin' bushes an' pap. Three seafood cocktails. Two very large steaks, ultrarare. A side of sautéed fungi. A large salad, with a simple dressing. A half bottle of wine, to help digestion. The waitress lifted an eyebrow when he finished, sighed, and announced he was now ready for part two of his meal, but said nothing. Part two was carbpacking. He stuffed pasta, in as many permutations as the menu offered, until even he could detect outward movement in his rotund belly. He drank heavily. Water. Pitcher after pitcher of it. Water-packing.

By the time he finished gourmandizing and rolled out, tipping well as Laird Kilgour ought, considering this might be his last *real* meal, it was getting on.

Now he was operational. The plan was running.

In an exclusive residential enclave he had cased several days earlier, he stole an expensive gravcar, easily subverting its alarm and ignition cutouts. He put the registration plate lifted from the bar's parking lot on the car, and that craft's legal plates on the gravcar just in front of it. Confusion shall *noo* be m' epitaph, he thought, and lifted the gravcar away toward his slum. That was a bit of a risk, as he left the out-of-place gravcar down the street long enough to grab his gear and bid a long, last farewell to the slum. Ah'd say thae's naught humbler, but Ah know, i' an hour or so, Ah'll be thinkin't ae aught havin' a roof wi' infin'te fondness.

Into the car, and away. He headed for his jumping-off point—the ultraluxury part of Fowler, the grand estates of the wealthy who sucked around the Emperor and his palace as closely as they could.

Now was when his registration switchy-swappy of a few nights before would pay off, if it had even been noticed yet. If it had been narked, and a copper bleeped him, they would be expecting a prankster, not a criminal. A pity for them, he thought, making sure the pistol in his lap was loaded and locked.

The Imperial Grounds around Arundel were walled and given every imaginable security device. Alex parked his stolen gravsled on the closest street to the wall, and shouldered his gear. Again, another justification for the swapped plates. When the gravcar was reported stolen, it'd be on every rozzer's hotsheet, since it belonged to a richie. Or, at any rate, its registration plate would be. And *that* plate was sitting on another vehicle entirely, back at the theft sight, adding more confusion to the situation.

Kilgour needed this expensive sporter of his to sit where he had parked it without being noticed for at least three days—and he knew that any money district, especially one as close to Arundel as this, would be patrolled. He also planned to use the gravcar for his slither-stage-left, with Poyndex, back to Ashley-on-Wye.

Confusion to m' enemies, he thought, sitting across the street from the wall, meter-metering the security precautions. In two hours, he had the Emperor's system nailed. A walking guard every hour/hour and a half, one well-trained enough to vary his appearances. One sensor just before the wall. One atop it. The coiled razor wire on the wall itself would be tagged. He thought he saw a tree-mounted sweep in a treetop on the other side. An aerial about every hour. A vehicle patrol in between on the street.

Amateurs, Kilgour sneered. A' th' rankest sort. A standard Mantis test was to break in—or out—of a max-security prison within one E-day. The test wasn't regarded as one of the section's more stringent.

It's time, lad. And he went across the street, through the security, over the wall, and was on the far side of that tree-mounted pickup in less than ten minutes.

Tsk, he thought. Th' Emp's noo only gaga, but he's hirin' brainburns t' boot.

Now it would get sticky.

There were twenty-seven kilometers of unpopulated

forest and glade between him and Arundel Castle.

What would be a morning's jog took him three days and nearly cost him his life on four occasions. Dogs. More autosensors, of every possible configuration, from seismic to UV to motion to anything the Imperial Household's Head of Security could come up with. Set in unlikely locations. Irregular patrols. Aircraft. It could have been worse, however. A weak point was that the Emperor had insisted his security *must* be as unobtrusive as possible. So this meant dead zones, killing fields, checkboard light-searches, and the like had been forbidden by His Eternalship.

Alex remembered a boast he had once made to Sten, saying he could do something, i' his sleep, draggin' a wee canoe. He felt as if he was doing just that, lugging the McLean-powered stretcher he had stolen from the ambulance that he planned to stick the unconscious Poyndex into, which would give Alex only a few kilos of weight to lug all the way back to the wall.

He moved a few meters at a time, checking his backtrail, sanitizing it when necessary. He never slept, but huddled under the camouflaged groundsheet now and again for a necessary breather and a return to full alertness. He defecated in streams and carried his empty ratpacks with him. Once he hid in a pond, trying to find the promised pleasure in gnawed jerky as a pack of hounds quartered the shores.

At last he saw Arundel, standing black against a blazing hot sky. Its cannonports appeared eyes, staring straight at him. And the crenellations of its battlements . . . he turned off his imagination.

Alex stashed the stretcher in an impenetrable thicket. He was right on schedule—it was midmorning of the first day of the weekend. By tonight, he would have to be inside its walls, or else go to ground for another week.

He would, if necessary. But he would rather not.

There was nothing between him and the 200-meter-tall, 50-degree-sloped walls of the castle's bailey, walls that actually enclosed offices and storerooms for Arundel's vast staff.

In the late afternoon there came a clamor, and he imagined the palace employees who had been stuck working on a rec day hurrying toward the pneumosubway that'd whoosh them back to Fowler.

Among them, he knew, would also be the lucky sods of the palace security who had been given passes.

All that would be left in Arundel would be the skeleton weekend shift, plus whatever personnel had pressing tasks that couldn't be put off for two days, the workaholics, and a full staff of palace functionaries, from cooks to bakers to laundry people to butlers.

Big clottin' deal, Kilgour thought. There wae a time whae th' staff'd be taken t' consid'ration, bein' ex-Guard, -Merc, or -Mantis. But wee Poyndex hae all ae *those* dismissed. An' replaced, so Senn an' Marr said, wi' other people, who's qual'fications dinnae be greater'n a droolin' adoration ae th' Emp.

Plus security.

Not Gurkhas—they were long-gone. Nor the Praetorians—they'd never been reformed after their colonel had converted them to a private army in a plot to overthrow the Emperor. Thae wae th' prob' lad, he thought to the memory of the deceased Colonel Fohlee. Y' were whae thae call a preemie antifascist. An f'r y'r pains y' got fed int' a meatslicer.

Now the guards were Internal Security. Poyndex's own. Which no one from Mantis or Mercury who'd encountered Internal Security was very impressed with.

Come night, we'll find oot, Kilgour thought, if the rankin's pure jealousy, or wi' grounds.

There were two other beings who would be in the castle.

Poyndex. Sten had been correct—he seldom left his quarters/offices in the castle.

And one other.

The Eternal Emperor.

Kilgour considered that, while he waited. W'd thae be the simplest solution, an' avoid all of Sten's moils, toils, an' machinations? An' c'd he e'en get wi'in striking distance? Most likely not. Gettin' ambitious, he reminded himself, most oft means y' bollix up th' whole clottin' mess, i'stead ae endin' wi' th' girl, th' gold haggis, an' all.

Poyndex i' th' lad, an' th' on'y lad.

Come night, after he had timed the overhead aerial patrols, he moved out, slithering up the 50-degree slope of the bailey's walls to just below its crest—to what's known as the military crest, just below the peak. He followed the line as it veed back and forth, to dead-end against Arundel's great wall that climbed 700 meters above him to the leering fangs of the battlements. Alex took off his boots, and tucked them into his pack.

An' noo f'r m' spidger act, he thought, and slid sideways, onto the wall. Notches between stone blocks . . . fingerjam . . . toehold . . . moving sideways, toward where huge blast doors closed off the main entrance into the castle.

'Twould be easier, he thought, wi' climbin' thread an' jumars. But he hadn't been willing to chance buying climbing gear in Fowler. And this wall was not exactly a jo-block fitting . . . He swallowed a gasp, a bit of stone coming away under his fingers, his toe sloppily crooked, coming off, hanging by two clawed fingers and his other leg, god *damn* it, hearing that tiny piece of stone land on the parade ground thirty meters below him, crashing, smashing, its echo ringing around the bailey, louder than an avalanche, louder than a cannonshot, almost as loud as Alex's hard breathing.

Back on the wall. Y' should'a done a few practice climbs afore y' left, lad. Where? Oop an' doon th' main hanger deck wall ae th' *Victory*? Keep on keepin' on.

He stopped just above and to one side of the blast doors. Noo, t' find m'self a home. He found a good one. He drove the thick blade of his knife into a crack for a place to stand. And a nice secure handhold, one that let all four fingers cling to the stone.

Ah c'd dance.

He checked his watch. Bare minutes, he thought, m'

timin's perfectamente, till th' first changin' ae th' guard.

The blast doors crashed open just at 1950 hours, and the changing of the guard commenced. Alex watched closely, as a professional.

It was as much a ceremony as a security process. The entire watch paraded out, with the officer of the guard and the watch commander at its head. The formation stopped at each guard's post, the guard challenged the watch—nice touch, thae, Alex thought. Thae's clottin' *clans* ae strange troopies clatterin' through Arundel ae an' evenin' an y' dinnae wan' t' be truckin' wi' strangers—the challenge was answered, and the guard relieved. He came to port arms, doubled to the rear of the formation, and his relief, at the formation's front, took the post. Then, with much crashing and bashing, the formation moved on to the next post and the next relief.

Alex hung happily overhead—he knew that no one in a military formation ever looks up, down, or to either side, in fear of Instant Disembowelment from a noncom or officer—and itemized Internal Security's stupidities.

Since this was a ceremony, IS's black uniforms—nice, functional, and unobtrusive at night—had been prettied up with a white sam browne belt, helmet, epaulettes, and gloves, plus white slings on their willyguns. At least, Alex thought, they'd junked the stupid parade-ground rifles, f'r chrissakes, the Praetorians used to parade with.

They were, he concluded, *most* inconspicuous. Especially when he listened, and realized someone had ordered pony and heel taps nailed on their bootsoles. It sounded spectacular against the stone, Alex thought contentedly. Y' c'n hear the clots comin' frae a country mile. Whaee'er a mile is.

Eventually the crashing of bootheels and -toes, the thudding of rifle butts against the ground, and the slap of gloved hands on riflestocks ended, and the old watch disappeared back into Arundel.

Noo, Alex thought, his amusement gone for a total focus, w'll see i' thae parade ground's a sham. I's noo, i's noo, i's noo, he thought in glee, damned near falling off his perch. Thae're ceremonial beings, throo an' throo . . .

Be sick, braw greatness, he thought, a memory from his days in school, an' bid thy ceremony gie thee cure.

Twa hours frae noo. 2200, an' Ah move.

The best time to mount an attack—or a snoop and poop— is either in the wee hours of the morning or else just before dawn, when energies are low and everyone's half-asleep. Normally.

But Kilgour was cagier than that. Which was why he had chosen a weekend as the perfect time to assault an essentially peacetime fortification. Everyone who's not got a pass is either broke, on a striper's drakh-list, lonely with nobody to go see, a lifer, or generally irked at it being their turn in the barrel. Plus supervisors normally take weekends off whenever *they* aren't on the duty roster.

Combine these two facts, and you end up with people going through the motions, generally just a little gruntled about things.

Kilgour, being a sophisticate, also chose the hour carefully. First shift is 1800–2000. These are guards who've been recently fed, but are fairly alert, if for no other reason than the officer of the guard will likely make his rounds on their watch. 2000–2200. Second watch. Not bad, but still a bit early. People are still out and about. 2200. Third watch's first shift. They're fed, had time to stir around the guardroom in boredom, or visit the canteen if the base has one—Arundel did, and it served beer and wine—for a consoling pint, or begin a card game. And then it's time to walk the post in a military manner, all the while realizing at midnight you will be relieved, you will go back to the guardhouse rather than being permitted to return to your own comfortable quarters and personal sack, and will be rousted out at 0400 for yet another tour before dawn. Perfect.

Kilgour's biggest worry was that IS was as subtle as the Gurkhas. They, too, had worked the same patterns when they guarded the castle, and had crashed and bashed with almost as much ceremony, even though they had worn parade-ground gear just on ceremonial occasions. And they had taken their duty very seriously, confining their on-duty canteen purchases to tea and a sweet. But the Gurkhas had their own, uniquely nasty touch, characteristic of the brown men from Nepal. They'd anticipated that some nefarious type, such as Kilgour, might have figured a parade formation is really easy to anticipate, evade, or avoid. So, behind the flashing panoply of the watch change swept a full platoon, in combat gear, weapons ready, at the bloodthirsty lurk.

Evidently IS hadn't gotten word of the twist. The troopies Alex had seen were all there were.

And so, at 2150, as *the guards' bootheels crashed louder and closer*, Kilgour kept himself from chortling aloud. The third watch came out—Alex heard a few out-of-step marchers who had hit the canteen—and moved through its roundelay. The formation came back, the relieved second-watch guards yawning, looking for a bit of a headdown.

Kilgour slid out of his web, dropped to the parade ground, and went through the blast doors behind the guard, just as the doors crashed closed.

He was inside Arundel Castle.

Now was the moment of maximum danger. Moment, quite literally, since he planned to be visible for not much more than that.

He eeled forward, behind the guard. Ahead was the guardhouse, and the stairs leading down, into the largely ceremonial dungeon far below. Alex *hoped* ceremonial— i.e., deserted. He had once been imprisoned there, as part of the twisting moils of the Hakone plot, with most of the Gurkhas.

The dungeon was his goal. A gaol f'r a goal, he thought merrily, and was suddenly surprised at his cheer. The feeling of doom was just as powerful. More so, really. And he was in greater and greater jeopardy, yet felt strong. Strong and even cheery. N' wonder, he thought with a bit of disgust, we Scots hae taken it i' th' kilt frae th' Brits. We hae songs an' merr'ment, an' they soljer on, grim-arsed, an' tread us int' th' dirt.

Och well. Roll on, death.

The guardhouse. Guard . . . halt. Order . . . harms. Carry . . . harms. Column of files from the left . . . for'd, harch. The watch went inside, followed by the officer of the guard and the watch commander. Shortly thereafter, Kilgour slunk into the guardhouse as well.

Clatter, shouts, the fresher flushing, rifles clattered into racks, mattresses being unrolled, noisy chatter of young men and women after two hours of walking froo and toe in a military manner.

Nobody even noticed the coverall-clad man who flashed past the open door and down the hall. The hall dead-ended at a thick door, dripping with elaborate locks. Elaborate and old-fashioned. It took less than a minute to pick the three that were locked, another minute to jimmy them so they looked to be still secure, and Alex was inside, at the head of the stairs leading down into the slammer.

He shut the door behind him, wedging it closed. He put his boots on and started down. The stone steps were worn— as if generations of prisoners and guards had trudged the *via dolorosa*.

Kilgour's flash illuminated the chamber at the base of the steps. Just as he remembered it, although memory was a traitor. But Marr and Senn had sworn Arundel had been rebuilt *exactly* as before. The door to the huge holding cell hung open—a lock he wouldn't have to pick.

Now, Ah rec'lect wee Sten came through th' wall aboot here . . . and he pressed.

Soundlessly, the wall slid away.

Alex moved inside.

This was the "secret" of Arundel, although not that much of a secret. Sten had discovered it years earlier, when he had been commander of the Guard. Arundel was honeycombed with secret passages. They ran from the Imperial chambers to bedrooms to the dungeon to seemingly pointless openings in main hallways. The tunnels had charmed both of them, in another time, with another Emperor. A proper castle had to have secret passageways, and they were impressed with an Emperor who so indulged his romantic impulses.

Now, the passages would be—if Marr and Senn had been right and they had been built exactly as in the old Arundel—one more step toward the Emperor's destruction.

Alex moved up the winding step and the bending low-ceiling passages, always keeping his carefully memorized picture of the castle's outside interior in mind. He wanted the passageway that led to the row of bedrooms.

Kilgour's mood had changed again. Now, and it might have been claustrophobia from the kilotons of stone and the darkness and the close air around him, he felt as if someone was waiting for him.

Up there. Up above.

Three times he discovered sensors and disarmed them. But this was easy going, moving invisibly, like a rat in the walls, past whatever security was patrolling the interior of Arundel. A rat that stuck *close* to the walls, as any experienced snoop did when climbing stairs and walking down corridors. Not just for cover, but because boards creak, and . . .

Stale air?

No. Suddenly fresh.

Alex looked for a ventilating duct. Nothing but gray stone, or some synthetic cast to look like it. Although Alex suspected the wallmarks, suggesting the passage had been hand-hewn by an ax, might well be genuine.

Definitely fresh air. Alex knelt, holding his palm flat. There. Around this one great flagstone. The stone was a trapdoor. Pressure-activated, most likely. He dug a millcredit coin from his pocket, and slipped it through a crack, and let go. *Ting . . . tiny . . . ting . . .*

a long way down.

An oubliette?

Alex thought of tripping the door, but decided against it. It might be hooked to an alarm. Or . . .

. . . it might be occupied.

Kilgour moved on, hastily, reading his mind the riot act. Ah'm i' th' catacombs, y' clot, an' y're comin' oop wi' dungeons wi' rats an' blind prisoners whae been cast doon i' the dark frae decades. It's nae but a garbage pit. Or a 'spection hatch. Or th' Emp put i' in frae authenticity.

Oh aye. The lad's such a stickler he puts holes i' th' cave no one'll e'er see, except f'r him, whae he hae t' fish one ae his fancy lassies or lads oot of.

Oh aye. Y' lyin' clot.

The long ramp came to an end, and a corridor, wider than the others he'd mazed through, opened.

This, Ah s'spect, i' th' floor Ah wan'. But Alex wanted to make sure. And, again, something was niggling at him. One floor above would be the Emperor's private chambers. And the Emperor would be in them.

Unless he was now hiding like th' ferret he's become, doon i' th' bunker, i' th' catacombs thae run doon t' th' gates ae hell below.

P'raps a wee check, his mind suggested innocently.

Somewhere around here, his mental chart said, should be a braw arch, an' marble steps leadin' oop t' th' mon himself.

There was no arch.

Just solid wall.

Alex touched it in several places, making sure it wasn't another secret doorway. It wasn't.

Aye, he thought. So th' lad dinnae built *ever'thing* ae i' was. Mad, paranoid bastard, he thought, but with relief. It kept him from indulging that wild urge to solve all, with one mad charge into the heart of the enemy.

So he went for the target he'd intended from the beginning.

Alex found one of the panels—intended for observation, perhaps—that swung out into the main outer passageway. He swung it open a trifle . . . and looked.

Ah. Two Internal Security sorts, standing in front of a double set of doors. Marr and Senn told him the entire floor had been

ripped apart and rebuilt. Only Poyndex occupied the floor.
Only Poyndex was entitled to be this close to the chamber.

Alex smiled.

A very different smile than before, when he hung above
the castle's entrance.

Now, the smile was truly on the face of the tiger.

Poyndex swore, but to himself. His frustration didn't show
on his face, any more than any other emotion would be
allowed to. He kicked out of the program he was running
and cut back to the top of the fiche.

He had a dull headache. His eyes felt as if they had been
sandblasted.

By rights he should have shut down and gone to bed. It
wasn't that late, but he had been putting in twenty-hour days,
between normal tasks of Internal Security, the Emperor's constant calls, and then this new mission of planetbusting all of
the rebel worlds' capitals.

He had considered and reconsidered the Eternal Emperor's
terror program.

At first, it seemed absurd. Not absurd, his mind corrected.
Wagnerian, in the sense of Götterdämerung. Like that
Earthtyrant, whatever was his name? Oh yes. Adolph the
Paretic. But that was impossible. The Eternal Emperor
couldn't be insane. Of course not.

He vaguely remembered one of his instructors in his youth
telling him about some dictator of the past, who had over-
thrown the old boss and was having his flunkies write a new
constitution, legitimizing his powergrab. The dictator had
rejected one draft, telling his subordinates the new constitution must not, in any way, interfere with the state's use of
terror as a legitimate ruling tool. Terror from above, it had
been termed. So there was precedent to the policy.

The problem was, he could not remember either the dictator's name, nor whether his reign had been long and lethal,
or brief and bloody . . . and he certainly did not have time
to do any idle research.

On further consideration, Poyndex thought the Emperor's plan meritorious. Might this flickering nonsense of a rebellion, which now, with its "liberator" dead, should properly be called anarchic, be quelled by a huge, nearly instantaneous application of force? Machiavelli, after all, had instructed his prince to ax all of his enemies at one time as soon as he'd seized power.

Not that Poyndex had ever entertained disobeying, or even questioning, this new Imperial policy. He served loyally. Perhaps not the Emperor, but the new fascination he had that it was possible to live forever. To live forever, and . . . and to rule?

The list was drawn up. The Cal'gata's capital world. The Honjo's six canton worlds. The seventeen area centers of the Zaginow. The Bhor capital of Vi. And on and on. The death roster ordered 118 worlds obliterated.

It could be done—the Empire still had far more battleships and completely loyal crews who'd murder an entire planet because it was so ordered.

The problem was the Eternal Emperor wanted the planet-bustings done nearly simultaneously.

On which clock, Poyndex thought, and whose calendar? Local? Zulu? Prime? By rights, he should have been able to rout out Admiral Anders and his planning staff. The navy might be a bit less than stupendous, but it would seem anyone with logistical training would know how to arrange things so that ships would arrive in the target system in time, but not early enough to arouse suspicion. But the Emperor had insisted this would be a totally secue operation, which meant only Poyndex and his own personal IS staff were even aware of the bloodbath to come.

Poyndex got up from his multileveled metal desk. It, and the rest of the technical apparatus he required, clashed with the ornate wood and silk wallpaper of the suite. But what of it? Perhaps, one day, when this was over, he would have it redone. This time with some of his own ideas, rather than what he had done before, letting some imbecile who thought the old ways were the prettiest handle things. When there was time, when there was time.

But there never was enough time.

Perhaps a drink, to get a little sugar in the bloodstream.

Poyndex walked to the small bar, and eyed the bottles. The Scotch the Emperor loved, and Poyndex couldn't stomach. That awful substance called "shine," and its even-worse companion, the ET beverage stregg, which the Emperor had reportedly once liked. Poyndex had tasted it once, and shuddered. No one but a soak or an ET could possibly drink that. He lifted the cut-glass decanter that held the multi-fruit brandy of his home world, which was about the only liquor Poyndex enjoyed the taste of, once a month or so.

No. That wasn't it, either.

He turned toward the doorway to his bedroom. *That* was what he really wanted. To lie down. To sleep. For a day, for a week, forever.

It took a moment to realize there was a man crouched in the doorway. A man wearing strange, camouflaged fatigues. His face was blackened. And he held a long-barreled pistol leveled at the center of Poyndex's chest.

"Y'll freeze," Alex said quietly. Normally he would've used a petrifying shout—but there were two sentries posted outside.

"Y'll noo breathe, 'cept on command," he went on, coming to his feet and moving forward, neither eyes nor gunbarrel moving from Poyndex.

"You're Kilgour," Poyndex said, trying, and hoping he succeeded, to keep shock from his voice. A flicker of pride—he didn't feel any fear.

"Aye."

"You know, killing me won't stop the Empire."

"Aye?" Kilgour asked, in polite disinterest. "Thae's noo m' plan. Y'r noo f'r th' big sleep, unless y' do someat daft, like cryin' oot.

"First, y'all step awa' frae th' bar, turn wi' y'r back t' me, kneel, an' clasp y'r hands behin' y'r head. Move!"

Poyndex turned. Started down, then stopped.

"The thought just struck me," he said. "If you're not on a personal vendetta . . . is Sten still alive? Did he order this operation?"

"Ah said," Kilgour repeated, still in a near whisper, "Ah wan' y' doon ae y'r knees, mate. Noo—"

Poyndex began to kneel . . . and lifted his arms, toward the back of his head. Alex's free hand came forward, the tiny bee sting of the narcdispenser ready. Poyndex's right hand shot out toward the bar.

Kilgour's reflexes cut in.

The heavy-worlder's left hand dropped the syringe, curled to hammerstrike, flashed out.

And struck. Just to the right side of Poyndex's neck. The snap was loud. Poyndex's head dropped to an impossible angle . . . and his body fell forward. Alex caught him by the collar before he could crash into the bar, and eased him down to the carpet.

Knowing he was wasting his time, he checked pulse. Rolled Poyndex over and peeled an eyelid back. Even, stupidly, held his ear to Poyndex's mouth, hoping for the slightest breath.

Nothing.

Y' clot, his mind savaged. Y' *know* bettern' thae! Are y' sarkers? Cannae y' control y'self? I' dinnae matter i' this i' th' lad whae killed Mahoney, or helped th' Emp slaughter who knows how many?

Y'r noo a professional, he thought in disgust. And started to get up.

Then his eye caught the button, mounted in the base of the bar. He looked closer. Nothing in the bar front. There. Above him. A snapaway panel, just like they showed him in training. Behind it would be what? A gun? A gas dispenser? An electrified net? Linked to a panic siren? Whatever it was, it would've been disaster.

Noo, did Ah *really* o'erreact . . . or did th' corner a' m' eye spot the switch? Balls, he thought. Kilgour resolutely refused to believe in any sense beyond the common. Then he realized, for the first time since that sleepless night on the battlements of Otho's castle, the night so long ago when Cind had been named to speak for the Bhor, that feeling of doom was gone.

By th' Stuarts, he thought. Ah been carryin't this death-sense wi me f'rever, stumblin' like a 'cruit i' th' Selection March ae Mantis. An' it's vanished, wi' Poyndex's dirty soul.

Are y' suggestin' his mind snickered, thae y' *sensed* thae wae a death owed? An' thae either you, or Poyndex, wh'd hae t' pay the price? Clot off, he thought. Ah hae noo time f'r Highland devils an' goblins.

Th' *real* question i' whae d' th' milkmaid do, whae she's kick'd o'er th' bucket, an' th' missus a' th' house dinnae hae a cat?

He had it.

He shouldered Poyndex's body and went into the bed-room, back through the panel into the secret passageway.

Feeling bulletproof, he trotted rapidly down it, to where that huge flagstone was. Noo, i' it's nae boobytrapp'd or alarm'd, he thought, Ah'm home free. He dropped Poyndex's corpse on the stone.

It fell away, and the body dropped into darkness.

No sirenscreech. No scurry of guards, if there'd been a silent alarm.

Just a thud. Silence. Another thud. Another silence, even longer. A splash, finally, as the late Poyndex hit bottom. Kilgour wondered, once again, just *what* was at the bottom of the shaft? He shone his tiny flash down into blackness. Nothing.

He touched the flagstone, and it smoothly swung back into place, waiting for the next weight to land on it.

Was it a garbage disposal? A sewer?

Alex shook his head.

He would never know.

He considered what had just happened and, after some reflection, nodded thoughtfully.

Assuming Poyndex's body wasn't discovered, at least for a while, what would the effect be? On Internal Security and, most importantly, the Emperor himself?

A wee bit scary, Kilgour concluded. I' fact, all thae's been sacrificed by giein' Poyndex a braw clout i' y'r original dreamscheme wi' th' brainscan.

Nae a bad night's work, he thought. Ah'm noo th' gowk Ah thought, a few min ago.

He allowed he deserved a pint and a dram. And perhaps a wee walk in the moonlight with Marl and Hotsco.

Feeling romantic—and thirsty—Kilgour headed for home.

CHAPTER THIRTY-SIX

THE CREATURE EYED Sten through its enormous compound eyes for a very long moment. Sten remained motionless, lying on his belly on the ocean's floor. Three meters above him, waves crested and crashed against a rocky island.

The animal had a three-segmented body, with hard jointed segments extending off in all directions. It looked hostile, but then, anything over a meter long with pincer-jaws usually was logged as unfriendly by Sten. Especially when it was about twenty centimeters from his face.

Eventually, some sort of sitrep was achieved by what passed for the creature's brain: You are the biggest thing in this ocean. No, you are not. There is something that is bigger than you. It is sitting just in front of you. You are a predator. You can devour anything that is in this ocean, No, you cannot. You tried to snag a morsel off this creature. Your pincers did not snag a morsel. This is not a familiar situation.

You are in trouble. You should go somewhere, somewhere this creature is not.

The huge "trilobite," or so Sten had labeled him, flurried its "legs," and was gone, vanished into a floating drift of algae.

Very good. Sten resumed his final mental briefing before he charged wildly off in all directions. It wasn't that the arthopod was any danger to Sten—especially since Sten was wearing a spacesuit. But those clotting pincers snapping on his faceplate made it hard to think.

That transmission beam that had almost been missed, 'casting from the mansion, had led the *Victory* farther out into the back of beyond, into barely explored space. It intersected no system or object for light-centuries.

But then there was a solar system. Three worlds, one moon, and a sun. Not a dead system, like the relay station Kyes had discovered, the relay station that had self-destructed on him. Life was just creating itself here.

Sten had kept the *Victory* on the solar system's fringes, terrified that one mistake would snap the thin lead, like so many others had before. Then, they would have to find another one of the luxury safehouses/way stations, and attempt to duplicate Cind's success. Or else follow that other beam far out into the unknown. It would probably take no more than a lifetime or two to find whatever pot of gold was at the end of that nearly infinite straight-line rainbow.

Freston again returned to his first skill, the com board. He had absolutely guaranteed Sten that the com beam from the mansion impacted on the second world from the sun.

Sten transferred Freston, Freston's com specialists, Hannelore La Ciotat, and himself to the *Aoife*, and again remoraed La Ciotat's tacship to the destroyer.

Very slowly, the *Aoife* closed on the world. Very young, indeed. Continents slowly sinking, seas shallowing and spreading across the world. Cambrian was the description, or so Cind informed him, suggesting that he might wish to take some basic geology courses one of these centuries, in his spare time.

They looked hard. Visually, electronically, actively, passively. It took an E-week before Freston had something. He had picked up some odd indicators from the coast of one of the small subcontinents in the southern hemisphere. Something was down there, something that appeared artificial. But every surface scan, from IR to scope, said the area was just one more rocky outcropping on the still-sterile land.

Freston chanced simulcasting a beam from the *Aoife* on the same freq as the continuous beam from the mansion, 'cast for less than a second. He picked up some bounced radiation. It was his theory that an antenna, or more likely several of them, had been inletted into the planet's surface in that area. Capable of receiving, transmitting, or retransmitting.

Sten thought about it. The moonlet Cind had visited had been hollowed out as it was equipped with antenna, a buried shelter, power, and supplies. The Emperor was smart enough to not choose the same sort of world for each relay station— but it seemed he would be using a similar construct for all of these stations, and, for safety's sake, putting most of the station underground.

Or underwater.

Freston sneered at that—why would you bother adding the additional interference of liquid, not to mention building sediment, crustaceans with claws, and all the rest? Sten nodded—right. The station—if this is where it was—would be just at the shore.

Freston then triumphantly produced his second piece of information. He had put a tight scan on the area, a few hours after nightfall. That really gave him something. Something a searcher would have to be specifically looking for, and looking in a very small area.

The rocks held their warmth for a long time. Far longer than air. That gave Freston some interesting images, particularly when they had been computer-enhanced by an operator with imagination. Here . . . the lines of the buried antenna, where the material the antenna had been made of held its heat even longer than the rocks. Over here, an oblong out-line, invisible without enhancement. Big. Freston thought that outline was a hangar door—the outline provided by cool air seeping through the door's edges. Over here—Freston's smile threatened to pass his ears and meet at the medulla oblon-gata—the door. People type.

All Sten had to do was get to that entrance, figure out how to pick the lock, and voilà.

Voilà, Sten said cynically. And then worry about how big a bomb is located inside. Freston *isk*ed. He couldn't be expected to do everything, could he? Being just an under-paid captain, and all.

Sten laughed and threw him out. Then he sat down to figure out the rest of the insertion plan. Thinking about under-water gave him the rest of the scheme. He sent for La Ciotat, kissed Cind, and moved out.

The tacship entered atmosphere in a trajectory exactly like that of a meteorite. A big one, but that couldn't be helped. It splashed down just beyond the horizon, but short of the bounce-reflection of any sensor on the subcontinent. La Ciotat sent her ship toward land below the surface, mutter-ing if she'd wanted to run a submarine, she would have been incarnated as a dolphin. Or a Rykor.

About a kilometer offshore, a reef rose to just below the surface. Sten ordered La Ciotat to bottom the tacship behind the reef.

He went out the airlock and began the long trudge toward shore. In the livies, the suit's little reaction jets would have worked splendidly in water and gravity, as they did in space, and sent him zooming like a speedboat toward his ren-dezvous with whatever. But even with the suit's McLean pack on full, mass was still mass. Sten chugged toward shore at the stately speed of a ferryboat, giving him plenty of time to tourist.

If the land above was barren, the sea was not. Algae in sheets. Ribbonweed thickets. Some things that looked like small crabs. Nautilus-coiled snails. And trilobites, from barely visible to . . . to large enough to make Sten think of big centipedes intermarried with scorpions.

As the bottom shelved, he cut power, and took her down. At three meters, he considered his situation and, until it wove away, the universe's biggest trilobite.

So far, there hadn't been any loud bangs that would indicate he had set off any of the booby traps he knew the relay station was equipped with. Very well. So they were still waiting for him. He wished he could figure out what those booby traps or booby trap could be. None could be that sensitive—the Emperor would hardly want his return slowed because a relay turned the fire on unexpectedly, and a heat sensor blew. Or a motion detector went crackers at an earth tremor. Trick stuff sometimes went off from its own cleverness. Nor, Sten thought, would the Emperor want to spend his time elaborately defusing some really sophisticated diabolism—he had heard the Emperor curse at puzzles and hurl them across rooms minutes after he had picked them up, back when . . .

Just back when, Sten. Stick to the subject at hand.

What the booby trap would most likely be, he concluded, was something the Emperor wouldn't have to worry about, but something that would send any intruder airborne in very small pieces. A retina-coded lock? A pore-pattern lock? Hardly, considering the device's reliability had to be conceivably measured in centuries.

Sten went ashore, wading through the surf, onto dry land. Dry rock. Nothing but rock, of various shades of gray and black. Dark sand at the water's edge. A beach, almost half a meter wide. Sten spotted something and knelt, his mission forgotten for a brief moment. There, just in the surfwash, was a bit of green. Life. Some kind of plant, he thought. Algae? He didn't know. Go on back to the sea, he thought. You don't know what you're starting.

He rose and trudged up toward the shelf where the station would be located. His suit's sensors said the air was breathable, although oxygen poor. But he stayed in the suit. Again, part of his caution. He didn't think that an infrared

sensor would be used to set off the self-destruct mechanism—
but the spacesuit would sure keep such a device from starting the Big Bang.

The ground flattened. Sten crouched behind a large boul-
der, and turned on the helmet display. He consulted the map
projected above his faceplate.

Over there would be the door. A slant of solid rock. Sten
moved as surreptitiously as the bulky suit would allow to the
closest cover. He was thirty meters away. He dropped binocs
down over his faceplate and minutely examined the rock.
Twice he stopped, eyes starting to see things that were or
weren't there.

At full magnification, his field of vision was less than a
third of a meter on a side. Back and forth, back and forth
his eyes moved, just like a photointerpreter scanning a
mosaic, looking for the camouflaged enemy.

Ah. Perfectly round. Which rarely exists in nature.

A keyhole.

Punched in the rock about where a keyhole should be . . .
for an Emperor-sized being.

All Sten needed was the key.

He went across the open ground like a trundling armadillo.
Expecting the shatterblast. Nothing.

He knelt next to the keyhole and unsealed a pouch. After
some thought, back aboard *Victory*, he had realized the key
would be the simplest part of this operation. The Emperor
couldn't wander around carrying some elaborate hex-pattern-
coded special key in his return to the throne. Or, anyway,
Sten wouldn't plan things that way, if he had been setting
this whole paranoiac rigmarole up. So the key would have
to be something that the Emperor could procure or have made
at the appropriate time. Also, the key wouldn't be part of an
exotic locking system that might be unobtainable or super-
seded by the time he returned.

Sten took out a standard, Mercury-issue electronic lock-
pick. Round, eh? He found a pickup of the correct size. He
fitted it to the analyzer and inserted the pickup in the hole,

wanting to put his fingers in his ears against the blast, even though the pickup was made of completely neutral Imperium X. The analyzer buzzed, and told him what code would open the door. Sten detached the pickup, and plugged it into the sender. He touched the TRANSMIT button . . .

. . . and the door lifted up, Sten tumbling back out of pure fear reaction, seeing a ramp leading down into blackness.

Sten waited until his heart began beating again. He took a flash from the pouch and, lying flat against the ground in the event *this* was the trigger, sent the beam around the inside of the passage. Nothing. He looked down. Just a ramp.

Sten set the flash's beam on full diffuse and started down, a centimeter at a time, a step taking a lifetime, moving forward as he had back on Vulcan so very, very long ago . . .

. . . and then he had it.

Or he thought he did.

All this slok about IR detectors, prox detectors, motion sensors, sensor sensors . . . that wasn't it. The Eternal Emperor had been an engineer. A good one. So his protection would have been conceived using one principle: Keep It Stupid, Simple.

Sten's foot came down more confidently, and he took another step. Another. Another.

The door dropped closed behind him. Sten flinched, but not much—he was increasingly sure he was right. An overhead light went on. There was a standard monitor panel against the wall. It showed an environmental system had gone on, and was bringing the shelter up to an E-normal condition. There was a counter display on the panel. The counter showed 0. Sten started past it, then saw, from the corner of his eye, the counter change to 1.

That *was* it.

There was a door in front of him. With a palmswitch. Sten touched it, and the door opened.

Living quarters inside. Small, but well-equipped.

Beyond them, a doorway.

Sten, trying not to hurry, went through it.

The room was huge. Instrument-filled. Coms and controls.

He'd done it! He was alive . . . and inside the relay station.

Unless something went bang in the next few seconds, Sten's dazzling perception had been correct:

What was the one thing the Emperor would do, but no one else would dare?

To show up solo. No one else would. Anyone smart enough and brave enough to get this close to the heart of power would have allies or subordinates. He didn't know where the sensor was—overhead, in the floor, or in the walls. There could be one, there could be many of them.

Christ, Sten thought with a chill. If Kilgour wasn't off on his run against Poyndex . . . he might have taken him along. Even Mantis killers like someone guarding their back, and Sten and Alex had been friends too long.

Count one . . . count two . . .

And this gleaming room would have been melted-down shambles.

He looked around at the keys to the kingdom. There were four secondary boards in the room. Reporting stations, Sten theorized. Three of them showed identical readouts, the fourth was zero/zero. That would be the station Kyes or Kyes's men had discovered, and, in the discovery, destroyed.

In the center of the room was a great circular control panel. Readouts and controls.

Sten touched nothing as he examined that carefully. Most of them were unlabeled—that wouldn't be necessary for one operator, the operator who'd designed the entire system. But there were enough marked so he could tell what the panel was intended for.

This *was* the secret of the universe. Sten felt a chill.

From here, the Eternal Emperor could turn the "power" on or off. Direct those great robot convoys to deliver the AM2 to the depot he directed. Increase the amount of AM2 for each depot. His decisions would be repeated at the three surviving relay stations.

And from here his commands would be transmitted out. Out toward another universe. Somewhere out there, somewhere beyond, was the discontinuity. All that was necessary was for Sten to plot the transmission coordinates of the beam from this station and send them up to Freston on the *Victory*. Simple triangulation with the beam from the mansion would locate the discontinuity.

"All right," Sten whispered, not aware that he spoke aloud. "All right, you bastard. It's all over now."

CHAPTER THIRTY-SEVEN

THE ETERNAL EMPEROR stormed down the corridor to his office. The long, broad hallway bristled with guards. On one side were the Internal Security thugs. On the other, a grizzled detachment of veteran Imperial Guardsmen.

He had a pistol at his belt and he kept a ready hand on the butt as he rushed by them. His eyes swept their ranks as he moved. At the slightest hint of a threat he was braced to draw and fire.

But not a being's eyes met his as he hurried to the relative safety of his quarters. They were all too busy watching one another. The atmosphere was so thick with suspicion, a sneeze would have set off a full-scale battle.

His chamberlain was writing by the door. "What are you doing here, Bleick?" the Emperor snarled. "I didn't send for you."

Bleick's weasel eyes took on a startled cast. "I was only here to report—"

The Emperor chopped in. "Search him!"

Bleick gave a bleat of fear as four guards—two IS men and two troopers—hurled him to the floor and put him through a humiliating body search. They followed this up with a thorough scanning, to make sure no assassination devices had been surgically implanted.

When they were done, Bleick scrambled to his feet. "I am so deeply sorry, Your Highness," he whined, "if my presence gave you even the slightest cause to worry."

"Shut up, Bleick," the Emperor said. "My orders were clear. No one is to come near me unannounced."

"But I thought—"

"Did I say you had permission to speak?"

"No, Your Highness."

"That's your problem, Bleick. You attempt to mimic the thought process. Instead of following orders."

The Emperor turned slightly to the side, so he could keep both Bleick and the corridor in view.

"All right," he said. "As long as you're here, you might as well tell me what you had to say."

"It's only about Poyndex, Your Majesty."

"Only? Only? What the clot's wrong with you, man? My chief of security disappears from the face of Prime World, and *you* call that only? For crying out loud, don't you—" He broke off, disgusted. "What a load of drakh. Okay. Speak up. I'm tired of making like a target in my own damned hallway."

"Yessir. I only came to report, sir, that I've just finished an exhaustive study of . . ." Bleick saw the Emperor was about to explode again, and dropped a few self-serving modifiers. "Uh . . . No one on the staff has seen him for some time, sir. I double-checked every room log in the castle. And personally supervised the follow-up interrogation of the staff."

"Who interrogated *you?*"

Again, that startled look. "Uh . . . Me, sir? Why . . . No one, Your Majesty."

The Emperor motioned to two of the guards. Since Poyndex's disappearance he had ordered them paired at all times, so there was always an IS man watching an Imperial Guardsman—and vice versa.

"Take him down to interrogation. Put the screws to him real good. I want to make sure he and Poyndex didn't do a little deal together."

Bleick squealed in alarm. "But, Your Majesty. I have certainly proved my loyalty over the—"

A beefy hand slapped over his mush, cutting off the rest of his nonsense, and he was hauled away.

The Emperor turned back to his door. Submitted himself to a thumb- and iris-print check. Then he tapped in the code that only he knew. The door slid open. He glanced around once more to make sure he wasn't threatened, then drew his pistol and stepped inside.

The door hissed shut behind him. He was alone. The Emperor carefully checked the new sensors he'd had installed. A little of the tension eased. His security was intact. No one had breached his office while he'd been gone. The Emperor holstered his weapon.

He crossed to his desk and pulled out some Scotch. He poured a glass. But before he drank, he slipped a small rod-like device from his pocket. Inserted it in the liquid. The pea light at the top of the rod beamed green.

The drink was safe.

He shuddered it down, then sagged into his chair. The Emperor was at the edge of exhaustion. He got out a syrette and pressed it against his arm. There was a slight stinging sensation, a tingling in his vein, then his heart gave a sudden jolt. And he was filled with drug-induced energy.

His hand shook as he reached for the bottle to refill his glass. The Emperor grimaced. It was one of the many downsides of amphets.

Another, he realized, was paranoia. A small laugh burst from his lips. There was a slight hysterical tinge to it that annoyed him. He'd have to watch it. Be very careful. Make sure his reasoning process was his own and not something out of a pharmacy.

On the other hand, as the man once said, even paranoiacs have enemies.

The Eternal Emperor settled back to take stock of his situation.

He had just returned from a personal tour of the interrogation rooms. His lips curled in disgust at the memory of the smells of blood, fear, puke, and body wastes. Only the loud screams of pain had given him any real sense of satisfaction. Not that he enjoyed that sort of thing. Not really. After all, that would be a symptom of madness.

The satisfaction came from seeing for himself that real effort was being put into solving the mystery of Poyndex's disappearance. He had also stressed to his interrogators it was equally important to uncover any conspiracy connected to the disappearance.

There had been a score or more confessions already. A few might even turn out to be true.

They had played a tape of Baseeker's hysterical babblings. She had admitted her disbelief in the Emperor's godhood. Confessed her motivations were only from greed. And then further revealed that Poyndex had suborned her. That she was directly working for him.

There were sure to be others. He would soon learn the extent of Poyndex's game playing.

He doubted Bleick was involved. But the Emperor was not willing to chance it. Of course, the man would be useless for any kind of position when the interrogators were through with him. He would have to find a new chamberlain. Ah, well. It was a price the Emperor was willing to pay.

The Emperor emptied his glass. He pushed the bottle aside. He would wait before having another.

It was time to put the crisis into perspective.

Poyndex's disappearance posed several possibilities—all of them nasty:

1. *Poyndex was dead. Slain by the enemy.*
2. *He'd been kidnapped.*

In either case, it was possible that he had been tortured and had spilled his guts to an agent, or agents, of the rebel forces. Which meant some of the Emperor's deepest secrets might have been revealed. Literally, considering it was Poyndex who'd supervised the removal of the bomb in the Emperor's gut. And that little secret could eventually lead to Alva Sector.

3. Poyndex had suddenly decided to defect to the other side.

4. Poyndex had been in league with the Emperor's enemies for some time, and fled because he feared his treachery was about to be uncovered.

5. If numbers three and four were true, it was likely Poyndex had co-conspirators within Arundel itself.

Internal Security certainly couldn't be trusted. And since Poyndex had crept into so many other areas, neither could any other branch of the Imperial Service. Once again, the Emperor's secrets were in jeopardy.

The most glaring fact—not possibility—of all was that:

6. Arundel, the most secure facility in the Empire, had been breached.

On that general topic, there was another item gnawing at him. And might not belong on the list. Although he would put it down anyway.

7. One of his safehouses had also been violated. The Shahryar mansion.

The full report on the incident had only just reached him. The enemy agent had obviously been supremely professional. This was one of the few times any of his sanctuaries had been invaded, by a burglar or otherwise. The agent was also professional enough to escape unscathed after wiping out his security force.

However, the report had assured him the woman had been unsuccessful in getting any useful information.

But, wait! What about the code word she'd attempted to penetrate the computer?

Raschid!

How did she know that name? The Emperor's secret persona?

Poyndex?

Possible. But, only if he had secretly joined the enemy some time before. Besides, how would Poyndex have known that name?

No. Highly unlikely. Just as it was unlikely that Poyndex was a longtime traitor. A mole. Nothing in the man's profile fit this. He'd been running his own, complex power game, but the Emperor was just as certain now as before that Poyndex's power yearnings were satisfied by being the most important member of the Emperor's staff.

Could the rebels sweeten that kitty?

Not a chance, the Emperor thought. Besides, Poyndex was the type to take the cash and let the credit go. Promises for the future by a rebel force had to be the rottenest credit in town.

There was one further item that argued against betrayal by Poyndex: the planetbusting program the Emperor had ordered. One hundred and eighteen planets and all their inhabitants had been targeted for destruction.

If Poyndex was in league with rebels, those planets would have been warned and their security jumped to the nth degree.

Intelligence assured him this had not happened. All transmissions and traffic from those systems were absolutely normal.

Good.

So, Poyndex was not a traitor.

Was he willing to bet his life on it?

Yes, he was.

This line of logic also erased the possibility Poyndex had been kidnapped. Or that he had revealed anything under torture. Because, once again, the intended victims would have been warned.

Very, *very*, good!

The Emperor rewarded himself with a drink.

As he was pouring, another possibility hit him. The trembling hand shook harder, spilling Scotch. He slammed the bottle down with such force that it shattered. Scotch pooled on his desk.

He didn't notice. Just as he didn't notice the sliver of glass in his palm.

The Shahryar mansion!

His safehouse!

What would be the worst-case scenario if the agent's mission had actually been successful? Even if the woman hadn't actually penetrated the computer, what could she have learned?

There was the tightbeam transmitter. Alone, it meant little. But there was a second clue the enemy might have uncovered. And that clue could lead to one of his AM2 relay stations.

From that point, it would be simple to get a fix on Alva Sector!

Oh, come on, he scoffed. That's foolishness. That's assuming an awful lot. That's seeing a level of professionalism rare in the history of his Empire. Who could possibly have—

Another gut-wrenching thought.

Sten could have accomplished it!

Yes. By himself, or he could have planned a mission to be carried out by one of his supremely efficient comrades. Alex Kilgour, for instance. Or that Bhor woman—what was her name? His warrior lover.

Could she have been the woman at the mansion?

No. That was ridiculous.

Wasn't it?

But . . .

Sten had been the very best he had ever had in his service. He had surpassed even that old warrior and spy master, Ian Mahoney. As an enemy, he had proven his deadly efficiency many times over.

Sten would have also been able to penetrate Arundel at will.

True.

But Sten was dead.

Wasn't he?

It was insanity to believe otherwise.

Wasn't it?

Another wrench of the gut. Bile rose. What was the proof of his death? There was no body. No witnesses.

Yes. But given the circumstances, escape had been impossible.

Hadn't it?

He felt a sudden chill. Hackles prickling like desert thorn.

The Emperor had a sudden certainly that it had all been a sham.

Sten was alive.

The Emperor drew a long breath. What should he do about it?

For the first time in his long reign, the Eternal Emperor was unsure what he ought to do next.

BOOK FIVE

ENDGAME

CHAPTER THIRTY-EIGHT

"ALL SYSTEMS GREEN. Entry to be effected in twenty seconds . . ."

There is a moment that confronts every sentient being. When moral imperative collides with survival in the shadow world that lies between decision and action.

The moment can be as simple as a choice between a lie and a self-destructive truth.

It can be as complex as a choice between the suffering of many or a moral and legal obligation to the few.

Theologians call it "free will."

There is no scientific term for this moment, although medical techs can trace with precision the effects of the inward struggle on the organism.

In humans, hormone and adrenal glands spurt their powerful mix into the system. Organs such as the heart and lungs speed up their actions. Fluid pressure and body temperature rise. Blood oxygen levels soar, especially in the muscles and the brain. Infection-fighting cells ready their chemical weapons to stave off attack. In extreme reactions, waste organs spasm empty—to lessen the chances of infection if the body is violently penetrated. The skin tightens to present a harder and smoother surface against a weapon. Sweat glands gape to pour out perspiration as the body's cooling system jumps to full readiness. The perspiration also acts as a lubricant between the limbs and the trunk of the body. In a man, the scrotum tightens and the testes rise to present a smaller, tougher target.

That's what science says.

Sten would have it said it was nothing more than plain animal fear.

He crouched alone on the small bridge of the tacship staring at the ship's monitor. Watching space rain fire. Sten had never seen or experienced anything like Alva Sector.

The tacship's voice rasped over the speaker: *"Entry will be effected in ten seconds . . ."*

His mathematical mind—the side that also contains poetry and music—acknowledged beauty. Saw wonder in the ultimate disharmony at play in the forces unleashed where two universes touched.

But his soul saw nothing but a hole into Hell.

"Entry will be effected in nine seconds," came the speaker voice.

Sten watched a small comet streak toward the discontinuity. Tendrils ablaze with scintillants snaked out for it. Enveloped it. The comet shattered with such violence, the pixels on the monitor screen exploded into white glare.

He steadied himself. Reached deep within and got a grip on the fear. He turned it this way and that, studying it by the light of his rational mind.

"Entry will be effected in eight seconds," the voice continued.

Sten wasn't afraid of sharing the fate of the comet. Well . . . to be honest . . . only a little afraid. The tacship—as well as every item that might be exposed to the raw anti-particles of the other universe—had been plated with Imperium X in a lightning stop on Vi—huge deposits of the substance lay just beyond the Wolf Worlds.

In theory, he should be able to slip through the discontinuity into the other universe unscathed. He'd already sent a probe through and it had returned unharmed.

Therefore . . . what was there to fear? The Emperor's security? The dogs he would have set to watch over his treasure? No. Sten imagined whatever he might encounter would be clever and fierce. But, he'd overcome those two dogs before, and trusted enough in himself to overcome them again.

"*. . . seven seconds . . .*"

What then? Sten sent his mind after that probe. Attempting to imagine himself on the other side. In an entirely different reality. An angry thing with a dripping red maw rose at him. He wasn't wanted. He didn't belong. Every thing . . . every minuscule particle . . . would be his enemy in that place. Even in his imagination, the hate was intense.

And he would be . . . absolutely . . . alone.

More than any other human had ever been. With one exception.

The Eternal Emperor.

"*. . . six seconds . . .*"

What made the fear burn hotter was that this was a choice he could reject. The crawling coward in him was weeping in its pit. Begging him not to go. Why must it be his responsibility? Let someone else do it. And if no one would, then clot them all. He could run and hide where the Emperor could not find him. And if he tracked him down, Sten could face him on braver ground. So what if the cause was lost? So what if everyone could be doomed?

They might die.

He might die.

But, at least he wouldn't have to go into that place.

All he had to do was hit the switch and the mission would be aborted.

"*. . . five seconds . . .*"

His hand lay just to the side of it. Sweating and cold.

"*. . . four seconds . . .*"

A twitch would shut that damned voice off.

"*. . . three seconds . . .*"

The coward in his gut shrilled, "It isn't too late!"

His fingers curled.

"*. . . two seconds . . .*"

Mahoney's voice floated up to him from the grave: "Make the devil into a fist, lad. And strike a blow!"

"*. . . one second . . .*"

Sten's fingers knotted down. Bloodless with effort. Fighting panic.

"Entry will now begin," the voice said.

Sten kept his eyes glued to the monitor as the tacship shot forward and closed on the gates of Hell.

    so small . . .
    piteous and small . . .
    and they all want to . . .
    kill me.
    i don't want to die here . . .
    please.
    no one knows me . . .
    here.
    no one . . .
    cares.
    my eyes are . . .
    bitter.
    and i taste colors on . . .
    my tongue.
    someone . . .
    someone is watching.
    where?
    i'm afraid.
    where is he?
    out there.
    who is he?
    i'm afraid.
    who is he?
    i don't know.
    he's watching . . . and . . . i'm . . .
    so small.

Sten vomited into the bucket he had put beside his seat. He snapped open a freshpac and swabbed his face and neck with a cool astringent. He rinsed his mouth with stregg and spit into the bucket.

Then he raised the bottle to his lips and drank. Deeply.

The stregg shuddered and boiled in his belly. But he kept it down. He took another drink. Felt the fire build. It was warm and comfortable and familiar. Like a hearth.

Sten rose from his chair and went through stretching motions. He felt the knots unsnarl and blood sing in his veins. Then he went through the complete Mantis warm-up. A half hour of blinding motion and violent ballet.

He went into the small sanitary facility and took a shower just below blistering temperature. He followed it with an icy blast that sent his heart racing and brought the blood up stinging just below the surface of his skin.

He put on a clean shipsuit, made caff, and padded back to the bridge, with a steaming black cup in his hand. He calmly eyed the data streaming in from the ship's sensors. The mainframe's control module winked and gurgled as the computer fed on the data. Once in a while it gave a red-light hiccup as it digested a more complicated bit.

Sten nodded. Good. He sipped on his caff.

Feeling quite normal.

In a few moments the computer survey would be completed. The basic laws of this universe would be deciphered. The ship's computer would redefine its own reality.

And Sten and the ship would no longer be blind.

He settled into his seat to wait, sipping at the caff, his mind clear, but settled on nothing, his eyes on the rushing stream of data as if he could actually decipher and make sense of anything moving at such speed.

Sten was carving out a place for himself in this new universe the only way he knew how. Which was—routine. It was an old soldier's trick. Someone experienced in constant changes of post. No matter how distant from home, or bizarre the inhabitants, strangeness can be overcome by establishing a routine. Little things. Familiar things. Selfish things. Like washing and grooming. The first hot, bitter cup of caff at the shift start. And the cool, uninvolved appraisal of the mission to be accomplished.

Then you rolled up your sleeves and plunged in, secure
in the knowledge it was only necessary to do this job well.
Greater and more complex responsibilities were on the able
shoulders of your superiors. Just do your job, and keep your
nose clean.

Sten eased back, relaxing. He had found his center now.
It was time to populate this place.

He smiled, thinking of Cind. And the warm arms he would
go home to when this job was done. Comfort in those arms.
Yes, and in that sharp mind as well. The way she had of
always finding a way around a problem that was vexing him.

And Kilgour. His brawny, near-lifetime friend and com-
rade-in-arms. There was a man to have at your back. Any
problem that stumped Cind would never get past his cunning
Scot's brain.

After them, Sten invited Otho and the Bhor. Applauded
as the Gurkhas marched on. Then Marr and Senn. Haines
and Sam'l. And his other friends and loyal crew members.

Soon, they were all trooping about in his imagination.
Cracking jokes. Slapping him on the back. Kissing him or
shaking his hand.

The computer chirped and went silent. Sten looked over
and saw the "Ready" sign blinking.

He took another sip of his caff and set the cup down. His
fingers flew over the control board. Then he sent the command.

Sten looked up at the monitor screen. Light began to fill
the blankness.

He leaned forward, eager to get his first look at this new
universe.

He had no fear of it now.

Because he was no longer alone.

He had found it!

The Emperor's glory hole!

The size of the operation seemed larger . . . but somehow
also smaller . . . than he'd imagined.

Big AM2 tanker ships moved in and out of the rubble of an old, destroyed system. On the rubble itself—broken planetoids, or moonlets—his probes showed huge mining machines, harvesting the basic stuff of this universe. Smaller shuttles laden with ore moved back and forth between the tankers. Once full, the tankers moved off—for the long voyage into another universe and back.

It was a vast, complex system—all operating automatically—to accomplish the Emperor's far-off purpose.

Part of him was disappointed in the size, comparing it to the gigantic mining operations he'd seen in his travels. This place would fit in a small corner of one such complex and still have room to rattle around.

He thought it incredible that something this small had such a profound impact on civilization for so many hundreds of years. But a whole empire had been founded on one small particle from an alien universe.

The second thing that amazed him was the age of the ships and machinery. They all functioned perfectly, going about their business as if they were just off the line. But their designs were straight out of a technology museum.

They were all big, clunky things, with sharp edges and many moving parts.

The final thing that startled him—and *this* most of all—was that so far not one shot, not one missile, had been fired at him.

Sten smoothed the tacship past a tanker, moving deeper into the mining complex.

As soon as he had spotted it, Sten had gone into extreme stealth mode. He had cut all extraneous power, maxed his shielding on all freqs, held sensors on passive, and dropped internal operations to the barest hum. Then, using a tortuous, grab-every-speck-of-dust-for-cover route, he had "crept" in. Not one enemy sensor appeared to have sought him out. Nor did he find a single trip wire to sound the alarm at his approach.

When he was more certain, he had dropped the shields

and begun an active search. Still, no reaction. Then he had
emerged in plain view—every gun port of his own open and
bristling for the attack. But the mining colony had gone about
its robotic drudgery without paying him the slightest notice.
This was very strange. Why would the Emperor leave his
treasure unguarded?

Perhaps because he felt quite certain it would never be
discovered. After all, it did lie in another universe. A universe that everyone until a short time ago had been led to
believe did not exist. *Could not exist.*

Sten frowned as he ran this through, half his mind occupied with the moonlet whooshing past him on the monitor
screen . . . Okay. He'd buy that logic.

Although, if it had been Sten's hidey-hole—no matter how
impossible to find—he'd have filled it with wall-to-wall trip
wires and booby traps. His paranoia had been ground in by
his Mantis trainers. Trust nothing to chance.

Sten thought of the Emperor's quirky mind, and felt easier
still. This was simple. The Emperor *liked* simple. Simple
meant it was harder for things to go wrong.

His mind clicked one large step forward. A simple system
would also have a single control. Which meant it was likely
the whole mining operation was run from one command
center. Next step . . . The Emperor would most likely set up
his living facilities at the command center. It wouldn't take
much space. Sten was sure the Emperor would always be
alone. There was no living being he could trust with this
secret.

Very, very good. Because this meant all Sten had to do
to stop the AM2 flow to the Empire was to hunt that command center down and blow it in place.

And goddamn the Emperor's eyes!

The big white ship loomed large on the screen. It was
older than his father's ghost stories. Space dust cobwebbed
its archaic lines. He saw sensor banks and antenna pods he
had only a dim memory of from his flight-school history

fiches. He saw other apparatus whose purpose escaped him entirely.

But there was no escaping the purpose of the weapon ports. Archaic or not, they were instantly recognizable. The Eternal Emperor was not entirely unarmed.

The puzzling thing was, the ports were sealed.

Sten kept a ready hand on the button that would send two Goblins hurling toward the ship. A hint of menace and he'd blast it to whatever hell existed in this universe.

Was this the place? Was this the command center? The Emperor's ultimate safehouse?

He probed it. The ship was alive, but running on a very dim intelligence. There was atmosphere. There was function. But there was no sign of life.

Sten sighed, wishing for the thousandth time that it had been possible to sail in here with the *Victory* and a full crew. With their skill and the *Victory*'s sophisticated sensor system, he would have been able to pick the white ship apart atom by atom.

He *thought* this was the right target. But he wasn't sure.

Sten would have to go on board to investigate.

He studied the white ship, looking for a point of entry. He dismissed the idea of docking with the ship. Or of using any of the main entry ports.

The Emperor liked simple. Booby traps are simple. Which equaled booby-trapped entrances and docking area.

He almost missed the hole back near the engine area. Sten zoomed in on it until its raw edges filled the monitor screen. A meteor impact point. It looked fairly fresh. No more than a few years old. Evidently the AM2 debris had impacted, then detonated on or near the outer skin.

Sten wondered how much damage it had caused. Was this the explanation for the closed weapon ports? The dimmed nature of the ship's operation?

Luck was still running with him. And clot Otho and his "there's only three" kinds: dumb, blind, and bad. For Sten, the first one was working just fine.

He studied the hole. Then felt luckier still when he realized it was large enough to give him his own private door into the ship.

Getting to it would be no problem. Alex and Otho had sheathed a complete spacesuit and accessories with Imperium X.

So if he encountered a stray particle of AM2 on the way over and back, he would not go bang.

Sten started gathering what he would need. Mentally figuring the size of the charge it would take to blow the ship, if it was indeed the Emperor's command center.

He would have to rig some kind of demo pack. With a one-or two-hour timer. No problem. Except—what to put the unit in. How would he get it there? Clutch it in his damned arms like a baby?

Then he remembered the pack Alex had put through the Imperium X plating. They hadn't much time, and Sten was impatient.

"What the clot's that for?" Sten had asked. "Am I supposed to pull it over my head when the shooting starts?"

"Y' noo ken, young Sten," Alex had answered, "when y'll hae need t' tote sum'at."

Sten had let it go rather than argue.

And now, thanks to Alex, he had something to put the demo unit in.

Pure blind luck.

The second on Otho's list.

He'd take it. No problem at all.

He floated out into that mad universe, ignoring the colordazzle he saw through the faceplate and navigating on the suit's own inertial system.

His luck stayed with him and he reached the white ship without incident. It took less than twenty minutes to widen the hole enough to get him and his gear inside.

Once inside, however, confusion was his temporary enemy. The ship's design was too ancient, too unfamiliar, for

him to find his bearings. He locked his boots on a work platform—in a cavity just beneath the ship's skin—and swung
this way and that. Poking his pinspot into the mouths of the
shafts that emptied onto the platform.

Finally, he got a sense of direction. Odd, how that term
sounds in another reality. Another universe. Sten shook off
this mind-buzzing notion. Direction was the shaft he chose.
The one he believed led to the engine room. This was all the
definition he needed. He'd save the other for long, philo-
sophical nights when he was deep in his cups with his friends.

He made his choice and kicked off. Floating upward into
blackness, moving gracefully, despite the bulk of the demo
pack on his back.

The engine room was a shambles. Twisted metal and cable
were evidence of just how much damage the meteor impact
had caused.

There was no atmosphere. But the ship's gravity was on—
he was standing firmly on his feet, with his boots' mag units
turned off. Readings on his helmet screen indicated signs of
mechanical life just beyond. There was no danger indicated.
No sign of a defense system sniffing for Sten.

Sten guessed the meteor's impact—and the resulting
explosive reaction of AM2 exposed to alien particles—had
only wounded the ship. It had reacted by reducing its functions to the barest minimum. That minimum most probably
included the AM2 mining operation, and transport. Assuming
this was the Emperor's command ship. Which he still was.

It was still probably capable of effecting repair, but had
reserved the power necessary for this to maintain those all-
important minimum functions.

In other words, Sten thought, it was too clottin' busy.

It suddenly occurred to him the damage he was looking
at might have something to do with what was so wrong about
the Emperor.

What was it Haines had said? The Emperor was the same.
But, not the same. Same, but different.

Maybe the meteorite had upset some sort of plan. Some sort of . . . He shook his head. This was pointless speculation.

To be saved for that far-off night with his friends.

He moved onward.

Sten slipped down the corridor, in increasing awe at the complexity of the white ship. Now that he was two damage-control locks beyond the damage zone, the atmosphere and temperature were E-normal. His helmet and gloves were off and snapped to his harness. He was breathing deeply, washing out the stale suit air from his lungs.

The air smelled fresh, with a faint sharpness to it. Pine? Yes, or something close to it.

This was the Emperor's place, all right. He was a great lover of nature in the raw.

Sten was following the main corridor. He assumed this from its large size, and the blue line painted down the center. Everywhere he looked were more corridors—smaller corridors—angling into this one. And there were doors. Many doors.

Some led into nothing more than masses of wiring and electronic gear. Some led into storage rooms crammed with equipment and parts. There was even a working repair bay for all the robots scurrying about the ship.

Sten stepped aside as one chugged past, waving a welding wand, intent on its small purpose.

The corridor suddenly opened into a high-vaulting atrium. And he entered a vast hydroponic farm. Filled with exotic plants and fruits and vegetables.

Things the Emperor would find delicious.

Sten kept to the blue line until the path became corridor again.

And that gave way to a large room. Smelling of antiseptics and medical purity. There was a long row of vats, filled with an unfamiliar liquid. The light in the room was oddly bright . . . and warm. He saw steel tables and surgical snap-ons for medical 'bots. The room made him feel quite uneasy. He moved on.

He came to the ship's control center. It was jammed with archaic equipment, all operating as smoothly as if this were the ship's maiden run.

Sten was absolutely sure, now.

This was the Emperor's command center. His safehouse. Blow this ship, and the AM2 would stop.

He unslung the demo pack and put it on the floor, next to an air-fresher vent.

This was as good a place as any.

He looked about, curious. Amazed at what the Emperor had accomplished. Actually, Sten knew he could only have a glimmering of the sophistication.

How had he done it?

Hell! How had he even gotten started?

Sten saw a door just down the corridor. It was marked Library. Maybe there was some kind of an answer in there. A clue to the mystery of the Emperor.

He walked along the corridor to the door. It hissed open and he stepped inside.

As the door shut behind him, he noted with some surprise that there were no banks of fiches. No shelves of books. Just a few tables and chairs.

Was this really a library?

The voice came from behind him.

"Checkmate," the Eternal Emperor said.

CHAPTER THIRTY-NINE

"YOU KNOW THE drill," the Eternal Emperor said. "Don't make a move. Sudden or otherwise."

His tone was light. Confident. Sten did not make the mistake, however, of thinking he was *over*confident. He stayed quite still.

"Now . . . Shed the spacesuit. Very slowly, please."

Sten's hands crept to the fastenings. A moment later the spacesuit was heaped at his feet. Now he was wearing only the overall-like shipsuit.

"Kick it away," the Emperor ordered. "A good sturdy kick, if you please."

Sten kicked, and the spacesuit went flying into a corner.

"Walk forward to the far end of the room," the Emperor ordered.

Sten walked. He stopped when his nose touched the wall.

"You can turn around now," the Emperor said.

Sten turned. His old boss had a haunch perched on a table. A pleased smile on his face. The gun in his hand was pointed steadily at Sten.

"It's good to see you," the Emperor said. "For a while I was afraid you weren't coming."

His free hand went to a bottle of Scotch sitting on a drink tray. Without moving his eyes from Sten, the Emperor poured himself a drink.

"Sorry I can't offer you any," the Emperor said. "But I'm sure you can understand my rudeness." He sipped from the glass.

Sten understood. Given a chance, he would turn anything handed to him into a weapon. A piece of paper would do just fine. A glass would be even better.

His Mantis senses had taken over the moment he had heard the Emperor's voice. Respiration and heartbeat calm and steady. Muscles at ease, but set on a hair trigger. Mind working clearly, taking in every object in the room.

Eyes measuring the distance between himself and the Emperor. It was a little far. But doable.

Why he was still alive, he didn't know. Or much care. He was completely focused, however, on remaining in that condition.

"You realize, I suppose," the Emperor said, "that you're going to have to tell me who else knows about this. And the disposition of their forces."

Sten shrugged, but said nothing.

"I won't bother with torture," the Emperor said. "Out of respect for our past relationship. Besides, I have a perfectly adequate brainscanner. A little elderly. A little careless with vital cells, sometimes."

He took another drink. "Nothing to worry about, however," he said. "If it turns you into a vegetable . . . at least you'll be a dead vegetable."

"Congratulations," Sten said. "It looks like you thought of everything."

The Emperor grinned. "Tsk. Tsk. No, 'Your Majesty' anymore? Or, 'Your Highness'? No respectful terms at all for your old boss?"

"It was an easy habit to lose," Sten said. "Once the respect was gone."

"No need for cheap insults," the Emperor said.

"No insult intended," Sten said. "Just a fact. Candidly admitted."

The Emperor chortled. "You won't believe this," he said, "but I've actually missed you. You can't imagine how dull and incompetent the people I have around me are."

"So I've heard," Sten said. "Especially that character you

had—what was his name?—the one who runs the boys in the storm-trooper getups?"

"Poyndex," the Emperor answered. "His name *was* Poyndex. Thanks for helping me out, by the way. I hadn't quite decided how to get rid of him."

"You're welcome," Sten said. "I'll be sure to give Kilgour a 'well done.'"

"Right now," the Emperor said, "I imagine you're thinking to play along. Spin it out. Delay the inevitable, until you get your chance."

Sten did not answer.

"If these thoughts amuse you," the Emperor said, "then, please . . . go ahead. Be my guest. Meanwhile . . . aren't you going to compliment me on my digs?" He gestured with his free hand, indicating the white ship . . . everything. "After all, I put a lot of thought and years into it."

"It's real nice," Sten said, dry. "Too bad about the meteorite."

The Emperor frowned. "A one-in-a-trillion happenstance," he said. "I'll soon get it fixed." There was a harsh edge to his voice. Indicating a vulnerability.

"Is that what fouled things up?" Sten prodded.

"Not really," the Emperor said. "There have been some difficulties, to be sure. But, on the whole, I think there's been an improvement."

"You're a lot happier with yourself, now?" Sten guessed.

"Yes. Yes, I am. Certain . . . weaknesses . . . have been shed."

"Like the bomb in your gut?" Sten hurled another missile.

The Emperor reacted, startled. Then he laughed. "So, you're on to that as well?"

"It wasn't that difficult," Sten said. "You can thank Kilgour again." He fixed the Emperor with a hard look. "Just like it wasn't hard to figure out the rest. Of course, Mahoney gave us a big leg up. Ian had just about everything figured."

"I miss him," the Emperor said, voice very low.

"I'll bet you miss a lot of people," Sten said sarcastically.

The Emperor surprised Sten. "Yes," he said. "Yes, I do. Mahoney, especially. He was my friend." He gave Sten an odd look. "And once . . . I thought you were, as well."

Sten barked laughter. "Is that how you tote up your friends?" he scoffed. "Put them on a death list and then number them from one to finish?"

The Emperor sighed. "It's harder being me than you think," he said. "The rules are different."

"Yeah, I know," Sten said. "The Big Picture. The Long View. The funny thing is, where you were concerned, I used to believe that stuff. Or at least didn't question it."

"There really is no other way to run things," the Emperor said. "I've done this for the good of all. There's been suffering. True. But life is suffering. Mostly, if you average it all out over a few thousand years, there's been a great many more good times than bad."

He reached for his Scotch, took a drink, and set the glass down again. "You should have seen what it was like before I . . . got started."

"Before you found the AM2?" Sten asked.

"Yes. Before then. You should have seen the inbred brain-dead clots who ran things. Hell, if it wasn't for me, civilization would still consist of a few stars and planetary systems."

"I'll take your word for it," Sten said.

The Emperor stopped, staring at him. "You think I'm crazy, don't you? Go ahead. I won't be offended."

Sten answered, not caring whether he was offended or not. "I don't think—I *know* it!"

"Perhaps I was . . . once," the Emperor said. "But, no more. Not since that meteor blessed this ship. As soon as I was . . . aware . . . I knew something was . . . different. Much different! And vastly superior."

"Superior to the *old* model?" Sten guessed, remembering the room with the biological vats and surgical equipment.

"I suppose you could put it that way," the Emperor said.

"The chain was broken. It was time to begin anew. With fresh ideas. To build a new order. Of course, there are sacrifices to be made. Nothing good ever comes without sacrifice."

"As long as it's not your own," Sten said.

"Do you really think that? Do you really think . . . I don't suffer as well?"

"The guy pulling the trigger," Sten said, indicating the gun, "never suffers as much as the person on the receiving end."

"You're too cynical." The Emperor laughed. "You were around me too long. But facts are facts. My . . . predecessor . . . had let things go into the drakh-house.

"Letting the Tahn get out of hand, for a start. And the privy council! How the clot did . . . he . . . allow those fools so much power? It was weakness, I tell you.

"The Empire was allowed to get too fat. Too sloppy. It was time to pare things to the bone. Put things back on the right footing. An Empire is no different than any business. The rules of capitalism require a periodic shakeout."

"Business leaders don't usually declare themselves God," Sten said.

The Emperor snorted. "Don't be stupid," he said. "The image was getting rusty. It wanted brightening up. Besides, there's a long tradition in rule by divine right."

"Then, you don't actually believe you are a god?"

The Emperor shrugged. "Maybe I do. Maybe I don't. However, last time I checked, immortality fits the definition."

"Gods don't climb out of vats," Sten said.

"Oh, really? Perhaps I was misinformed. But, since you've obviously met so many gods, I bow to your wide experience."

The Emperor took another drink, then replaced the glass on the tray. "You won't live to see it," he said, "but I do promise you things *will* be better. You can take comfort in that."

"Better than what?" Sten growled. "You're just a new wrinkle on an old, ugly face. I've led too many kids to their graves for that face. Hell, I've *filled* whole fields of graves, myself. For what? Twenty or thirty centuries of lies?

"You like to think of yourself as unique. The greatest Emperor of the greatest Empire in all history. Well, from where I stand—poor mortal that I am, with only a few years to spend—you're no better . . . or worse than any other tyrant."

"This is a very stimulating conversation," the Eternal Emperor said. "It's been a long time since I've had such an enjoyable exchange. I wish there were some other way. I really do."

He raised the pistol. Sten's mind shrilled alarms. Wait! What about the brainscan? There was supposed to be more time.

"I've decided," the Emperor said, "that it would be too risky for me to move you from this room. So, to be absolutely safe, I'll have to make one of those sacrifices I was mentioning . . . by killing you now."

His trigger finger tightened.

At that moment a voice blared out, "The two organisms aboard this ship are ordered to stand in place."

Sten gaped. What the clot was going on? He saw the Emperor's face. Bewildered . . . and frightened. But the gun remained steady.

"An analysis of the intentions and makeup of these organisms is now complete," the voice continued. It had to be the ship's command center talking.

The Emperor's judgment machine.

"The Prime Organism's directive to permit the intruder organism's presence has been found in error and has been overridden. The alien organism is an enemy. And shall be killed."

Big clottin' deal, Sten thought, a little wild. Dead by the gun. Or dead by the ship. What's the difference?

"The Prime Organism has also been found wanting," the ship's voice said. "It has been declared flawed. And it, too, shall be killed."

Sten saw the Emperor jump in even greater surprise. The gun drooped.

It was Sten's first and only break.

He dove for the Emperor.

CHAPTER FORTY

STEN TUCKED IN middive, shoulder scraping the deck, sending him in a backflip to one side as the Emperor fired and the AM2 round blew a jagged hole in the deck and metal shrapneled. Feet first, he slammed into the Eternal Emperor and sent him tumbling. The Emperor took the fall, pistol aiming. Sten scissor-kicked and the gun spun away. The Emperor double-rolled and was on his feet, wrists instinctively up in a V-block as Sten's knife came out of his arm and slashed. The block caught Sten's knife-hand and he lost balance, recovering his stance by dropping into a momentary crouch.

Sten lunged . . . and the Emperor threw himself back, across the tabletop, whirling, and was on his feet.

Feint . . . bob . . .

The Emperor doublefist-smashed the table and the plas shattered. Sten's knife flicked out . . . and first blood ran down the Emperor's forearm.

The Emperor backed away, hand scooping up a razor fragment of the tabletop, nearly forty centimeters long. He held it low, close to his right side. Sten chanced a look away from the Emperor's eyes. Noted the Emperor held the shard in the relaxed thumb-forefinger fencing grip of a trained knife-fighter.

Shiphum. Feetshuffle as each of them moved, circling toward his opponent's offside.

Sten realized he was being maneuvered . . . and caught the Emperor's goal. The pistol. The Emperor sliced at Sten, and Sten back-leaned . . . away from the cut . . . chanced a riposte of his own, missed, recovered.

The Emperor's eyes flickered, giving away his next strike, and Sten's arm wasn't where it'd been a moment earlier. Too long, Sten thought. You haven't been in a real brawl in too long.

But neither have you, Sten.

Sten chanced a bravo's flip, tossing his blade from right to left hand—and the Emperor attacked. Sten damned near lost the knife, reeled back, cursing himself for even thinking of a grandstand play. Again he slashed at the Emperor's wrist, recovered, slashed, blade slicing off a long curl of the plas, and Sten's hand flashed to the deck, came up with the pistol, and the Emperor underhand-cast the plas, and it cut into Sten's shoulder, muscle spasm on the trigger, round going somewhere, missing, pistol flipping out of his hand from recoil and . . .

Darkness.

The voice was calm. "I have determined that the intruding organism is more dangerous to my assigned duties than the aberrant one that was created. His termination will be given priority."

Jesus. It hurt. Sten put his knife between his teeth, clenched on the machined crystal, and pulled the long shard from his shoulder. Waves of pain. Put the plas down. Wipe blood from your fingers. Feel the wound. Bleeding? Some. Badly? Not to worry about. For a while. Pain?

Sten mumbled the mantra he had been conditioned with years before, back when he had been a Guards trainee, and his body forgot the pain. He went prone on the deck. Slowly let his fingers move across the deck, looking for that pistol. It could not be far.

Across the chamber, a clatter.

Laser aircrackle *blast* as the round hit somewhere. High, and left.

Sten's fingers touched something.

The pistol butt.

Clot. So the Emperor had a backup gun.

"Stand by," the voice announced. "I have the intruding organism located. Prepare to fire."

Twin lights flashed on, glareblind, and Sten shot twice, explosion, dying into darkness, the Emperor shooting a little late, the bullet smashing down where Sten had been a few seconds earlier.

All right, you bastard, Sten thought, and, concentrating on where those lights had been, sent five rounds rapid into the general area, rolling and spinning as he fired.

If the Emperor shot back, Sten didn't know it, as thunder rocked the room and alarms screamed. Sten thought he heard a shout. The strange voice that had to be the ship itself? The Emperor? He didn't know. Smoke boiled, fire flashed, lights strobed. A panel was sliding closed; Sten snapped a shot through it, buckling the door.

Sten started after the Emperor, trying to stop him before he got to whatever nasty surprise he was heading for in this, his ship. Stopped, damned himself for a fool, and headed for his spacesuit. He tugged it on, but left helmet and gauntlets clipped to the belt. Before he sealed the suit's chest opening he touched his medkit to his arm, and the box clicked, clicked, feeding painkillers and disinfectants into the wound. He sprayed a dressing across it, then buttoned up.

Take your time, he thought. Better to let him get a bit of a lead rather than stumble into something.

"Ship," he panted, feeling very much a damned fool.

The voice did not respond.

Sten blew two more rounds into the biggest wallcrater. More alarms, and the flicker of flames, and the hiss of extinguishers.

"Ship! I will not harm you," Sten lied. "You can continue your mission."

Toneless: "Does not compute. Organisms other than the created organism are hostile and to be destroyed. Basic program applies."

Okay, try to kill me then, Sten thought. If you can.

He went to the buckled doorpanel and started to kick it open. Stopped, cursing himself for still not having his head on correct, picked up a chair and hurled it through the plas. *Gunslam*, and an AM2 round blew the panel away. Remember, that could of been you.

He sent a doubletap down the corridor for confusion's sake and went through. He was about to go after the Emperor when a thought struck him.

He aimed back into the ruined compartment and blew five carefully aimed shells into the deepening hole in the wall. He flashaw metal peel/girder strips/smoke boiling into another chamber and then the smoke and fire closed in as a new alarm *DEE*dawDEEdawDEEdawed . . .

This one he knew. This one was standard—*Ship holed/Atmosphere being lost.*

His ears popped as the ship lost air. Sten scrabbled for his helmet. He had it on and was ready to slam the faceplate when pressure returned to normal. The ship was self-repairing. Having given the ship something to busy itself with, Sten ran down the corridor after the Emperor.

He understood none of the rooms he searched, any more than he had the first time through. Some were tiny, yet packed with consoles and equipment. Others were huge and completely bare.

It was in the first of those that the ship tried to kill him, as the McLean generator went off, and Sten floated up toward the ceiling, and then gravity slammed back on, but you didn't wait enough to let the fall kill me, as Sten dropped back, landing cat-quick on his feet. He put two rounds, out of spite, straight down, into the deck. One worry he did not have was ammo—the ammo tube contained five hundred of the 1mm-diameter AM2 rounds in their Imperium X shield.

The blast tincanned the decking, and Sten looked down,

into another level. He quickly ran a three-D prog in his head. The Emperor would probably be farther along this deck I'm on, so if I can get down there and circle up behind . . .

Sten dropped through the hole.

"The intruding organism is now on Golf Deck," the voice narked. "Proceeding toward medical station."

Clot. He looked around, to see if he could spot a telltale eye to shoot out. Nothing.

Okay. Bad idea. He would just as soon be back where he had come from. Idea. He stepped into the middle of the passage, the rent in the decking just above him, and the ship took its lead and spun the gravity yet again, sending Sten falling "up" toward the hole he had come down through. But as he fell he thumbed a bester grenade out. Heard it *tink* against the passageway's upper deck. He fell through the hole toward the overhead deck now twenty meters above/below him, locking a bootheel under a curl of debris, and gravity went back to normal as the grenade went off.

Sten waited—but the voice said nothing about his return. Did the time-loss grenades operate against it? Improbable.

Now what? The Emperor could be anywhere in this great polygon of a ship/station. He would have a spacecraft decked somewhere—probably in the same place that ships would be parked for the Emperor to use to begin his return journey.

This is his turf, not yours. Exactly. And it is his to defend. Therefore:

Return to your first plan. Except you don't just want to turn off the AM2 now.

The control room is . . . Sten reoriented himself . . . one deck up. And back a short distance. We'll do it the easy way. Don't worry about the ship—just don't let it get you into wide open spaces, and it can play up with down all day long. If that's the worst it can manage, it wasn't that great a danger. Sten wondered why it hadn't been built with some sort of robot gun-cars or something—and then he realized the ship would have to be suicidal to allow shooting in its own "body." But he still worried—this last bastion wasn't well defended at all.

A few seconds later, the ship made its first real attack.

The corridor was long. Closed hatches led off to unknown compartments at periodic intervals. Somewhere down near its end, Sten thought he would find a stairwell leading up to the control deck. He heard a sound, like a hundred locks banging closed. Then he saw the far wall of the corridor was coming toward him. As was the near one, he saw, glancing behind him. We'll just divert through this hatch . . . which is bolted. As were the next two he tried. Sten knelt, held a two-handed firing stance, and sent four rounds slamming into the four corners of the oncoming wall.

Blast, smoke, fire . . . but nothing else. The "piston" kept closing in the cylinder.

Imperium X. Used as armor-plating. Why not? If you had enough of it . . .

The moving walls, he guessed, weren't a livie nightmare impossibility—they were most likely intended to help the ship repair itself. Close off an injured section, and send in repair robots.

So the ship was improvising and learning how to modify its resources into weapons.

Sten shot a door panel apart, as the moving walls were only a few meters away, and darted into the compartment. It was bare. Outside, in the corridor, the two walls stopped on either side of the doorway.

Stalemate. The ship would likely let Sten sit here for the rest of his life. The air was thick, he noticed. The ship must've shut off the corridor's air circulation. He could close his suit's faceplate, which would give him another, what, six E-hours before he ran out of air?

Fine. So get out as you got in. He went to the doorway, made himself into a smallish target for ricochets, and fired once at the far wall.

A smashing explosion, and shards of metalloid sang around the room. A crater. Not a hole. And the blast had eaten even more of the oxygen. Sten coughed in the smoke. How long would it take him to shoot through the wall, even if he buttoned up the suit? Unknown, but certainly longer than it would take pieces of shrapnel to finish him.

Could he use his knife to cut his way through? Possibly, given enough time, and enough leverage. Not probable.

Up there. A vent duct.

Too small.

But as he thought it, his knife was in his hand, slicing the grille away.

The duct was tiny. Sten would never fit. He looked into it—his forehead touching the top, his chin the bottom. Not only was it not much more than a forearm wide, but it turned through 90 degrees about an equal distance in.

Sten's palms were sweat-drenched.

He told his mind to shut up, and stripped naked. He kept the pistol ready. Hell, you can always shoot yourself.

Head turned to the side, he forced himself into the vent. One shoulder cocked forward, palms finding a hold on the smooth metal, pulling, pulling, legs flailing in the room behind him. He pulled himself three centimeters forward. Then another three. And another.

Then he stuck.

His chest and mind swelled in panic. Stop that, he told himself. You can't be stuck. You can always go back in the room and start over. You can always crawl out of anything you can crawl into.

That was a physiological lie.

Don't flail. Don't hyperventilate. Exhale. Wriggle. Exhale again. The lungs are empty. Goddamn it, no they aren't! Lose here and the Emperor wins . . . *clot* the Emperor, and with a great squirm he was in the vent, around the bend, and writhing, writhing down the tight passage not thinking, just moving, pushing his clothes and suit ahead of him, and then it opened down into a wider duct, and he could bring up a knee, and lift his head, and then it widened again, and again, and he was up, feet and hands sending him forward, bear-walking, and hell, now he could move upright, standing, this was just like the ducts you used as a private throughway back on Vulcan, when you were a Delinq and it wasn't so bad back there, was it? You've been through tighter squeezes, you lying clot, and isn't this about right? You *do* want the control room, don't you?

Sten unconfused his mental map. And agreed. He found a grille with an empty room on the other side, cut the grille away, and dropped inside.

A messroom. Tables. Cooking gear over there.

Then he heard it.

It sounded like a voice.

Sten quickly dressed, and moved silently toward the voice.

It was the Eternal Emperor.

He stood in the center of a large, bare compartment. Just in front of him was a shallow pool, now dry. There was a bare stand beside it.

The far wall was a monster screen, sensesmashing with the colors/not colors of N-space.

His back was to Sten. His arms hung empty.

Who had he been talking to? Himself? The ship?

Sten lifted his pistol, then hesitated. It was not any misguided sense of fair play—he'd shot many an enemy from behind without warning in his life.

But . . .

"In my end," the Emperor said, "is my beginning."

Sten jolted. The Emperor laughed, but did not turn.

"Of course, would there even be another beginning is the question?" the Emperor said, in a near monotone. "Or would the next refute beelzy, and return to that long line of milksops it took to breed me?

"And even if the ship bred true again, what would the path be? Would he . . . would my . . . perhaps you might call him my son . . . find his way, alone, back? Would he be able to cut out the telltale inside as I did, without it detonating?

"But," and the Emperor's voice slowed, "it's a question that'll never be answered, will it?

"Either way"—and as he spoke, he whirled, dropping into a gunfighter's crouch, Sten realizing here was the trap, the

Emperor's right hand flashing for his belt, gun coming up, reflexpoint aim . . .

Sten fired, and the projection flickered, holograph flashing off, and then the real Emperor came around the corner, close, too close, real pistol about to fire, Sten's foot up, leg blocking, the Emperor's arm thudding against the bulkhead, painshout and somehow his own pistol was gone, knife coming out of armsheath, into hand, and it was very slow:

Sten's right foot slid forward, just clear of the ground. It found a firm stance, half a meter in front of his left, as that foot precisely turned toe outward, and slid backward on its instep.

His knife-hand came up and forward, just as Sten's left hand caught his right, just at the wrist, clamped for a brace, as his hips swiveled, shock-impact and he full-stretch lunged, needlepoint attack lancing out, going home.

His knife buried itself in the Eternal Emperor's throat. Mouthgape. Bloodgush.

Sten recovered as the Emperor stumbled backward, backward, then fell, fell through all time and space, and his body struck the deck with the limp thud of a corpse.

Sten took two steps forward.

The Emperor's face held a look of vast bewilderment.

It softened, toward blankness.

And then the mouth that had ordered too many deaths twisted. Deathrictus—but Sten thought it to be a smile. The eyes that had seen too many years and too much evil saw nothing, looking straight up at the chamber's overhead.

Or perhaps they saw everything.

Time ran free again, and Sten was moving, diving for his pistol, and in a crouch. He was firing, firing like a madman. Into that empty pool, into that wallscreen, and, in now-realized carefully spaced shots, around the room.

An end . . .

. . . there would never be another beginning for the Emperor.

Fire gouted from the walls, and multicolored smokes whirled.

The ship screamed.

Emergency alarms . . . distorted metal . . . self-destructing cybernetics and electronics . . .

Perhaps.

But the ship screamed.

And Sten ran for the control room.

Sten swung the targeting indicators across the bulk of the ship. One here . . . two here . . . three here . . . four here . . . five here . . . six here . . . seven targeted here.

One reserve.

Fire when . . .

. . . the first charge blew, the screen told him, the demo pack in the control room that Sten had set for a fifteen-E-minute delay as he fled toward the meteor hole and his ship.

One blast, and the robot mining ships brainlessly processing AM2 somewhere in the distance would be stopping. But they could be reprogrammed and recontrolled, if anyone wished. Later.

Sten slammed fingers down onto firing keys, a dissonant chord of hellfire.

Seven nuclear-headed Goblin XII missiles spat from the tacship's launch tubes, and, ignoring the jumble of N-space input their sensors shouted to them, homed as ordered on the Emperor's birth/death ship.

Sten's ship was too close when they impacted.

All his screens blanked, went to secondary, blanked again, and then, probably because they were jury-rigged to give computer enhancements of N-space, stayed dead for long seconds.

Finally, one imaging radar came to life, and adjusted its input to the enhancement program.

Colors/not colors.

Nothing else.

It was as if the great decahedron had never existed.

The Eternal Emperor was gone.

Sten stared for a long, long time at that emptiness, perhaps wishing many things had never been, perhaps making sure the void would not take form.

Finally, he turned to his controls.

He fed in his return course, and went at full drive, for the discontinuity.

And home.

It was over.

CHAPTER FORTY-ONE

FOUR SCREENS YAMMERED HIGHEST PRIORITY—IMMEDIATE ATTENTION. Three others flashed with CRITICAL—PERSONAL messages for Sten, using his private access code that supposedly only Cind, Alex, and Sr. Ecu had ever been given.

All of them—and other coms outside Sten's suite in Otho's castle—wanted one thing, in various categories: Sten. Sten's appearance, Sten's advice, Sten's prognostications, Sten's orders, Sten's suggestions, Sten's emissaries.

"Doesn't anybody want to do anything for themselves?" Sten wondered. "I mean, the Emperor is dead. Go for it, people."

"Th' Zaginows're feelin' frisky," Alex said. "Ah hae logged a un'lateral declaration ae independence an' non-alliance frae th' lads. T' be present'd ae th' Imperial Parl'ment, if i' e'er sits again. Th' copy thae sen' you, f'r inf'rmation on'y, has a wee pers'nal note. Sayin' thanks, an' i' y' e'er hap by their part ae' th' universe, *i' an un'fficial capac'ty*, their emph'sis nae mine, drop by f'r a dram."

"It's like an infected tusk," Otho said. "It hurts, and it hurts, and then it falls out. And your tongue keeps seeking the gap, wondering where the tusk went, and maybe even missing it a trace."

There were only two other beings in the chamber—Cind and Rykor.

But there should have been more:

The dead: Mahoney. Sr Ecu. Others, stretching back into the dimness of Sten's memory, soldiers, civilians, even bandits and criminals, who had died for the mask of freedom that they never knew concealed the skullface of tyranny.

The living: Haines. Her husband. Marr. Senn. Ida. Jemedar Mankajiri Gurung and the other Gurkhas. A woman, long ago, named Bet.

And just as there had been invisible beings with Sten before he entered the discontinuity, all these were now in this chamber.

Waiting.

"Cind," Sten wondered. "What will the Bhor do?"

"I will no longer be speaking for them," Cind said. "I'll be traveling. With a friend." She smiled at Sten, a promising smile.

"The Bhor will accept my retirement. Even if I have to grow a beard to cut."

She nodded across the room. "I rather imagine Otho will be the speaker once more, even if he has to be drafted."

Otho growled. "Perhaps. But only for the moment. I have seen as much of the slow dry death of politics as any being could wish for his worst enemy.

"Perhaps I shall outfit a ship, as I did when young. There will be great chances for a trader now, with freedom instead of Empire.

"Perhaps I shall go looking for those strange human friends of yours. The Rom, I believe they called themselves? You know that none of them remain on Vi? They departed before your return from that other place . . . leaving no word as to their intent."

Sten was silent, surprised. Ida, gone? Evidently without even a farewell. She didn't even stick around to see that the good guys won. He remembered words of hers, said over her shoulder: "Freedom cannot be served by making laws and fences . . ."

Otho got up. "Or perhaps I shall take up sewing," he said. "But enough of this, by Kholeric. I am thirsty and hungry, and a bit angry. I shall butcher out your incompetent staff, Sr Sten, and inform them when you wish privacy, there are no alternative choices."

Otho banged out, and a few seconds later, Sten heard loud growls. All of the screens blanked.

But in his mind he still saw their pleas.

He was suddenly, irrationally, angry.

"What the hell," he near-snarled, "do they want? Me to declare myself the new Eternal Emperor? What, the tyrant is dead, now put your necks down for the iron boot again?"

"Some of them wish exactly that," Cind said softly. "Muscles get lazy when they aren't worked. And it's always easier to let somebody else make the decisions, isn't it?

"I know. All that my forebears had to do was obey—absolutely—the Jannissar general. He would tell them when to eat, when to sleep, who to kill, and when to die. If they obeyed—absolutely—they were rewarded, and had a place after death guaranteed.

"Right," she said. "That was all."

"Both a y' appear a wee bit hard ae our allies," Alex said, his face carefully composed. "Thae'll hae t' be somebody ae th' top, aye? T' oversee th' changes an' th' transition. There cannae be an empty throne, e'en i' thae's but a caretaker gov-'mint. Can there?

"F'r beginnin's, who's t' divvy th' AM2?"

Again, Anti-Matter Two, hell and heaven, riches and death.

There was a splash from Rykor's tank. She was watching Sten, her great compassionate eyes wide. But she said nothing of the common secret they held.

"A caretaker," Sten mused, his anger gone. "What? You think I should soldier on? At least until somebody figures out who should run things? Maybe until we put together some kind of coalition like Ecu would have overseen?"

"To most beings," Cind said, "that'd be the most comfortable. The hero slays the dragon . . . and helps the people begin their lives anew."

"Just like in the livies," Sten said cynically.

Cind shrugged. "Why do you think they're so popular?"

"How does that play, Rykor?" Sten asked.

Rykor considered, whiskers fluffing. "Logical. Psychologically welcome, as Cind said. Certainly you have the experience for it. How many times did your ambassadorial duties in fact mean you were the entire government in a cluster? I know you hardly bothered getting the Emperor's approval for every decision."

No, Sten thought. He hadn't. And he had run things with, he thought pridefully, a certain measure of success, assuming clotheads hadn't gotten in the way, clotheads who just didn't understand what was supposed to happen, and that their best interests would be eventually served.

Christ. With no one second-guessing his decisions after the fact from afar. Not a section commander. Not a general. Not even an Eternal Emperor.

Not anyone.

A chance to correct a lot of those wrongs he'd seen across the years, wrongs too big or too distant to confront. And there would be the time—Sten could easily train a diplomatic equivalent of a general staff that would be able to carry out Sten's policies.

All those dictators some mythical thing called Policy or Expediency said should be supported. All those crimes that Pragmatism told him to ignore. All the beings who stole and murdered from their lessers, beings that Sten had never had the opportunity to confront and destroy.

Call it caretaking.

If you wished.

Now, that would not be a bad way to *really* serve the universe, would it? Especially after all those decades of blood and slaughter.

It would also be an example for those who came later, that someone could rule for a while, and then, when his charges reached maturity, step aside. Pass the reins along.

"Say I agreed," Sten said. "Sorry, that's the wrong way to put it. Say that when the smoke cleared that a lot of worlds wanted me to act as some kind of, what? 'Regent' isn't the proper word. 'Manager'? I guess that'd be it."

"There would be few if any systems that would object," Rykor said firmly.

"Right. Now. If I did this, agreed to serve for a few more years, until the time was right and everybody realized that they had to rule themselves . . . would you stay with me?"

Rykor wallowed in the tank without answering. Then: "You would be welcome to my advice, such as it is, for as long as I am able to offer it."

Sten noted her answer.

"Alex?"

The tubby man looked at him for a very long moment.

"Y' hae m' word, boss," he said finally. "Ah'll sign on agin, ae y'r strong right bower. But thae'll be a time whae Ah'll be retirin't, Ah'll hae t' warn you."

Twice.

"Cind?"

"I'll stay," she said, without a hesitation. "As long as you're caretaker. As long as you're Sten."

Three times.

There it was.

Sten saw, once more, the smile on the Emperor's corpse, and icy fingers moved down his spine as he wondered if this moment explained the gioconda smile.

"I just wonder," Sten said, "if anybody ever knows when that time is? Or," he said, being as honest as he knew how, "if every time somebody gets offered a crown, he always thinks that he's taking it just for universal good?"

The chamber was silent, very silent, as silent as the icy, frozen night outside.

"Ah dinnae knoo aboot thae," Alex said, finally. "Thae's Phliposophy, an' thae's noo Scots sol'jer permitted t' think ae that, 'r thae toss him oot ae th' pub an' make him' drink piss wi' th' Brits.

"But Ah hae a wee tale. Call i' a par'ble, i' y' wish.

"Thae wae a mon. Always wanted t' prove himself, aye? An' he hears thae' th' mos' fearsome sort ae huntin' i' on Earth. Ae a wee island, i' a north' ae froze ae Vi.

"Huntin' th' bear. Cind, thae's a—"

"I know what a bear is. You've called Otho one enough times. GA," she said.

"A'right. So, he goes oot i' th' forest, wi' a rifle, an' a sharp eye. An' sooner come later, he spots th' bear. Binga-banga-bonga he shoots, an' th' bear goes't doon.

"An' he bounds o'er, an' to his vast sur'prise an' dismay, thae's noo bear.

"Tap tap on th' shoulder, an' thae's th' bear! An' th' bear growls, an' says, 'I' y' wan' t' live, y'll be giein' doon ae y'r han's an' knees an' committin' a disgustin' sexual act ae m' bod'.

"An' th' hunter goes eech an' ech an' och, but th' bear's fangs are braw, an' his claws are great. An' he goes doon ae his knees . . .

"Noo, when he gies back t' his camp, he's fill't wi' disgust. Wi' loathin'. He's aboot t' suicide. But first, he thinks, Ah'll hae th' skin ae thae bear!

"An' next mornin, he goes oot t' th' forest agin, an' pret' quick, he spots th' bear. An' its bompa-bompa-bompa, an' agin' th' bear goes doon.

"An' th' hunter goes clip-cloppin't' th' site, knowin' he hae th' revenge . . . but thae's no bear.

"Tap tap on th' shoulder . . . an' thae's bear! Loomin't o'er him!

"An' th' bear says, 'I' y' be wantin' y'r life, y'll be disrobin't, an' turnin't aroun', an' Ah'll be performin't a revoltin' sexual act wi' y'!'

"An' yeesh an' bleah an' yargh, but th' bear's claws are braw, an' his teeth are great. An' so th' hunter drops hi' trews . . .

"Thae's it. Thae's all. Th' hunter slink't back t' camp. He feels worsen' a Campbell. H's th' lowest ae th' low. Killin' himself i' th' best fate he c'd dream of.

"But firs' . . . th' bear mus' die! Wi' oot fail, wi'oot question.

"An' so, th' next morn, just ae dawn, th' hunter's oot i' the woods. An' *agin* he sees th' bear. An' again he raises his rifle. An *agin* i's blastawayblastawayblastaway all. An' agin' th' bear goes doon.

"An' agin' th' hunter rushes oop.

"An' agin', thae's noo clottin' bear!

"But agin, thae's a tap tap on th' shoulder.

"An', knowin't whae he's aboot t' see, th' hunter turns aroun'. An' thae's th' bear!

"An' th' bear eyes him, an' says, 'Lad, y' dinnae coom f'r th' huntin' noo did y'?'"

Sten stared at Kilgour, who, after a space, smiled a gently benevolent smile.

"Right," Sten said.

He turned around.

"Rykor. From the abstract of my brainscan, could you help some engineers put together a synth on Project Bravo? A how-to-do-it on AM2?"

"I could."

"That's my first request. We'll bring in some hotshot—maybe that woman reporter, Ranett, who used to give the Emperor the kolrobbies—and let her disseminate the information.

"I want that to go out on every livie, vid, and broadsheet possible.

"Second. Ask Otho to get the voyage tapes from my tacship. That should give a fair triangulation to the discontinuity and the Emperor's treasure.

"Put that out, too. Let anyone who wants AM2 know where to find it."

Rykor thrashed in her tank.

"Intellectually, I approve," she said. "And personally, caring for a single being named Sten, this is good. But considering its effect on the masses—"

"I can't think for them," Sten said. "I can barely take care of myself.

"All I can do is say . . . Here. Here's the AM2. Here's the keys to the kingdom. Every being can make himself a king, or a bloody despot. Let them make the universe as they like it. A paradise or a desert.

"That's not for me. I'm not going to play God. Not now. Not ever."

Sten thought he heard a murmur from all those beings, dead and alive, who had been in the chamber. Of agreement? Disappointment?

But they were gone. Gone forever.

Sten looked back at Alex.

"Do you think anybody'll grudge me the *Victory*?"

"Ah dinnae think so, lad. An' thae'll be clots like Otho'll be glad t' serve. Y'll hae t' beat 'em awa' wi' a blackthorne."

"Good. Now. I'll ask you again. About staying with me."

"Ah'll hae need ae a few weeks, boss. T' intr'duce twa lassies t' m' mum. An' t' hae th' banns posted, assumin't Ah'll be able t' coerce a wee pulpitbanger. C'n Ah hae a' month?"

Sten nodded.

Alex beamed. He went to the door where Rykor waited.

"Ah, lad. It'll be braw. It'll be braw. Thae's entire *galaxies* thae dinnae ken aboot spotted snakes."

And he and Rykor were gone.

"You left me for last," Cind said.

"I did."

"Are you going to ask?"

"Surely. You got any conflicting plans for the next couple of centuries?"

Cind didn't answer.

She kissed him.

Then she took him by the hand . . . and they walked across the chamber to the door to the balcony. She opened it and they went out, into the clear, frost-chiming night.

Neither of them felt the cold.

They looked up and out, far and beyond, at the unknown stars that stretched on forever.

An Explanation Of Sorts

The idea for Sten came to us a few years back. It was encouraged by the fact that, at the time, very few people were writing the kind of science fiction we grew up reading and appreciating—a situation that's changed for the better of late, we're delighted to observe.

But the main reason was out of general pissoff.

Science fiction, for some unknown reason, has always been overly enamored of social and political fascism, primarily because of ignorance, we suspect.

Our irk was best expressed by Damon Knight, in his classic collection of essays, *In Search Of Wonder*, when he was busily ripping the lips off of A.E. van Vogt, Scientologist/confusionaire extraordinary:

"It strikes me as singular that, in van Vogt's stories, nearly all of which deal with the future, the form of government which occurs most often is the absolute monarchy; and further, that the monarchs in these stories are invariably depicted sympathetically, (one of his heroes being) a 'benevolent dictator' if you please.

". . . I shall not say what I think of a man who loves monarchies . . . neither do I think it relevant that these stories were written and published during a time when both van Vogt's country (Canada) and ours were at war with dictatorships . . ."

". . . The absolute monarchy was a form of government which evolved to meet feudal economic conditions everywhere, and which has died everywhere with feudalism . . .

Modern attempts to impose a similar system on higher cultures have just been proven, very decisively, to be failures . . . It is no crime for van Vogt as a private citizen to wish this were not so; but ignorance, for an author, is a crime . . ."

Just so.

The second quote is far better known:

John Emerich Edward Dalberg, Lord Acton, in a letter to Bishop Mandell Creighton, 1887:

"Power tends to corrupt; absolute power corrupts absolutely."

Equally true.

And so it was absurd for us that science fiction, in spite of its loud bannering of thinking of the future, in fact spends all too much of its substance sucking the empty husk of a false past.

Therefore . . . *Sten.*

We used all of the hard, cynical knowledge that we'd gained in fourteen years *each* in mainstream journalism of just how politics and raw power works.

We would create an empire, we decided, that would be big enough and old enough to contain all our bizarre notions of that great, dark, comic figure, the Human Race. We would see this empire through the eyes of an ordinary, working-class man who is overtaken by extraordinary events.

He would be just smart enough, swift enough, and—this was most important—have enough of a sense of humor to survive. And grow into a bona fide hero. Or, at least, our idea of a hero—someone with enormous clumps of clay for feet.

It would be a long story, we both agreed. It would take eight books to tell it all. One novel—in eight parts.

We guessed it would take about a million words.

Today we passed that mark.

And the story is done.